a faith abbey mystery

A MATTER
of ROSES

DAVID MANUEL

PARACLETE PRESS
Brewster, Massachusetts

Library of Congress Cataloging-in-Publication Data

Manuel, David.
    A matter of roses / David Manuel.
       p.   cm.
    "Faith Abbey mystery."
    ISBN 1-55725-234-3 (hardcover)
    I. Title.
    PS3563.A5747M38 1999
    813'.54–dc21

                                               99-39525
                                                CIP

The book is a work of fiction. Except as noted below, names, characters, places, and incidents either are products of the author's imagination or are used fictitiously. Any resemblance to actual events or locales or persons, living or dead is entirely coincidental.

Faith Abbey, is in spirit quite close to the Community of Jesus, the ecumenical religious community of which the author has been a member for 28 years. Father Horton Chambers is as close as words allow to the late Hal M. Helms, who served as Chaplain of the Community of Jesus from 1989 until his death in 1997.

10 9 8 7 6 5 4 3 2 1

ISBN 1-55725-234-3

Published by Paraclete Press
Brewster, Massachusetts
www.paraclete-press.com

Printed in the United States of America.

A MATTER
of ROSES

prologue

IT TOOK EIGHT MINUTES FOR EASTPORT'S yellow-and-white rescue truck to reach the Tomlinson residence on Village Cove. Had the response time been any greater, it is doubtful Maurice Tomlinson would have survived. As it was, he had gone into anaphylactic shock, and the EMT crew had to work feverishly to save him.

"Get that oxygen mask on!" shouted the team leader, his fingers on the stricken man's carotid artery. "I'm losing him!"

They had parked the truck on the lawn next to Tomlinson, and now another orange-jacketed EMT opened the bleeder valve on the green canister. He placed the plastic mask over the patient's nose and mouth, while the leader loaded a syringe with .3 cc's of adrenaline and plunged it into Tomlinson's upper arm.

As this tableau played out at the edge of the Tomlinsons' rose garden, the third member of the team, a woman, was trying to calm the patient's wife. Shaking uncontrollably, Sarah Tomlinson was nonetheless determined to explain what had happened. The words came in bunches, in the soft Virginia accent of her childhood. "It was so warm! More like June than mid-April. He was in shirt sleeves. Pruning along the fence." She pointed to the old split-rail fence atop the bluff overlooking the cove. "Oh, God, is he going to be all right?"

The EMT observed the work of her teammates. "Looks like it," she nodded with a smile. "Close, though. Good thing you called us when you did."

"Can I go to him?"

"There's nothing you could do that they're not already doing. But you can come with us to the hospital." She paused. "You were telling me how it happened."

"I was in the kitchen and just happened to be looking out the window when he was bitten. Suddenly there were bees every-where! And that doesn't make sense!" Sarah exclaimed angrily. "We don't get bees here, even in the middle of summer!" Her blue eyes filled.

"It's all right," said the EMT, putting a hand on her shoulder.

"No, it's not all right!" cried Sarah, shaking off the hand. "That's what I'm trying to tell you: He has this terrible reaction to bee stings, so we always keep a bee-sting kit on the shelf by the kitchen door." She paused and then continued with a trace of pro-fessional pride. "I'm a nurse myself; I know about these things."

The EMT nodded.

"But the kit wasn't there!"

"Could you have put it somewhere else?"

"No! In fact, I'd just replaced the epinephrine last month!" She turned to the EMT. "Thank God you people are fast!" She started to cry.

"Fast enough," agreed the EMT, not taking her eyes off her teammates. "Looks like they've got him stabilized now."

Outside the truck, the other two orange-jackets eased their patient onto a gurney. One stayed with him, while the other went to the truck's cab to call the hospital. He alerted the duty intern of Maurice Tomlinson's condition and the procedures they had already done. What was ETA at the emergency room? He checked his watch: Since there wasn't much traffic on the Mid-Cape, they should make it by 3:35.

The EMT beside Maurice looked down at the 53-year-old man. His neck was purple and bulging where the bee had stung him; his

eyes were swollen almost shut. But his expression was peaceful:
The powerful sedative was doing its work.

The EMT's gaze was drawn to a movement in the dense brush
beyond the garden. Was it just a shifting in the pattern of leaves
and shadows? Or—the EMT suddenly shivered.

"You felt it, too!" whispered Maurice, who had been watching
him through puffy eyes. "So did I. Just before the bees."

1 | mac the knife

MAC CURTIS DESPISED WEAKNESS. He despised it in others, just as his father had despised it in him. His father had named him for the general under whom he had served in the Pacific, and had expected great things of his son. But the boy had turned out to be puny, often sick, and his father, in charge of highway maintenance for three counties in western Massachusetts, had little use for him. The senior Curtis required his foremen to get a full day's work out of their crews, and as far as he was concerned, young Mac, whose mother insisted on calling him MacArthur, was far from putting in a full day's effort.

The boy had tried, as hard as he knew how. But the harder he tried, the more his father ignored him. He went to Springfield, his father's college, and tried out for football, his father's sport. But when he failed to make the varsity, he switched to swimming. With sheer determination—and so many laps that he once calculated that he had swum clear to Hartford—he had made the team. His father never came to a meet.

Finally something inside of Mac snapped. The yearning for his father's approval was transmuted into implacable hatred.

Physically and mentally Mac Curtis hardened himself, until nothing could hurt him. After Army OCS he went to Viet Nam as a Special Forces volunteer who had been through Ranger' and Paratrooper training.

In combat he had emerged as a natural-born warrior. Most men took no delight in drawing recon duty. Not Mac; he volunteered for the most extreme assignments and sometimes thought them up. He liked nothing better than engaging the enemy, ideally in a stalking situation, taking him by surprise and dispatching him at close quarters. Each member of his outfit was issued a combat knife with a reverse curve on its upper edge, reminiscent of the legendary Bowie knife. But the blade was only seven inches long, and Mac wanted something with a little more heft.

So he had one custom-made for him by a knife maker in Mississippi. The blade was ten inches long, of 1005 carbon steel that he could sharpen in the field, with a powder black finish that would not reflect light. The handle was tooled leather, and when it was finished, it was a handsome, lethal piece of craftsmanship, ideal for the silent kill.

There were two ways to take out a sentry from behind: the one they taught, where you clapped a hand over his mouth and slit his throat, or the one Mac had perfected, where you suddenly stepped around in front of him and gutted him. Mac preferred the latter; he enjoyed seeing the horror in his victim's bulging eyes, as his bowels spilled out over his belt. In the big knife's leather handle, he carved a notch for each man he thus dispatched. By the time he came home, there were eight notches, and he had earned the sobriquet "Mac the Knife."

Many Viet Nam combat veterans had difficulty adjusting to peacetime civilian life. Not Mac; there were other ways to destroy a man than physically. He had become a real estate developer, a profession that could be notoriously cutthroat if the practitioner was sufficiently ruthless. Mac was.

Two times in his life, his heart had almost softened. The first had been in 1970, at Pleiku, where he met Sarah Hillman.

≈●

Sarah Tomlinson, née Hillman, had always done everything her mother wanted. Her father, whom she adored, died when she was eight, and life went downhill after that. As soon as she was old enough, she was shipped off to Rosemary Hall, her mother's finishing school, after which she made her debut in Richmond society the old-fashioned way: Her grandmother held a formal tea for her, at which she was introduced to that city's doyennes. While the hand-lace quaintness of her coming out may have seemed anachronistic in 1968, it in no way diminished her popularity. For one piece of her mother's endless stream of advice had proven wise and timely.

Sarah was fine-boned and graceful, like one of the porcelain figurines on her grandmother's mantel. But her best feature was her large, blue eyes. Her mother had warned her: Take care never to appear as smart as whichever gentleman you might find yourself in conversation with. And so Sarah, who was very smart, was careful not to let her quick mind show. She would gaze up at whoever was speaking, and just let those blue eyes do their work. Into them fell the long, the short, and the tall; she was by far the most popular debutante of her year. In her grandmother's day, it would have been said that her dance card was always the first one filled.

Sarah possessed a buoyant cheerfulness, and being without guile, she was as popular with women as she was with men. At Sweet Briar (her mother's college) she had seven beaus from Washington & Lee and even one from VMI. But it was a wide receiver from the University of Virginia who caught her fancy.

Unfortunately, he failed to make a similar impression on Mother, who did some "inquiring," as she delicately put it. When she had prepared her dossier, she explained to her daughter that the boy's father was a tradesman (he owned a hardware store), and his mother worked (as an accountant). Neither came from any family to speak of, nor was there any money to speak of, new or old. In fact, Mother suspected that the boy's parents had made quite a sacrifice to send their son to The University.

Sarah could stand it no longer. "We're not living in a Jane Austen novel!" she exploded. "You'd better join the twentieth century, Mother, before it becomes the twenty-first!" But as always her mother's will proved steely and indomitable, and eventually Sarah's resistance collapsed.

The experience made her all the more determined to have a life of her own, a life that counted for something, giving to others, instead of the life of well-mannered indolence for which she was being prepared. Without her mother's knowledge, let alone approval, Sarah Hillman enrolled in nursing school. And refused to disenroll when Mother found out about it.

While on the surface her mother seemed to accept this show of defiance with equanimity, quietly she went about making certain Sarah married well. The husband she had in mind was Bryce Lee Harlow, a scion of the FFV (First Families of Virginia), whose ancestral tree claimed none other than Robert E. Lee. Moreover, Bryce Lee stood to inherit Brentworth, a large if gloomy Tidewater plantation. To Mother and to Bryce Lee's mother, and to Bryce Lee himself, there was not a finer match in the Old Dominion. But to Sarah, the insufferably pompous BLH was incapable of thinking of anything but himself for more than three seconds.

With sad certainty Sarah knew that while the wheels of Richmond society might grind slowly, they ground exceeding fine. In six months, a year at most, she would be the mistress of the willow-shrouded, white-columned mausoleum she referred to as Toad Hall.

Then the possibility of escape presented itself. The conflict in Viet Nam was escalating. Her great-great-grandfather, who, according to Mother, was the prize fruit of their own ancestral tree, had been the first doctor from Richmond to join the Army of Northern Virginia. Very well, she would be the first nurse from Richmond to accompany the Navy to Viet Nam.

When she announced that she would soon be leaving to join the Seventh Fleet, her mother didn't believe her. Sarah triumphantly produced her set of orders, which her mother took from her. As she perused them, her eyes narrowed and her lips compressed into a white line—an expression which had hitherto reduced her daughter's spine to jelly. "Nothing is irreversible," Mother observed in words chiseled from ice. "I'll just call the Governor and have this—" she waved the document with contempt, "annulled, or whatever one does with such things."

"Not this time!" announced Sarah gaily, snatching the orders back and feeling freer than she ever had in her life. She felt so free, in fact, that as she drove away, she remembered looking down at her arms, to make sure they were not butterfly wings. For she felt as if she had just fought her way out of a chrysalis.

ॐ

In the summer of 1970, Nurse Hillman reported to the base hospital at Pleiku. The moment Mac Curtis met her, he regarded her as a military objective, a hill to be conquered and held. When Sarah made it clear that she intended to play the field, instead of attempting to dissuade her, Mac quietly let it be known around the Officers' Club that as far as he was concerned, it was *not* an open field. And since he was Mac the Knife, the other players soon changed their mind about romancing Sarah Hillman. Before long the Belle of Richmond had only one name on her dance card.

One warm May evening in 1971, when Mac had been off the line for three days and was reasonably relaxed, he took her for a walk up the hill behind the club. There he kissed her, and when she kissed him back, he assumed that a whole lot more than kissing lay ahead. But Sarah made it clear that that was as far as she intended their relationship to go. His eyes turned cold, but he kept control of his temper. Okay, he told her, she had been brought up by an old-fashioned code; he would respect that. Besides, he had come to think of her as someone with whom he might spend the rest of his life.

Whoa! she replied. But since he had been that honest with her, she would be no less with him: She liked him, because in him she could see the terribly hurt boy who had grown such a hard, protective skin. It was that boy who appealed to her, and it was to him she was willing to reach out, in the hope that one day he might emerge.

Mac was stunned. No one had ever spoken to him that way. No one had ever seen in him what she could see. For the first time since he was a child, there were tears in his eyes. He blurted out that he loved her and always would and wanted her to be his wife.

She told him that was way too fast for her. She liked him, but that was all, so far. Whether it would ever grow into love, they would have to wait and see. He laughed; waiting was something they could easily do; they had a whole nother year in that godforsaken place.

2 | witches' brew

MAURICE TOMLINSON HAD NO BUSINESS being in Viet Nam during that war; he was a botanist. But the Midwestern university of whose Biology Department he was a member, was approached by the Government with a research grant so large that it could not refuse the offer. All the university had to do was develop a new, more effective chemical defoliant, which the Army was anxious to put into service as soon as possible. Under normal circumstances the testing would have taken at least two years. In the spring of '71, however, circumstances were far from normal. The need for the defoliating agent was so urgent that the Army decided that testing would have to be done in the field, meaning Viet Nam. A team of scientists from the university would have to go for first-hand observation, reporting back to the lab.

The team was to have been comprised of the senior men on the project. But unlike the senior chemist and the senior microbiologist, the senior botanist had a strong aversion to going anywhere bullets were flying. Though the Army insisted that he would be perfectly safe at all times, the senior botanist was adamant; young Tomlinson was just as capable as he was, and besides, he himself would be needed back in the lab to analyze the results.

Maurice had no strong feelings about the war, one way or the other; it had simply not affected him. Now it did. And he found himself caught on the horns of irony: He had joined this university because it was leading the field in green engineering, making significant advances in crop yields. It did not take a professional botanist to see that the populations of third-world countries were expanding so rapidly that unless their food supply managed to keep pace, in another generation there would be famines of Biblical proportion. That had been enough to draw Maurice into a career in botany in the first place.

Now his Government was waging war in just such a third-world country, and he was being sent there to create the ultimate defoliant, a witches' brew capable of destroying all vegetation for generations.

Could he refuse to go? When the chief botanist presented Tomlinson with the "challenge," he assured him that his willingness to participate would be duly noted in his academic file and would, no doubt, be a significant factor when he came up for tenure. The reciprocal, of course, went unstated: Unless Maurice now demonstrated that he was a team player, his career at the university—and perhaps in botany—would be effectively over.

Thus it was that on November 22, 1971, in the middle of the rainy season, Maurice Tomlinson was hard at work in a makeshift lab in the base hospital at Pleiku. Following modifications that had been radioed that morning from his superior at the university, he was concocting a new batch of chemical stew. Things were not going well. The stuff killed vegetation, all right, but it was not heavy enough. It came out as too fine a mist, and kept getting borne away and dissipated by air currents. The colonel in charge was apoplectic. Their objective was to deny the enemy ground cover, and all Tomlinson and the others had been able to give him was a few bald patches.

Maurice was fed up. Tenure, even his career, was not worth this. So what if he wound up teaching science in the same Iowa high school from which he had graduated; *anything* was preferable to this.

Five minutes to take-off. He went over to the big spraying Huey, whose giant rotor was slowing turning. As the most junior (and only un-married) member of the scientific team, he found himself picked to observe the actual lay-down. Okay, he thought, as he clambered aboard, as soon as this flight returned, he would tender his resignation, effective immediately, and catch the first ride home.

Their target that morning was a suspected transfer depot en route to the Ho Chi Minh Trail. The colonel had ordered the chopper's pilots to go in so low that the only way they could get a denser distribution would be to paint the agent on each leaf—and he was thinking of having them do that next.

The pilots took him at his word, performing the lay-down less than 50 feet above tree level. The only problem was that at that height, any kid in black pajamas with a Kalashnikov could hit them. And one did. Built to withstand terrific punishment, the Huey could have made it back to base, except that another Viet Cong with another AK-47 picked up where his comrade left off. Several bullets hit the rotor's gyro mechanism, and the chopper flopped down like a wounded duck, right through the layer of orange mist it had just released.

They hit hard; all on board were turned upside down and shaken together. Maurice had his leg broken at the ankle and the bottom disc of his spine herniated. He was lucky; the pilot was killed.

The copilot managed to radio their position, and a couple of gunships arrived in time to beat off a swarm of VC. They provided air cover while a rescue chopper's team extracted the crew. All of this was related to Maurice later; in shock and doped up with morphine, he found that his recollection was surreal at best.

When he came fully to his senses, he was in a hospital bed, immobilized in a back brace. He glanced down at his leg. It was in a cast, but still there; others in the ward were not so fortunate. He tried to tell them of one more symptom: His lungs felt raw and burned from the defoliant he had inhaled. But they were more concerned with his leg and the possibility of nerve damage in his spinal column.

How long was he going to be there? he had asked the day nurse. Oh, a few weeks, she told him cheerily. Her name was

Sarah, and she was short and blonde and Southern, with eyes so blue that they made him wonder if he might still be feeling the morphine. He watched her make her rounds, wishing he could have thought of something clever to say. He had never been very good with women, especially the good-looking ones; words just dried up inside of him, as if they were drops of water and he a desert. The nurse who was now down at the far end of the ward was the most beautiful woman he had ever seen. And that was *not* the morphine talking, nor the fact that he was trussed up like a turkey. She really was.

And she was coming back; she would pass by his bed on her way out. Say something. Anything! But if the words had come hard before, it was Death Valley Days now.

"Hello, again," he managed inanely. She smiled at him and went out the swinging door.

The one thing he had was time, so he began to plan sentences and complete thoughts for the next time she came around. It took almost a week, but eventually he discovered that she loved roses. He beamed; his doctoral thesis had been on developing hybrids.

Intrigued, Sarah lingered, and then came back after she had finished her rounds. Maurice confided that he had almost gone to work for a rose developer, but he wanted to do something to help alleviate the coming global famine.

His next discovery had been that she liked poetry—something else they had in common. Sarah was able to scrounge up a volume of Emily Dickinson, and that night when she came off duty, she returned to his bedside and read to him. Dickinson was followed by Frost and Yeats, and after a week Maurice requested a clipboard and a pen; he was tired of just listening and wanted to start composing.

His poems revealed all that he could never put into spoken words. And when one described her as a newly emerged white butterfly with healing in her wings, her blue eyes had moistened, and she had kissed him.

After that, he had a new poem waiting for her every evening. And finally she showed him one that she had written, about a lepidopterist with a touch so gentle he did not disturb the fragile chromatic dust on the wings of the specimen he had just captured.

The following evening, however, she arrived with a troubled look on her face. When he asked her about it, she said there'd been some trouble over at the Oak Club, but nothing she couldn't handle. Maurice worried about that, and when a new nurse came in her place the next day, he worried even more.

Finally he had a word with the head nurse who filled him in on the situation. Apparently there was a Special Ops captain over at the club who was not at all pleased with how Sarah was now choosing to spend her evenings. The night before, he had had too much to drink and had forced a showdown with Sarah. She had decided to take a few days' leave to go down to Saigon to visit a nurse friend, until the captain went back on the line.

Much relieved, Maurice started another poem. But then the head nurse came to him again, this time with wonderful news. About him. He was being shipped Stateside in the morning. She was surprised at his less than enthusiastic response.

Leaving a good-bye poem for Sarah with the head nurse, he spent the next month in Bethesda Naval Hospital. When he was finally released—on a cane, with a mobile back brace—he was told that it would be a year before he regained the full use of his leg. In the meantime, the coughing had begun, and the hospital had no means of healing it; indeed, they seemed to think it was a direct result of his pack-a-day cigarette habit.

Throughout his convalescence, the university was solicitous, covering all his expenses and giving him a generous disability allowance. But then he made the mistake of venting his qualms about his assignment in Viet Nam. A Washington *Post* reporter got wind of it and came over to the hospital and interviewed him. Maurice thought he was giving an even-handed presentation of the mission and his dilemma, but when the story was published, it was anything but. Under the headline WITCHES' BREW, it was widely reprinted and even touted for a Pulitzer. The university, which the reporter portrayed in a most unflattering light, fired him and curtailed his disability allowance.

Maurice returned to his parents' home in Iowa, where he continued to convalesce—without getting a whole lot better. And then in April of 1973, Sarah showed up. She had been looking for him for four months, ever since she had mustered out. The hospital had no forwarding address, and the university, gun-shy after all the bad publicity, had been less than cooperative. She had finally tracked him down through a monograph on roses he had published some years before.

She came, she said, to marry him.

He tried to talk her out of it. His health was obviously broken and was only going to get worse. But she was determined, and she enlisted his parents on her side. Her own mother, who had contracted lung cancer from a lifelong addiction to menthol cigarettes, regarded this as her daughter's final act of betrayal, in a life whose sole purpose was to humiliate her. She refused to come to the wedding, much less give it, and would have disinherited Sarah had the cancer not taken her before she could meet with her lawyers.

Sarah buried her and sold the antebellum ancestral home that had been built by her great-great-grandfather after his service with the Army of Northern Virginia. But she did not sell her mother's summer retreat cottage on Cape Cod. She took Maurice there. She had been his nurse when they met, and had remained his nurse ever since.

3 | a chance encounter

TWO WEEKS AFTER HER HUSBAND'S NEAR-DEATH experience with the bees, Sarah Tomlinson was behind the wheel of her old, green Camry wagon on a mission of mercy. Maurice was still not fully recovered, and she wanted to find him a gardening book he didn't already have. Normally the soul of patience, this morning she was in a hurry. And the little old lady, the top of whose head was barely visible in the blue Taurus in front of her in the traffic circles, was clearly not.

As they approached the turnoff for Eastport, the Taurus slowed. Then it sped up, only to slow again before the Mid-Cape Highway's westbound exit. Sarah felt compassion for its driver, as she obviously struggled to remember where she was going, before she had to go around again. Sarah was only 50, yet the same sort of thing was beginning to happen to her, as well.

With apparent misgivings, the driver of the Taurus finally decided to go west towards Hyannis. Albeit slowly. Perhaps a bit shaken, she never accelerated above 40–a good ten miles per hour below the posted limit in the two-lane, no-pass zone, and 15 to 20 miles below the speed at which most people drove in it. Unless the

Taurus got off before the road widened to four lanes some 16 miles ahead, this was going to be a slow trip.

After a few minutes, Sarah flashed her lights to encourage the Taurus to go a little faster, but its driver, perhaps a bit self-righteous as well as forgetful, refused to speed up or let her by. Any lingering compassion Sarah may have felt was now supplanted by the faint, brackish taste of incipient road rage.

So absorbed had she been in the drama unfolding in front of her, that she failed to notice the one in her rearview mirror. As she exited the rotary, a bright red Porsche Carrera nipped in front of the car behind her, nearly hitting it. Then it abruptly slowed until Sarah was almost out of sight, before matching her pace. So when she did look in her mirror, there was nothing behind her but empty road. That was a little odd for the middle of a busy weekday morning, especially at such a slow speed, but Sarah had other things on her mind.

She got off at Exit 9 and headed south. So did the Porsche. She turned into Patriot Square Mall, parking in the closest available space to Sovereign's, the megabookstore nearest to Eastport. The Porsche parked at the far end of the same row.

Before entering the bookstore, Sarah paused to check her reflection in the door. Her short blond hair was in place, the blue Liberty scarf showed just enough, and her heels added two inches to her 5'4" frame. Her raincoat, just warm enough for late April, nicely hid the two inches that had crept onto her hips.

Entering the store, she smiled at the aroma of hazelnut coffee brewing in the back. She liked these big new bookstores; she could almost always find what she was looking for. The trouble was, there was so much else to find that she invariably wound up spending three or four times as much as she'd intended.

She went straight to the gardening section. Maurice, her master of roses, read such books for pleasure, the way some who were skilled in the culinary arts read cookbooks. But now, as she scanned the shelves, she frowned; there was nothing here that he'd not already read. Well, no matter; on her way in she'd noticed a display of magnetic poetry—which might be even better. . . .

"Sarah?" said an astonished man's voice near her. "Sarah Hillman?"

She turned and looked at the man addressing her. He was big, over six feet, well tanned though it was still April, with powerful shoulders and big hands. But it was the cold, gray eyes that brought an involuntary shudder. "*Mac?*"

He nodded.

"How *are* you?" she said, feigning surprise. She had seen his picture in the paper, in connection with his real estate ventures, and had followed the development of Teal Pond with dread. As long as he didn't find out she was on the Cape. . . . But now he had.

"Oh, pretty good. I thought I recognized you, but I couldn't be sure."

"This is incredible!" she gasped. "It must be—28 years! Do you *live* on the Cape?"

He nodded. "Down in Eastport."

"You're kidding! That's where we live!"

"We?"

"I'm Sarah Tomlinson now. Have been for more than twenty years."

"Oh," he said, disappointment briefly crossing his face. "I'm married, too." Then he brightened. "Listen, we've got to get together."

"Where do you live?" she said, not responding to the suggestion. "I'm surprised we haven't run into each other; Eastport's not that big a town." Actually, she thought, it's not that small, either—four thousand in winter, and ten times that, when all the summer people come on board.

"We've just moved there." He smiled and tapped the side of his head. "That explains it!"

"What?"

"Last month, I was in Eastport on business and thought I saw someone who looked like you, coming out of Baxter's Pharmacy."

"It probably *was* me. That's where I fill my prescriptions." She tilted her head and looked at him. "I can't get over this! Mac Curtis! Whereabouts do you live?"

"Over on Teal Pond."

Her eyes widened. "You live in Teal Pond?" The last she had heard, he was living in Centerville, 25 miles away from her—just far enough to preclude a chance encounter. Begun in 1994, Teal Pond was a planned paradise of luxury homes, townhouses, and condominiums surrounding a golf course, with a clubhouse, pool, and tennis courts. In all the Middle Cape, only Ocean Edge in Brewster surpassed it. Even Teal Pond's smallest condos went for a quarter of a million.

"We live *on* the pond." He made the distinction carefully, then added, "Sarah, I *built* Teal Pond."

She stared at him.

Smiling, he nodded at the shelves next to her. "What are you looking for?"

"Oh. I was hoping to find a new book on roses. My husband breeds them."

"Your husband's not *Maurice* Tomlinson?"

"Why, yes," she looked at him, her head tilted. "How do you—"

He chuckled. "I'm cooking up something with the town. For the kick-off of the Bicentennial on the Fourth of July. We're going to have a contest for a new rose, the Eastport Rose. All the hybrid rose growers in Eastport will be invited to submit the best of their new strains. I've heard your husband's an accomplished rosarian." He leaned closer. "But don't tell him about this; it's supposed to be a surprise."

Sarah laughed. "You obviously don't know Eastport very well yet, or you'd know that if three people know about it, within a week the whole town will."

Curtis looked chagrined, then smiled. "Then I expect we'll be seeing you sooner than I thought. I'm planning a little reception to announce the contest," he confided, "and that *is* a surprise. So please don't say anything to Mr. Tomlinson." She nodded in collusion.

He checked his watch. "I've got to run. Amazing, running into you like this, after all these years!"

"It certainly is!" she said, still a little dazed as she watched him depart.

She did not see him walk quickly to the far end of the parking lot and climb into the red Porsche with the vanity plates that said TEALPOND.

When she got home, Sarah let herself quietly into the house and was pleased to see Maurice out in the garden again. Hiding the magnetic poetry in the cleaning closet, she curled up in the easy chair by the window. She loved to watch him tend the roses—they were like children to him.

৯

At three, Maurice Tomlinson came inside to get something cold to drink and sit down for a bit. Finding his wife dozing in her favorite chair, he gazed at her and shook his head. How could she still love him? How had she ever loved him enough to marry him?

He could have stood there indefinitely, but he felt an episode coming on. Trying to make no noise on the creaky stairs, he hurried up to their bedroom, barely getting the door shut before the coughing began. It was a dry hack at first, almost controllable. But it got deeper and heavier, until it wracked him and left him gasping for breath. He staggered into the bathroom and spat the collecting phlegm into the toilet.

When the coughing finally subsided, he was pleased to see there was less blood in the bowl than last time. He tried not to think about the fact that these spasms, which had once come weekly, were now occurring almost daily. Shaking and totally spent, he collapsed on the bed and closed his eyes.

But sleep would not come. With a sigh he got up and went downstairs as quietly as he had come. Relieved to see he hadn't wakened Sarah, he went over to her and brushed the back of his hand across her cheek—so lightly that he did not disturb the fragile chromatic dust.

Without opening her eyes, she smiled and reached for his hand and brought it to her lips.

4 | good-bye, old bull

FROM THE SOUTHEAST CORNER of Massachusetts, Cape Cod juts out into the North Atlantic and then up, as if the state were signaling for a right turn. To get further east, you would have to go clear up to Bangor or Bar Harbor. If you planned to sail there and were favored by a warm breeze out of the southwest, you might just run downwind the whole way—going "down east" to Maine.

New England names and directions can be quirky that way. Take Eastport, on the Cape's inner elbow, between Eastham and Orleans: The harbor from which the town derives its name is actually on the west side of the peninsula, looking out on Cape Cod Bay. The name strikes visitors as odd, until they learn that Eastport had originally been part of Eastham. When the men who lived around the harbor returned from the War for Independence, they decided there were enough of them to break away from Eastham and form their own town. It took them sixteen years to convince all who needed convincing that this was so, but finally, on the Fourth of July, 1799, the town of Eastport was officially incorporated. Some had wanted to call it East Harbor, but those with greater vision prevailed. After all, had they not defeated the mightiest military power on earth?

Yet, despite its grand name, the harbor never grew. What kept it small was the tide. In the six and a half hours from low tide to high, it rose a full nine feet, flooding the marsh creek that meandered inland from the harbor. At low tide, however, the channel outside the harbor was only knee-deep, which meant that for two hours on either side of dead low, it was virtually unnavigable.

Losing access to the bay for a third of each day ensured that Eastport would never be more than a fishing harbor. In the 1960s it was populated by a dozen seasonal charter fishing boats and a few commercial draggers and scallopers. Those who dwelt around the harbor and its marsh appreciated its quiet charms, and hoped the summer people would continue to be drawn to the more glamorous oceanside communities of Chatham and Harwichport and Hyannis. But it was not to be. In the summer of 1969, the discovery of Eastport began. The price of a four-hour charter-fishing trip then was $51; thirty years later it was $325. And the number of charter boats had more than doubled. There were so many now that they could no longer parallel park along the dock, but had to be backed into slips.

In the summer, the harbor's paved parking lot teemed with visitors. Many came to watch the gleaming, white charter boats come in or leave, which they did together in a long, stately procession. Or they came to watch the sun set—in one of the few places on the Eastern Seaboard where one could see the sun go down over water.

A few came to launch their own boats on the peaceful waters of Cape Cod Bay, there being no other place to launch south of Wellfleet. Invariably on a busy summer weekend, a newcomer would be in too much of a hurry to bother reading the notice posted next to the launch ramp. It warned one and all of the low tide, though it neglected to say how quickly the water disappeared—as if someone had pulled a plug in that corner of the bay. The emerging sand flats extended more than a mile, and a too-hasty skipper might have his craft beached on its side for a few hours.

Though Eastport's harbor never grew, the town did. Like Orleans, it eventually stretched all the way across the Cape to the ocean. There were now a number of magnificent new homes sprinkled among the old family cottages overlooking the North Atlantic. Between Lighthouse Beach and Nauset Beach, the Eastport section known as East Bluffs boasted some of the most spectacular ocean vistas on the National Seashore.

In the middle of Eastport, between East Bluffs on the ocean side and the harbor on the bay side, was a spreading colony of condominiums. Most were owned by retirees who had decided that the Cape, ideal in the summer and mellow in the fall, was not a bad place to spend winter and spring as well. They soon discovered, however, that during the Cape's cruelest months, a damp, 40-knot wind swept in across the bay. That, coupled with a temperature well below freezing, made the Cape in winter a mighty bleak finger of land. Those who could afford to, departed for warmer climes, the richest leaving for condos in Naples or Scottsdale, soon after the first line of geese passed over the bay.

One oceansider who would never retreat was Commodore Wilson Peters, USNR, ret. At least, that was how his calling card announced him. But in point of fact, the U.S. Navy had retired the rank of Commodore at the turn of the century. And while it was true that the thin, beak-nosed, bespectacled Peters had served in the Naval Reserve, he had never risen above the rank of lieutenant. Indeed, after he had managed to run the battleship *Missouri* aground in a training exercise, the Bureau of Personnel had encouraged him to seek early retirement.

It was also true that Wilson Peters had served (briefly) as Commodore of the Sandy Hook Yacht Club in southern New Jersey. His father, Folsom J. Peters, a real admiral who had spent thirty years in the blue-water Navy, had upon retirement accepted the leadership of that obscure yacht club, serving as its Commodore until his fatal heart attack. So beloved had the elder Peters been, that the members invited his son to fill his shoes until the club's next scheduled election two years hence. After one month of his hand on the helm, they advanced the election by a year and a half.

A fool and his money are not so quickly parted, if the fool has a wise father. Sadly aware of his only child's shortcomings, the old admiral had so structured his sizable fortune that his son could receive only a quarter of a million a year.

Lightly regarded in southern New Jersey, ex-Commodore Wilson Peters moved his family to his father's summer residence on East Bluffs, and there assumed his fantasy in earnest. For the late admiral's "cottage" was a ten-room house built to resemble a warship. Its most prominent feature was the captain's bridge that jutted out over a foredeck in the shape of a ship's prow. Galley, wardroom, and captain's cabin were aft of the bridge; the crew's quarters were below.

On the foredeck was a white nautical flagpole, complete with yardarm, from which the old admiral had flown a large American flag and, directly beneath it, his own battle ensign, three white stars on a navy-blue field. He had also seen to it that each grandchild and ultimately great-grandchild had his or her own pennant, to be hoisted from the yardarm whenever he or she was aboard.

Wilson Peters carried on this tradition, but he did so alone, after his wife of thirty years had decided she could no longer play the ship game. She had moved to Bar Harbor, where she made quilts to her heart's content. Her younger daughter informed her that going to Maine to do quilting was a cliché, but she didn't care; ever since she'd seen the article in *Yankee* magazine, she'd wanted to do it. And she had company—four other quilting widows who had sought a refuge there.

The Commodore's children were willing to put up with him for a month or two in the summer. They had grown up in this house, and though they had moved to other states as soon as possible, they loved to come back to the Cape in the summer and could not afford to stay anywhere else as comfortably. Besides, one day they would come into their inheritance; their grandfather had seen to that. In the meantime, they endured the slings and arrows of the Commodore's outrageous eccentricities, as he strode about in his "Dress Blue Bravo" uniform—white yachting cap, blue blazer, and white ducks. With his hands clasped behind him, Hornblower fashion, he barked orders salted with words like "avast" and "belay" which no one understood. His grandchildren thought "Gampa Com" was cute, except when he would bellow at them: "Stow that gear in the starboard bulkhead, you little lubber, and swab the deck where you spilled that jelly!"

One tradition instituted by the Commodore himself caused his neighbors considerable consternation. Being less than gifted at small boat handling (to say nothing of large boat handling), he had sold his father's 53-foot yacht before moving to the Cape. But he had retained its squat, solid brass cannon with which the Admiral had started the yacht club's Sunday races. It was not large—about the size of a seated English Bull Terrier—yet when its lanyard was yanked, its report could be heard for more than a mile.

Early on those summer Sunday mornings that his family was with him *(very* early, since the Cape extended almost into another time zone), the Commodore, followed by his grandchildren, would emerge on the foredeck. The moment the tip of the sun appeared on the eastern horizon (which could occur as early as 0447 hours), the Commodore sounded reveille on his bos'n's pipe. Then he ordered his party to attention and all held a salute while the designated colors-steward raised the American flag, the navy-blue ensign with the single star, and the appropriate pennants. When all colors were aloft, the Commodore would yank the lanyard, and Old Bull, as he affectionately called the cannon, would roar.

Windows rattled up and down the National Seashore, eliciting muffled groans and curses from neighbors rolling over in bed and wondering why this nightmare kept happening on the one morning they could sleep in. At length, the Commodore's tradition elicited another response—a visit by Officer Otis Whipple of the Eastport Police Department. Alerted of his coming, the Commodore escorted him to the bridge, where an enlargement of Eastport's original by-laws was laid out on the chart table. And since next year on the Fourth of July, the town would launch its bicentennial celebration, the red-circled statute had clearly been on the books a very long time. Its gist: With the exception of the town's militia, there would be no training or maneuvering with cannon, howitzers, or other field pieces by the citizenry of Eastport. There was one notable exception: "The discharge of a cannon on ceremonial occasions shall be allowed."

Out of his depth, Officer Whipple had reported back to Eastport's Chief of Police, Dan Burke, who reluctantly decided that he himself would have to pay a call on the Commodore.

Driving out to East Bluffs, Dan shook his head, feeling far older than his 48 years. He loved this town; he'd grown up here. But lately it seemed as if Eastport consisted mainly of grandparents who were behaving worse than their grandchildren—and someone had put him in charge of kindergarten.

The sun had burned away the fog that shrouded the bluffs, and a brisk northwest wind made everything sparkle. It was shaping up to be a magnificent morning, but he was in too foul a mood to appreciate it. He had been sour for days—to the point where Peg had grown concerned. So they'd had a little talk last night. She thought that with Tony, the third of their four sons, having left for the Marine Corps, and only Danny left at home, he was—lonely. That had made him mad; what about her? But she had all those women at church, while he could hardly fraternize with the officers of the Eastport Police Department.

The talk ended inconclusively—petered out, really, due to the total lack of cooperation of one of the participants. And now he was left to chew the cud . . . empty nest syndrome . . . the loneliness of command. . . . What a great morning this was shaping up to be!

He turned the old, white Oldsmobile Bravada, the department's only four-wheel-drive vehicle (which he used as his own car), into the Commodore's driveway. There he was, standing at the front door in his dress-blue attire. With a sigh, the Chief got out and greeted him.

"Mr. Peters, you know why I'm here."

"Commodore."

"What?"

"It's Commodore Peters."

"Oh. Well, Commodore, we can't have you waking up half the Cape on Sunday mornings, so—"

"Yes, yes," the Commodore nodded, motioning him inside, "there's coffee on the bridge; a fresh pot was made at the changing of the watch."

"Huh?"

"At 0800. Join me?"

"Uh, sure," the Chief shrugged and followed him. The view, he had to admit, was outstanding. The bridge's windows bowed out, so that to port it was possible to see the high cliffs of Lighthouse Beach, and to starboard the rolling dunes that stretched away to the south.

After a mug of coffee, they arrived at an understanding that the Chief felt the Commodore's neighbors could live with. Old Bull could be fired on the following five ceremonial occasions: Memorial Day, the Fourth of July, Washington's Birthday, the Admiral's birthday, and the Commodore's birthday. But only at high noon. Never at dawn. And never on Sunday. If this agreement was ever broken, Chief Burke warned the Commodore while climbing back in the Bravada, the consequences would be swift and severe.

Peace reigned—for about a year. Then, on one perfectly gorgeous April Sunday sunrise (ten days after Maurice Tomlinson was attacked by the bees), the Commodore, thrilled to have two of his grandchildren aboard and overwhelmed with the splendor of the coming dawn, could not resist. Old Bull roared again. And so did the neighbors, every one of whom called the Chief. At his home. On the one morning he could sleep in.

After the fifth call, the Chief, madder than any of the callers, phoned Officer Whipple.

"I'll pick you up in five minutes."

"Where are we going?" yawned Otis, still half asleep.

"Bulldogging."

"What?"

"Just be ready. And Otis? Wear your uniform."

Once again, the Commodore was awaiting them, this time the soul of contrition. "I can't tell you how sorry I am!" he exclaimed, as soon as they alighted from the Bravada. "I don't know what came over me!"

The Chief said nothing. He went around to the back of the vehicle and opened the rear door.

The Commodore's eyes widened. "I'll pay any fine you deem appropriate," he pleaded.

The Chief shook his head. "There's only one way to make sure this never happens again: We're taking that cannon into custody. Where is it?"

A meek Wilson Peters led them to the foredeck. The Chief towed it on its little brass wheels as far as he could, then he and Otis lifted it and carried it up to the Bravada. Barely. Old Bull weighed close to four hundred pounds.

"How long will he be in the brig?" the Commodore inquired.

"You'd better not count on seeing him any time soon," the Chief scowled. "Remember, you were warned."

As they pulled away, in his rearview mirror Chief Burke could see the forlorn blue-blazered figure staring plaintively after them.

5 | faith abbey

OVERLOOKING EASTPORT'S HARBOR on its south side was a series of low, white-clapboard buildings of vaguely Dutch Colonial architecture, fronted by an expanse of well-kept green lawn. Visible behind the buildings was the upper level and roof of a major work in progress—a basilica sheathed in stone the color of the sand on the flats.

This was Faith Abbey, a residential ecumenical community of some 350 people, counting the children. Not visible behind the white buildings were a convent residence for 70 nuns, and a friary for a Brotherhood of 30 monks. Completing the Abbey were some 36 private homes, each housing two or more families, none more than a ten-minute walk from these buildings.

On this balmy Wednesday morning in late April (ten days after the incarceration of the Commodore's cannon, and the same day that Sarah went to the bookstore), only one person was visible on the Abbey's grounds—a man of medium height with close-cropped, iron-gray hair, in a light blue work shirt and khakis. He was trimming rose bushes in front of the low, decorative stone walls that edged the lawn.

Brother Bartholomew straightened and gazed out at the mirror-calm bay. Indeed, it so matched the milky haze above that it was impossible to tell where sea met sky. The only sound came from behind him, and he turned and shaded his eyes as the builders eased one of the last stones into position. *Lapides vivi*—living stones. He smiled. They had prayed so long for this church that each stone did seem alive, though the Latin phrase referred to the members of the Abbey who were being formed by God into a living church. For eight long years they had implored his aid, and it had seemed like nothing was happening. Now suddenly it *was* happening—so fast, it left everyone breathless.

Brother Bartholomew turned back to the little harbor which had been his home since he was a boy. Of the 30 Brothers in the friary, he was the only one from Eastport, and one of three from Cape Cod. The rest came from all over America and Canada. With a sigh, he brought his pruning clippers to bear on the next of the rose bushes he had planted a month before. *Snick, snick*—the sound of the clippers blended with the drone of bees and crickets, as he recalled how he had first come to this place twenty years before.

He had been born in 1951. His name had been Andrew then. His father was Buck Doane, first mate of the *Annabel Lee*, a commercial fishing boat out of Chatham. She was a gill-netter, which meant that his father would often be gone for days at a time. But when he came home, after he got reacquainted with Andrew's mother Isabel, he would take his son surf casting on Nauset's Outer Beach. And if he were home for longer than a few days, he would take him camping. With tent and canoe and all their gear in the back of the old red pick-up, they would head for a tract of virgin forest near Orford, New Hampshire, owned by a friend of Buck's. There Buck would teach his son the important things—how to track deer, how to pitch a tent and start a fire in the driving rain, how to survive in the bush if he ever ran out of food, how to paddle into a headwind. These were things Buck's father had taught him when he was Andrew's age. They weren't things you could learn in school.

In those days his mother had been an English teacher at Nauset Regional High School, and she had felt strongly that Andrew should go to college, specifically to Dartmouth, where her father had gone. Buck hadn't thought college was necessary, but he loved Isabel, and he agreed. Then, as his son turned eighteen, the Viet Nam draft had begun, and the day before his notice arrived, young Andrew Doane joined the Marines. Buck had taught him never to kill anything he wasn't going to eat, so Andrew volunteered to become a corpsman, which meant he would go into combat carrying a stretcher instead of a rifle. He spent his tour pulling wounded Marines out of trouble and trying to keep them alive, until he could get them to the med-evac choppers at the Landing Zone. Given the high mortality rate for corpsmen, it was not long before Andrew was a sergeant and the leader of his own team. After one engagement in which only his coolness under fire kept everyone from being killed, his commanding officer put him up for the Silver Star.

The worst thing that happened to Andrew in Viet Nam did not occur in combat, though. It was a letter from his mother: His father's ship, caught in a terrible gale over the Georges Bank, had gone down with all hands. Andrew got up and walked into the bush, not coming out until long after dark. When he emerged, he wore the blank expression of some of the men he had rescued.

When Andrew would not talk about it, his commanding officer sent him to see their chaplain. In Nam, chaplains were often the butt of bitter humor, but this one had been wise and compassionate. Andrew began to talk. He saw the chaplain often, and gradually the latter opened his eyes to another dimension in life, one in which a loving God existed—a God who could take his father from him and still be loving.

The summer Andrew returned home, he was changed—like everyone who had seen combat in Viet Nam. He had been quiet before; he was even quieter now. His mother took him to see his father's memorial stone—they had never found his body. The next morning he found his father's surf-casting rod in the basement and took the old pick-up to the Outer Beach, where all he did was stare at the sea. For hours. Until the dying sun fired the crests of the breakers an iridescent emerald green, exactly as it had been the last time he had been there with his father. Then he left.

The next day he went back again. And the next, until his mother, who had a summer job as hostess at Norma's Café, got on his case. If he was going to Dartmouth in the fall, his application was already late. But his grades had been good, his SAT scores were high, and he had that medal; they would probably make an exception.

"I don't see any reason to go," he finally said.

"What are you going to do with your life, then?" his mother demanded.

"I don't know," he said at length. "I thought I might get a job on a commercial fishing boat."

"Oh my God!" she shouted. "You are not going to do that! We worked too hard, too long, saving for the tuition, for you to throw your life away!"

He did not shout when he replied, but his eyes narrowed and his jaw tightened. "Are you saying that Dad's life was a waste?"

She had never seen him that angry before, and she caught her tongue. "No," she replied, her voice lower, "but we had agreed you should go."

"I was not party to that agreement," he said.

But in the end, because he loved her, he went.

After Viet Nam, life as a Dartmouth freshman was an adjustment. Though only four years older than his classmates, Andrew felt like the Ancient Mariner. On football weekends while he tried to study, the guys in his house would drink beer till they had to lean out their windows and puke. Though fond of them and bemused by their antics, he never joined them. When he needed a break, he took the old pick-up up the Connecticut River to Fairlee, where he would cross the little bridge into New Hampshire and head up into the hills, where he and his father used to camp.

To his housemates, he was a mystery. Since he would not talk about the war, they construed elaborate fantasies which he bore in good spirits; indeed, his gentle sense of humor disarmed more than one dispute before it got out of hand.

Despite Isabel's hope that he would become an English major, Andrew felt more comfortable in Dartmouth's superb forestry program. Upon graduation in 1978, instead of joining the others in seeking assignment in the great national parks out

West, Andrew applied for service on Cape Cod's National Seashore.

Back in Eastport, he told his mother he was going to rent a room.

Isabel was hurt, and when he explained that he wanted to give her space in case she ever wanted to date, she was even more hurt; after his father, she could never love anyone else. But she saw that *he* needed space; it was time he started doing some dating himself.

That summer of '78 Andrew found himself drawn to the long, low chapel at Faith Abbey. The Sunday services reminded him of the Episcopal ones over in Wellfleet to which his grandmother had occasionally taken him. The Abbey's worship was traditional (some said old-fashioned)–strong on liturgy and formal prayers. Several of the 15 clergy on staff would take turns preaching sermons that were mercifully short and usually to the point. Andrew particularly liked those of the eldest minister, Horton Chambers, who reminded him of the chaplain in Viet Nam.

In the monastic tradition, the Abbey also observed the liturgy of the hours, starting the morning with Lauds before Mass, then a combined service of Sext and None at noon, Vespers in the late afternoon, and Compline in the evening. Some people found it odd that the Abbey used Gregorian chant during these services, but Andrew felt drawn to it. On Monday, his day off, he sometimes went to the noon service and Vespers, as well as Lauds and Mass. While he did not understand the Latin, he had no trouble understanding the peace that emanated from the haunting melodies, rising and falling like the ebb and flow of the surf at Nauset.

They also put a yearning there, and he began to think about the monks and nuns who sang the chant, how they lived and how they had come to be there.

One Sunday morning in the spring of 1980, it had been Horton Chambers' turn to preach. After the service, Andrew lingered to ask him if he might come speak with him sometime. How about tomorrow, on his day off? So their Monday talks became a regular thing.

In October of the following year, on his mother's birthday, Andrew took Isabel to her favorite place, Gordie's, which was as close to an Irish pub as one was likely to find on Cape Cod. Since it was a Thursday, the group known as *Skellig Michael* was playing, and his mother, who was half-Irish, loved it. It had been a perfect evening, she declared as he took her home, the best she'd had since his father died. And then, over a nightcap of Black Bush in her kitchen, he ruined it.

"I think God's calling me to become a Brother at the Abbey," he said quietly. "I've been doing a lot of thinking about it, and I'm going to enter their novitiate to find out."

At first she couldn't speak. "When are you going to do this?" she finally said, her voice scarcely above a whisper."

"Probably in two weeks, when the next novice class begins."

She looked at him, then down at her folded hands. Tears started down her cheeks. "This is some birthday present!" she cried. "How can you think of throwing away everything that you—that we—worked so hard for?"

Andrew made no reply.

And then she hit him with something he had not anticipated. "You realize, this means there'll be no grandchildren! Have you any idea how much I have longed for them?"

He was speechless. Then he got up. "I'd better go."

"Yes, you'd better!" She slammed the door behind him, as he left, and that was the last memory he would have of her for a long time.

But there was someone even more upset about Andrew Doane's decision.

6 | laurel

LAUREL WINSLOW WAS LIKE AN AUTUMN BREEZE. Tall and willowy, with long, auburn hair, green eyes, and high cheekbones, she was at once striking and elusive. There was a wispiness to her, like smoke curling up from raked leaves, and when she spoke, her voice sounded like a breeze stirring maples.

In her youth, fresh out of Sarah Lawrence, she had gone to New York to become an actress. She had answered every casting call, but the parts usually went to the sexy ones or the strident, pushy ones; not many roles were written for wisps of smoke. At length, she had returned to Plymouth, Massachusetts, to care for her widowed father, a newspaperman dying of emphysema. And there, where she would least have expected to, she found work—as one of the interpreters at the historic reconstruction of Plimoth Plantation. It was total interactive theater, the audience being tourists and school groups. The interpreters so immersed themselves in their roles that they became Miles Standish or Governor Bradford, John Alden or William Brewster. They had to answer visitors' questions while remaining in character, rigorously faithful to the year 1628. It was tricky work sometimes (cameras were "magick picture boxes"; tobacco, the "sot weed"), but for Laurel, it was pure Method acting, and she loved it. She never got to play her ancestor, Susanna Winslow, but she did a credible job as the plantation's romantic lead, Priscilla Mullens.

She was not particularly fond of Plymouth, however, which at the peak of the tourist season was like living in a badly overcrowded theme park. She longed for solitude. And one day, as part of the new interpreters' orientation, they were taken down to Cape Cod, to see on the ocean side where the *Mayflower* had first sighted land, and on the bay side where the Pilgrims had first encountered the Nauset Indians.

The North Atlantic seacoast was wild and windswept, and as soon as her foot touched the sand, her heart told her she was home. But she could not go there right away, not as long as her father clung to life. Years before, she had given up smoking to encourage him to quit, and he had honestly tried. But in the end, the sot weed took this thoroughly decent man from her.

When it did in 1978, she quit her job and sold the house, which brought the money to buy a little cottage in Eastport—not enough for the ocean side, just enough for the bay side. That was fine with her, because Laurel was a night person. She preferred to watch the sun set rather than rise, especially when dawn came at such ungodly hours in the summertime. Laurel was a sleepy, languid riser—like a long cat with slow-motion stretching and at least one great, delicious yawn.

Speaking of cats, she had two that she had acquired in New York, after seeing "Cats." (She would have given anything to be a member of *that* cast—and play herself for months on end.) In the spirit of that show, she named her first feline Episcopuss, and the second, Phantasmata, the Magnificat. Puss and Phanty were her only companions, and that was fine with her; a relationship with a director in New York had left her a bit leery of men.

She continued to act. The Cape had an unusual number of good theater groups. For day work, she became the assistant librarian of the Eastport Library. Though the converted farmhouse was a far more modest facility than Orleans' grand Snow Library, it nonetheless had its own display in the Fourth of July parade—a goat pulling a child's red wagon which carried a sign inviting Eastport's children to come to the next "Poetry Read."

Long before it became trendy, Laurel had created a "Cozy Corner" in the library, furnishing it with well-broken-in, overstuffed chairs, and setting up a coffee and tea bar. Gradually a reading club formed, and there would often be two or three older folk who dropped in each morning, to join her in her favorite pastime.

Her monthly Poetry Reads for the children on Saturday mornings were an immediate success. Starting with T.S. Eliot's cat poems for his nieces, each month she would introduce them to another poet. She also encouraged each of them to bring a poem of their own, one of which she would post on the bulletin board until the next Read. And she inaugurated a Yuletide tradition: reading to them (and their parents) her favorite tale of whimsy, *The Thirteen Clocks*, written by James Thurber for *his* nieces. It had nothing to do with Christmas, of course, but that was Laurel.

 è

One cold Monday afternoon in late May, 1981, three years after she had bought her bayside cottage, Laurel had felt a strong urge to take a walk on the wild side. That was what she called going over to the Outer Beach to stroll in the lee of the sand cliffs and watch the waves pounding on the shore. Such wildness appealed to her dramatic nature, especially on a day like that one, when the fog would be billowing in. It made her feel very Irish, and she wound herself into the great woolen shawl that her grandmother had knitted, hooding her head so that she looked like a wraith.

That afternoon, drifting with the fog, she walked much further down the beach than usual. She assumed that what lay before her was as empty as what stretched behind, and when the fog parted briefly, she was surprised to see a lone surf caster far ahead. He stood motionless, except to fling his lure over the silver spindrift that the wind whipped off the waves. Then the fog closed in again.

Eventually she reached him. When she emerged out of the vaporous billows, he was startled, then relieved to find she was mortal.

"Have you caught anything?" she asked softly.

"No," he smiled.

"But it doesn't matter," she said.

"No."

"I know," she smiled.

And as simply as that, Andrew Doane and Laurel Winslow had fallen in love.

He taught her how to fish, took her up to New Hampshire and walked with her over his favorite trails. They camped by the lake, and he taught her how to talk to birds and bake bannock bread in a reflector oven by a campfire—all the important things.

Those were halcyon days. Time did its accordion thing: Perfect moments would expand so that everything seemed to happen in super slow motion. Each of these moments would receive a full page in the album of forever memories. Then, when he wasn't with her, time would compress, with everything happening all at once and jumbled together. Then he would be coming to her, and time would expand again. An hour would take days, and it seemed like an eternity before he actually got there.

They had a song—Judy Collins singing "Both Sides Now." She played it so often, the needle seemed to find its own way to the band. She taped it so she could hear it in the car. They danced to it on her little deck at sunset, woke up to it in the morning, let it weave a golden thread into the tapestry they were making.

It was a blissful summer and a soft fall. Indian Summer came three weeks later to the Cape than the mainland, because it took that much longer for the water around it to cool down. (Of course, the reverse was true in the spring.)

She loved him more than she had ever thought possible—so much that she didn't want to think about it. But there was one part of him she could not reach, a place where she could not accompany him. At first she assumed it had something to do with the death of his father. She wanted to ask him, but kept silent; he would tell her in his time.

One evening towards the end of October, staring into the campfire on what would be their last trip up north that year, he described the things he and his father had done together, how his father had been a man of few words, how wonderful it had been to be the third member of that family. From the sound of Buck Doane, Laurel decided he must have been much like his son. She hugged Andrew's arm, resting her cheek against his scratchy lumberjack shirt, and joined him gazing into the fire.

But it wasn't his father.

She wondered then, if it might have to do with his time in Viet Nam. And the next night, she asked him about the war. He told her what he had never told anyone else: what it felt like to have a man die in your arms and not be able to do anything but just hold him. Tears came to his eyes, and he could barely get the words out. She put an arm around his shoulder and was wise enough not to say anything.

But it was not that, either.

The following morning she would have slept until the sun on the tent made it warm enough for her to get up. But the local chipmunk was of the opinion that every visitor to his domain ought to be up to greet the dawn. And since theirs was the only tent, he scolded it and scampered on it, until he heard her groan and roll over.

Andrew was already up. Peering out the flap, she saw him seated over on the large boulder that overlooked the lake, his hands clasped around his knees. He was watching the sunrise, not moving. A tremor went through her; he had gone to that place again.

She got dressed and joined him making breakfast–blue enamel mugs of steaming coffee brewed in his father's battered tin pot, bacon, oatmeal with raisins and brown sugar, bannock with strawberry jam, and two little trout he had caught just before dawn.

It was perfect. And then he said, "We've got to go back."

"Why?" she said, startled. "You said Dana would sub for you till Wednesday, and Sheila's covering for me at the library."

"I know," he nodded. "But we have to."

She knew him well enough to know that if he were going to explain, he would have. She loved him well enough not to try to find out anyway.

Their last day was happy; they both wanted it to be. But it was sad, too, and as they packed up and started the long drive back to the Cape, she was struck by a premonition: They would never do this again. Ridiculous, she told herself. He loved camping, and now so did she. But the sense of foreboding haunted her. Open your mouth, she told herself. Say something. Lift the rock and let sunlight send the dark things scurrying. But she did not break the silence, and the dread built within her, until she had to bite her lip to keep from crying.

The worst thing was, she didn't even know why.

Then on the radio, they played "Both Sides Now," and she couldn't hold back the tears. He *must* know what she was feeling. . . .

But all he did was keep driving, eyes on the road. And that was the worst of all.

That evening, sitting on her little deck after supper, feet up on the railing, without taking his eyes off the red grandeur that filled the horizon in front of them, he finally told her. "I'm going to join the Abbey's Brotherhood."

"Fine," she laughed, "then I'll become a Sister."

But she realized at once that he was serious. And that the greatest happiness she had ever known—that she had never dared believe she could know—was about to come to an end.

"How soon?"

"Monday."

"That's only two days."

He nodded.

She started to cry, silently. He put an arm around her shoulder, but nothing he could do could ease her pain.

Watching her life crumble into that magnificent sunset, Laurel did not know what to make of God. No one had ever told her that He was real; as a child, she had never imagined Him up there. The sum total of her contact with Him had been when she, like her friends, used His name as a mild expletive. Until now. Now He was real. He was about to take her beloved.

There was no question He was real to Andrew. This wise and thoughtful man next to her, the kindest she had ever known other than her father, did not do things casually. He thought about them, weighed them, and then did the right thing, whatever it cost. Like her father.

Only this time it was going to cost her life.

Without speaking, they gazed at crimson turning to scarlet, to lavender and magenta, and then deepest purple. She shivered, and he stood up. It was time to go.

They went inside, and he took her in his arms and kissed her. It was a long, sad kiss—a kiss good-bye.

She had promised herself she would not beg. But she couldn't help it; she loved him. "Andrew, please"—the tears returned—*"please.* Don't go."

"I've got to," he said, his own voice breaking, "or I never will."

After he left, she put on the windbreaker he had given her and went back out on the deck. It was dark now. There was no moon, but the stars were out. She sat down and looked up at them and told God that she hated Him. He was taking away the best thing that had ever happened to her—that could ever have happened to anyone.

She cried herself to sleep that night. Puss licked her face, and Phanty curled up at her stomach, but nothing they could do could ease her pain.

7 | father horton

THE NEXT MORNING, LAUREL WINSLOW stared at the telephone. Everything in her shrank from what her will was telling her she had to do. Finally her flinty New England stock strengthened her resolve. She had to do it; her entire life was in the balance.

She called Faith Abbey.

She was put through to the Abbey's office. "I need to speak to the person in charge," she said to the young woman who politely inquired if she might help her.

"May I ask what it is in reference to?"

"It's a personal matter," Laurel said, quietly but firmly.

"Perhaps one of our clergy—"

"No!" she exclaimed, surprised at her own temerity. "I want to speak to the person who runs that place."

"One moment, please." She was put on hold. Another voice came on the line, an older woman, calm and precise. "May I help you? Mother Michaela's away with the choir. I'm her assistant."

"I said it was personal." She fought to control of her emotions. "It still is."

There was a pause. "In that case, I really think you ought to speak to one of our clergy."

"Fine. But I would like to *see* him. In person. This is *not* something that can be handled on the phone." She hesitated, then added, "And I need to see him today, not tomorrow."

"Hmm—I think perhaps the person you should talk to is our chaplain, Father Chambers. Hold the line, please." She came back in a moment. "He can see you in his study at the rectory at four o'clock."

"Thank you," she said, managing to hang up before the tears came.

᠅

Back in the fall of 1981, the chaplain's study used to have a bird feeder built into the window, so that finches and chickadees could seemingly eat on the sill, yet fly away in an instant. Horton Chambers was particularly fond of cardinals, and there were usually one or two waiting for the smaller birds to finish. Behind his desk were shelves of books, two of which he had written, along with a number of spiritual classics that he had edited and, as he put it, "mildly modernized." On the sideboard was a tray with a silver Thermos on it, and two mugs.

Any church would be blessed to have a man like Horton Chambers on its staff. The senior clergyman in residence at Faith Abbey, in his later years he had come to personify the compassion to which most dedicated Christians aspire but few achieve. He had the rare gift of pouring oil on troubled waters; indeed, just his presence in the boat seemed to have a calming effect on the turbulent seas around it.

But on that afternoon in late October of '81, Father Horton was about to encounter a wrath which could not be turned away by a soft answer.

Laurel glanced at the chaplain as he showed her to a chair with a view of the bird feeder and the garden beyond. He was an older man, with a pair of horned-rim reading glasses and gray hair–seventy-ish, she guessed, though these days with the new exercise-and-low-fat regimens, it was difficult to tell.

He asked her where she was from and what she did, but she cut the pleasant preamble short. "Father, this is not a social call. I'm upset about something that's just happened, for which you people are indirectly, or maybe directly, responsible."

"You're going to have to tell me what we've done," smiled the old chaplain, "before I can attempt to defend us."

It was a reasonable request. Laurel calmed down, but only a little. "Do you know Andrew Doane?"

"Yes."

"Do you know him well?"

"We've talked on a number of occasions."

She took a deep breath. "I thought *I* knew him well. Until yesterday. I thought we would probably get married."

Father Horton peered over his glasses. "Then you're the girl he was speaking of."

"He told you about me?"

The chaplain nodded.

"What did he tell you?"

"That if he didn't enter the novitiate, he would marry you, if you would have him."

"*Have* him? All he had to do was ask!"

Father Horton got up from the desk and went to the sideboard. "Would you like some coffee?"

"No. I mean, yes. What the hell, I didn't sleep *last* night; I might as well not sleep tonight, either."

"It's not high-test," he smiled. "After lunch, we only serve decaf."

After their first sip, he said, "You love Andrew very much."

"You could say that," she replied, sarcasm edging her voice.

"And he feels the same about you." It was not a question; he was stating the case. "But he also loves God. And he wants God's will for him."

Laurel put her mug down on his desk sharply. "Well, why isn't it God's will for us to be together?" She looked out at the garden and shook her head. "I mean, if there even *is* such a creature as

God, and if He *does* muck about in people's personal lives, why did
He let us fall in love? Was it only to destroy that love? What is He,
some kind of celestial sadist?"

Father Horton put the tips of his fingers together and took his
time before replying. "I don't know why the two of you met. I do
know that God wants only what is best for you—for *each* of you. For
Andrew, that may be to serve him in a special capacity."

Laurel leaned forward. "And what does He want for me? To
live alone with my cats for the rest of my life? Because I'll tell you
this: Andrew has ruined me for anyone else! He's just too—good!"
She started to cry.

Father Horton withdrew a box of Kleenex from a desk drawer
and offered it to her. As she took some, he got up and went to the
window. "I wonder how much you really love him," he mused, looking out at the lavender iris, transmuted to stained glass by the low
sun behind them.

"Didn't I just tell you?"

"Well, if you really love him, then the thing you want most,
above all else, is for him to be happy."

"Of course!" she exclaimed. Then she saw where he was heading. "But what about *my* happiness? Don't *I* have a right to be
happy?"

"Certainly. But for the moment, we're speaking of Andrew.
Suppose you got married and raised a family. And all that time, in
the back of his mind he would wonder: Had God had another calling for him?" He paused and looked at her. "Would he be truly
happy?" He held up his hand. "Before you answer, let me say that
I have known others with similar calls on their lives who refused
them; none of them was ever content."

"But I could make him happy!" she declared. "I know I could!"

"Could you?" he raised his eyebrows. "Can you reach the deepest corners of his heart?"

She stared at him; how could this man know—?

"And what if you couldn't?" Father Horton gently continued.
"What if he felt he had missed something terribly important. . . ."

As his voice died away, Laurel remembered Andrew on the
rock the day before. Wherever he was, she could not go there.

But wait a minute! Her knuckles whitened on the arm on her chair. They were talking about the man she loved! "What if it turns out God *isn't* calling him to be a Brother? What if he gets stuck in there," she nodded in the direction of the friary, "and it's not right, and he can't get out?"

Father Horton nodded. "That's why we have a novitiate. A novice lives like a Brother for at least a year, more often two, testing his call to the religious life. It's a rigorous, demanding call, to a life of service and obedience. One's time and one's space are no longer one's own. But if God has called him to it, then He provides the grace necessary to live it. And believe me," he smiled, "if Andrew is not called, he'll know it."

"So what am *I* supposed to do? Sit around and wait for two years?"

"No," said Father Horton gently. "It would be better to assume that he *is* called. Because that is the likelihood." The mantel clock on the bookshelf behind him struck the three-quarter hour. "In the meantime, you might consider asking God what His plan is for *you.*"

Laurel got up and shook her head. "No, thanks, not if this is how He treats the ones He supposedly loves."

In subsequent years, when she occasionally saw Andrew in the distance—and in a small town it was impossible not to—she took pains to avoid him. Gradually the ache in her heart subsided, and the void where he had been became a place she did not visit.

But Laurel never married. From time to time other men became interested in her, but compared to Andrew, they simply could not measure up, and she refused to settle for second best.

8 | from this day forth

ON A QUIET SUNDAY AFTERNOON, eighteen months after entering the novitiate, Andrew Doane sat at the polished study table in the friary's paneled library, at work on a legal pad. The work was not going well; half a dozen crumpled sheets of yellow paper lay on the floor beside him.

He was composing a letter to his mother, inviting her to church two weeks hence, Sunday afternoon, June 12, 1983, to the service in which he would take his formal vow and enter the Brotherhood. Regarding that ceremony as the most important threshold of his life, more than entering or graduating from Dartmouth, he wanted her to be there. In a way, it was as if he were getting married.

Which is why he was not inviting Laurel. Father Horton had spoken with her, and apparently she had understood, for she had made no attempt to contact him. And that had been a relief, as there had been more than one time when he was less than certain that this was how God intended him to spend the rest of his life.

But he was certain now, and he wanted his mother to share this special moment. The trouble was, they were not on speaking terms.

Twice during the past year and a half, he had attempted reconciliation. Twice his overtures had been rebuffed. The last time, she had accused him of rejecting her and all that was normal in the world. He could still hear her words: "All right, go and shut yourself off and live with your celibate friends! But don't expect me to understand or approve! Because I can't, and I won't!"

Father Horton had helped him to understand that she was reacting out of hurt and loneliness. And *love*—of her dead husband who had left her too early, and whom she could see so clearly in her son. In a sense, she had been abandoned twice by the same man, whom she had loved totally, and it was more than she could bear.

Finally, Andrew wrote simply:

> Mother, this coming Sunday afternoon at 4:00, I am entering the Brotherhood of Faith Abbey. Three other novices are entering the Sisterhood, and there will be a service of sacramental vows. It will be a closed service, but the immediate family of the novices are invited.

He hesitated, then added:

> It would mean a great deal to me if you were to come.

ৈ

Isabel Doane had stood over the kitchen trash can, staring at the letter from her son. Her first impulse had been to discard it with the junk mail. She could hurt him deeply by not going, and to do so would not begin to pay him back for the hurt he had done to her. And then she sighed. There was a ball of bitterness down inside her, like the ball of string her grandmother used to collect, and she realized that she had grown tired of adding bits of twine to it. She was his mother; she would go.

Isabel had never seen the inside of the Abbey's long, low chapel. It was somehow more austere than she had expected—white walls, dark red carpeting, dark brown rafters. A small icon of Jesus was visible in front of the organ on the right, and behind the altar hung a large banner of Christ seated in majesty, the Book of Life open on His lap. On either side of the banner, sunlight streamed in through two tall flanking windows and fell on the white altar cloth, making it so bright it was almost painful to look at.

The altar was decorated with white chrysanthemums, and there were more in the two brass planters on pedestals against the back wall. With a start, Isabel realized that the chapel looked as if it were decorated for a wedding. That impression was enhanced by the program, which an usher handed her as he showed her to a front pew. In it, printed with utmost simplicity, were the vows that the novices would take.

At the organ a Sister was playing a Bach motet, as Isabel raised her eyes to the altar area. There, in choir pews facing each other across the center aisle, knelt robed Brothers and Sisters—Brothers on the right, Sisters on the left. Their heads were bowed, their eyes were closed, and Isabel realized they must be praying for the novices about to join their ranks. In the congregation, the first two rows had been reserved for the novices' families; the rest were filled with abbey members, a number of whom Isabel recognized as parents of children she had taught, or customers at Norma's Café.

Abruptly the music shifted to a piece by Purcell, as down the center aisle processed an older Sister. In her outstretched arms she bore the folded robe which would become the habit of the novice coming behind her. On top of the robe was a plain wooden cross, which she would wear around her neck. There were three such pairs, and Isabel noted that the novices were all in white, carrying little white bouquets. It really *was* like a wedding.

Then came her son, preceded by Brother Anselm, the oldest Brother in the friary, who was carrying his folded robe. Andrew's eyes were straight ahead, and she had never seen him looking so solemn. She smiled as he approached, but if he saw her, he gave no notice.

One at a time, the novices knelt before the altar, where the abbess, joined by Father Horton, laid hands on the head of each and led them in their formal vows, in which they relinquished the right to own, to choose, and to marry, and were given their new religious names. *Do you solemnly swear,* thought Isabel; that was not what they were saying, but that was the sense of it.

Then, to Isabel's surprise there were warm embraces all around—motherly hugs, for the abbess would be their spiritual mother from now on. Isabel felt a twinge of jealousy then, but when Andrew's turn came, her eyes brimmed. She was very glad she'd come.

It was all very strange, she thought, and yet—to her surprise she felt at peace about it. Well, she sighed, from now on her son would be Brother Bartholomew, and she would have to get used to that.

There was no receiving line at the reception afterward, but there were many hugs. She watched Andrew/Bartholomew from afar, being congratulated by his friends and teased by his new Brothers. He was radiant; there was no other word for it. And as she watched, what remained of the ball of bitterness within her—unraveled.

Finally she went up to him herself and gave him a great hug, and with tears in her eyes kissed him on both cheeks and wished him a happy forever.

His eyes, too, were moist, as he thanked her. She left then, and as she drove home, she realized that for the first night since Buck's death, she would not need a pill to get to sleep.

The next morning a rose bush arrived at the friary for Brother Bartholomew. He recognized it as one of the two prize bushes that grew on either side of his mother's front door.

9 | norma's café

SNICK, SNICK—AS BROTHER BARTHOLOMEW FINISHED pruning the last rose bush, he straightened and tried to stretch the ache out of his lower back. That vow service had been back in '83; he, or at least his back, was middle-aged now. Hearing a footstep on the crushed-shell path, he turned and smiled. It was Brother Anselm, who was more than middle-aged. The Senior Brother surveyed his handiwork. "These new ones seem to be coming along very well," he smiled. "Frankly, I didn't think they'd make it."

Bartholomew nodded and gently lifted the head of a full bloom, as if it were a child's. "Roses are hardier than most people realize. And if they know you care. . . ."

Anselm's smile faded. "Brother Dominic and I have another plant we want you to care for. We feel that you should take Brother Ambrose under your wing for a season."

Bartholomew started to object, but the Senior Brother put up his hand. "I know what you're going to say; just to be around him is exhausting. No one plunges from mountaintop to valley faster than he. We've all had a turn on his roller-coaster."

"And he talks incessantly," added Bartholomew, reflecting on how much he might have preferred the life of a silent contemplative.

Anselm nodded. "We feel that he needs one person to relate to, and of all the older Brothers, you're the steadiest. We're not requiring this of you, Bartholomew; we're asking you—for the Brotherhood's sake, for his sake, and who knows, perhaps even for your own."

Brother Bartholomew sighed. "What will it entail?"

"Take him with you, wherever you go. Let him be your shadow. You've been asking for an assistant groundskeeper; apprentice him."

"When does this begin?"

"Now."

"Where is he?"

"At the goat barn, mucking out the stalls."

Bartholomew put away his pruning clippers. "I've got to go out to Cartwright's to pick up some perennials. I'll swing by the barn on my way." He paused. "But Anselm, you owe me one."

Brother Ambrose was twenty-four and rail-thin with quick, dark eyes. He was balding prematurely, to the point where he had to wear a cap out in the summer sun. His personality was mostly sunny, though storm clouds could spring up out of nowhere. His emotions were in perpetual motion, either scaling the face of enthusiasm or dashed on the rocks of despair.

When Bartholomew informed him of his new assignment and invited him aboard, Ambrose was delighted. "Great! I've wanted to learn horticulture and bee-keeping—all those things you do." Climbing into the old red pick-up (not the same as Buck Doane's, but surprisingly similar in character), he chattered happily on, while Bartholomew retreated further into silence.

As they turned into the long dirt road that led to Cartwright Landscaping, Ambrose asked, "Did you always know you were going to be a Brother? I mean, when you were young?"

Bartholomew shook his head.

"What were you—before?"

"A park ranger."

"Where?"

"The National Seashore."

"Right here? What made you change?"

"God, I think."

"Did He speak to you?"

"Not in so many words." And then, realizing that short answers were not going to turn off this spigot of inquisitiveness, Bartholomew elaborated. "I started coming to church at the Abbey. I got to thinking about the Gregorian chant and the people who sang it, and wondering why they were here. Then I started meeting with Father Horton, and. . . ." He shrugged and smiled.

"Did you ever doubt you were supposed to be a Brother?" asked Ambrose, trying in vain to make the question sound casual.

"Of course."

"What did you do?"

"I went out on the flats—so far out that I could yell at the top of my lungs, and no one would hear me."

"And then?"

"I yelled at the top of my lungs."

"What?"

"I told God that I wasn't going to play mind games. I wasn't going to try to convince myself that He hadn't called me into the Brotherhood, or that I'd been confused, or emotionally unstable, or had somehow been coerced into joining."

Brother Ambrose waited, then blurted out, "Well, what *did* you do?"

Bartholomew shifted into second, to tiptoe the truck around the potholes. "I asked Him to rescind my call."

Ambrose recoiled. "And?"

"Well," Bartholomew chuckled, "I'm still here, aren't I?"

They jounced along in silence. Then Ambrose mused, "Sometimes I think about being back in Nebraska, driving the John Deere. I used to love to plow; it was the one thing I could do better than my father. The showpiece of our farm was the two hundred acres alongside I-80. It was directly under the approach path to Lincoln's airport. Everyone in window seats would see the field just before they landed. My father used to let me plow that field, because my furrows were straighter than his."

Bartholomew said nothing, as they passed though the chain-link gate and pulled up at the first fiberglass Quonset hut. But instead of getting out, he fixed Ambrose with his gaze. "Do you believe God called you here?"

"Yes," came the unhesitating reply.

"Then don't look back. You've put you're hand to *this* plow; do your plowing here. It's about time you took responsibility for what goes on in that head of yours." Then he smiled. "A wise friend once told me an wise old Chinese proverb: 'Just because a bird flies over your head, it doesn't mean you have to let it build a nest in your hair.'"

Ambrose started to speak, but the older Brother put up his hand. "Just listen: The trick is to take each thought by the scruff of its neck and march it up to Christ. That's harder than you think," he smiled, getting out of the truck, "but it's about time you started developing some spiritual muscle." He opened the door. "In the meantime, use some physical muscle and give me a hand with these flats of mums."

They loaded them in the rear of the old pick-up and headed back out the dirt drive. All at once, Bartholomew started to chuckle.

"What's funny?" asked Ambrose.

"I just realized: you've got a hidden talent! You know, that lawn out in front of the friary is a little over an acre, and it takes me a couple of hours to mow, when I'm catching the cuttings." He grinned. "Congratulations: You've just become 'Brother Straight-furrow!' From now on, one of your responsibilities as assistant groundskeeper will be to make that lawn look as good as possible. And by the way," he laughed, "I don't know if you ever noticed, but our lawn tractor's an old John Deere."

For once, Ambrose was speechless.

"C'mon," said Bartholomew, "we'll stop at Norma's. I'll buy you a cup of coffee to celebrate."

&

Being a thriving resort town, Eastport had many excellent din-ing facilities in the summer and fall, but only a few that stayed open year round. Of those that did, each had its own loyal clien-tele. At Norma's Café, you could get a hearty, high-cholesterol breakfast as early as 6:30, or a box of take-out for your crew, if it was your turn to get the doughnuts. For lunch, you could have fresh-caught striped bass or a steaming mug of clam chowder that was so good, they sold it in large jars by the cash register. You could even have a no-fat, no-fun veggie-burger, if you really wanted one, up until they closed at 2:30. But at any time, you could be sure of getting the best cup of coffee in town.

Norma hadn't been in the place for several years. Pretty much bed-ridden, she left the running of things to Isabel Doane, who had long since retired from her teaching job. She knew all the charter fishermen and construction workers, all the shopkeepers and town hall clerks, all the lawyers and police officers. For them, Norma's was the heart of Eastport, and Isabel Doane was the heart of Norma's.

Just now she was pleased to see her son come through the creaking screen door, followed by a younger Brother whom she didn't recognize. As they sat down at the counter, she pulled a mug of coffee for Brother Bartholomew, then smiled at his friend. "And for you?"

"I'll have what he's having," Brother Ambrose said.

"Black, no cream or sugar?"

He nodded.

When Brother Bartholomew produced two dollars, Isabel just folded her arms and shook her head.

"Mother, we go through this every time," her son pleaded. "Let me pay for the coffee."

She shook her head. "I'm in charge here; I decide who gets free coffee. You want to pay? Go somewhere else."

"You know I can't," he smiled. "No one else's is as good as yours."

"Well then, enjoy."

He took a sip and turned to Ambrose, who was sampling his. "You see?"

Ambrose nodded appreciatively.

Isabel turned to her son. "How are those new hybrids I sent you last year doing?"

"Not as well as I'd hoped. They don't seem to care much for the salt breeze off the bay."

"Are they getting enough sun?"

"I think so, but the shadow from the guest house hits them after noon."

She frowned. "Sounds like they ought to be around on the south side. Look, I'm going to ask a friend of mine, Maurice Tomlinson, to stop by there and—"

"Mother, please. Don't do that."

"He's the best rosarian on the Cape, and he wouldn't mind."

"But *I* would!" exclaimed Bartholomew. "I have no desire to become a rosarian, whatever that is. I'm just an amateur, where hybrids are concerned, and—"

"I was, too, once," she replied, wiping her hands on her apron. "It won't hurt you to just meet the man and listen to what he has to say."

"All right, all right," he said, finishing his coffee and getting up. "Let's go, Ambrose. It's time you met a friend of mine named Mr. Deere."

10 | teal pond

EVERYONE KNEW THE FIRST THREE RULES in real estate development: location, location, and location. But the fourth—timing—was the one that made or broke the major players. In the 1980s on Cape Cod, Mac Curtis's sense of timing had been unerring. Like a world-class surfer, he'd had an uncanny feel for the huge wave he was riding. His company, Curtis Investments, had caught the real estate boom just as it was beginning to build, and CI had had a long and sparkling ride—luxury townhouses in Hyannisport, condominiums in Orleans, assisted-living retirement communities in Centerville and Yarmouth.

It had been a fast, steep wave. When Laurel Winslow moved to Eastport in 1978, she had paid just under eighty thousand for a modest two-bedroom cottage with a deck on a half-acre of mostly salt marsh, overlooking the bay. Four years later, it was worth more than a hundred thousand, but that was mostly natural accrual. (As old baysiders smugly put it, God was not making any more water-front property.) Then, almost overnight, it seemed everyone had become convinced that Cape Cod was the only place on earth they wanted to spend the remainder of their days. In two years,

Laurel's home had doubled in value; in two more it had doubled again. By March of '88, a friend in real estate informed her that her cottage was probably worth three-quarters of a million dollars. (Unimpressed, she had no intention of selling.)

Cape Cod real estate had, in fact, become one of the hottest land speculations in the country. Construction workers flocked to the Cape to get in on the action. Houses they built on speculation were sold before they could frame them in. It was an across-the-board frenzy, and the flood tide was lifting *all* boats. Houses coming on the market were snapped up, sometimes *above* their initial asking price. Condominium developments were fully subscribed before their prospectus went out. Financiers in New York and Boston instructed their brokers to buy land on Cape Cod, sight unseen. Whatever they paid, it would be worth ten percent more in a month.

And then in August of '89, the bubble burst. A year before, the Federal Reserve, phobic about the return of double-digit inflation, had so clamped down on the money supply that there was none to borrow anywhere. But the Roaring Eighties had kept barreling along, seemingly impervious to the fact that the brakes were now being applied so hard that the pads had worn off, and steel shoes were scoring steel drums.

Economic forecasters had spoken wistfully of a soft landing, but a few older, wiser heads knew this was going to be a crash-dummy experience of the worst order.

On the Cape, prices in July had suddenly leveled off. The big city brokers had stopped calling. Nobody wanted the builders' spec houses. By August the market had gone completely sour. By September those who had been building on credit (which was practically everyone), had to reckon with their creditors. By October, the construction industry, one half of Cape Cod's economic mainstay, had collapsed.

The recession was nationwide. It was not just a hard landing; it was a crash landing, one that some deemed the worst since the Great Depression. It hit the Cape with a terrible impact. People decided to vacation in their backyards, and summer traffic over the two bridges leading to the Cape fell by 30 percent. With it went the Cape's other mainstay, tourism.

A national survey showed that the Northeast was the hardest hit. Of all its states, Massachusetts was the worst off, and of all her districts, Cape Cod had the highest bankruptcy and unemployment rates. Wiped-out builders left their spec houses unsold and headed south. Some of the largest and oldest lumber supply companies went under. Retailers caved in, until downtown Hyannis resembled a smile with half its teeth missing. The value of Laurel's cottage fell to a third of what it had been eighteen months before.

By the end of 1990, the real estate tide had flowed so far out of Cape Cod Bay that an armada of boats, large and small, found themselves beached on the sand flats—with no indication that the tide would ever return.

Not even Mac Curtis's golden touch could protect Curtis Investments. Along with all the other major developers, CI took a staggering hit in 1989, and for the next four years, it was all they could do to keep afloat. Stretching payments, pleading with banks, leveraging with collateral which at times was ephemeral at best, they wrote new lyrics to the pop hit "Stayin' Alive."

But they survived.

11 | a most untimely end

As a boy, Mac Curtis had come to the Cape on vacation with his family, and seeing its long-term growth potential, in 1982 he moved Curtis Investments to the Cape. He set up its main office in Centerville, where he bought a home. A year later he expanded CI, inviting two independent developers, Tobin Hatch and Randall "Cal" MacAllister, to join him as full partners. Together they would be the Three Musketeers—one for all, and all for one.

Then the wave crashed. But Mac Curtis had not lost his surfer's sense, and in 1993, his intuition told him another wave was coming—possibly even as big as the one before. His partners could not see it. To them, it looked as if the economy—and with it, the confidence of the vacationers and condo buyers—would never recover. Corporate America was downsizing the very people who had once dreamed of retiring on Cape Cod. But Mac would not be deterred. The next boom would arrive in 1996, and CI was going to catch it before anyone else and ride it farther than anyone else.

He had a scheme—so over-the-top that it might one day rival Brewster's Ocean Edge Resort. He intended to develop 320 acres, including 12 acres of bayfront property and 30 around a small

pond carried on old maps as "Wallace Sink." As soon as he had
acquired enough of the property around it, he would change its
name to "Teal Pond"—and even import some teal ducks to legiti-
matize the new, more romantic name. In fact, he would call the
whole development Teal Pond. It would be a gated community
around a match-play golf course, complete with a country club,
tennis courts, indoor and outdoor pools, and a corporate convention center. There would be elegant townhouses and condominiums, and two, three, and four-acre estates available for building. At
its heart would be Teal Pond itself, about three-quarters of a mile
in from the front gate and half a mile from the clubhouse.

But when he presented the scheme to his partners, he had
barely finished the broad-stroke outline, when he stopped. They
were not with him. "All right," he said, glaring at first one, then the
other, "what's wrong?"

Cal MacAllister spoke first. "The whole thing's too big, Mac.
It'll take too long to get to the pay-off. If we start on all fronts at
once, like you want to—which will take half a billion dollars, by the
way—and never look back, we won't finish until 1998. That's six
years!"

Mac said nothing. Where he gripped the edge of the teak
boardroom table, his knuckles whitened. He turned to his other
partner and waited.

"I agree," said Tobin Hatch. "The exposure is too great for too
long. With too many variables in play. Granted, the market's been
going nowhere but up. And the economy's starting to follow suit.
But it can't possibly sustain that kind of growth for another six
years! Meanwhile, we're stretched so thin, you can see light
through us!"

From Mac's expression, it was obvious to Tobin that he was
not getting through. Nevertheless, for the sake of the partnership
he persevered. "Look, why can't we do it in stages? Start with the
golf course and the club, but don't finish until the membership is
fully subscribed. Do some of the townhouses and condos, and
then sell them before doing the rest. Ditto, the luxury estates. And
wait on the convention center and the tennis courts and the indoor

pool, until everything else is done. That way, if your wave is a year or two late–"

"We can simply scale back and stretch out the timetable," Cal concluded. "Honestly, Mac, it only makes sense to–"

But Mac had heard enough. He stood up and slammed the table, so hard that the black onyx sculpture of a coiled cobra jumped. "Before I invited you two on board, I did a little checking. Cal, you led the student protest at Amherst against the war in Viet Nam. And Tobin, you were Bowdoin's great football hero." He looked at them. "You both peaked while you were still undergraduates. Life in the real world was a lot less sexy–before I came along. Then I made you rich."

When the other two started to react, he reacted first. "Do you really think you had anything to do with CI's success? You were useful, when it came to dealing with the yacht club and private dining room crowd. They were more comfortable with you two. But I was the hard-ass down in the engine room, making it happen. And your posh friends knew it. They might have preferred to invite you to their clubs, but they wanted me driving the deals!"

Cal and Tobin were angry now, but Mac didn't care. "You were window dressing! But–don't feel too bad; I made you twice as much money as you would have made on your own!"

He sat down and smiled at them. "If you don't have the," he paused and rephrased his words in yacht club language, "*intestinal fortitude* to follow me to the plate and take your cuts, then get out of the on-deck circle. There's plenty of heavy hitters who would give anything for the chance I've given you!"

When they didn't answer, he prodded them: "In or out, boys? If you're the men you like to think you are, you'll tell me off, walk out that door, and never turn back. Your income will drop in half, but you'll have salvaged your self-respect."

He watched their backbones stiffen, as they inwardly told themselves that very thing. But he didn't wait too long, or they might actually leave, and he still had need of them. "On the other hand, if you're the men *I* think you are, you'll swallow your pride and come with me–one more time, for all the marbles–while I make you rich beyond your wildest imagining."

They stayed.

CI opened a branch office in Eastport, where Tobin already had a home, and where Cal now moved his family. On March 27, 1994, as soon as the ground frost had released its iron grip on the Cape, the bulldozers started to sculpt Teal Pond—all of it, all at once.

And everything went better than they had dared hope. Major investors, remembering CI's track record in the last boom, were ready to back Mac's play. And sure enough, early in 1998 Mac's new wave did begin to crest. While it had arrived later than he had expected, he was right about its size. It was going to be every bit as big as the eighties' wave. The previous fall, the Fed had cut the prime three times. Mortgage rates were the lowest they had been in thirty years—and could be locked in for thirty more. In a single year the number of new mortgages doubled.

In Teal Pond, half the townhouses and all the luxury estates were bought before they became available to the public. The Teal Pond Country Club, despite an entrance fee of $60,000, had eighty-two of its limit of two hundred members. Of the twelve lots surrounding the pond, eleven had been acquired, including one on which Mac himself began building a trophy house. Now he changed its name, and at considerable expense imported three families of teal ducks.

Cal MacAllister and Tobin Hatch began to relax. By the time Teal Pond was finished, on schedule in August, of '98, its paper value had increased 46 percent. Cal and Tobin even threw a party for the backers in the new clubhouse, at which they congratulated MacArthur Curtis on his extraordinary foresight—"No, call it what it is: *genius!*" And they laughed at how cold their feet had been.

But there were hairline cracks on Teal Pond's smooth façade, and they were beginning to spider across it. The pools and convention center had run 53 percent over cost projections. The principal backers had reluctantly anteed up to cover the overruns, making it clear there would be no more help. Moreover, there were no reserves. Having put up every scrap of collateral he owned, Mac had called on his two partners to do the same. CI was so heavily leveraged that if the sale of the remaining condos did not continue at the record pace they had been setting, their partnership could actually go into default.

And then CI's biggest backer, Commonwealth Securities, experienced a palace revolution on its board of directors. The new board was convinced that there was more money to be made buying and selling Internet companies, so on April 29, 1999, they informed Mac Curtis that in thirty days they would be withdrawing their support—all $150 million of it. That sort of news could not be hidden, and was sure to spell the untimely end of Curtis Investments.

12 | tobin

TOBIN HATCH WAS THE FIRST TO ARRIVE for the partners' emergency meeting. Entering the CI boardroom, he collapsed into one of the green leather club chairs around the oval table of polished teak. As its centerpiece, there was a highly stylized, black onyx sculpture of a cobra coiled to strike. To Tobin it was chilling, but Mac was immensely proud of it, having parted with a month's pay to acquire it in Saigon in '71. But now the snake was about to bite him.

Tobin had little doubt about the purpose of this meeting: Commonwealth must be pulling out. Which meant it was "game over." He would lose the $14 million he had worked 23 years to accumulate. At least he and Andrina would keep the house; it was in her name. As it should be, he reminded himself; it was bought with her money. Or rather, her parents' money. In the early years, they had bought their daughter and son-in-law everything—houses, cars, club memberships. At the time he'd been grateful, but as the years passed, he had come to resent it bitterly.

They had made it all far too easy for them. Andrina was their only child, and the Brocks of Booth Bay Harbor had an awful lot of money—old money, with only her to spend it on. They had wanted

Andrina to follow her mother to Vassar, but while she had dutifully gone to prep school at Ethel Walker's, after graduation she determined never again to relinquish control of her life. Having persuaded her father to give her a bottle-green Jaguar in lieu of a com-
ing-out party, she opted for her father's college and went to
Bowdoin.

Tobin had met Andrina on the Brunswick campus, where he
was the football team's center linebacker and captain. He was tall
and rangy, quick in mind and reflexes. And he was popular; after
a sack or a solo tackle, his mates in the stands would begin to
chant: "To-bin, To-bin, To-bin!" And he would be inspired to even
greater feats of daring-do.

When Andrina first saw him, she had no idea he was a campus
hero. She admired his easy grace and light-hearted confidence,
and like Lola, whatever Andrina wanted, Andrina got. They were
married right after college, honeymooning at Cap D'Antibes on
the Riviera.

The trouble was, reflected Tobin, the honeymoon never ended.
On the Cap they ran into Neil and Marcia Carrington, who had a
huge sailing yacht with a crew and were about to visit Majorca
before returning to England. Marcia had been a classmate of
Andrina's at Walker's; now she and her husband urged the newly-
weds to accompany them. To Andrina, sailing along the Riviera on
this magnificent yacht sounded like the adventure of a lifetime,
and she persuaded Tobin to see it her way.

But when they put in at San Rafael where Neil's family had a
villa, and started calling friends all over Europe to join them for an
impromptu house party, Tobin had had enough. In the privacy of
their cabin, he insisted that they go home and get started on their
life. Unused to having anyone insist that she do anything, Andrina
threw a fit, an ugly one—so ugly, that it shook both of them.

Tobin was stunned. But if she thought she was going to cow
him, she was mistaken. The former linebacker took a deep breath
and dug in.

Seeing that rage was not working, and that he might actually fly home without her, thus ending the marriage, Andrina
relented. Her parents considered Tobin the best thing that had

ever happened to her. Petulantly she agreed to return to America, but she withheld herself from him for three months, so that he would never forget the cost of crossing her will.

Tobin joined an industrial real estate firm in Portland, where he discovered that being captain of Bowdoin's football team was not exactly a liability. He learned fast and did well—so well that a top Boston firm made him an offer he could not refuse: a partnership with equity.

The Brocks bought them an eighteenth-century home in Marblehead, and through relatives arranged a membership for them in the exclusive Marblehead Yacht Club, so that Tobin would have a place to keep his beloved *Dream Away*, the 33-foot sloop that had belonged to his father.

When it came to decorating, Andrina had taste and talent. It took her a year to restore and redecorate their home, but eventually it was featured on the cover of *American Antiquities*. She filled her days with workouts at the gym, shopping, lunch, and tennis, and her evenings with going out to dinner. Occasionally Tobin's desires would prevail, and they would go to a movie instead. But they never did what he really wanted to do, which was to spend a quiet evening at home with a good book and a fire. His idea of heaven was her idea of hell.

Finally, one evening over fettuccini at Toscano's, Tobin wondered aloud if it wasn't time they started a family. Andrina's fork stopped on its way to her mouth, and she stared at him. Did he really think that, after she had worked so hard to pummel her body into submission, she should actually throw all that away? There would be plenty of time to have children, once she reached thirty.

Only there wasn't. And there never was. And so Tobin got a golden retriever puppy named Tiffany and threw himself into his work, making his first million by the time he was thirty. True to his down-east heritage, he did not enlarge his lifestyle. He kept plowing his gains back into his ventures, rolling an ever bigger snowball and looking forward to the day when he could spend all his time at the helm of *Dream Away*. His work ethic prohibited him from going on more than one trip a year with Andrina—who began finding excuses to travel alone.

In 1983, when CI was making a killing on conventional development of malls and condos, Mac Curtis invited Tobin to join Curtis Investments as a full partner. To his surprise, Andrina welcomed the idea; at last, she could build the house of her dreams. All his money would be tied up in CI, but as her parents had recently died, she had plenty of her own. Though it would mean a forty-minute commute for Tobin, she purchased a six-acre oceanside estate in East Bluffs for two million dollars, and worked with Paul Harrison, an architect in the Eastport firm of Better Creations, to bring her dream to reality.

When it was finished, for her house-christening party she persuaded her friend Peter Duchin to come over to do the music and school friends to come from up and down the East Coast. Complete with fireworks, it was the most lavish party Eastport had ever seen. She basked in its afterglow for weeks, but eventually it faded, and she began to travel again. For the past month, she had been with Neil and Marcia, cruising the Greek Isles.

Friends in Eastport took pity on Tobin, making sure to include him when they did fun things, but increasingly he spent his spare time on his boat with Tiffany, who was now eight now and a seasoned sailor. Not much of a life, he thought, looking at the snake, when a man's best friend really *is* his dog.

The boardroom door swung open. It was Cal.

"Hi, Tobe, is he here yet?"

"Not yet," shrugged Tobin. In addition to being partners, the two men over the years had become close friends. As tall as Tobin, Cal was also in his mid-fifties, but slighter and narrower, with horned-rim glasses, gray-flecked hair, and a bow tie. "You think it's Commonwealth?" he asked.

Tobin nodded. "Couldn't be anything else."

"Well," he sighed, "it's not as if they didn't warn us."

Tobin slumped back in his chair. "Yup."

There was a commotion in the hall, and Mac Curtis burst in. Seeing their expressions, he grinned. "Hey, it's time to send the paid mourners home! Gentlemen, I bear glad tidings: We are about to attend a wedding, not a funeral!"

They stared at him in disbelief. "What are you talking about?" demanded Tobin.

"I'm talking about a new player! One who's going to pick up all of Commonwealth's marbles, and maybe then some!"

"Who is this king of glory?" exclaimed Cal. "I thought we'd beaten all the hedges and byroads."

"We had!" Mac laughed. "This one came to us! It's Boston Fiduciary. When the Chinese took over GennTech last week, they invited BF out. Suddenly BF's awash in liquid assets, and they want something that's hot and close enough to keep an eye on. Nothing's hotter or closer than the Cape right now, and with Teal Pond about to rise from the ashes," he paused and looked at them, "*we* are Boston Fi's next great adventure!"

Tobin was dumbfounded. In the twinkling of an eye, they had gone from looking up at a tidal wave to riding its crest. But there had to be a downside.

Cal was apparently thinking the same thing. "How much do we have to give away?"

"Nothing!" declared Mac. "That's the beauty part! They want the same terms as Commonwealth!"

Cal shook his head. "You mean, all we have to do is—"

"Keep on trucking!" concluded Mac.

But Tobin was still not on board. "When do we see the money?"

"They have their next board meeting in two weeks, and Arthur Hallenbeck, my man at BF, says he can't see anything to keep it from being a done deal."

Tobin frowned. "Then why do I have the feeling there's still something you're not telling us?"

"Well, there is one caveat," Mac admitted. "One of their directors, Arthur won't say which one, has apparently lived on the Cape forever, somewhere over in Chatham or Harwich. Anyway, they're concerned that Teal Pond's relationship with the town is entirely compatible. Seems they've had some unfortunate experiences in the past with contrary town meetings." They all chuckled.

Cal relaxed. "Well, if that's all it is, we shouldn't have a problem. We've generated a lot of employment for local people, and we've all paid our bills on time—so far."

"Even so," said Mac, "I've got a little something else in mind, to warm the cockles of Boston Fi's heart. We're already sponsoring the Bicentennial Fourth of July fireworks down at the harbor; why not do something to ice the cake? Something lasting and positive, that will be admired for years. Curtis Investments is going to sponsor a contest for the Bicentennial: We are going to offer a prize of $2,000 for a new hybrid rose."

He paused to let them savor it. "The Eastport Rose! Awarding it will be part of the Bicentennial events on the Fourth. And to showcase it, we're also going to give the town a memorial planter. It will go in front of Town Hall, where the Eastport Rose will be on permanent display."

"A memorial?" asked Cal.

"To all the sons of Eastport who have died in the defense of our country."

"Mac," said Tobin, at last smiling, "I've got to hand it to you! This is really good!"

"I'm not finished," grinned Mac. "Next Wednesday at my place, we're going to have a reception for the families of the town's eight serious hybrid rose breeders, one of whom is going to be the winner, and for the five judges who will make that decision."

Tobin chuckled. "And the press will, no doubt, be in attendance?"

Mac nodded. "I've promised Barry an exclusive." Barry Jones was editor and associate publisher of the *Revelator*, one of the two bi-weekly newspapers serving the Middle Cape, the other being the *Cape Codder*. Mac had decided to play ball with the young, aggressive editor/publisher, but it was a gamble; Jones was known for his independent thinking. If he thought you were wrong, no amount of persuasion would keep him from saying so. But he was also fair-minded; if he was behind you, he would stay with you all the way. "Sounds like fun," Cal said.

Mac nodded. "We'll pull out all the stops on this one. I want it to be a night to remember."

13 | allie

WHEN MAC GOT HOME from the meeting with Cal and Tobin, he was pleased to see his wife's white Saab in the driveway, though less pleased to see she'd left it out with the top down, when it was about to rain. The main thing was, she was home; he needed her to do something with him this afternoon. He put his car in the garage, then hers, and went in the house.

Allie was in the shower, so he made her a vodka-and-tonic and poured himself a Coke. He walked out on the deck and put the drinks beside their chairs, then settled into his. He pulled his Day-Timer from his hip pocket and smiled; Allie's was so cumbersome, it practically filled her handbag, but this was all he needed. Turning to Wednesday, May 5, he went down the guest list for the reception. There were three columns: judges, rose breeders, and social guests.

At the top of the first column was Chief Burke. The scuttlebutt in town was that he could be considering running for sheriff in the next election. Even if he wasn't, he was widely respected and well liked—a good friend to have. Next was Laurel Winslow, who had just been made Eastport's chief librarian and who wrote the

"People & Places" column in the *Revelator*. A key shaper of local opinion, she was another good friend to have. Ditto, Barb Saunders, running for selectman. The fourth name was that of Roland Royce, their neighbor on the pond. He detested Royce, but he owned the only piece of pond property that Mac didn't. The last judge would be Wilson Peters. The "Commodore" was an eccentric old coot, but a recent profile of him by Laurel had miraculously transformed him and his odd house into a unique and prized bit of local Cape Cod color. Besides, his daughter Pat was more than comely—and just happened to be Mac's executive assistant.

Lining up the next column had been harder. From Bill Finn, at whose garden supply store and greenhouse most of Eastport's amateur and not-so-amateur horticulturists bought their supplies, he had learned of Isabel Doane's long-time interest in roses. The day before, he had dropped in at Norma's Café, taken her into his confidence, and enlisted her aid. From her he had gotten the names of the seven other hybrid growers in town. One, it turned out, was her son, a Brother at the abbey. And one—which was why he had dreamed up the contest in the first place—was Maurice Tomlinson.

He glanced up at their bedroom window. It was not that he didn't like his wife; he did. But Sarah Hillman Tomlinson, his once and future obsession, had consumed him ever since he'd caught sight of her coming out of the pharmacy a month ago.

Allie came to the window now, and called to him. "I'll be down in a minute, hon; soon as I dry my hair."

He thought back to how he had met Allison White four years before. Struggling to hold Teal Pond together, he was flying back from Washington, where he had gone to see if Bill Clinton's Asian friends might be interested in an excellent land investment on Cape Cod (they weren't). He always flew in first class (second row, aisle), where he would erect a cone of silence around him. If the person in the window seat felt chatty, he would give polite, one-word answers until he or she gave up.

But on this flight, the person next to him did not show up until they had almost pushed back from the gate. By that time the overhead bins were full, and there was no room for her laptop or carry-on, except under the seat in front of her. After he helped her stow her gear, the attendant offered her some champagne, which she accepted, joking that she needed it to calm her nerves. Then she managed to spill it on Mac.

Vexed, he nonetheless found himself intrigued with this apparently scatterbrained yet obviously competent executive. She was, he guessed, in her mid-forties, with short, unnaturally blond hair and darting brown eyes. Based in Roanoke, she was on her way to Boston to staff the new regional headquarters of a rapidly expanding telecommunications conglomerate. Having noted how quickly she picked things up, Mac decided to break his rule. He folded the *Wall Street Journal*, got her talking about herself, and settled back to listen.

Over a not bad dinner she told him her story. She was Jewish, from the Bronx. She had married an accountant and spent many years in Bridgeport, Connecticut, raising two daughters. Then she had discovered that her husband actually loved the man she had assumed was merely his best friend. After the divorce she had poured herself into her children, who had finally come to accept that beneath her super-control beat a heart of pure love.

To celebrate her divorce, she had gone in for the hammer throw, as she put it, spinning and letting fly with a legal sledgehammer that had shattered her conglomerate's glass ceiling. She was now their first female vice-president, responsible for all their personnel in the northeast corridor.

Mac congratulated her—so formally that they both laughed. Then, realizing they did not know each other's names, they formally exchanged business cards—and laughed again.

Three days later he drove up from the Cape to take her out to dinner on her last night in town, and persuaded her to add a couple of days to her next trip, to visit him. While he awaited her return, he realized how lonely he was. She must have been thinking along similar lines; six months later, in the fall of '95, they were married.

For Allie, it was not an easy decision. Good at her job and fiercely independent, she was afraid to be vulnerable again. So she decided to have it both ways, persuading her conglomerate that she could perform her tasks just as easily flying out of Logan or

Providence, as out of Roanoke. From Mac's home in Centerville, it was about an hour and a half to either airport.

And then a month ago, he had suddenly announced that they were moving to Eastport.

"What?" she'd exclaimed. "Why?"

"Because I'm sick of commuting! This morning I got stuck behind a little old lady who refused to go over 40 the entire way! I had to shift down to third, to keep the car from lugging."

He neglected to tell her that the car he was following was actually a green Camry.

"Well," she said brightly, getting on board this new train, "we'd better start looking at what's available. Since I'm already taking the month off, why don't I go down to Eastport in the morning and—"

"You don't have to. We'll live in the Teal Pond house."

"I thought you were trying to sell it."

"I was. It hasn't sold. We're moving in."

"Why don't you just lower the price? Six million's a little steep, even in this market."

"Look," he said, letting a corner of his impatience show—something he had never done before. "I want to live there, all right?"

"But it's so big! We don't need that much—"

"I said: I want to live there!"

She was speechless. If he'd slapped her, she could not have been more shocked.

Seeing her expression, he suddenly beamed. "I was planning it as a surprise for our fourth anniversary, but—I'm giving you the house! I've put it in your name!"

Allie was flabbergasted—and now quite chagrined at her reaction of a moment before.

"Mac," she stammered, "I—don't know what to say!"

"Then don't say anything," he smiled, taking her into his arms. As she nestled there, overwhelmed, he added softly, "You don't really think it's too big, do you?"

"No," she laughed, "it'll be just fine."

"Good! Tomorrow we'll go down to Eastport and sign papers. I'm also deeding over to you the ten pond lots—for tax purposes."

She pulled back and looked at him, still smiling but question-ing. "I thought they were part of the Teal Pond development."

"They are. We're just doing these a little differently."

She hesitated. "It is legal, isn't it?"

"Of course!" he assured her in a tone that registered surprise she would even ask.

"And Cal and Tobin think it's the right thing to do?"

His smile faded, letting her know that he did not appreciate her questioning his judgment. "It's legal, but not entirely ethical. And as my partners are not always comfortable with the way I do things, I would appreciate your not mentioning this to them—or anybody. Understood?"

She nodded, a little shaken by this glimpse of a side of him she'd not seen in their four years together. His smile returned, and he again held her, until he could feel her soften and relax, as she decided to trust him.

Good. She must never guess what precipitated their sudden move to Eastport.

The month before, when he had happened to see Sarah going into Baxter's Pharmacy, he had nearly hit a parked car. Pulling over, barely able to breathe, he had felt like throwing up. It couldn't be her! Not after all these years! But it was.

He had never gotten over Sarah. And now it all came back in a rush—the night he had drunkenly confronted her. She had told him the truth, that she had never meant to hurt him, but she had no more control over her heart than he had over his.

At that, he had lost control and had started shouting. Two other officers had tried to calm him down, and he had nearly anni-hilated them. That might have been brushed over, but a Marine colonel had stepped in at that moment, and Mac had decked him, too. Had the colonel made an issue of it, there would have been a court martial, but even without one, Mac's military career was effectively over.

Well, he thought, as he sipped his Coke now and gazed out at the pond waiting for Allie to finish her hair, he may not have been able to control his heart, but he could control everything else. That night 28 years ago was the last time he had ever touched alcohol. Not because he had a problem with it; simply because it clouded his judgment. Life was a jungle, and he could not afford to be to be less than 100 percent sharp, even for an instant.

In Pleiku the next day, he had gone over to the hospital to apologize to Sarah, only to find that she had gone down to Saigon and would not be back until after he was back on the line. The day afterward, he decided to pay the botanist a visit, but they had just shipped him stateside.

His outfit had been shifted to the Cambodian border, and by the time he got back to Pleiku, Sarah had finished her tour and gone home. He had never seen her again—until now.

After the war was over, Sarah had become an obsession with him, until a very expensive psychiatrist had persuaded him to put her behind him and get on with his life. He had, becoming one of the prime movers in large-scale Boston and then Cape Cod development. Until he had met Allie, he had been too busy to marry. But that had worked out well, better than he had expected. He had even begun to enjoy married life. . . .

And then suddenly, none of it mattered. He had seen Sarah, watched her go into that store. Snap out of it, he commanded himself. Improvise! Just like you used to, on recon. In an instant he was back in the jungle, a warrior stalking his prey.

When she came out, he noted that she had a prescription parcel in her hand. Waiting until she had driven off, he took out a twenty dollar bill and entered the pharmacy. When the pharmacist was occupied with a customer, he approached the cheerful young school-girl, chewing gum and chatting on the phone at the cash register behind the drug counter. "The woman who just left," he said to her, nodding toward the front door, "dropped this as she got into her car." He held out the twenty. "I'd like to return it to her. Can you—"

"Oh, that's Mrs. Tomlinson, picking up her epinephrine," said the girl. "She lives over by the cove, on—"

Just then the pharmacist threw her a fierce scowl, and she shut her mouth. But Mac had learned all he needed: Tomlinson . . . by the cove . . . epinephrine, the antidote for bee-stings. . . .

Sweet Sarah, she was going to be his, after all. The shrink was wrong; some obsessions were magnificent. And this one—

The sliding door opened behind him. "Thanks, hon, is this for me?" Allie, in a white sun-dress, reached for the vodka-and-tonic on the table beside her chair.

"Yes, but it'll have to wait till we get back."

"Where are we going?"

He nodded to the cottage across the water in the distance, the only other dwelling on the pond. Though the rest of Teal Pond had been landscaped, and the other pond lots would soon be developed, for the moment the densely wooded area surrounding the pond might have been part of a vast wilderness. "We're going to visit our neighbor."

"I thought you and he weren't on speaking terms."

"Well, it's time to bury the hatchet. That's why I want you to come with me."

"Are we going to drive?"

"No, we'll walk. It'll seem more neighborly." He shook his head. "He's probably watching us through that telescope of his right now."

"What telescope?"

"He's got a big one on his deck. Through my binoculars, I've seen him watching us. Incidentally, you'd better be more careful with your shades."

She nodded. "And why do we want to seem neighborly?"

"I want to buy his property."

"I thought you said he refused to sell under any circumstances."

"He did. But I intend to soften him up by making him a judge of the rose contest and inviting him to the reception. Or rather, I want you to invite him." He looked at her knowingly. "Pull out all the stops; we need this one."

Allie smiled and glanced across the pond. "Can you actually walk around there?" While the lots surrounding it had been staked out and optioned, the clearing of them had not yet begun. The pond was still a virginal ecosystem—though not for long.

He nodded, getting up. "That path down there goes all the way around the pond. You'd better bring your windbreaker; it looks like rain."

14 | rr iv

THROUGH THE LONG BARREL OF THE ANTIQUE BRASS TELESCOPE on his deck, Roland Royce IV watched his neighbors descend their three acres of neatly trimmed lawn and start along the footpath around the pond. They were coming to see him.

He had no desire to see Curtis, who was probably coming to persuade him to change his mind about selling. The cottage was not for sale at any price, and never would be! And yet—he was bringing his wife, so ostensibly it would be a social call. Mrs. Curtis, he *did* look forward to meeting.

He felt like he knew her already. Through the 'scope he had begun watching her whenever she was home. She hadn't bothered to pull down shades; the bedroom, dressing room, and bathroom windows looked out on nothing but pond. So he knew how she felt about herself, and he disagreed with her; she was perfect. (If they had any idea how powerful this old telescope was!)

Getting up, he quickly covered it with the tarp that not only protected it from the elements but also camouflaged what lay beneath it, and went inside. He should offer them something. What? From what he'd seen, she preferred tall, clear drinks, probably gin or vodka tonics. He would explain that without a refrigerator, all he could offer them was herbal tea.

He put another stick of kindling in the wood stove and moved the copper pot over on top of the firebox. Then he looked around the one-room cottage, pulled up the covers on his bed, hid the dirty dishes under the sink, and hung the smelly bag of dirty laundry out the bedroom window.

That done, he got three dirty mugs out from under the sink, rinsed them, dried them with a dirty T-shirt, and got out some Red Zinger tea bags. It would take them another ten minutes to get here; was there anything else that needed doing? Should he cover the computer? No, he would explain that he was a selective Luddite. He could do without most of the conveniences of the techno-revolution, but he was a writer, and it was imperative that he have the best tools available for that craft. He was even plugged into the Internet.

He would not tell them that the Net was where most of his readership was. There were other ultra-environmentalists out there, who felt exactly as he did. In fact, a number of them had come to depend on his insight, expressed in his weekly newsletter. He had 21 disciples out there—17 in the U.S.A., two in Canada, one in France, and one in New Zealand. They devoured the newsletter, forwarding it to friends of similar persuasion. Then, at his invitation, they would join him in a chat-room forum to discuss his key points. The New Zealander and two followers in Montana were already discipling others, but always under his supervision, coming to him with any problems. He was, in effect, the patriarch of a new cyber-green family, and he smiled as his eye fell on the photograph of his own family. In that portrait, his father was frowning, as if he had just thought of something else that displeased him about his eldest son.

Roland Royce III had gone to St. Paul's and Harvard, as had all the Royce men. He bore an astonishing resemblance to Cary Grant, and it was this, as much as the brace of fine British motorcars in his father's garage, which had caused him to be nicknamed Rolls. The name fit. He did everything with grace, style, and panache, and the good things in life seemed to come easily to him.

RR III had hoped that his son would also be called Rolls by his school chums. But when RR IV arrived at St. Paul's, he was a bit of a chub, weighing in at 236, to be exact. So they called him Roly, as in roly-poly, and like all unfortunate nicknames, it stuck. At Harvard, trying out for the crew (all the Royce men rowed), he eventually got down to 185, but he was still Roly. He did not make the freshman boat or even the JV, and after winding up in the fourth boat as a sophomore, he quit. He was accepted into Porcelain (all the Royce men had been members), but he was barely tolerated; in fact, his undergraduate career was something that he (and his father) wanted to forget as quickly as possible.

In the business world, it was expected that he would follow the other Royces into the banking and brokerage firm of Boston Fiduciary. He stuck it out for six months, then informed his father that he was leaving the firm to become a writer. His father had just shaken his head; his son might as well have told him he was running away to join the circus.

Back in the 1920s, the first Roland Royce had bought a piece of land on a wilderness pond in the middle of Cape Cod and put up a rustic cottage on it—a pleasant escape from the elegant but formal town house on Beacon Street. RR II had built a much more sumptuous summer home in Chatham, overlooking the ocean. RR III had made it a year-round residence, adding a guest cottage, a four-car garage with servants' quarters (he had retained his father's chauffeur and housekeeper and moved them to the Cape, along with his father's now-priceless vintage motorcars). But the young Royce siblings loved the little pond cottage and begged him not to sell it, so it had remained in the family.

It was in this cottage that, Roly announced to his family, he intended to live. There he could work undisturbed and would not have to pay an exorbitant rent. His mother had pleaded with his father to give him a portion of his inheritance early, so that he could winterize the place and put in the modern conveniences he would need.

But his father had refused; some day, young Roland was going to have to grow up and take responsibility for his life. And to ensure that day came sooner, his father decreed that he was going to have to support himself at his bizarre chosen profession. There would be no annual remittance from the family. He would have to get by on the income from the trust fund his grandfather had established for him—plus, of course, whatever he could earn by selling what he wrote. His father had laughed out loud at the unlikelihood of that. Roly had moved in at once, and to his credit, he persevered at his writing. But after four years he had little to show, beyond a desk drawer full of rejection letters. As manuscript after manuscript was returned, often with only the first two or three pages disturbed, he began to withdraw. He visited his family seldom, though they were only twenty minutes away.

Each morning he would get up early and work diligently at the keyboard of his computer, then spend much of the afternoon sitting on the deck, watching the pond. He refused to think of it as Teal Pond, but he didn't care much for "Wallace Sink," either. In his mind, it was his own Walden. From the days of his childhood vacationing here, it had been home to a family of large snapping turtles. Now, during the seven years he had lived here, he had studied them so thoroughly with his grandfather's telescope that he had come to know them intimately.

The patriarch he named Old Mose. He was so big that on land he was almost helpless. But he bossed the others around, and they each had personalities—there was St. Agathe, flighty and impractical, and St. Honore who could never seem to get enough to eat, and Young Mose who looked forward to the year when he would finally be big enough to supplant his father.

Roly had come to love them and regard them as his own family. It was perhaps inevitable that he would start to write about them. And to fantasize—*this* would be the manuscript that would be accepted. By the end of his second summer, it was book-length and he had sent it off, to the same publisher who had done that quail book by another Cape Codder, writing on a pond not far from his own. While he waited, Roly dreamed of his book becoming a bestseller, as hers had. When they made the movie of it, the studio would bring his family to New York for the opening night. They would be put up at the Waldorf, and before the limousines came to take them to the theater, there would be a black-tie dinner at which he would receive an award. And at long last, his father would be proud of him.

But the publisher of the quail book did not feel that *Old Mose* "met their publishing needs at this time," nor did any of the other houses to which he sent it subsequently. After two years, he gave up and withdrew even more, coming to regard the turtles as his only true friends.

During his seven years on the pond, he had become increasingly sensitive ecologically, until he was finally the most environmentally correct person he knew. He recycled everything, ate only fruit and vegetables, many of which he grew himself, and used his old Volkswagen Beetle sparingly, preferring to bicycle where he needed to go. The one area in which he ventured forth into society was on behalf of various projects to preserve what was left of Eastport's open spaces, before they were consumed by developers like his new neighbor on the pond. And if the need were great enough, he would even speak out at town meetings.

As he fought the good fight to protect the wetlands and their endangered species, he had come to see himself as Mother Nature's champion, sometimes her chief defender. His writing had taken the form of long environmental polemics—which neither the *Cape Codder* nor the *Revelator* had felt any inclination to print.

And then he had discovered the Net. He had started his own environmental newsletter, and to his delight had soon found that it was receiving several hundred hits a week. That was all the encouragement he had needed. As he tapped away in the solitude of the little cottage, he crossed an unseen line: He began to preach that the preservation of nature had become an end that justified any means.

≥▲

Looking out the window, Roly caught a flash of white in the brush near the cottage's clearing; they would be here any moment. He went out on the deck to greet them.

Their last exchange had been anything but pleasant. Friction had been growing between him and Curtis ever since 1994 when the latter, having purchased all the other property around the sink, had changed its name to Teal Pond. And imported three families of teal ducks. The only problem was, in the spring when the teal families produced ducklings, the little creatures had begun disappearing.

Assuming that foxes or hawks had been making meals of them, Curtis had grudgingly replaced them. Then, one morning three weeks ago, shortly after he had moved into the mansion across the pond, just at dawn he watched the latest batch of new ducklings as they followed their mother into the water and paddled in a line after her. Suddenly, the last duckling in the line—disappeared. Had it been taken by a large fish?

In a moment he was back with a pair of high-powered binoculars, and saw that it was not a fish at all, but a giant turtle. The next day an exterminator's truck had appeared at the Curtis mansion, and as Roly watched through his telescope, a man in gray coveralls spread nets as a trap and baited them.

Roly jumped into his VW and rattled over to the Curtis place to protest in person. The two of them started shouting at each other, but since Curtis badly wanted to acquire the Royce property, he could not afford to alienate the cottage's occupant. So with fists still clenched, he told the exterminator that his services would not be required after all. Had Roly simply left then, the rift between them might have been repaired. But he could not resist pointing out to Curtis that he had been wrong to tamper with nature's balance—first by putting in a lawn where there had been only pristine virginal growth, then by importing a species into a habitat to which it was clearly alien.

Curtis had accepted this lecture in seething silence, and they had not spoken since.

But now, judging from the smile resolutely painted on Curtis's face as he emerged from the brush surrounding the footpath, he was determined to proffer an olive branch. Very well, Roly would graciously accept it.

"Hello, the house!" called Allie cheerfully.

"Hi!" responded Roly, descending the steps from the deck with his hand outstretched, as if they were old friends. He shook hands with her, then with Curtis, but his eyes never strayed from her. Inviting them inside, he offered them herb tea, which was brewing on the stove. Curtis grimaced, but Allie said, "We'd love some," and he poured them each a steaming mug.

Taking hers, Allie studied the large topographical map of the Middle Cape that was tacked on the wall. On it were many notations in fine handscript, referring to various ecological infractions that their host had noted. "I gather you're an environmentalist," she said with a smile.

"I play my little part," he demurred, nodding toward the side window, through which Allie caught sight of his vegetable and herb garden.

"Well," Allie launched in, "since growing things is what you are expert at, and since there will soon be a contest announced to select a new rose for Eastport's Bicentennial, we wondered if you would be willing to serve on the panel of judges." She gave him the full benefit of her most radiant smile.

Roly was stunned. This was not at all what he'd expected. And as he gazed into her wide brown eyes, he knew that he would say yes to anything she asked. "I would be honored," he managed.

"Good!" she replied, taking his hand in both of hers. "Then we'll expect you for our little dinner reception for the rose breeders and judges, next Wednesday at seven o'clock."

Roly nodded. "I'll be there."

When they said good-bye, Roly realized that it was the only time Curtis had opened his mouth. He shrugged, as he watched Allie follow her husband down to the path. Yes, she was perfect.

15 | a wisp of smoke

MAC CURTIS STOOD OUT ON HIS DECK, sipping a soda and watching the eastern sky deepen. Already the trees and brush surrounding the pond were in silhouette, and its surface was a glistening black slate. He looked down, adjusted his cummerbund, and smiled; thanks to the club's fitness center and twice-weekly private sessions with its trainer, he had not gained an inch.

It was a perfect night, he thought, warm enough for the guests to be out on the deck, and about a month ahead of the no-see-ums. Good. It was the most important night of his life. For five years he had struggled to hold Teal Pond together, and now with the almost-certain influx of fresh capital, he could at last be sure of its survival. Tonight would be the beginning of positive coverage in the *Revelator,* of the sort that could be presented to the BF board member concerned about Teal Pond's relations with the local community.

But that was not what made tonight so special. Sarah was going to be here. In his house. After all these years. He put a foot on the deck railing, leaned forward and stared at a light in the distance, across the water. The light was not red like Jay Gatsby's, but it would do. As he watched, it went out; Royce was on his way over.

Allie came up behind him and slipped a hand under his arm. "Everything's ready," she said. "The harpist is setting up in the dining room. The caterers have the hot hors d'oeuvres waiting to go in the oven the moment the guests come."

"They're good," he nodded. "That's why they have day jobs at the club." He put an arm around her. "I'm counting on you to change Royce's mind about selling."

She smiled. "Leave him to me."

The door chimes rang. "There's the gun," she laughed, leaving to greet the first arrivals, and with that, the evening commenced.

Allie had done a magnificent job. Everything was soft candlelight, fresh-cut flowers, gleaming silver and crystal. And the harp music enhanced the setting, like an old gold frame on an elegant portrait.

The first guests were not really guests; they were co-hosts—Cal and Karen MacAllister and Tobin Hatch. The three of them had been talking about sailing, as always, and as soon as they had been greeted by Mac and Allie and had drinks in hand, they resumed, with the MacAllisters inviting Tobin to join them on the water on Saturday.

At the door were Wilson Peters, wearing a white turtleneck and a navy-blue blazer, and his daughter Patricia, in a silver lamé gown. "Good evening, Commodore," hailed Mac, extending his hand, "Glad to have you aboard. Pat has told me a great deal about you." Both were lies, but the old man appreciated them. So did Pat, whose hand he held a moment longer than necessary. Separated from her husband, she had returned to the Cape six months before, and was living with her father. As it happened, his executive secretary had abruptly quit in February, and the placement service had sent him Pat.

The moment she had entered his office, something clicked. Short, brunette, and well-proportioned, she was the only prospect he interviewed. And after the fiasco with her predecessor, Mac had been careful not to say or do anything inappropriate. But he was nonetheless confident that she was aware of his desire for her. In fact, he suspected she might even be one of those ladies who appreciated a little sexual tension in the workplace. With Pat, unlike with Sarah, his interest was purely physical.

The rose breeders arrived in a clump, led by Isabel Doane. With her was her son, Brother Bartholomew, wearing a monk's abbreviated brown robe over khaki trousers. The last of the rose breeders was Maurice Tomlinson, a frail, sickly-looking man with a bad cough, accompanied by the one for whom all of this had been arranged. Sarah wore a diaphanous, cream-colored gown that took Mac's breath away. He greeted them cordially, being careful not to show her any undue attention.

Now Barb Saunders and her husband Matt entered, followed by Barry Jones and a cameraman from the newspaper. "Is it all right if Larry takes a few pictures?" he asked. "We'll need them for the story." Roly entered then, abashed to find himself the only guest not in black tie. Allie went to him immediately, took him by the arm and assured him that his brown corduroy jacket was entirely suitable for the occasion. Beaming at him till he believed her and relaxed, she offered him a glass of Pinot Grigio. Then she asked him what he was working on, listening with rapt attention as he outlined the key points in the newsletter he was composing.

As soon as he paused to take a sip of wine, she slipped a hand inside his elbow and steered him over to Barry Jones. "Do you know our neighbor, Roland Royce?"

"I've heard the name," Barry smiled. They suspected he hadn't, but it didn't matter.

"Well, he has some fascinating thoughts on the ecology of the Middle Cape in the coming millennium."

For the sake of his hostess, Barry feigned interest, while Roly, ecstatic at the chance to talk to a live editor, began to explain to him what would inevitably happen to the fragile dune grass at the northern edge of the harbor, year by year.

The reception was well under way when Laurel arrived. As a former actress, she was well aware of the entrance she was making, and she was indeed striking, her auburn hair gathered in a French twist, her tall, spare frame swathed in glowing, topaz silk. Mac stared at her, then managed to say, "I, um, haven't read any good books lately; what do you recommend?"

"Why don't you come in sometime and see for yourself?" Laurel smiled.

Seeing her, Barry Jones came up. "Laurel, I didn't expect to see you here. Are you gathering material for P&P's?"

"No," she smiled, "I've been asked to be one of the judges. By the way, you're not going to like my next column."

"I didn't like your last one!" he grimaced. "When did you become such a feminist?"

"Selective feminist," she corrected him. "I'm still an old-fashioned girl at heart. Besides, newspaper editors aren't supposed to think like that any more."

At that moment, Allie drew Mac aside. "Don't you think we ought to start serving dinner? It's been more than an hour since most of the guests got here."

"Chief Burke isn't here yet," he replied, "and I want to do the pictures and make the announcement before everyone gets involved in eating."

"All right," she shrugged. Then she whispered, "I just don't want anyone getting loaded. Most of these people don't know each other, and if they're nervous, they'll drink more than they should."

"They'll be fine," he said, patting her arm, "and frankly, the looser they are, the better."

⁊⧫

Out on the deck, Brother Bartholomew was staring at the pond. A May moon was coming up, full and round and yellow-orange with promise, like the moon that once cast its spell on Camelot, when the lords and ladies went a-Maying. It made a path of rippling light, right to the deck where he was standing.

It wasn't fair, he thought; she looked so breathtaking, after all these years. She should look middle-aged. Her hair should be gray, her face lined, her figure thicker at the middle. She should have steel-rimmed glasses and crow's feet at the corners of her eyes. And maybe creak a little at the joints, like he did. She should look like a *librarian*, not some movie star!

Why was he reacting this way? Because she looked as good as the last time he'd seen her? The night she'd buried her head in his chest and begged him not to leave?

And then, because he always tried to be honest with himself, he had to admit that she actually looked even better now; she had grown into the woman she had promised to become.

He finished the glass of cabernet and shook his head, as if to clear it of the images forming there. He shouldn't have come. But how could he possibly have known she was going to be here?

He took a deep breath and let it out. Well, it didn't matter; that was eighteen years ago. He was long over it, well at peace in his chosen vocation.

And then he caught a delicate scent he had never expected to smell again. He turned, and she was standing beside him. She, too, was looking out at the pond. "Seems to me," she said softly, "that we were looking at water the last time we were together."

"I guess that's right," he said, half-smiling, as if the thought had not just crossed his mind.

"How are you, Laurel?" he asked in a tone he might have used, had they both served on an erosion-control committee many years ago.

She fixed him with her gaze. "Do you really want to know?"

"Maybe not," he chuckled, determined to keep it light. "I hear you're a chief librarian now."

She nodded. And then she laughed. "And I hear you're a quite the hand with roses."

He didn't reply at first. Her laugh was a spray of tiny crystal notes that shattered against the beam of moonlight and disappeared.

"In fact," she went on, "I hear you might win this contest."

He shook his head. "I don't think so. Mother's better at roses than I am, and she says Maurice Tomlinson is better than any of us."

"But you know one of the judges," she said, laughing again.

He tried to join her laughter, but his notes were heavier. They just sank into the moonbeam and drowned.

Then he made the mistake of looking up and into her eyes— and eighteen years vanished like a wisp of smoke.

16 | a night to remember

IN THE STUDY, ALLIE BROUGHT Roly a fresh glass of wine. She thought if she heard one more word about piping plovers or open spaces she would scream. But she was on a mission. So when there was an opening, she said, "I know how much you love our pond. I love it, too. But I'm afraid it isn't going to stay this way much longer. The other nine lots are optioned, and it won't be long before there'll be bulldozers in here, knocking down trees, gouging out huge holes."

She paused, letting him see the scene. "Then the cement trucks will come, and the builders, hammering up the frames, bringing in their blaring rock music."

She let the cumulative horror of it sink in, then gave him an even worse vision: "Our delicate ecosystem will be replaced by big houses with new lawns. And when the houses are ready, there'll be kids and dogs and swing sets and pool parties, and jet skis on the pond—Roland? Are you all right?"

He nodded glumly, looking as if he was going to be sick.

"But," she smiled, "you *can* have the isolation you need to pro- duce your best work. Not here. Up north. In New Hampshire. You could have—perfect peace." She smiled at him, encouraging him to believe that the continuation of his writing was the most important thing on her mind that evening.

"I don't know," he said, shaking his head. "My family has owned it for three generations."

"But that was then," she held his eyes, "and this is now. Only now doesn't have to be tomorrow."

"I'll think about it," he said, finishing the glass of wine. She said nothing, just watched his face. And let him watch hers.

"You know," he said finally, "trying to preserve this pond, our pond, would be like trying to hold back the tide." He sighed. "But I could never afford to duplicate what I have here," he murmured, his eyes downcast.

"Roland," she said in a mothering tone that showed she felt his pain. "We don't want you to suffer. We want you to have—all that you have here. The compensation we are planning to offer is so generous, you could buy your own pond in New Hampshire—*and* build a cottage on it! You could even take your turtles with you."

For a long time he said nothing. Then, when he raised his eyes, they were shining. "My father would have to approve it," he said with new life in his voice. "The family controls the land. But come to think of it, he's on the Cape this week." Allie beamed at him. "In fact, it's Mother's birthday tomorrow, and I'm supposed to be there for lunch. I'll ask him then." Allie gave his arm a squeeze.

At last Chief Burke arrived, two hours late and apologizing profusely. His youngest son Danny was the Nauset Warriors' pitcher and captain, and the team had a game over on the Vineyard that afternoon. He and his wife Peg had gone to take it in. They would have been back in plenty of time, except that the ferry had chosen that time to break down, and they'd had to wait for the next one. They had debated going home to get into formal attire and decided that since they were so late already, they'd better just come as they were.

Mac called everyone into the living room and formally announced what they all knew: that there would be a contest to choose a new hybrid rose for the Bicentennial, the Eastport Rose. Reading from the script that Isabel Doane had helped prepare, he introduced the eight finalists and the five judges. The photographer took pictures of each group, as well as the partners of Curtis Investments, and filling his pockets with canapés, departed.

Allie invited the guests, a number of whom were now so relaxed that they were no longer hungry, to partake of the elaborate buffet in the dining room. As they did so, Mac saw the opportunity he had been waiting for all evening. Maurice Tomlinson had taken his plate over to the window seat, where Isabel Doane had joined him. Sarah was about to make it a threesome, when Mac intercepted her. "It's a shame to waste such a beautiful evening," he said quietly. "Come outside."

She hesitated, then pointed out that he didn't have any dinner.

"I'll get some in a minute. Sarah, I haven't seen you in ages! I often wondered what happened to you. I want you to tell me everything that's happened to you."

She looked at him, her head tilted. "I'm not sure that's such a good idea, Mac," she said, still smiling. "Besides, there's nothing to tell, really."

"Oh, come on," he insisted with a laugh. "I'm not going to bite."

With a sigh, she went out through the screen door he held open for her.

They had the deck to themselves. "Let me look at you," said Mac, leaning back and putting a hand on her shoulder. "You look wonderful!"

She said nothing.

"Well, come on," he urged, "what happened after you left 'Nam?"

Sitting down on the railing bench, she took a forkful of Lobster Thermidor and savored it. Then she looked up at him. "Well, I spent a couple of years trying to find Maurice, and when I did, I married him. Then when Mother died, we moved to her summer home on the Cape. And that's it. End of story."

"End of story?" he exclaimed. "But...." His voice trailed off as he gazed at the ribbon of moonlight on the pond that seemed to reach right to them.

He felt cheated. He had replayed this scene so many times. But in his script, she mentioned him—not once, but several times. With a certain wistfulness, for what might have been. But she was not on the same page. She was not even in the same script. And never had been.

Sarah kept her eyes away from his. If she sensed what he was going through, she gave no indication.

What he was going through was hell. For twenty-eight years, despite the long, expensive therapy sessions, he had imagined this moment. But it had all been just that, he realized, just imagination. A gossamer castle built on a moonbeam. And now the moonbeam had shifted.

He had thought the dream was stronger than that. He had wanted so badly for it to be true, that over the years in his mind it had *become* true. It was no longer an article of faith; it was actual. All he had to do was bring the players into juxtaposition. And now he had done that. But the castle was in fragments, sinking slowly beneath the surface of the pond.

Sarah shivered and looked toward the warmth of the house. But he could not bring himself to give it all up. Could the castle still be salvaged?

"I don't think there's a day that's gone by, that I haven't thought of you," he said at length, putting a hand on her arm. "Even when I was getting married, I imagined it was your face looking up at me—"

"Mac, listen," Sarah said, cutting him off and pulling away. "Whatever might have been between us, it was over years ago. I tried to tell you—"

"Not for me, it wasn't," he said with bitterness.

"I explained to you how I felt, before I left," she went on, determined to get it said. "You knew exactly how I felt," she paused, and then continued with as much emphasis as she could and still keep her voice down. *"And nothing's changed."*

"Nothing's changed for me, either," he hissed. Then seeing the alarm on her face, he forced himself to smile. "You know, in a way I did all of this for you," he gestured to the house and grounds behind him. "I knew that some day I'd find you—"

"Mac!" she exclaimed. "You're married. So am I."

"What," he glanced through the window at Tomlinson, "to a half-dead ex-botanist? That's not a life, Sarah. What I'm offering you is—"

She put her plate down and got up. "I think it's time we went home. Please thank Mrs. Curtis for a lovely evening."

As she turned to go in, Mac grabbed her arm. "No!" he cried, no longer caring who heard him. "You walked out on me once; you're not going to do it again!"

The screen door opened, and Allie came out, visibly shaken. Conversation inside had stopped; everyone was peering through the picture window at the darkened deck.

"Come inside," said Allie brightly, taking Sarah by the arm. "You don't want to miss this. They're about to bring in the *Tiramisu.*" Leaving with her guest, she threw a dark look over her shoulder at Mac, hoping to check him before he turned the evening into an unmitigated disaster. But by then, he was beyond caring.

He went into the pantry, where Tommy was putting the liquor away.

"I want a martini, Tommy. Make it a double."

"Mrs. Curtis asked me to close the bar."

He considered countermanding her order, then said, "Never mind, I'll make it myself." Taking the pale blue bottle of Bombay Sapphire Gin, he filled a large tumbler with it. He reached for the small vermouth bottle next to it, then smiled and left it there. This would be a very dry martini.

By the time he joined Pat Peters in the library, the tumbler was half empty. She had been talking to Barry Jones, who had just excused himself. Mac leaned forward and asked, "Are you having a nice time?"

"Oh, yes!" she replied, apparently unaware of what had just transpired on the deck. "It's—beautiful."

"So are you," he whispered. "I've thought so, from the moment you started working for me."

Pat stared at him, mouth open.

"Don't look so surprised! You've known from the beginning how I felt about you!" Again his voice was carrying, and again he didn't care.

Thinking to rescue the situation, Barry Jones now returned and gestured toward the living room. "What's the story behind that knife?" He pointed to the modern, Bowie-style knife mounted in a glass display case over the mantel. The case was edged in walnut, backed with green velvet, and lit by a spotlight in the ceiling. The leather handle had been oiled, and the polished blade gleamed.

Barry went into the living room, and Mac followed. The other guests fell silent. "It's Government Issue, what they gave to Green Berets and recon units," he announced so all could hear. "One of the most efficient killing devices ever designed. You see the reverse curve on the top of the blade? That's so it can be used with an up-thrust," and he demonstrated, holding an imaginary knife in his hand. "Of course, it's also an excellent slashing weapon." He demonstrated that, too, cutting a backhand swath across the face of an imaginary enemy.

There was an awkward silence in the room. It grew prolonged, till the only noise was the pendulum of the cherry wood grandfather's clock. Some of the guests felt like they were watching an unwanted horror program which they were powerless to turn off. All of them wished they could fast-forward to the point where they could go home. But their host seemed to be caught in the grip of some *Götterdämmerung* impulse, which was propelling him forward.

"You see the eight notches on the handle?" He gestured for the guests at the back to come forward, so that everyone could have a clear view. "There's one for each life this knife has taken. They taught us that the best way to eliminate an unsuspecting sentry is to slit his throat from behind." Again, he showed how it was done.

"But I disagree," he said thoughtfully, as if reflecting on faulty doctrine. "I say the best way is step in front of your enemy suddenly, like this, and in that split-second before he can react, you—gut him." He thrust the imaginary blade forward. "You have to be careful to go in low, deep in the belly, or you risk the sharp upper edge of the knife catching on one of his ribs. Then, when you're in deep enough, you angle the blade upward," he showed them how, "slicing through the lung, till the point finds the heart and penetrates."

His guests were aghast. One woman looked ready to faint, another as if she were about to lose her *Tiramisu*.

"You have to keep a knife like this as sharp as a surgeon's scalpel," the lecture went on. "Here, let me show you," and he fumbled a key ring out of his pocket. Taking the smallest key, he started to unlock the case, when Allie came up to him. "Mac, please! I don't think they're interested."

"Of course they're interested!" he replied, pushing her away. "How often do they get to see a knife that's killed eight people?"

He opened the case and withdrew the knife, then began tossing it rapidly from one hand to the other, and now there was genuine fear on the faces of some of his guests. He just smiled; he was a jungle fighter again, back in the dense foliage, blending with the shadows. Back where nothing could defeat him.

His eye caught Maurice Tomlinson's. "You're thinking it's not that sharp, aren't you." Tomlinson shook his head vehemently, but his host continued. "Here, you want to see sharp?" And though no one did, he pushed up the left sleeve of his dinner jacket, tearing open his shirt sleeve, sending the cuff link flying. Then, with the lower edge of the blade, he started dry-shaving the hair on his forearm.

"I'm leaving!" exclaimed Roly, starting for the front door.

"Yeah, go back to your turtles," Mac called after him. "You don't have the stomach for a man's game!"

When others started to follow him, Mac shouted, "Go ahead, all of you! But you're going to miss seeing that this is also a throwing knife!"

"Okay, Mac," said Tobin, calm and smiling. "I think show time's over. Let's put the knife away." He started towards his partner, who now dropped into a crouch, balancing his weight on the balls of his feet.

"You think *you're* man enough? You want to try me? C'mon," he said, beckoning Tobin with his free hand. "Or do you have to hear the grandstands chanting, 'To-bin, To-bin, To-bin' before you can be a hero?"

At that, Tobin started towards him, as Mac knew he would. "Well, come on, hero, let's see what you're made of!"

Before it could go any further, Chief Burke stepped between them. "All right, that's enough!" he commanded. Then, more calmly, to his host, "Now put that thing away." When Mac made no move to comply, he added, "Do you really want to wind up this evening as *my* guest? In our slammer?"

"For God's sake, Mac!" pleaded Allie.

The jungle faded, and the enormity of how far things had gotten out of control gradually seeped into Mac's awareness. He looked at his wide-eyed guests, then at the knife in his hand. He was not one of those Viet vets who periodically went off his rocker. He had never had post-traumatic stress syndrome; for that matter, he had never had the knife out of its case before.

Crestfallen, he returned it now and locked it. "Sorry, everyone," he said to them, "it was just a joke."

Some of the guests nodded, and a few made an attempt at thanking their hostess. But everyone was politely pressing toward the front door, like the *Titanic's* first-class passengers in their dinner jackets and gowns, heading for the boat-deck.

It was a night to remember.

17 | brother anselm

THE BEST THING ABOUT BROTHER ANSELM was that he was a good listener. He did not interrupt or jump to conclusions, or attempt to come up with the perfect answer. He listened—and before responding, he weighed what he was about to say.

So it was to him that Brother Bartholomew went with his dilemma. Brother Anselm, the Senior Brother, was the oldest, and coincidentally, the wisest of the Brothers in the friary. Together with Brother Dominic, he was responsible for the Brotherhood, reporting to the Abbess, Mother Michaela.

He found him in the barn, inspecting the hurt hoof of one of their goats. "Anselm, I need to talk."

The older Brother looked up at him, and seeing his face, straightened and wiped his hands on the barn apron. Then he went over and sat on the milking bench, where the younger monk joined him.

"Something happened a long time ago," Bartholomew got the words out with difficulty. "Something I thought I was free of, but now suspect may have been merely dormant all this time. Anyway," he sighed, "it's not dormant now."

He paused in case Anselm had a comment, but the latter just listened, waiting for him to continue.

Bartholomew took a deep breath. "When I came here, there was a girl. If I hadn't become a Brother, I would have married her. And for seventeen years I never saw her, except at a distance. But I've seen her now," he shook his head, "up close. And personal. And what I feel for her—*still*—is so strong, it scares me."

He waited for Anselm to say something, and when he didn't, he anticipated his friend's first question. "I've prayed. I cannot get her out of my mind, and believe me, I *have* prayed!"

Finally, Anselm replied. "Why do you suppose this has happened now?"

The younger Brother looked at him. "I've no idea. Maybe things were just going too smoothly," he added sardonically.

"You're *angry* at God, aren't you." It was a statement, not a question.

"What? Why should I be?"

"For upsetting the status quo. For allowing this to happen to you. For disrupting your tranquillity."

Bartholomew thought for a moment, then nodded.

"Well, believe it or not," his older friend went on, "this is love."

"*Love?* Then how come I feel torn apart inside?"

Anselm hesitated. "Let me put it a different way: Why do you suppose this has happened now, instead of, say, five years ago? Or even last year?"

Bartholomew shrugged.

"It could be time for healing, and—it may also be a test. A test that you might not have been ready to face five years, or even a year ago. A test you may be barely ready to face right now."

Bartholomew slammed his hand on the bench. "It's not fair! I've taken my final vows! I took them eleven years ago! My call, my celibacy, my spending the remainder of my days in this place, in this Brotherhood—all that was settled a long time ago!"

Anselm smiled sympathetically. "Then why do you feel so—unsettled?"

The younger monk had no answer. He just shook his head, his eyes filling.

"Look," said his friend, his own eyes full of compassion, "God has allowed this to happen, because He knows there's unfinished business deep in your soul. And now is the time for it to be resolved. I do believe He has called you to be a Brother, and—"

"I believe it, too!" cried Bartholomew.

"Well, our call is like a marriage. Only it goes beyond death; it's for time and eternity." Bartholomew nodded. "Every marriage I know of," continued Anselm, "has some rocky places in it." He sighed. "And a lot of times they come after the marriage has been doing fine for years. There's even a saying about that: *Beware the dogs of noonday.*"

Bartholomew looked at him, his brow wrinkled.

"When we're young in our call," Anselm explained, "the dogs of morning don't bother us; we're on fire for Christ. But when we reach middle age and look down the corridor of years awaiting us, with each not much different than the ones before, we can be tempted to feel lonely. Or empty. Or to wonder: Is this all there is?" He paused. "At such times we are vulnerable. And Bartholomew," he looked at the younger monk, "this is your noontime."

Turning away, Bartholomew stared at the goats grazing in the yard.

"You've been a good Brother," his friend concluded, "more steady in your ways and in your growth than most of the others. That's why we felt you were the one to take on Ambrose."

And then he chuckled. "But I've always thought you were a little *too* good. I almost wished you had inordinate pride, or an ego that could get loose at times, or a problem with jealousy or anger. Or even that you were, God forbid, perpetually irresponsible or tardy." He shook his head. "But you were none of those. If we had a recruiting poster for the Brotherhood, you'd be on it."

Bartholomew smiled and shrugged, attempting to join the joke, but his friend's smile faded. "The trouble is, perfect Brothers don't bend. And so they have a tendency to break, or shatter—perhaps because they've never failed before. The enemy particularly enjoys testing them—and God allows him to. But not until they are strong enough to withstand him. And stand with their Father, if they so choose."

Anselm got up and took off his apron. "Bartholomew, you made a hard choice when you came here seventeen years ago," he said. "And now, it seems, you face the same choice again. Only this time, I fear, it will be even harder." He looked at him. "I will pray for you every day."

18 | in cold blood

AS HE COASTED PAST the Chatham Bars Inn and swung left into the short driveway of his parents' home overlooking Pleasant Bay, Roly checked the computer on his handlebars: 32:16—not his best, but close. He rang the doorbell, and when the ancient handyman, Horace, opened the door, he gave him the bicycle, which was too good to leave outside. From his backpack he removed his mother's present, a leather-bound collection of his newsletters. It wasn't wrapped, but she wouldn't mind.

"Is my sister here?"

"Yes, sir," Horace replied, "everyone's in the drawing room."

"People don't have drawing rooms any more, Horace."

"Yes, sir, but that's what your mother calls it."

"Well, it *is* her birthday. Her house, too, come to think of it. I suppose she can call it anything she wants to."

"Yes, sir."

Roly hastened toward the living/drawing room. He had counted on his sister being late, but for once she was on time. Probably because she knew he would be counting on her being late. She'd won again.

In the drawing room a cheery fire flickered in the hearth, though it was the sixth of May and warm enough outside for him to have ridden over in a polo shirt. But Mother loved fires, and it was her birthday. "Sorry I'm late," he murmured, "headwind."

"Well," his father said, deciding not to admonish him on this happy occasion, "now we can open the champagne." From a silver ice bucket signed with the signatures of his ushers, he withdrew a well-chilled bottle of Schramsberg, uncorked it, and poured four glasses. When they each had one, he raised his glass to his wife and pronounced: "Mary, as you have brightened so many of our days, let this day be a very bright one for you. And may this coming year be your best yet. And so say all of us."

"Hear, hear," said Roly and his sister. He even *sounds* like Cary Grant, Roly thought. His mother was delighted. All twittery and chirpy in her white chiffon party dress, she reminded him of Billie Burke as Glinda the Good.

Horace's wife Harriet appeared in a black dress and a starched white apron and passed a silver tray of hot hors d'oeuvres. The sight of them brought the previous night back to Roly so vividly that he emitted a groan.

"Is something the matter, Roland? You look as if you're about to be sick."

"Sorry, Father. I was just remembering last night."

Everyone waited for him to explain. "A little party at my neighbors' on the pond."

"Who are your neighbors, dear?" his mother asked. "Are they anyone we might know?"

Roly smiled dourly. "I don't think so, Mother. He's a real estate developer named Curtis."

"Of Curtis Investments?" asked his father, putting down his glass.

"He's the head of it, I think. He renamed the pond. It's Teal Pond now, to go with some big development he started five years ago."

"Interesting," said his father, and in truth he seemed more interested than in anything Roly had said in years. "You say he had a party last night? What sort of party?"

Roly related the reception, adding that they had asked him to be on the panel of judges. "I think because they want to buy the cottage; it's the only lot around the pond that they don't own. And last night, Allison—Mrs. Curtis—almost had me convinced it was a good idea. The pond is about to lose all its charm, and she indicated that they were prepared to be extremely generous. In fact," he concluded, "I was going to recommend that the family consider it."

"What changed your mind?" his father asked.

Roly told him of the knife episode, and of Chief Burke having to put a stop to it.

"Before that," his father asked, "what was your assessment of Curtis?"

Roly was pleased; his father was actually seeking his opinion. "Well, before he started doing his Rambo thing, I just thought he was an obnoxious, self-made egomaniac. Now I think he's a dangerous sociopath."

Roly's mother waved her hand. "Please! Let's not have any more of such talk! It's my birthday! I want us to talk about happy things!" She raised her glass. "I want each of you to know how much you have meant to me, and how grateful I am for each one of you." She may sound like Glinda, thought Roly, but she really means it. He reached over and patted her hand.

Roly's father got up. "Mary, excuse me for a moment; I have to make a business call."

"Can't it wait, dear?"

"Afraid not. But don't worry; I'll only be gone a minute." He went in to the adjacent library, and Roly heard him put through a call to his brother, who was Boston Fiduciary's CEO. Then his father closed the door.

❧

Allie looked out the bedroom window at the pond and tried to shut out the hideous memories of the previous evening. It was no use; they seemed to be on an endless loop. It had been the worst night of her life. And this morning had seen little improvement.

She had expected her husband to have a horrible hangover—and then, as the realization of what he had done became clear to him, she had anticipated that he would implore her to forgive him. Together the two of them would get to work at damage control, to see if somehow their ship could be saved.

But that was not the way it played out. He had gotten up before her, and had been sullen and withdrawn, barely speaking to her, when she had come down. And then he had closeted himself in his study, and she had gone back upstairs to make the bed and read.

Now, on the deck below, she saw movement. It was Mac, with a scoped hunting rifle. She watched him attach the sling to his upper right arm, then rest the barrel on the deck's railing and start sighting through the scope.

She cranked open the window. "Mac! What are you doing?"

Turning to look up at her, he scowled and said slowly, "Just go back in, and shut the window."

In his voice there was a steel she had never heard before. With a shudder, she closed the window. But she watched. He was aiming at something across the pond. My God, was it Royce? No, he had gone to his parents'. What then? The turtles! Her hand reached for the window crank—and stopped. She realized that she was afraid of him.

Half an hour later, after six shots had been fired, she came downstairs and found him in the gun room. With a ramrod, he was slowly, methodically running an oiled patch down the barrel of the rifle. Holding a thumbnail into the open breech to reflect light up the barrel, he inspected it. Then he looked up and saw her standing by the door.

"Don't start with me," he warned. "They've had it coming, ever since I caught them eating my ducks. The little creep's had it coming, too, walking out on my party and leading everyone else away."

"Mac, what's gotten into you? You were so drunk last night, you almost took on the chief of police!"

"It wasn't that bad," he replied scornfully.

"Not that bad?" she shouted, forgetting her fear. "You managed to insult every guest at the party! And then that macho business with the knife was totally over the edge! Until that moment, I had Royce ready to sell us his cottage!"

He glared at her sullenly, then went back to cleaning his gun, now rubbing down the wooden stock with another oiled patch.

She looked at him, her eyes narrowing. "You started on the booze right after you were out on the deck with Sarah Tomlinson. It's got something to do with her, doesn't it?" He made no response. "Last night wasn't the first time you'd met her, was it?" Another statement. "In fact, I'm beginning to wonder if you didn't cook the whole thing up for her benefit. Did you—"

Mac laid the gun aside and got up. "Don't go any further," he whispered, raising a finger.

ë

That afternoon, as he turned his bike into the yard of the pond cottage, Roly sensed something was wrong, terribly wrong. But the front door was still locked when he tried it, and the computer was still there, when he went inside. He noted that a few e-mails had arrived from his disciples, but nothing to put this sense of dread in his stomach. Unable to shake it, he went out on the deck—and emitted a deep, agonizing groan. There, on the grass at the edge of the pond, was Old Mose. His neck had been almost severed, but he was still alive. He was trying to reach St. Agathe, whose shell had been shattered but who was still twitching. Floating in the water upside down a little ways from shore, were St. Honore and Young Mose. The entire family—his family—had been wiped out, massacred in cold blood.

Sobbing, Roly stumbled down the steps and went to Old Mose. He dropped to his knees beside the great, dying turtle, picked him up, and cradled him in his arms, rocking back and forth and wailing.

19 | the collapse of teal pond

MAC WAS STARING OUT THE BOARDROOM WINDOW, hands clasped behind his back, when Cal and Tobin came in. He did not turn around.

"What's up?" asked Tobin. "Is one of our guests suing us for cruel and unusual punishment?" Not having spoken to Mac since the reception two nights before, he now made a joke of it, to show that as far as he was concerned, they were still the Three Musketeers, and there were no hard feelings.

Cal chuckled in support, but Mac remained silent. Then, without turning, he said quietly, "Boston Fiduciary has just turned us down."

"Oh my God," murmured Tobin. "There goes the ball game."

Cal was too stunned to speak. At length he managed to whisper, "Why?"

"Arthur, my man there, said that with the stock market so volatile, the board did not feel comfortable having that much capital tied up for so long in one venture." Now he turned, and they could see that his face was black with rage. "He said their decision took him by surprise; two days ago they could not have been more keen." He glared at first Tobin, then Cal. "It sounds like someone told them about Wednesday night." They way he said it, there was no doubt he suspected it was one of them.

Tobin met his gaze. He said nothing, but at his sides his hands slowly drew into fists. Standing next to him, Cal gently touched his arm, then said, "Mac, that's crazy. If this is the end of Teal Pond, it's the end of me. You know I'm leveraged to the eyeballs. So is Tobin."

But Mac would not be mollified. "Mr. All-American's wife is so rich," he sneered, "he doesn't have anything to worry about. It might be worth a few million to him, to see me go down in flames."

Both men stared at him, as if he had lost his senses. Then Tobin took a deep breath. "All right, Mac, I'll level with you: I don't care a whole lot for you. And you obviously feel the same way about me. But when I joined this partnership, I said I would give it one hundred percent." He paused. "Up in Maine, a Hatch's word is worth something." He looked Mac in the eye. "I'm going to tell you this once: I said nothing to anyone about Wednesday night."

Shaking his head, Cal sought to put the moment behind them. "Do the other investors know?"

"You can't keep something this big quiet very long," Mac replied, nodding in the direction of his office. "Just before you came, Pat got a call from Ed Finlay over at BankBoston. I think we can assume the word is out."

Cal put a hand over his eyes. "Then it's over." He sighed and walked over to the window, murmuring to himself, "What am I going to tell the boys?"

"What do we do now?" asked Tobin. "I've never faced bankruptcy before."

"Our investors will send their auditors," answered Cal from the window, "to go over our assets."

"Like vultures picking at carrion," commented Mac.

"Well," Tobin observed, "it's been quite a run. One for all—and all for naught."

Speaking as much to himself as to the others, Cal wondered how he was going to break it to his family. "I've got a son at Andover and another at Princeton. That's fifty grand a year. For openers." He stared at the black onyx cobra. "We can sell the house, of course, but how long is that going to last?" His voice trailed off into silence.

Tobin looked at Mac. "Is there *anything* we can do? Any rabbit we can pull out of the hat?"

Mac picked up the onyx snake and turned it slowly. "I've looked in every hat I can think of. No joy. That noise you heard as you came in was the fat lady singing." He replaced the sculpture carefully on the table.

"Well," said Tobin, "if there's nothing we can do here, I might as well go and be morbid on my boat." He turned to Cal. "You want to come?"

"Not today; I've got to break the news to Karen. But we're still counting on you for tomorrow."

Tobin left, and Mac was about to follow him, when Cal said, "Can I speak to you for a moment?"

The other man turned back. "Well?"

"Look, Mac, I, um—I'm a little short on cash just now." The words came out slowly, as if each were wrapped in barbed wire and tearing the inside of his mouth. "I wonder if you might lend me a hundred thousand to tide me over."

"Tide you over?" responded Mac, not making it any easier for him. "Till when?"

"Well—until I can land something," Cal finished lamely.

"Do you think you'll be able to?" Mac said, still turning the sculpture. "I think you're going to find that guys in their fifties are a glut on the market just now. Corporations are hiring kids for a third as much, figuring they can pick up the experience they need on the way." He put the sculpture back on the table. "Sorry, Cal, but you'll be lucky if you can land a job managing a convenience store."

Cal said nothing.

"And on that pay scale," his partner concluded, "you'll be dead long before you could pay me back."

Cal exploded. "I can't believe this! You almost seem to be enjoying it! You've got to be hurting, too—maybe not as much as us, but—"

"Because I'm not as much of a fool," Mac explained. "I had a very wise colonel in Special Forces. When we were part of a defensive perimeter with other forces, he taught us to link up with them but at the same time encircle our own position—so that if they collapsed or got overrun, we'd still be protected."

Cal's eyes narrowed. "What are you saying?"

"You know those lots around the pond? Who do you think owns them?"

Cal just stared at him.

"Not Curtis Investments. A little company called ACA—Allison Curtis and Associates. It was all there in the fine print, but you and Tobin were too busy to bother reading the boiler plate."

"We *trusted* you!"

Mac shrugged and smiled. "That's not my—"

Cal lunged at him, but his swing never connected. Instead, faster than he could register the blows, he received the edge of a palm across his face and an elbow to his chest that sent him flying over the table and onto the floor.

When he came to, Mac was gone. He groaned as he tried to move, and then, despite his split lip, he smiled. There on the floor beside him was the onyx cobra in a dozen pieces.

 è♠

The view from the end of the harbor parking lot could not have been more dreary, thought Cal, as he parked the Volvo wagon. There was no wind; the surface of the bay had a greasy, gelid look to it and perfectly reflected the heavy overcast. Everywhere it was gray, unbroken, with no horizon. Just like his life. Once there had been the wreck of the target ship to look at out there on days like this. But it had rusted away, and now there was—nothing.

Which pretty well summed it up. Mac was right; there was nothing out there for him.

The thought reminded him that the pain on the outside was at least as bad as the pain on the inside. He took inventory of where he hurt, starting with his left front tooth. He touched it and sighed; it was definitely loose in its socket. Did they grow back, if you left them alone? He hoped so. He didn't have the $1500 to cap or replace it just now.

He sighed again and winced; his chest ached. Gently probing, he decided that there was at least one broken rib, maybe two. He ought to sue him, he wryly thought; his hands—and palms and elbows—were lethal weapons.

Except, he reminded himself, he had made the first move. Better get back to the business at hand.

He had come here to sort things out, before going home to break the news to Karen. He would follow it with a realistic but positive appraisal of their situation, only he was having trouble with the positive part. Thank God they didn't owe anything on the house, and that he'd had the presence of mind to put it in Karen's name. She would have to sell it, of course; including taxes, it cost nearly $30,000 a year just to run it, and that was with him doing most of the yard work. Plus, it needed new shingles and a new roof, and the windows needed replacing—there was another $30,000 right there.

At least, whatever they could sell it for would be free and clear.

But the market was softening again; it would probably bring no more than half a million. Most of which would have to go into an educational trust fund for the boys. Randy wanted to go to med school, and Judd always did what his older brother did. Plus, they would need to live somewhere, and in Eastport you couldn't get a decent two-bedroom condo for under $200,000.

Something white in the gray sky caught his eye. Two gulls were flying together—stark, white silhouettes against lowering clouds. He watched them as they soared and wheeled, circling higher, then diving down and away. When one gull turned, the other would bank right with it, so smoothly it was like they were dancing—a breathtaking *pas de deux*. He could almost hear the music.

He forced himself to leave them and return to earth. Now, as for work, he would find something. In real estate. Even if he had to take an entry-level job. He had twenty-five years' experience, and he could soon parlay that into—what? Who was he kidding?

From beneath the bulkhead doors of the root cellar in the back of his mind, there was a scuffling noise. No! He was not even going to look in that direction. But the scuffling grew persistent, and at last he went over and drew back the bolt and allowed the thoughts to enter his consciousness.

Twelve years ago, when the money was coming in faster than he could wisely invest it, his estate planner had advised him to put as much as he didn't need into a life insurance policy. It was a way of passing it on to his family without them having to pay estate taxes on the interest or go through probate. And they would get it right away. It didn't seem like all that much at the time, only half a million. But it was two million now—under the present circumstances, a small fortune.

There was movement up in the sky, and his eyes went to it. It was one of the gulls. He scanned the skies for the other, but the gull was alone now and flying farther and farther away.

20 | karen & cal & tobin & (not) andrina

TOBIN'S SUBCONSCIOUS TRIED TO WEAVE the ring of the telephone into the dream, so he would not have to wake up. It couldn't, but he didn't mind; it was a lousy dream. In it he was calling everyone he knew, to see if they would give him any money. They wouldn't.

"Hullo," he mumbled.

"Tobin?" It was Karen, sounding far too perky for so early in the morning. He told her so.

"Come on, Tobin; it's eight o'clock already! We're going sailing today, remember?"

He had forgotten. And he did not want to remember now. He had consumed a bottle of Tyronnell single malt Irish whiskey last night, and though he normally loved sailing, it was the absolute last thing he wanted to do this morning. His head felt like an overripe watermelon that someone had dropped. The thought of being on a small, pitching sailboat in the bright sun all day nearly sent him into the bathroom for another turn at driving the porcelain bus.

"Look, Karen, let me beg off. Please. You and Cal go. I'm really not fit company for man or beast."

She laughed. "We're not exactly bubbling over, ourselves. From the empties in the recycling box, I'd say we made a fair dent in Cal's collection of vintage wines last night. All the more reason why we really need to do this. We'll meet you at the launch ramp at nine."

"But—"

"No buts. Just be there." And before he could muster a firm refusal, she hung up.

With a groan, Tobin swung his legs over the side of the bed and started to sit up. Not a good idea: Waves of nausea lapped on the shores of his consciousness. Seeing he was up, his golden retriever came over, rested her chin on his knee, and looked up at him. Smiling in spite of himself, he patted her head. Good old Tiffany; she always understood. "Okay, old girl, come on."

He eased himself upright, and gingerly made his way to the kitchen door, opening it and putting her out in the back yard.

Then he gazed at the kitchen clock, trying to make it make sense. It wouldn't; in fact, it seemed to be staring back at him, waiting. With a deep breath, he wrapped the pull-cord around the flywheel of his mind and gave a hefty tug. Nothing happened. It needed some choke. From the refrigerator he produced a bottle of Mexican beer, popped its top, and took a deep swig. Now he pulled the cord again, and this time the motor caught.

Let's see. . . . Twenty-two minutes to get over to Chatham, which meant—less than 22 minutes to get ready. First, brush teeth. Next, hot shower. Now the watermelon is parboiled! Eat something. Ugh. But sailing with a hangover on an empty stomach was disaster. He forced himself to eat a bagel and washed it down with another Dos Equis. That was better; he finally began to feel like he could actually do this thing.

Putting Tiff in the kennel and making sure she had fresh water, he backed the old Morgan out of the garage. The royal blue English sports car, breathtakingly restored, was his secret mistress. He took her out only on weekends, and she never failed to lift his spirits. Well, this was a Saturday—and by the time he got to Ryder's Cove, the landing on the way to Chatham that his friends always launched from, he felt at least tolerable.

They already had the *True Love* in the water, and Karen, dazzling in a navy windbreaker and white ducks, was forward, ready to raise the jib. Beside her was a wicker picnic hamper brimming with sandwiches and goodies, none of which had the slightest appeal now, but all of which would taste wonderful after three hours on the water. Cal had an ancient, battered cooler to which Tobin added two six-packs of Dos Equis, his contribution to the outing.

He admired the lines of the *True Love*, as she rocked gently at the dock. She was a lovely old teak Thistle, beautifully finished and varnished, a true open-boat classic. Cal and Karen were justifiably proud of her; if there were such things as antique boat shows, the *True Love* would win best in show.

He thought of his own boat, a Hinkley Bermuda 40, moored at Chatham's Stage Harbor, and Karen read his mind. "Ours may not be as big as *Dream Away*, Tobin," she gaily laughed, "but she's the yarrest boat in this harbor!"

He smiled and nodded—and thought: And her skipper has a wife who enjoys going out in her.

Climbing aboard, he raised the mainsail for Cal who had mentioned that he had hurt his ribs, while Karen put up the jib. In a few moments they were under way, with Cal at the tiller, nosing her out of the channel, close to the windward rocks, but not too close. Once they were clear, they encountered a steady northeast wind of about six knots, gusting to eight or ten—brisk enough to keep them moving, but not enough to kick up whitecaps and force them to concentrate more than they cared to. It meant they could tack up the coast and into Pleasant Bay and then have a bracing run home. Above them, cumulus clouds scudded across the sky, providing brief but welcome respites from the bright sun. A light chop thumped the bows in a gentle, steady rhythm. It was a perfect day.

Karen caught Tobin grinning, and called, "You see? I knew you'd be glad."

She was right: He was already beginning to feel the tension and frustration draining away. As she turned to watch the sand cliffs disappearing in the haze off their port bow, Tobin gazed at her. This wind had dislodged a strand of hair, and it played around the firm line of her jaw, until she absently brushed it back where it belonged.

Taking a deep breath, he told himself to forget it; she was the wife of his best friend. He glanced back at Cal, whose eyes, barely visible under the long bill of his faded sailing cap, were fixed on the shoreline ahead. Tobin realized that what he really yearned for was not so much Karen, as what the two of them had.

They enjoyed being together, and nowhere was it more apparent than when they were sailing. Anticipating the needs of the boat, they would move without speaking, one shifting position while the other tautened the jib. Each knew what the other was about to do, and they flowed together with such grace that they reminded Tobin of ballroom dancers.

He tried to remember if Andrina had ever enjoyed being with him. She had at first, though she always made him feel as if he were some kind of trophy that she'd won. He was handsome and a hero, she'd told him, and every girl from Bangor to Booth Bay wanted him.

And Andrina—she, with the wide, almond eyes and honey-blond hair and a haunting, far-away look—had gotten him. Her great-grandfather had founded a shipyard on the Maine coast, and her grandfather had run it brilliantly during World War II. As a result, Andrina had more money than she could ever hope to spend—which was saying something, as she was very good at spending it.

"Tobin? Want to take her?" Cal offered him a turn at the helm, and Tobin, startled, nodded. Moving carefully in the small boat, they changed places.

"You want a beer?"

Tobin squinted aloft and frowned. "Sun's not quite past the yardarm."

"Never stopped us before," smiled Cal, fishing one out and opening it for him.

Tobin took it gratefully, and pointing the *True Love* up a bit, went back to his ruminations. After she'd finished building the house, Andrina had wanted to get him a bigger boat, more in keeping with their new lifestyle. She would prefer a power yacht, but since he had such a thing for sailing, she allowed as how it could have masts. Only it had to be at least sixty feet, so that it could have staterooms and a crew and a proper kitchen, and a deck big enough to dance on.

He had asked her: If he got such a boat, would she sail across the Atlantic with him? She had looked at him, amazed. That was what crews were for! You flew over and went aboard when the boat was safely in the harbor; Neil and Marcia had taught her that. He told her then that *Dream Away* was all the boat he needed.

After one endless summer of back-to-back houseguests, Andrina had decided that Eastport was beginning to lose its charm. She called Neil and Marcia to see if they were doing anything fun, and with their kibitzing she fashioned their next *divertissement.* Gathering a bunch of their friends for a trip down the canals of France on a small flotilla of barge boats, when they reached Champagne country Andrina had a surprise for them, cooked up with her old chum, Buddy Bombard. She arranged for an early-morning festival of champagne-breakfast balloons, which made for a gorgeous double-page spread in *Condé Nast.* Overnight, Andrina was an international celebrity in her own right—the new savior of the bored and the restless.

Her next coup was to do Africa in a small fleet of Lear jets, and after that, Moscow and Saint Petersburg. She never had trouble lining up fellow travelers, not with so many fun people saying to her: "Listen, if you ever put together another adventure, call me first!"

At the moment she was leading a squadron of four ocean-going yachts through the Greek Isles. Neil and Marcia's was the flagship, of course, but there was no question who was the commodore.

"Tobe! Watch it!" called Cal. "Don't you see those shoals?"

"Sorry." He pushed the tiller hard over, narrowly avoiding the patch of ripples ahead of them.

"It's all right," said Karen gaily. "We've all got a lot on our minds. Who's for lunch?"

Tobin threw her a smile of thanks. It struck him that that was the first kind word any woman had said to him in—he couldn't remember how long. She looked stunning, and the longing for her returned. He sternly told himself that the only reason she'd invited him was that she had felt sorry for him, and probably also that she thought it would be good for Cal, who was getting morose.

They gathered aft, around the hamper which Karen had covered with a bright, red-checked tablecloth. The two of them had Chardonnay; Tobin stuck with beer.

It was he who brought their troubles back on board. "It's my fault," he said, shaking his head. "I never should have let him bulldoze us into that conference center. I knew the market was getting spongy."

"We both knew it, Tobe," said Cal. "It's my fault as much as yours."

Karen scowled, then shrugged; if they were both determined to ruin her party, she might as well join in. "But what you don't know," she said to Tobin, "is that Mac has come out of the cesspool, smelling like the Eastport Rose!"

"What are you talking about?"

Cal told him what he had learned yesterday about who owned the pond lots, and why he was now sporting a swollen lip and a black eye.

Tobin opened his mouth, but no words came out.

"Not a bad parachute, wouldn't you say?" Cal concluded.

"God," muttered Tobin, "what fools we were!"

"No!" declared Karen. "You were not fools! You were decent men. But you were dealing with a snake."

From their faces, it was obvious she was not getting through. "Look," she said, trying again, "a partnership is built on trust. It's like a marriage: If you don't have trust, you don't have anything."

At length, Tobin nodded. "She's right, Cal. We *had* to trust him. It might have been a mistake to have ever gotten involved with CI, but once we were in, we were in."

"But *I* got *you* in!"

"Don't beat yourself up over it. I was a big boy with a lot of experience," Tobin smiled ruefully. "And I *did* check him out, and I *did* know that he was a slippery character. I just didn't think—"

But Cal wasn't listening; he stared at the water running past the boat, and Karen threw Tobin a pleading look.

"C'mon, Cal," cried Tobin, "he's not worth it!"

Cal looked at him then. "Even if we sell the house," he murmured, "I don't see how we can keep the boys on track for med school."

"Okay!" announced Karen decisively. "Pity party's over. You guys either have another drink, or we're going home!"

"Might as well do both," Tobin smiled, joining in. "Ready about?" he called. "Hard a lee," and he swung the *True Love* south and ran before the wind.

But in the scant hour it took them to reach Ryder's Cove, Cal said not a word.

21 | andrina's farewell

THE STANDING LAMP behind the cracked burgundy-leather easy chair made a warm pool of light. No other lamp in the paneled study was on, but for Tobin, slumped in the chair with his legs stretched out on the matching footstool, one was enough. He could see the old engravings of great racing yachts, one of which, the *Atair*, had been owned by his grandfather. And the color enlargement of his father winning the Monhegan Race in *Dream Away*. And the black-and-white photo of his father, much younger, in the cockpit of his Corsair on the deck of the *Essex*.

Andrina hated this room. It did not go at all with the decor of the house and completely disrupted the flow of a first-time guest's aesthetic experience. Yet since it was to be his study, Tobin had been adamant: He wanted a replica of his parents' library, right down to his father's old leather chair. Over the years it had acquired a patina and a certain scruffy charm, and if a house could be said to have a warm center, this was it. Visitors invariably gravitated here, so whenever Andrina was entertaining, she kept the door shut, pretending it was a utility closet.

Tobin gravitated here, whenever he needed a fix on who he was. But tonight the room wasn't working. He picked up the phone and called the overseas operator, asking for callback operator number 41.

"Mr. Hatch, I was about to call you. With good news: I've located Mrs. Hatch. She's not on Skorpios; she's on Mikonos. But it's 1:30 over there; are you sure you want me to put you through?"

"Go ahead. I doubt Mrs. Hatch will be asleep."

And when Andrina came on the line, clearly sleep was the furthest thing from her mind. "Tobin? Is that *you?* Darling, how *sweet* of you to call!"

In the background he could hear a bouzouki band playing. "Sounds like you're having fun," he said, trying to match her cheeriness.

"It's a masquerade dinner party in a palace that's being excavated! No one's ever done such a thing, until I came. They weren't going to let us, until I persuaded Ian—he's the resident archeologist, a charming boy on loan from the British Museum—with an enormous gift to the excavation fund. And so, as the greeting cards say, here we are, having a *wonderful* time!"

Wish you were here? Apparently not. "Listen, Andrina, this is important: Curtis Investments has just lost its principal backer. And with it go all the others." He paused. "We're done for."

The bouzouki music seemed to grow louder, as he waited for her to respond.

"Well," she finally said, "that's too bad."

"You don't seem to get it: We're bankrupt."

In the background, they were playing "Never on Sunday."

"What I don't get is, what do you want me to do about it?"

He could not breathe, let alone speak.

"Oh, I see! You don't have any money! Well, *nema problema*, as they say over here. I'll wire my bank to put $10,000 a month in your account. Will that be enough?"

"Andrina, it's not the money," he said, his voice breaking. "I want *you*. Here. With me. I *need* you."

Now they were playing the theme from "Zorba the Greek."

"But darling, we haven't finished Mikonos. And Monday Ian has re-arranged his schedule to take us on a tour of the caves on Siros and—"

"Did you hear what I said? I really need you"—his voice fell to a whisper—"probably more than I ever have."

She did not respond at first, but he could feel her surprise and embarrassment; he had never been so vulnerable. Finally he had to ask, "Can you come home?"

More silence.

"Andrina?"

"Well, I can't possibly leave now; I have obligations." She thought for a moment, then said brightly, "Look, I'll be home in about three weeks, how's that? We were planning an Ireland adventure in June, but I'll just put it off. I'll spend the whole month with you."

"I need you *now.*"

"I just told you, darling: I can't." A note of irritation crept into her voice, as if she were dealing with a demanding child.

He was about to hang up, when he caught himself; his entire marriage rested on what happened next. "Andrina, you're my wife."

"Now, darling, you really are getting a bit tiresome." He could hear other voices in the background. "Oh, here's Neil and Marcia!" she exclaimed. "They send you their love, but they're telling me that Ian is about to do the unveiling. Kisses, darling; I've got to go." And she did.

Tobin stared at the dead receiver in his hand.

æ

Cal did not have a rich wife. Yet in Karen, he was far richer than he supposed. While he was cleaning up the *True Love* in the barn and making some minor adjustments to her rigging, she ran a couple of errands. At Baxter's Pharmacy she got the latest copies of the *Cape Cod Times*, the *Cape Codder*, and the *Revelator*. Then she stopped by Bill Finn's garden supplies and bought a rose bush.

When she returned, she brewed some coffee and got out their mugs—his with the blue sailboat on it, hers with the head of a

Springer Spaniel. It was a liver-and-white Springer, not a black-and-white like Pepper, but it was close enough. Next, she spread the help-wanted sections of the papers over the counter like war maps. At the top of a fresh legal pad, she wrote POSSIBILITIES. Then she called Cal in from the barn.

"Welcome to the war room," she smiled, handing him his mug. "This thing has hit us like Pearl Harbor!" (She'd just read John Tolland's book.) "They think they've finished us, but they're in for a terrible surprise. For an aroused America," she said, imitating FDR, "is a fearsome adversary! The only thing we have to fear—is fear itself!"

Cal chuckled, and Karen joined him; it was the first time she'd seen him smile in two days. "You want to go first?" she asked, pointing at the newspapers.

He just looked at her.

"All right," she said, resolutely cheerful, "I will." She scanned the ads, reading aloud anything that might suit her capabilities, and every so often throwing in something so completely outlandish he had to laugh. "Thank God Judd got me over my computer phobia, before he went back to school! I can still type, and I can even balance my checkbook on the thing."

When she was finished, she had circled three ads with a red marker and written down the phone numbers under the column headed *Karen*. "Your turn," she smiled, tapping the *Cal* column.

With a sigh of resignation, he started reading. And reading. "Well?"

He looked up at her, and the hopelessness in his face made her want to cry. "Karen, we've got to face it: There's nothing out there for a 56-year-old bankrupt developer. And the moment they hear I'm a former partner of Curtis Investments, it'll be the kiss of death."

"You can't just give up!" she pleaded. "At least contact a placement agency, and if that doesn't work, you can go to the different Realtors yourself. I just know you're going to find—"

"No, you don't know that," he retorted. "And you obviously don't know about Terry Armbruster."

"Who's he?"

"Who *was* he." He took a sip of coffee. "A dozen years ago, Armbruster was a developer down in Falmouth. I met him at a Realtors convention. Nice guy, about my age. We had a drink together. He had kids in prep school and college; none heading for med school, but there were three instead of two. Like us, he'd gotten overextended and lost everything. He drew blanks with an agency, and started doing what you want me to do, going around with résumé in hand. At least, that's what he told his wife he was doing."

He looked out the window at the shadows of twilight rapidly filling in the shrubbery that surrounded their back yard. Karen said nothing.

"Day after day, Armbruster would go down to Cotuit harbor and just park and watch the gulls. And then one night he parked somewhere else—in their garage, with the door down and the engine running."

Karen inhaled sharply. "How do you know all this? I mean the part about him going to the harbor."

"Someone I know in the business went to the funeral; at the reception afterwards, his wife came apart and told him everything. One of her friends had seen her husband down at the harbor several days running, and had mentioned it to her. She'd confronted him, and that was the night he did it."

Then he added with a wry smile, "That's when I let Steve talk me into that big policy."

Karen stared at him, eyes widening. "Randall MacAllister!" she almost shouted. "Don't you even—"

"Don't worry," he grinned. "I wouldn't do anything that stupid."

But the sense of grave unease would not leave her.

"All right," he said cheerfully, "let's see that paper." He quickly found an ad by a local Realtor and circled it, writing the firm's name and number on the pad. "I'll go see them tomorrow."

Trying to look reassured, she refrained from pointing out that tomorrow was Sunday. "Okay," she said, matching his bright tone, "now come outside for Part Two."

Mystified, he followed her out. She pointed to the rose bush in the back of the wagon. "We're going to plant that, right in the middle of our back yard! In years to come, we'll look at that big old bush and remember that this night was the start of our new life together."

She strode toward the barn, calling over her shoulder, "You get it out of the back and figure out where it's supposed to go; I'll get the shovels."

By the time they had gotten the bush in the ground and watered it in, it was almost dark. They went inside and checked: Their brave little earnest was clearly visible from the kitchen counter, leaning on its support stake. To show that he was as committed as she, Cal got out the best bottle in his small cellar, a '91 Opus One. With exaggerated ceremony he uncorked it and let it breathe, while Karen found some aged Volpetti parmesan, some extra virgin olive oil, and a sourdough loaf she'd been saving for supper.

Filling two big-bowl wineglasses a third full, he gave one to Karen and raised his to the little bush outside. "To our new life."

And then unaccountably he started to cry and soon was wracked with silent sobs.

Oh, my God, she thought as she went around the counter to put an arm around his shoulders, he's never done this. And she struggled not to join him.

Oh, my God, what am I going to do now?

22 | kyrie

THE MACALLISTERS ARRIVED at the chapel ten minutes early, only to find it already two-thirds full. Local choral aficionados knew that when the abbey's choir gave a concert, the downbeat came at precisely the time announced, not five or ten minutes later.

As they settled into seats at the end of a pew by one of the windows looking out on the harbor, Karen was glad they had not come any later. They had almost not come at all. When she'd broached the possibility that morning over bagels and the Sunday *Globe*, Cal had made it clear that the last thing he wanted to do that afternoon was sit in a stuffy chapel listening to classical music, and he didn't care how good the choir was. As his bumper sticker put it, he'd rather be sailing.

But Karen had persisted. Her husband was sinking into a slough of despond, which seemed to have no bottom. She was losing him. The night before, when she had begged him to talk, he had said there was no point and had gone to bed.

Just before falling asleep herself, she remembered something that had happened when she picked up the rose bush at Bill Finn's. Brother Bartholomew had been there, picking up feed for the abbey's goats. Remembering him from the reception three days earlier, she had greeted him warmly, and he had helped her pick out the rose bush. When they parted, he mentioned that the abbey's choir was giving a memorial concert tomorrow afternoon at three, if she and her husband would like to come.

Maybe a good concert would help, she thought; at least, it couldn't make things any worse.

So now, despite Cal's grumping, they were here. She opened the program and read that the concert was in memory of a recently deceased Russian composer named Georgy Sviridov. She had never heard of him, let alone any of the works by him that they would be singing that afternoon. No, she thought on closer inspection, that wasn't true. She *had* heard the first piece by Sviridov: three choruses from the play *Tsar Feodor Ioannovich*, music which according the program had been used on the sound track of "Lorenzo's Oil." She and Cal had seen that movie. She went back over it in her mind and decided it must have been the haunting background for the candlelight service in the cathedral. But first they were going to sing something she definitely knew: the Fauré "Requiem." She turned to point it out to Cal, but he was staring out at the bay.

At 2:55 the 45-voice choir filed in, the men in black tie, the women in full-length gowns of blue silk. They took their places on the risers, calm and poised—without fidgeting, Karen noted. A bit austere for Cape Cod, she thought; this was hardly Carnegie Hall. She'd heard they were that good, though, and they did tour all over the place. She herself had never heard them, because truth to tell, she, too, would rather be sailing.

But she was not unacquainted with choral singing. At Smith, she had been in the choir and also in Smithsoons, the *a cappella* group for which she had done some of the arranging. If this choir was world-class, as one New York critic had called them, she would know it.

At 2:59 the choir's conductor, Mother Michaela, who was also their abbess, came out and took her place facing the four ranks of singers. She wore a black gown, and her gray hair was cropped fairly close. A minute later they began—and Karen was enthralled.

Balanced, beautifully blended and articulate, their rich sound reminded her of—what? Dennis Brain's French horn recordings.

Visually, two things impressed her: first, the hands of the conductor; moving in unbroken, fluid motion, they evoked, alerted, calmed and summoned. They *were* what the music was, and ultimately they brought out all that was in the music—and in the hearts of the singers.

The other thing Karen noticed was the expressions of the choir; their eyes never strayed from the face and hands of their director. They were holding music, but they obviously knew it by heart. And in their faces she saw total commitment. They were not 45 voices, she realized; they were one voice, coming through 45 people.

The Fauré came to the lyrical Kyrie movement, and now, as it soared and lofted, overcoming the oppressive acoustics of the low-ceilinged chapel with its massive cross-beam rafters, she stopped assessing and let her heart soar freely with the music. And then she was twelve, back in Montana on the Gallatin River, with her father in the stern of the canoe. The fly rod in her hand was forgotten, as she watched a pair of eagles above them. They weren't hunting; they were circling and diving in the wide, blue sky, rolling over on their backs and peeling out of the heavens, plunging earthward for the sheer, sun-dazzled enjoyment of it. Now, listening to the Kyrie, she could see them again.

She threw a sidelong glance at her husband, who was still gazing out the window. But he was listening; tears were flowing down his cheeks. He would brush them away, but more kept coming. Seeing them, it was all she could do to keep from crying herself. Her right hand sought his left and held it.

When the "Requiem" was over, there was a pause before the Sviridov. Cal whispered to Karen that he could not take any more and had to leave. She nodded, and they got up as unobtrusively as possible and left by the side aisle.

Standing in the corridor, watching the concert from the doorway at the back of the chapel, was Brother Bartholomew. As they passed him, Karen paused to thank him. So did Cal. "It was beautiful," he whispered. "I just—can't handle it right now."

Brother Bartholomew nodded understandingly and returned his attention to the stage, where the choir began the first piece by Sviridov. The ethereal lament now carried into the corridor and caused them both to stop. "Listen to that!" murmured Cal in awe. "If we'd stayed, I would have lost it totally," and he hurried to get beyond the reach of the music.

Outside, the sky had turned dark gray. They went down the white shell path to the harbor parking lot, but as Karen went to her side of the car, her husband said, "Let's not go just yet. Let's go out to the end of the breakwater." Raw and windy, this day felt more like February than May, but since it was the first thing he'd suggested doing in the last three days, Karen acquiesced.

The harbor was protected by two rock jetties, like arms reaching out to the bay in silent supplication. Picking their way over the massive boulders, they stopped on the last one and looked down at the dark waves a few feet below. Out on the bay, whitecaps were beginning to form, which meant the wind had picked up to at least 12 knots. She shivered, and Cal, standing behind her, wrapped his arms around her. "I love you," he said.

She trembled from a chill that had nothing to do with the wind. "I love you, too," she said, patting his arm. She could not remember the last time either of them had spoken such words aloud.

"Now we can go," he said, and they went back to the car.

They drove home in silence. As they pulled into their driveway, he looked at his watch. "Still time to get a sail in."

"Are you sure?" she replied. "Isn't there a storm coming up?" They'd both seen the green blob moving towards them on the Weather Channel.

"It won't get here until after dark, and I'll be home before then."

She sighed. "You know I'm a fair-weather sailor, but if you really want to, I'm game."

"I thought I'd go out alone this time," he said, not looking at her. "I'd like to get my head together, and nothing does that like the *True Love*. Besides," he said with a wry laugh, "I'm not very good company just now, anyway."

She tried to smile, but all she could feel was an icy hand closing over her heart. Everything in her wanted to beg him not to go.

To spend this afternoon and night at home, with her. But she could think of no logical reason, and he was the best sailor she knew. So she just nodded.

She stood by the kitchen door, watching as he pulled their little boat on its trailer out of the barn and hitched it to the Volvo's bumper. She smiled and waved, and he waved back. "You be sure to get home before dark," she called after him, then clamped her mouth shut to keep from crying.

23 | home before dark

KAREN SAT AT THE COUNTER, staring out the kitchen's bay window. In the gathering twilight, the little rose bush was a silhouette—until a flash of lightning from the gathering storm starkly illuminated it. It looked so fragile out there, sagging against its supporting stake, trembling in the quickening wind.

She glanced at the clock above the wall phone and could barely make it out, yet she refused to turn on the kitchen lights. It was an act of faith; he said he would be home before dark. Besides, if the lights were on, she would not be able to see the little bush out there.

Streaks of rain began to slash the window, and heavy drops drummed on its copper flashing until they became a steady roar. There was no longer even a second's delay between lightning and thunder; the storm was directly overhead. Shaking off the desire to believe that everything was still all right, she went to the back hall closet, pulled on her slicker, and dashed for the car—his car, because he'd used her wagon to haul the boat. She got in the musty old Buick, then realized she'd forgotten the keys.

Back she ran out into the rain, into the house, grabbed the spare keys off the key-shaped board that Judd had made in sixth grade shop, back out to the car. Then the darned thing wouldn't start; the battery could barely turn the engine.

"God, I *hate* this car!" she shouted, slamming the steering wheel with the heel of her palm. Since it was a '48 Roadmaster, she hit the horn ring, and the sound of the horn startled her.

Calm down! she told herself; *think*, for God's sake! Then she remembered a trick she'd learned another time in the rain, when her own car wouldn't start in the mall parking lot. A nice man had suggested she turn on her lights. It made no sense; there was so little juice left anyway. But he'd said to trust him; the activity would stir up the battery and sort of remind it what its job was. It had worked. And it worked again now.

She drove the fifty-year-old relic over to Ryder's Cove as fast as she dared. Which wasn't very fast; the windshield wipers were losing their battle to keep ahead of the deluge. She veered all over the road; it was lucky no one else was out on a night like this.

When she got to the cove's parking lot, it was empty. But they *always* launched from here!

With a deepening sense of dread, she backed the old car around and headed for the one landing he should never have used with a storm building in the northeast: Stage Harbor.

When she got there, the only vehicle there was her wagon with the boat trailer behind it. No sign of Cal. Leaving the Buick's motor running, she got out and tried the door of the Harbormaster's office. It was locked; everyone had gone home. Now what? She got back in the Buick and drove over to where its headlights would shine towards the entrance of the harbor. They didn't reach very far in this rain, but it was pitch black now, and if he were trying to find his way into the harbor, they might help.

Through the smearing, feeble efforts of the windshield wipers, she stared out at the waves. They looked malevolent and angry, and she tried to hold down the panic rising within her. It was 6:15; she would give him another half-hour, and then—what? Call the Coast Guard, she guessed.

She imagined him out there, trying to keep the *True Love* from swamping. It was an open boat and awfully tippy, really not good in heavy weather. In a huge blow like this one, his only defense would be to keep her pointed into the wind as much as possible. And since the wind was from the northeast, that meant he would have to head *away* from the harbor. He had no choice; if he broached to, or if a rogue wave came over the gunwales, the game was over. Then he would have to wait until the Coast Guard could find him and pick him up. And since the Gulf Stream wandered off into the mid-Atlantic, instead of rounding the elbow of the Cape and heading north along its coast, the water would be in the low 50s. How long could he survive out there before succumbing to hypothermia?

That settled it; she wasn't waiting any longer. Where was the nearest phone? Then she remembered her cellular phone in the glove compartment of her car. She jumped out, taking the spare keys with her, and ran over to her car. Inside, she turned on the engine, which caught right away, got out the phone, and plugged it in. She called 911 and was patched through to the Chatham Coast Guard station, which was less than a mile from where she was parked.

Seaman Beatty took her information, then Petty Officer Dodd, the duty officer, got on the line. Calmly he outlined what would happen next: They would call all the Harbormasters, to make sure Mr. MacAllister had not tucked in somewhere else, and they would send out an urgent marine assistance request to all ships who had their radios on. If anyone had seen her husband, they would know within the next fifteen minutes. "And since he's an experienced sailor and is three hours overdue, I'm sure he'll authorize the rescue boat leaving immediately."

"How long before we will know something?" It was an awfully big ocean, and they were looking for an awfully small boat.

"That's hard to say, ma'am, since I'm afraid we have no way of knowing which way he was heading. When the cox gets out there, he will do either a parallel line or expanding square search. In a couple of hours—"

"A couple of *hours?* Petty Officer Dodd—what do you think his chances are?"

"There's no way of telling, ma'am. We could get lucky and find him right away. Or, it might take—longer." He changed the subject. "You're in your car?"

"Yes, at the harbor."

"I think you should go home and wait there. If he *is* able to make it to shore somewhere, the first thing he's going to do is try to call you, to tell you he's all right."

"Of course!" she exclaimed. "I'll go right now."

"Good. We have your home number. I'll call you as soon as I know anything."

Without thinking, she put her car in gear—and then remembered it had the boat trailer behind it. If Cal did make it back here, he would be looking for the wagon and trailer. She turned it off and left it as she had found it, running over to the Buick and hoping it would start. It did.

Half an hour later, she was back at the kitchen counter. This time the kitchen lights were on, and she was watching the clock, as its hands pulled through invisible glue. After twenty minutes, she started pacing through the darkened house. A few minutes before ten, the phone rang. It was Petty Officer Dodd. "I don't have anything to tell you," he said. "We have two other boats out there now, the one from Brant Point and the one from Wood's Hole. They've been over their areas twice, and no one's seen anything." He tried to sound more cheerful. "There is one piece of good news: The cloud cover's beginning to break up. And Otis has said they will send their helicopter at first light. I'll call you as soon as we know anything."

"Thanks," she said. The way she said it, the word sounded ungrateful, but she didn't know how else to say it.

"It's okay, Mrs. MacAllister; it's our job. And we do know how hard this is for you. All of us do."

"Thanks," she said again, her voice breaking.

"Oh, there is one thing," added Petty Officer Dodd almost apologetically. "I have to ask this: Did he have a life jacket with him?"

"Of course. We never sail without them."

"Okay, ma'am; we'll get back to you as soon as we have anything."

Karen hung up and looked out at the barn for a long time. Then she got up, put the slicker back on, and took the flashlight from the top of the refrigerator. The storm seemed to be letting up, she noted, as she went out the back door. Inside the barn, she went straight to the shelf in the back, where they kept their nautical gear. The empty sail bags for the *True Love* were there, and next to them, just beyond the paddles for the kayaks, were something that shouldn't have been there: four orange life vests—two for the boys, and two for themselves. There should only have been three.

"You liar!" she screamed, "I was afraid you'd pull something like this! You said you wouldn't, but you did! You did!" She shouted it over and over, beating the flashlight against the shelf until it went out. Hurling it to the ground, she ran out of the barn, wailing into the stormy night.

&a.

At 6:30 in the morning, the phone rang. Karen, her mind fogged by two Seconals, groped the receiver off its cradle on the nightstand and mumbled something into it.

"Mrs. MacAllister, it's Petty Officer Dodd. The helo hasn't sighted anything yet, but," he tried to sound hopeful, "the fog's lifting; we should know something soon." He paused. "How are you doing?"

"I don't know. I just woke up."

"Well, it's good you could get some sleep."

"Mm." The fog in her head had not begun to lift. "Petty Officer, if you had the duty last night, how come you're still on this morning?"

"Port section's got the weekend duty." He hesitated. "Listen, is there—anyone who could be with you? I don't know what we're going to find, but whatever it is, it should be in the next couple of hours."

"I'll call someone," she lied.

"Okay. You'll hear from me again at 0800, if not before."

Karen hung up and rolled over and stared at her husband's unused pillow.

She must have fallen back asleep, because the next thing she knew, the phone was ringing again, and the digital numbers on the clock radio next to it said 7:45.

It was Petty Officer Dodd. "Mrs. MacAllister, we've found the boat. Foundered. *East* of Monomoy; in fact eight miles out in the Atlantic. That's why we couldn't find him. . . . Anyway, the mast is gone, and I'm afraid there's no sign of Mr. MacAllister."

Karen started to cry.

"Of course, in a life vest he could have drifted a long ways from the boat," the petty officer said, sounding as optimistic as possible. She did not tell him that all vests were present and accounted for. "So we're extending our grid," he concluded, "and there's still a chance. . . ." They both knew he was lying.

After that, Karen needed to call someone. But who? My God, they had lived in this town for 14 years; didn't she know someone well enough to want them with her? She realized that Cal and she had been so close, she'd never felt the need of girlfriends. And now, when she really needed someone here to keep her from going crazy, there was no one.

In the end, she called the one person she could bear to have around, and who also cared about Cal. She called Tobin.

Sitting in the silent kitchen waiting for him to come, she glanced at the empty stool at the end of the counter, next to her. Cal's stool. They'd worked out so many things here. Except the last, most important thing.

She should call the boys, she supposed. But not until the Coast Guard gave up the search.

"Cal!" she cried at his stool. "I don't want your policy! I want *you!*" And she started to cry again.

Her eyes went out to the rose bush. Battered by the storm, it drooped against the stake.

From there, her gaze wandered to the butcher's block knifeholder next to the sink. The sight of the black handles reminded her of the episode at the Curtises' the other night, when the real Mac Curtis, beyond drunk, had acted out his hatred. Of whom? Of everyone, apparently. He was the same Mac Curtis who two days ago had turned down Cal's request for a loan— after Cal had been his partner for fifteen years. And then he had broken two of her husband's ribs. But worse than that, the unforgivable part, was that he had also broken Cal's spirit. Cal had been crushed, destroyed, and nothing she could do would resurrect him.

And all the while, he had feathered his own nest so carefully that the devastation they were suffering barely affected him.

Her eye came to rest on the empty stool. Mac Curtis was the reason it would be forever empty. On an impulse, she withdrew the steak knife and tested its edge with her thumb.

TOBIN CAME IN THE KITCHEN DOOR, just as Karen was hanging up. "That was the Coast Guard," she said, her voice breaking. "They're calling off the search."

Without a word he held out his arms, and she collapsed into them, shoulders shaking. Guiding her to a stool, he took a paper towel from the roll near the sink and gave it to her. Then he took the stool at the end of the counter.

When she had collected herself, she said, "The duty officer, Petty Officer Dodd, just told me they'd covered the entire area in a ten-mile radius from where they found the boat."

"Still, it's possible they might have missed something. Maybe a different crew would—"

She sighed and shook her head. "I trust that duty officer; he stayed up all night to direct the search."

Tobin stared out the window. "So," he murmured, "he's gone." And now his eyes filled. "I should have done something. I should have picked up on the boat that he was—"

"It wasn't your fault, Tobin," she said, putting a hand on his arm.

"But I might have—"

"There was nothing you could have done."

For a long time neither of them spoke.

Then Tobin said, "Curtis did this. That rotten excuse for a human being does not deserve to walk this earth!"

❧

The memorial service was held Wednesday morning in the side chapel of Saint Enodoc's. The MacAllisters were not churchgoers, but their boys had been confirmed there. They were both able to get home, and they flanked their mother in the first pew, along with Cal's mother, who had come from Connecticut, and Tobin. In the next pew were sailing friends and members of the Orleans Yacht Club, and behind them, Curtis Investment employees. Also present were more than a few townspeople, from Orleans and Eastham as well as Eastport. For someone who had lived on the Cape a relatively short time (and one had to be at least third-generation Cape Cod to be considered a local), Cal had made a surprising number of friends. Mac and Allie Curtis were also present, though they were not ushered to a forward pew.

In his eulogy, the young rector made some surprisingly pertinent observations—surprising because he had no personal knowledge of the deceased, beyond what he had been able to gather from a visit to his widow. Afterwards there was a coffee reception in the fellowship room, at which the mourners paid their respects and lingered an appropriate amount of time, sharing reminiscences of Cal. After about half an hour, most of them had left, and Mac took the opportunity to have a private word with Karen.

"I can't tell you how sorry I am," he began, taking her hand in both of his. But she just stared at him icily, until he stopped. "Well," he finally said in a low voice, letting go of her hand, "when the insurance people come around—"

"What insurance people?"

He leaned forward and whispered, "With a policy that size, they're bound to come around, looking for any excuse to keep from paying the maximum. Just don't say anything about Cal's being depressed."

"But he *was* depressed!" she hissed. "You, of all people, should know that. You were the reason!"

Seemingly oblivious to her anger, Mac continued in his unctuous tone, now resting a comforting hand on her arm. "If they suspected that—"

At that moment Tobin came over. "I think you'd better leave, Mac. Right now."

"I was talking to Karen," he replied with a quiet intensity, his jawline tightening.

"Yeah, well, another time."

Mac took a breath, then smiled and relaxed. "Yes. Another time."

ъ♨

Curtis Investments had closed for the memorial service and remained closed for the rest of the day. But Mac had prevailed upon Pat Peters to come into the office at 4:00, to help him prepare for the accountants who would be descending on them first thing Friday morning.

Though apprehensive about being alone in the office with him, especially after his coming on to her at the reception a week ago, Pat could not deny the pressing work needs. Putting on her loosest sweatshirt, an old pair of baggy jeans, and no make-up or perfume, she arrived promptly at 4:00. She found him in the boardroom, with papers all over the table and others strewn about the floor. He told her he'd been at it for three hours and had gotten the presentation pretty well together—well enough to try it out on her.

But when he read it to her, she kept interrupting to ask the sort of questions she assumed the accountants would want answers to, and before long it became apparent they had a great deal more to do than he'd supposed. She suggested that they go back to the beginning and present a detailed timeline of the company. It was such a logical solution, Mac expressed surprise that he'd not thought of it himself.

They worked steadily for an hour and a half, then Pat said, "I'm afraid I've got to go. I promised my father I'd take him to dinner."

"You can't quit now!" Mac exclaimed. "Not when we've finally got a handle on how to do this! Can't you do the dinner another night?"

"It's his birthday."

"Well, it's CI's death day," he said bitterly, "and frankly, I really need your help to give it a proper burial."

"I'm really sorry," she said, getting up, "but he's been counting on it all week. I can't let him down."

"I'm sorry, too, Pat," he said with an edge to his tone, "but you can't let me down, either. In half a year, I've never had to ask you for emergency help, and you've got to admit this is an emergency." Then seeing her stiffen at his peremptory tone, he softened it. "Look, how about just postponing it a couple of hours?" When she hesitated, he quickly added, "I'll arrange for you to be my guests at the club for dinner."

"Not the club," she shook his head. "His favorite restaurant is Captain Morgan's."

"Fine, I'll call and have them send me the bill—including a bottle of their best champagne."

"Well—"

"Call him, Pat. Use the phone in my office."

She did, returning in a moment with a smile. "He said to tell you that you can relax; he doesn't like champagne."

Two hours later, though still not finished, they were clearly in the home stretch. A couple of more hours in the morning should finish it, and she could ready the final copies in the afternoon. She brought them two mugs of coffee, gave him his, and then clicked cups in a toast to what they had accomplished.

"Pat," he said warmly, "I cannot remember every being so grateful to anyone, as I am for what you've just done."

She shrugged and smiled. "That's what you pay me for."

"It's been more than just work." He paused. "We've been a team, you and I. And I'd say pretty a damned good one."

"It *has* been fun," she admitted. "I just wish we weren't presiding over CI's demise."

He put his mug down and drew closer to her. "Curtis Investments may be finished, but I'm not. I can promise you: I'll be back in play within a year. And when I am, I want you with me. Not as my assistant; as a full-fledged associate."

She smiled. "That would be—well, great."

"Consider it done."

"Thanks, Mac," she smiled, gathering her purse and windbreaker.

"Do you have to go?" he asked softly.

Uh-oh, she thought. "You know I do," she said brightly. "My father—"

"Your father can wait a little longer," he said, moving still closer to her.

"No, really, I—"

He put an arm around her and drew her close.

"Whoa!" she said, being careful to keep it cheerful, and gently but firmly pushing him away. "We'd better keep this on a professional basis."

"You can't tell me," he said, his voice tightening, "that the thought that something might happen between us never crossed your mind this afternoon." He was trembling with the struggle to keep himself under control.

"It might have," she admitted. "But you're married, and I'm separated, and let's leave it at that."

He reached for her again. "Sarah, you can't tell me that you don't want this as much as I do."

"Sarah? Who's Sarah?" Pat demanded. "Look," she said, raising her voice. "I'm leaving! Right now!" And she pulled away and started for the door.

"No, you're not," he announced, blocking her way. "You're not doing this to me again, Sarah."

She tried to push him aside, but he was much stronger. He gripped her arm and twisted it. She tried to hit him, but he easily warded off the blow. Then he hit her. In the face. Twice. Hard. The blows hurt, but they did not stun her, and she vaguely sensed they were controlled. He was letting her know how much he could really damage her, if she continued to resist. She tried to knee him, bite him, kick him, but he laughed as he countered every attempt.

"Enough foreplay!" he grunted, throwing her on the floor. She fought him as hard as she could, but he was the strongest man she had ever known. She did manage to rake his face once with her nails, before he pinned her arms under her. She screamed at the top of her lungs, but there was no one to hear her. Then, realizing that her struggles were only heightening his enjoyment, she went utterly limp.

When he was finished, he stood up and reached down to help her up. She spat in his face, and he hit her again. Then he warned her: "You tell anyone about this, and it'll be your word against mine. And as soon as people hear about what you were involved in over in Poughkeepsie, nobody's going to believe you. And I will also make sure you never work in this town or in real estate again."

She said nothing. Inside, she was screaming. She held it in, until she got out in the parking lot and was safely locked inside her car. Then she let the scream out and screamed all the way home.

25 | let no man tear asunder

WHEN HIS DAUGHTER CAME IN, the Commodore was down in the CIC. That was what he called the below-decks room which housed his computer, his stereo, and his 36-inch television set. Save for the huge monitor, the room was darkened—exactly as the Combat Information Center of a modern warship, illuminated with strategically placed infrared lamps. Tonight he was watching tapes from his collection of the endless Victory at Sea series, until his daughter returned. He had just reached the Battle for Leyte Gulf, when he heard the front door open.

"I'm down here, honey," he called, and heard her coming down the stairs. She looked in, and in the faint reddish light, he did not see the bruise on her left cheek, or her split lip.

"Daddy, would you mind terribly if we didn't go out tonight? I know it's your birthday, but I really don't feel up to it."

"That's fine," he replied, "it's a little late anyway." He paused. "You okay? You don't sound so good."

"I think I'll just take a shower and go to bed. But we'll celebrate tomorrow, I promise." And she started back up the stairs.

Then he did just what she didn't want him to; he came upstairs, too, and into the hall. "Honey, I don't care about the birthday. Let me get you some hot soup and maybe a sandwich and—oh, my God, Patricia, what *happened* to you?"

"I don't want to talk about it!" she sobbed, and ran down to her room. He went to her door and asked her if she wanted to talk about it. She didn't. But he could hear her crying, and he had a pretty good idea what had happened.

After a long time, she came out and found him in the living room. "I love you, Daddy, but I want to go up to Bar Harbor and see Mom." "And your job?"

She shuddered. "I'm never going back there again!" She left him and went back to her room. And he stared into the cold, dark fireplace. He had been at the reception; he had seen Curtis unmasked, as it were. The man was a monster—and now he had beaten up his daughter—and obviously worse. In a perfect world, he could go to Chief Burke and tell him what he was pretty sure had happened. The Chief would investigate, and Curtis would wind up in jail, where he belonged.

But the world didn't work that way. Pat would have to file a complaint and give testimony, which the defense attorney (and Curtis could afford the best in Boston) would do his utmost to discredit—along with her character. And his daughter, if she were willing to press charges (which he was sure she wouldn't), would never stand up under that. It would put her back in Payne-Whitney, and this time she might never recover.

In this far-from-perfect world, predators like Curtis were allowed to roam free. But there might be another way.

The Commodore was well aware that he was regarded as an eccentric. It didn't bother him; he enjoyed his eccentricities. And they afforded him more tolerance than would be shown most people. He could park where he shouldn't, say things he oughtn't, be loud when he should be quiet. Behind his back, people might smile indulgently at each other and circle their fingers at their temples. But he was no fool.

And now, as his eye traveled upward to his father's ceremonial dress sword over the mantel, he smiled.

≀●

Across the breakfast table, Allie looked at the back of the front section of the *Wall Street Journal*. "I think I'm going to go up to Kennebunkport for a few days," she said to it. "Joan's gone up early this year, and she's invited me to join her. I told them at work I was taking the month off, so I might as well enjoy it."

If she held out any hope that there might yet be a return to at least a semblance of normalcy, it flickered and died in the ensuing silence.

Finally she didn't care. So she asked the one question guaranteed to permanently extinguish the possibility of hope ever being rekindled: "How did you get those scratches?"

He turned the page without answering. But the knuckles holding the newspaper whitened. She no longer cared about that, either. In the last eight days, she had come to see that the man sitting across from her was not the same man she had met on the airplane and fallen in love with. That man had been an adventurer in life, who had wanted her to share the adventure with him. And they *had* shared it—until last Wednesday when she realized whom he really wanted to share the adventure with.

At the reception she had been as shocked as any of their guests, to see what lurked beneath the surface of MacArthur Curtis. Dr. Jekyll's potion had been emerald green; her husband's Sapphire blue. But the latter's Mr. Hyde was no less horrifying. The next morning, still clinging to the shreds of fantasy, she had tried to treat the previous evening's disaster as some kind of nightmarish aberration that judicious spin control might yet put right. But his ruthless slaughter of the turtles had shown her once and for all: From this nightmare there would be no awakening.

In the following week, they had scarcely spoken, even going to the memorial service for Cal yesterday. He had not come home from his office until after midnight, long after she was certain to be asleep. She wasn't, of course, but she pretended to be, because when it was show time she wanted to be fresh and sharp.

It was show time now. Taking a sip of coffee, she asked again: "I want to know how you got those scratches."

Now the paper did come down, and he was wearing a look that warned her that the cracking noise she was hearing was the ice under her skates.

When he saw she was unfazed, he spread some marmalade on his English muffin and said, "I got them raping my secretary last night."

She winced inwardly but was careful not to let it show. Had there been a corner of her heart that might have been resuscitated, he had just driven a stake through it.

"Our marriage is over," he said, taking a bite of muffin. "We both know it. You shouldn't have turned me down when I suggested a pre-nuptial agreement. You would have found me far more generous than I'm inclined to be now."

She remembered that hazy sunny afternoon when he'd brought it up. It had seemed like a dark cloud on a distant horizon, and she had wanted none of it. Unable to think of a reply, she took another sip of coffee.

"Alex Cooper is out of town and won't be back until tomorrow, but I've called his secretary and will be seeing him first thing in the morning. Don't worry," he said, patting his lips with his napkin and picking up the paper again, "I won't leave you penniless. And you still have your job. You'll be all right."

Suddenly she hated him. "You've forgotten the Teal Pond properties," she said softly with a cold smile. "They're in my name."

Down came the paper again, but he, too, was smiling. "Anticipation, Allison. Everything is in the anticipation. Whether it's a pre-nup or a dummy front, there's one cardinal rule: No matter how unpleasant, you need to anticipate the unthinkable. I anticipated that you might turn on me. So—I took a precaution." He studied her face for a response, but she refused to give him the satisfaction.

"Remember all those papers I had you sign when we set up the holding company with you as president?" Again, he paused. Again, no reaction. "Well," he went on, "you did read the first five or six documents pretty carefully. But as I'd anticipated, after that your eyes glazed over, and you just skimmed the rest. By the time you got to the fourteenth, which was an agreement to sell the afore-mentioned properties back to me one year from that date, for one dollar, you were just signing them."

He beamed; she was reacting now.

How could she have been so blind? Not about the documents, but about marrying him! She jumped up from the table. She would have liked to hit him, or better, fling the toaster at his face. But he would anticipate that, too, and would dodge, and then break her arm or something.

She went over to the window and looked down at the pond. "You know what you are?" she said finally. "*Despicable!* As creepy as anything that ever slithered out of that pond! And some day you're going get what you so richly deserve!"

He chuckled behind the newspaper. "Too bad you won't be around to see it."

Maybe, she thought. And then again, maybe not.

26 | he who lives by the sword. . . .

CAPE CODDERS HAD CALLED the first one, "the no-name storm," because it had sprung up out of nowhere. Building over Georges Bank, it come roaring out of the northeast so suddenly that no weather station had the presence of mind to think of a clever name for it. In no time, it was on top of them, mauling them, savaging the fragile sand cliffs of Lighthouse Beach like some monstrous circus cat gone berserk. On north and east-facing shores on both sides of the Cape, it wrought more havoc than Hurricane Bob or hurricane anyone, and year-round Cape Codders loathed its memory.

Now on Thursday afternoon, they were about to be hit by another—the second "hundred-year weather event" in a decade.

Mac Curtis had no time to put the deck furniture in the garage, no time to run into town to pick up batteries or extra gas for the generator. He had just barely time to close up the house and put rolled-up towels at the sills of the east-facing doors, where water was sure to be driven in.

Stuffing the towels tight against the door to the deck, he was reminded of Allie. For the winter, she had bought stuffed calico versions to keep the cold winds out, informing him that they were known as Cape Cod snakes. He was going to miss her. But not enough to keep her. There was only one who deserved to be by his side in this house.

He glanced at the row of wind instruments by the deck door. The wind was already holding at 40 miles per hour out of the northeast, with gusts up to 50. And the barometer was in free fall. Outside there was an eerie gray-green gloom, and it was almost dark—two hours before sunset. This was going to be a hell of a storm!

He had time to do one more thing. His teals were going to be disoriented by the storm and awfully hungry when it was finally over. Going into the garage, he grabbed the pail of dried corn kernels and went out into the gathering darkness. Leaning against the wind, he made his way down to the edge of the pond. He peered out at the water to see if any of them were still out there, but the visibility had so deteriorated he couldn't be sure. They were probably snugged down under the brush and shrubbery that bordered most of the pond.

He cast the kernels liberally out in the open, right down to the marshy grass at the edge of the pond, where they would be sure to find them. The sky was streaked with yellow and frequently whitened by lightning just beyond the nearest cloud bank. He shuddered and bent to his task, flinging out handful after handful of corn like Daumier's sower, until the pail was empty. Then as the first drops of cold, hard rain lashed the surface of the pond, he turned to go back to the house.

The knife thrust took him completely by surprise. Dropping the pail, he brought both forearms up, even as the blade plunged in low, under his rib cage. Ripping into his intestines, it angled up, slicing through his stomach, and up, its tip reaching for his heart.

He reacted instantly, bringing both forearms smashing down on the arm of his assailant. He had not practiced the counter-move in thirty years, but his instincts served him well. His attacker let go of the knife.

But it was too late. The sharpened point of the blade pierced the epicardial shield and probed deep into the left ventricle chamber. The stricken heart went into spasm; its owner had perhaps three seconds of life remaining.

He seemed to know that, even as he clutched the buried blade with both hands, trying to extract it. Lightning flashed again, blasting everything white and giving him a stark view of who had done this to him. "Not *you!*" he gasped, lunging for his attacker, who was circling behind him. Then he slipped on the newly wet grass, and, twisting, he fell face forward into the pond.

His assailant now moved towards the twitching legs, to recover the knife, but at that moment the main power line to Teal Pond was severed, and in the garage the big generator roared to life. The sound startled the assailant, who slipped quickly into the thick underbrush at the edge of the pond.

èa

The second no-name storm lashed the Cape for three nights and two days. Trees and power lines were down everywhere, and the great sand cliffs which had taken the brunt of the Atlantic's fury now bore deep scars. Fifty feet of cliff front had been lost, and had the lighthouse not been moved inland two years before, it would have perished.

By the dawn of the third day, the surface of Teal Pond was calm. At its edge, a family of ducks, ravenously hungry, foraged for food. Fortunately, it seemed to be in abundance, kernels everywhere, right on top of the grass. In the first rays of morning light, two of the ducklings found morsels around twin obstructions protruding from the pond's green scum—a pair of khaki-clad lower legs that ended in white running shoes with "Nike" stamped on their soles.

27 | the scene of the crime

SWINGING THE BRAVADA BY DOC FINLAY'S OFFICE, Chief Burke was about to honk, when the wispy, bespectacled General Practitioner appeared, black valise in hand. Climbing into the four-wheel-drive vehicle, he put the valise in the back seat. "Should I have worn old clothes?"

"I don't know, Doc; I haven't been out there yet."

"I had to reschedule Millie Foster and Agnes Cunningham," Doc smiled, "but first things first. And this sure is a first!"

"Damned crowded for two weeks before Memorial Day," grumbled the Chief, not seeming to hear him. He considered using the siren and blue light, then decided against it. No point in drawing undue attention. Too damned many people were discovering Eastport's hidden charms and telling their friends. "What do you mean?" he asked Doc, whom he'd heard, after all.

"Well," his friend explained, "it's our first murder in thirty years, isn't it?"

"Since '47, to be exact," said the Chief, not sharing his passenger's enthusiasm.

"Fifty-two years! That's even more impressive!"

"Look, Doc, I don't want to make a big thing out of this." He suddenly frowned. "You didn't tell those two busybodies *why* you couldn't see them, did you?"

"You know better than that, Dan."

The Chief glanced at him. "Well, what *did* you tell them?"

"I had Angie call them. She told them that I'd been called away for an emergency."

"And that's all?"

Doc thought for a moment. "Well, she did say it was police business." He paused again, then sheepishly added, "urgent police business."

"Oh, great! It'll be all over town."

When they got to the Curtis mansion, Car #2 was already parked at the end of the gravel driveway. With yellow police tape, Officer Whipple had cordoned off the back lawn leading to the pond. Having already shot of roll of film of the crime scene, he was taking a preliminary statement from Mrs. Curtis. It was she who had discovered the body and had phoned the station half an hour earlier.

The Chief parked the Bravada and got out. "Good job, Otis," he called to the young officer. "I'll talk to Mrs. Curtis in a minute. Doc and I are going down to have a look at the body." He scratched his head. "Call the rescue truck, will you? And have them take the body down to the hospital for an autopsy. You'd better call the hospital, too, to let them know it's coming."

He lifted the yellow tape for Doc to duck under, then followed him. "Slow down, Doc; he's not going anywhere. Besides, I want to take it easy, going down there. I want to see if we can see anything."

"What are we looking for?" asked the smaller man, waiting for him.

"I don't know," replied the Chief, a little irritated. "I just want to take a nice, long look at the crime scene."

The two men slowly approached the body sticking out of the pond, scanning the lawn for anything that might prove significant. But there was only sodden grass and a few kernels of corn.

"What do you make of those?" asked Doc.

"Well, judging from that pail over there," the Chief pointed to the empty container, "I'd say he was probably feeding his precious ducks when it happened."

"When what happened?"

"I don't know! That's what we're here to figure out!"

"Okay, okay," Doc soothed him. "I've never been to a murder scene before."

"Well, neither have I!" Then the Chief relaxed and ruefully chuckled, "So let's try to act like we know what we're doing."

At that moment, all he could think of was the bungled police work in the O.J. Simpson and JonBenet Ramsey cases, which got spread all over the media. That was the last thing Eastport—or he—needed.

They reached the edge of the pond and gazed down at the half-submerged corpse. The water was clear, and in the afternoon sun, they had no trouble making out details. The man's navy-blue polo shirt and the stomach underneath it were sliced open in front, and out of the cut protruded his bowels. Severed ends had drifted away from the stomach cavity. These were being nibbled on by a few little fish, which darted away as they leaned forward. The victim's face was under a foot of water, and its eyes had been eaten. But they had no trouble seeing that it was Curtis, and that his expression was contorted—and now frozen—in rage.

Gazing at the scene, the Chief was surprised that the human body contained such a quantity of entrails.

Doc interrupted his reverie. "Is that a footprint?" he pointed to an impression in the mud, next to the left leg.

The Chief peered at it. "Yup," he said. "And it's not Curtis's. It's someone smaller and lighter."

"The murderer?"

"More likely Mrs. Curtis, when she came down here."

He straightened and pointed to the incision. "What do you make of that?"

Doc rubbed his chin. "Well, it's a really big cut."

"Thanks, Doc; I can see that for myself."

"I was just thinking out loud," the latter reflected. "It was probably a big knife—and unusually sharp."

"What makes you say that?"

"Well, look: It was as sharp as a scalpel."

"Why?"

"The cut in the shirt—it's not torn or ragged. It's—sliced. A blade would have to be awfully damned sharp to do that."

The Chief nodded appreciatively. He'd had to bring Doc, to certify the death. Now he was grateful he was here. "Go on."

"Well," said the smaller man, hunkering down on his haunches (something the Chief had not been able to do since he was a little kid), "you see how both ends of the cut in the shirt are clean? No loose threads or puncture-stress in the weave?" The Chief nodded. "I think the blade was double-edged."

Thoroughly absorbed now, Doc looked up at the Chief. "Mind if I push the shirt up?"

"Be my guest."

Doc stood up and took off his suitcoat, which he handed to the Chief. He took off his shoes and socks and rolled up his pants and shirtsleeves. Then, moving carefully so as not to disturb the footprint, he stepped into the water, next to the corpse. After gathering the floating ends of intestines and tucking them into the stomach cavity, he pushed the shirt up, exposing the corpse's full torso.

He stood up and pointed to the long cut, as if he were giving an anatomy lesson in a medical school's operating theater. "You see the length of the incision? The blade entered down here, practically at the groin, and moved upward. Its upper edge was enlarging the incision even as its tip was reaching upward for the heart." He paused. "Whoever did this knew what they were doing."

"Is that what killed him?"

"Oh, yes. They may discover water in his lungs, but the knife was the cause of death." He shook his head. "That must have been some knife!"

"It was," muttered the Chief under his breath. When Doc tilted his head at him, he quickly added, "What do you make of those scratches on his face?"

The smaller man frowned. "They might have been made by finger-nails. But that doesn't make sense: Whoever did this to him would hardly have been wrestling with him. Not if they had that knife."

"Last question," the Chief said. "Can you give me any idea how long he's been dead?"

His friend shook his head. "I wish I could give you one of those amazingly precise estimates—but the truth is, I haven't a clue. Judging from the advanced state of rigor mortis, I'd say he'd been dead at least two days, maybe more. Whoever does the autopsy might be able to give you a better estimate, but don't count on it."

"They may not have to," the Chief mused, staring intently at the body's left wrist. "As long as you're already in there, see if you can get his watch off."

Doc reached over and lifted the left arm out of the water, undid the gold link band, and handed it up to him. The Chief turned it over. A Patek Philippe. Very expensive but hardly waterproof. The hands were stopped at 5:13. There was even a tiny window for the date. The Chief squinted at the numerals: 13. MacArthur Curtis was murdered sometime on Thursday afternoon. Probably while he was feeding his ducks. Probably just before the storm.

For the first time since they'd gotten the call, the Chief smiled. "You know, Doc, no one deserves to be this lucky." From the side pocket of his windbreaker, he produced a Ziploc sandwich bag and dropped the watch into it.

Just then the yellow-and-white rescue truck arrived, and the Chief said, "Look, Doc, you take charge of sending the body down to Hyannis, will you? Show Officer Whipple where the footprint is, and don't let anyone mess it up. I want to talk to Mrs. Curtis. Then I'll buy you a cup of coffee."

He found Allie up on the deck, pacing back and forth, nervously running a hand through her short blond hair.

"Hello," he said smiling. "Hard to believe I was here not that long ago, under more pleasant circumstances." Seeing her shudder at the memory, the Chief modified his comment. "At least they started off pleasantly." He looked at her. "It was the knife, wasn't it."

Shocked, Allie brought her hand to her mouth. "How did you know? I haven't told anyone about that yet."

"Well, suppose you tell me now."

"I'll show you," she said, getting up and crossing the deck. He followed her into the living room and over to the mantel. The display case was shattered; shards of glass were strewn over the mantel and the floor. The knife was gone.

"This is exactly the way I found it, when I came in here," Allie said. "At first, I thought they were trying to get at the safe."

"What safe?"

"This one," she replied and, pushing something on the side of the display case, she swung the case out, revealing a small wall safe.

"What do you keep in there?" asked the Chief.

"Deeds and documents, passbooks, birth certificates—and a couple of thousand in cash." Anticipating his next question, she added, "I checked; it's all there."

"Then whoever did this was after the knife."

Allie shuddered. "Can we go back outside? I'd like to be in the sun."

The Chief held the door for her. Down by the pond, the rescue squad had brought their gurney, and under Doc's supervision they were lifting the body out of the water.

The Chief turned to Allie. "Why don't you tell me exactly what happened this afternoon."

"When I got home," Allie said, perching on the arm of a chair, "I put my car in the garage, next to my husband's, and—"

"About what time was that?"

"About two, maybe a little after."

"Wait a minute," the Chief apologetically, taking out his Pearlcorder and propping it on the deck's flat railing, where it could pick up both their conversations.

She looked at it and hesitated. "Should I have a lawyer?"

"Why? You're not a suspect. I'm just trying to get a handle on what happened here." Then seeing what had prompted the question, he chuckled. "Don't worry about that thing; I use it because I'm so lousy at taking notes. I write down stuff that isn't important and miss stuff that is. Also, I'm so slow that I make all kinds of abbreviations to keep up, and then when I get back to the station, I haven't the foggiest idea what they mean."

He smiled, but she was not amused. "What do you want to know?"

"Let's start where you left off: You saw your husband's car, so you knew he was home."

"That's right," she nodded. "I called for him when I came in the kitchen, to let him know I was back." She recalled the moment. "When he didn't answer, I figured he might be upstairs, taking a nap. I went in the living room, and that's when I saw the case."

The Chief was watching the men on the lawn put the body in a black plastic bag and load it onto the gurney. Turning to Allie, he asked, "Did you ever know him to take the knife out of the case, other than at the reception?"

"Not in the four years we've been married."

"When you saw his car, did you wonder why he was home in the middle of a work day?"

She nodded. "As a matter of fact, that thought did cross my mind. But he's in the middle of bankruptcy proceedings, and I figured maybe he'd had about all of the office he could take."

The Chief turned to her. "What did you do, when you saw the case?"

"I was scared! I yelled for Mac and ran upstairs to see if he was in the bedroom. He wasn't. That's when I happened to look out the window and...." She put her hands over her eyes.

The Chief gave her a moment, than asked, "Did you go down to the pond?"

"Not at first. But when he didn't move, I called the police."

"About what time?"

"About 2:30."

"Where had you been?"

"Up in Maine. At a friend's house in Kennebunkport."

"How long for?"

"I went up Thursday."

The two of them watched the rescue squad push the gurney up the lawn to where their truck was waiting.

"What time did you leave here?" the Chief asked.

"I guess about 2:00."

"And Mr. Curtis was alive when you left?" She looked at him as if he'd just asked a particularly stupid question, and with chagrin he realized she was right. "That *was* dumb," he admitted, and they both laughed. But then the tension re-asserted itself.

"Who's your friend in Kennebunkport?"

"Joan Mason," she said. "We went to school together." And she gave him her number.

"The next questions are going to be a little uncomfortable," he advised her. "You don't have to answer, if you don't want to."

"All right."

"How were you getting along with your husband?"

Her eyes went cold. "You were here that night; what do *you* think?"

"Were things any better the next day?"

"Not really."

"Did they ever get any better?"

"Not really."

"When did you decide to up to Kennebunkport?"

"When Joan called Wednesday," she sighed, "I thought that maybe, if I could get away from here for a few days, it would give the air a chance to clear."

"Do you think the bankruptcy was the reason for your husband's—um, losing control the night of the reception?"

She thought for a moment. "It had to have had an impact on him."

"But you don't think it was the main reason."

She stood up. "Now I *am* getting uncomfortable."

"Okay," the Chief smiled, turning off the tape recorder and slipping it into his pocket, "that's enough for today. Thanks, Mrs. Curtis; I'll be in touch." He turned to go.

"Uh, Chief?" He turned back. "Am I going to be safe out here?"

"I think so. Whoever killed your husband had it in for him, not you."

She hugged her arms. "It feels a little creepy out here, just now."

He nodded. "Tell you what: I'll have a patrol car come by here every couple of hours. When you hear crunching on the gravel, it'll be them." He started down the steps, then paused. "One more thing: Don't touch anything around the case, till I get someone to dust it for fingerprints."

"Mine are all over it now," she said.

"I know. I'm looking for someone else's."

As he turned to leave, this time for good, he noticed a momentary glimmer in the distance across the pond, as the afternoon sun briefly reflected off something.

28 | the buzz at norma's

THEY WERE HALFWAY BACK to town before the Chief said anything. "You got time for a cup of coffee, Doc? Or should I take you back to your office?"

The smaller man yawned. "I'm through for the day," he said. "If you'd rather have a beer, I've got a tab at Gordie's."

The Chief shook his head. "*You* may be done, but I'll be lucky if my day ends before midnight. I do have time for coffee though, and I'd like to buy you one: You were a real help today."

"I was? How?"

"By describing the murder weapon."

Doc turned to him and raised an eyebrow. "You've seen it, haven't you."

"Yup." Then he turned to his friend. "Look, Doc: I don't want you talking about this—*any* of it—with your wife or Angie or anyone else! Understood?"

"Understood."

"Anyone asks you about it, you just say it's police business, an ongoing investigation, and you're not free to discuss it. You got it?"

"I got it. Lighten up, will you?"

"I'll lighten up when–" Then he shook his head and smiled. "Sorry, Doc. Hey, will you look at this thing?" he chuckled, pointing at the steering wheel. "Every time we go by Norma's, it turns in automatically."

They took a table by the door, and Isabel Doane came over. "Regular with double sugar, Chief? And how about you, Doc?"

"I think I'll have a little fizz in my caffeine; how about a Coke?"

"Coming up." In a moment she returned with their order. She lowered her voice. "You boys been on 'Police Business'?"

"How'd you know?" exclaimed Doc, before the Chief could catch his eye.

"Yes, how *do* you know, Isabel?" asked the Chief, quietly.

"Well, if it's such a secret," she retorted out of hurt, "why is Emmet Adams holding a press conference over at the station?"

"*What?*"

"At five o'clock! Just in time for the Cape's evening news."

The Chief flung down a five-dollar bill and said to Doc: "I've got to go!"

"No problem," his friend replied. "I'm not that far from home, and I can use the exercise."

The Chief tried to get his emotions under control, but the tires of the Bravada still complained as he exited the parking lot. Lieutenant Emmet Adams, his second in command, was tall, blond, and a loose cannon. He was bright–without a scrap of wisdom. Ambitious–without the sense to keep it from showing. Jealous–of everything the Chief did, and utterly convinced he could do it better. Whenever the Chief implemented a new policy or procedure, Adams could be counted on to let it be known that there was a better way to do it.

Worst of all, Emmet Adams had one of the town's three selectmen, Vic Malcolm, openly encouraging him. Matters had reached a head last winter when the Chief had actually suspended Adams for insubordination. Adams had fought it, appealed to the town board, and with Malcolm's help had gotten himself reinstated. So now the Chief was stuck with him.

Entering the station, he found chaos. As one of the field crew from Channel 38 adjusted the lighting, a gaggle of reporters from the *Cape Cod Times*, the *Cape Codder*, and the *Revelator* clustered around Lieutenant Adams, who was making a few off-the-record remarks before issuing a formal statement.

"Lieutenant!" the Chief bellowed. "In my office!" He turned to Sergeant Bascomb. "You, too, Leo."

As soon as the door was shut, the Chief got two inches from Adams's face and yelled: "What the hell do you think you're doing? There's never been a press conference in the history of Eastport! And I've got Sergeant Bascomb here, so don't think you can distort what I say, like last winter."

Under the withering blast of his superior's fury, Adams was completely unfazed. He even smiled, as he explained, "I assumed you'd be out at the Curtis place all afternoon, Chief, and I knew you wouldn't want to miss this opportunity for the department to gain a few good headlines."

The Chief was shaking with fury. But he was still in control. "The department, my ass! Emmet Adams wanted his picture in the paper!"

"That's not true!" Adams insisted. "I wanted people to know that we're on top of the situation, a thoroughly professional—"

"Cut the crap, lieutenant! The people of Eastport know we do our job. And I don't give a rat's patootie what anybody else thinks! You—" he caught himself before calling him what he felt like calling him. "I'm surprised you didn't alert the Boston papers and TV stations."

"I did. The *Globe* is sending a stringer tomorrow. Channel 4 is using a local crew from Yarmouth. And Channel 5 is sending their mobile unit down in time for the late news."

Twenty seconds elapsed before the Chief trusted himself to speak. Then, in a voice quivering, he said, "From now on, Sergeant Bascomb is in charge of media liaison. And you are hereby removed from this case! You are to have nothing to do with it, and that means any contact with any of the officers working on it. And that," he looked at Leo Bascomb, "is a direct order. Is that understood?"

"Yes," said Adams, without adding "sir." And then, incredibly, he smiled again. "Chief, just because you personally are extremely uneasy with the press, doesn't mean that this is not a landmark opportunity for this department. Why this—"

"I don't believe this!" The Chief's eyes widened. "Did you not hear anything I just said?"

"Well," Adams went on blithely, "what are you going to do with those reporters out there? I mean, the story's out now, and it's hot. There's no way you're going to get it back under wraps." He held up a typed page. "And I have a prepared statement here."

His smile was almost a smirk, thought the Chief, as he slowly raised his right hand. One well-placed shot would send a few of those beautiful teeth flying—and at the last moment, wisdom prevailed. He'd sue me. And win. And poor Leo would have to testify against me, and I would be summarily dismissed. Then the town would have Emmet Adams as their new Chief of Police. Slowly the hand came down.

There was a timid knock on the door. "What is it?" demanded the Chief. The door opened a crack. It was Trish Allen, the newest, youngest member of the force. "It's two minutes to five," she said in a small voice. "And Chief, they can hear you out there."

"What a mess!" he scowled at Adams. Then to Trish: "All right, tell them I'm coming."

The Chief left the office and went into the conference room, where the local media, such as it was, was gathered. The Chief stepped to the head of the conference table. "I'm afraid you people have been called here on false pretenses. We can't say—"

He was cut off by a stringy-haired woman counting, "Five, four—" The last three digits were silent, as she threw out the appropriate number of fingers and then pointed at the Chief.

This was exactly the sort of thing he detested! And now he was caught in the middle of it. By sheer force of will, he took control of the situation.

"This afternoon we have begun an investigation into the apparent homicide of an Eastport resident, MacArthur Curtis," he extemporized. "Mr. Curtis was the Chief Executive Officer of Curtis Investments, primary developer of the Teal Pond complex. At 2:13 this afternoon his body was discovered on the grounds of his estate on Teal Pond. The apparent cause of death was a knife wound. A formal investigation is now underway, and until such time as we have positive developments to announce, I must ask your patience. I *will* contact you, as soon as we have something to report." With that, he started to leave.

"Chief? One question before you go?" It was Barry Jones.

"Sorry, no questions."

"Is it true that the murder weapon was a specially-designed combat knife that belonged to the victim?"

"I said, no questions." He tried to keep the shock out of his response.

The lights went down, the reporters started to leave, and the Chief took Barry Jones aside. "Where did you hear that?" he asked in a voice too low for anyone else to pick up.

"Chief, you know I can't reveal my sources," he smiled. "But thanks for confirming it."

About to respond, the Chief thought better of it. He asked Leo Bascomb to expedite the departure of their guests. Then he addressed the department. All but two of the 14 officers were present.

"What you have just witnessed," he told them, "is *exactly* what I was hoping to avoid. I do not want this thing blown up any further. Understood?" He looked around the room. They understood.

"As long as my name is on that door," he pointed to his office, "this investigation will be conducted with dignity. Our department will maintain perfect decorum—and tactful silence."

He had calmed down enough now, to deal with what was really on his mind. "Which of you told Barry Jones about the knife?"

No one answered. There was some nervous shuffling of feet.

"Listen, people, we're not going home, until I find out. And I mean, we'll stay here all night, if necessary."

More silence. No one wanted to rat on a fellow officer.

"All right, we'll do this another way." He turned to Officer Whipple. "You were the only one, other than myself, who even knew about the knife. Is that correct?"

"No, sir."

"Who else did?"

"Officer Carey, who came out with the fingerprint kit and with the plaster, to make a cast of the footprint."

"And you called him?"

"Sure, Chief, just like you asked me to."

"Did you talk to him directly?"

"No."

"Well, who *did* you talk to?"

"Officer Carey was on the phone, but then Lieutenant Adams took over the call."

The Chief nodded. "I thought so." He looked at them all, one by one. "All right, listen up: From now on, Lieutenant Adams is to be out of the loop. He is to have nothing whatever to do with this case. He will continue in his administrative capacity and is to be shown the fullest respect. Do what he asks and do it promptly, with a good attitude. But anything to do with the Curtis case will go directly to Sergeant Bascomb or myself. No one else."

"We'll see about that!" shouted Adams, looking far from blithe as he stormed out the station's front door.

The Chief sighed and sat on the edge of a desk. "I'm sorry you all had to be party to that. But you're not dummies; you've known it was coming for a long time. I've been a member of this force for almost twenty years, as patrolman, sergeant, and lieutenant, before making Chief. And a few of you, like Leo, have been here almost as long. You know the way I do things, and how I like to see them done—the old-fashioned way, low profile. We do our best for the people of this town, and they know it, and that's all the recognition we need."

He tapped the desk with his forefinger. "Until such time as the town gets another chief, we're going to continue doing things my way."

There was a muted chorus of affirmation.

He looked around the room. "Some of you may be sympathetic to Lieutenant Adams's position. If you are, I ask you in good conscience to remove yourself from this case. We cannot let this thing divide the department more than it already has." He stood up. "In the meantime, what are you all doing here? We've still got a town to serve and protect, remember?"

29 | in the folds of God's protection

COMPLINE, THE LAST OF THE DAY'S "OFFICES," as the abbey's prayer services were known, was Brother Bartholomew's favorite. He felt a little guilty about this, as he donned his robe for the evening service, because he suspected it had something to do with its proximity to the time he would get horizontal. The older he got, the more he appreciated the gift of sleep, particularly at the end of a long day—and these days seemed to be getting steadily longer.

The other reason he looked forward to Compline was for the Grand Silence which immediately followed it and which would remain unbroken until the community assembled for Lauds before Mass in the morning. He loved his Brothers, but sometimes he would just like to click the mute button on all of them. Especially tonight, with all of them caught up in the news that evening of Eastport's first murder.

Thank God, the Church had foreseen the need for the interposition of Grand Silence ages ago. And so, each evening there was a time before retiring, when he could read, study, contemplate, or if the spirit moved him, even write some poetry. Now, as the Brothers formed up for procession, he wondered if other monks over the centuries had felt guilty pleasure, anticipating the Grand Silence.

They entered the darkened sanctuary, two by two, robed silhouettes in solemn procession, just as they had for as long as he could remember. There was something comforting and reassuring about shared traditions, faithfully observed. He imagined other monks, in other times, feeling similarly–content.

He did not always feel this way. Some evenings he would be frustrated at having to leave a nearly finished project. His mind, restless as an unruly child, would be anxious to get the office over with, so he could get back to it. Or he would be preoccupied, struggling to solve a thorny problem or resolve a sudden conflict.

Yet as the years passed, he had gradually come to accept Compline as a time to let God put the church to bed, and bring his closure to the day. There would always be interruptions and problems and conflicts. But Compline would outlast them all. And so he would relax and let the service enfold him in God's protection for the night.

As the monks and nuns entered the lighted area before the altar, they separated into pews that faced each other on either side of the center aisle, Brothers on the right, Sisters on the left. They shared this office, as they did Vespers and the offices at noon. When he had come here, the Brothers had done Matins before Mass, and the Sisters had done Lauds afterwards, but there was just one morning service now, Lauds, and it, too, was shared.

All of these offices, considered together, reminded Bartholomew of the ebb and flow of the tide throughout each day, gently reconnecting each of them with God, and with their reason for being here.

The civilian members of the abbey were encouraged to attend as many offices as they could, and most managed to get to at least one, in addition to Mass. Some had joined the corps of cantors who led the chant, and came as often as they could. Some of these were here tonight, as well as other civilians in the regular pews.

He longed for the day when the great stone basilica now being constructed behind the Pastorium and the retreat house would be completed. Then their Gregorian chant would waft up into the high rafters, wreathing them like the smoke of incense, circling and returning, echoing and resonating, and lingering in the mind long after the singing had ceased.

He had heard the choir sing chant in great cathedrals, had heard what it *could* sound like—and what could happen to the heart that heard it. Some day. . . .

They were starting. *Deus in adjutorium, meum intende*—O God, come to my assistance. The familiar Latin phrases rose and fell like the cadence of the sea. And he remembered a long time ago, when chant was just beginning to become part of their lives, Mother Michaela had urged them to go over to Nauset Beach on a quiet day and just listen to the surf as it broke and receded. He had not thought much of the idea—until he actually did what she had suggested. Since then, he could never hear chant without being reminded of the sea.

After twenty years the responses had become ingrained in the community's corporate being. He imagined they could sing them in their sleep and suspected that occasionally a few sometimes did.

The service continued, and with each new psalm the stresses of the day receded further, until the final prayer: *Divinum auxilium maneat semper nobiscum, et cum fratribus nostris absentibus*—may the divine assistance remain with us always, and with our absent brethren.

Compline was ended.

As he joined the others filing out, he realized that once again, he had arrived at peace. He smiled, bemused to think of all the monks through all the ages who had sung these same phrases in this same way at this time of day. Did they, too, feel as agreeably reconciled?

Slipping out of his robe, he was surprised by Brother Ambrose who whispered: "Phone call for you."

Bartholomew shook his head and put his finger to his lips. Grand silence had begun.

But Ambrose wouldn't let it go. "It's the Chief of Police," he whispered.

With a sigh Bartholomew followed him to the phone in the retreat house kitchen. "Hello?" he said into the receiver.

"Andrew, is that you?"

"Brother Bartholomew," the monk reminded him.

"Yeah, well, I need to see you."

"I can't now."

"In the morning, then."

"All right."

"How early can you make it?"

"As early as you like, after 8:00. That's when we finish Mass."

"Okay, 8:15. At Nauset Beach. The south end. And bring a rod."

"A rod?"

"A fishing rod. I want it to look like we're fishing."

"I'm not sure I can find one."

"Never mind, I'll bring one for you. Just be there."

"What's it about?"

"I'll tell you when I see you."

"All right," said Bartholomew, hanging up and resuming silence.

Later that evening, as he gently but firmly moved the friary cat, Pangor Ban, over to his corner of the foot of his bunk, he wondered what Dan Burke wanted. And hoped it had nothing to do with the murder.

30 | rounding up the usual suspects

NAUSET BEACH WAS COLD, BRIGHT, AND DESERTED when Brother Bartholomew got there. With the wind out of the west, the breakers were too small to entice wetsuited surfers to cut their first class at Nauset High. He and Dan Burke had been classmates at Nauset, more years ago than he cared to remember. They had been on the soccer team together and had both had a crush on Peg Foster. In their senior year, Andrew had been elected the team's captain, but Dan had gotten Peg, and Andrew would gladly have traded places. Like most of them, Dan had gone to Viet Nam, where he joined the military police. That started him on a career in law enforcement, nearly all of it in the Eastport Police Department.

Bartholomew looked around for his friend, but the beach was empty. Dan and Peg had four sons, all soccer players, all better than their father had been, or himself, for that matter. At Dan's invitation, he had watched one of their games and had been impressed with their ability. Dan had confided that there were some excellent colleges in New England, which seemed to have extra scholarship funds available for a good striker with a decent GPA.

Other than at the occasional soccer game, Bartholomew had not seen a whole lot of his friend. Each summer he invited Dan and Peg and their boys to one of the abbey's pops concerts. As the boys grew older, they were usually busy with summer jobs, but Dan and Peg would come. He still felt close to Dan, but they just lived in different worlds now, even though they were in the same town.

He was startled by a noise behind him. "Sorry I'm late," said the Chief, trying to manage two rods under one arm while carrying a tackle box. "You wouldn't believe how hard it is just to get out of your own home, when one of your cars is in the shop and you have to work out the day's transportation. Here, pick one," he said, opening the tackle box.

They selected lures and attached them to the end of their lines. The Chief got his on first, and cast it out about thirty yards, barely clearing the nearest combing breaker. Then Bartholomew effortlessly sailed his lure far out over the line of breakers.

The Chief stared him. "I thought you'd given up fishing!"

His friend grinned. "I have. That's the first time I've done that in 18 years." He chuckled. "I guess it's like riding a bike."

"Yeah, right!" exclaimed the Chief with disgust, trying again with little better success than before.

"Dan, this is fun!" his friend teased him. "But—why are we out here?"

The Chief looked at him, surprised. "You heard about the murder."

"Sure, everyone has. But—"

"Well, believe it or not, you're one of the suspects."

"What?"

"The way I figure it, it's got to be someone who was at that reception for the rose-growers." He tried another cast, which went no further than his previous attempt. "So, I've got to ask you: Where were you last Thursday afternoon, a little after five o'clock?"

"Last Thursday?" Bartholomew laughed. "At the friary, robing for Vespers, with 29 other guys dressed exactly like me."

The Chief frowned, but his friend could not contain himself. "I'm sorry, but this is incredible!"

"That's one word for it," his friend said sourly. "I won't offend you with the others I've been using lately." He picked up a bit of dried seaweed, then let it blow away, to see where the wind was coming from.

Then he said thoughtfully, "Andrew—Brother Bartholomew—if I were to talk to you confidentially, would that be like—talking to a priest in confession?"

His friend stopped laughing. "What are you saying, Dan? If you tell me something in private, will I keep it that way?"

"Something like that."

"Then the answer is yes."

The Chief sighed and looked as if a great weight had been lifted from him. "Good! Because I've *got* to talk to someone who won't leak what I say."

"And there's nobody at work?"

The Chief told him about what had occurred at the station the night before.

"What a mess!" Brother Bartholomew exclaimed.

"You're telling me! And on top of that, I've got to run a murder investigation."

"How's it going?"

The Chief looked at his friend, making up his mind. "Okay. I'm going to tell you *everything*. I've got to trust someone, and it's not fair to Peg to dump it all on her. But if you ever—"

"I won't," his friend cut in, "you have my word."

The Chief told Brother Bartholomew of his theory: Whoever killed Mac Curtis used the same knife, exactly the way he had shown them eight days before. Ergo, the killer had to be someone at that reception, who was in town last Thursday afternoon, and who hated him enough to kill him.

"Motive and opportunity," the Chief concluded, "just like they taught us at the academy." He shook his head and added wryly, "I should have taken better notes."

"Don't beat yourself up, Dan," said his friend. "I think you've done pretty darned well, narrowing it down that far, that fast. Assuming you've put me and the other rose-growers, including my mother, on the sidelines, then rounding up the usual suspects shouldn't be that big a deal."

The Chief was unconvinced.

"Look," Brother Bartholomew said, taking the handle of his fishing rod and poking a hole in the sand. "That's Curtis's wife." He made another hole. "And that's his partner, the one who nearly took him on that night."

"Tobin Hatch," muttered the Chief. "And you better make one for Karen MacAllister, the widow of his other partner."

The monk made another hole. "What about the neighbor, that Royce person?"

"Yup," the Chief nodded. "He gets a hole. Though he doesn't seem like the type."

"Is there a type?"

"Hell, I don't know," growled the Chief. "This whole thing is new to me. The most I've ever had to contend with is a drunk driver, trying to convince me he only had a couple of beers. And kids dealing marijuana down at the harbor. And some jerk of a construction worker, taking out his frustration on his wife." He looked out at the ocean. "This is light years beyond them."

"Okay," said his friend, "we've got four holes. Who else?"

"Well," said the Chief, thinking for a moment, "there's his secretary, Pat Peters—you know, the daughter of the self-styled Commodore?"

Bartholomew made another hole.

"And there was that woman he was talking to out on the deck—which may have been what set Curtis off that night. She was the wife of one of the rose growers—Tomlinson, I think."

Brother Bartholomew whistled appreciatively. "Chief, I've got to hand it to you: For somebody who wants people to think he's not too plugged in, you don't miss a trick. I think you've been watching Columbo reruns."

The Chief smiled, his first one for the day. "I had a hunch that talking to you was going to be a good idea."

His friend had the rod handle poised. "One hole or two? Because if there was something going on between Curtis and Mrs. Tomlinson, you might have to add her husband to your list—although I wish you didn't."

"Why?"

"Well, I know Maurice Tomlinson. My mother asked him to come over to the abbey to help me get our roses started. He's a really nice guy, kind of fragile and awfully sick."

"In other words, not the type," the Chief cracked, and they both laughed.

"Okay," said his friend, making another hole. "Anybody else? What about Barry Jones?"

"Nope," replied the Chief, "he was at the paper, overseeing the storm coverage." He paused. "But there *was* somebody else who spent time out on the deck, also in fairly deep conversation."

"You mean Laurel? She didn't know Curtis," Bartholomew added quickly.

"How do you know?"

"I—don't."

"Then she gets a hole, too—at least, until I can talk to her."

Brother Bartholomew made the hole and looked up. "Is that what's going to happen next?"

The Chief nodded. "Motive and opportunity. I'm going to talk to," he counted up the holes, "the eight of them, one on one, and see where we are."

He gathered up the tackle box and poles, and they headed for the parking lot. "Can't anyone at the station help you?" asked his friend. "At least do some of the leg-work for you?"

The Chief hesitated before replying. "If you want to know the truth, there's only a few of them that I trust to keep their mouths shut, and even fewer who have the moxie to do an investigation like this." He sighed. "I guess that makes me conceited."

"Not in my book," said Brother Bartholomew. "It's just common sense: The person doing the interviewing, watching the body language, listening to how they sound, and even more to what they *don't* say—that's the person who ought to be doing *all* the interviews."

The Chief said nothing until they'd reached the parking lot. Then at the door of the Bravada, he said, "You know, we think alike." He stuck out his hand. "Thanks. You've been more help to me than you know."

His friend shook his hand. "Any time."

"I was hoping you'd say that," the Chief chuckled. "As I expect we're going to be doing a lot of fishing, before this thing is done."

"Where are you going to start?"

"I don't know," murmured the Chief. "I'm going to trust my intuition, and see where it takes me. It's worked pretty well for me over the years; of course, it never amounted to much more than asking a driver to open the trunk of his car."

"Just out of curiosity: Have you got any idea right now about who did it?"

The Chief hesitated, then said, "Well, I guess there's no reason not to tell you, since I've told you everything else. I think it took a big man to take down someone like Curtis. You saw him at the party: He was like an animal. There was only one man strong enough to—"

"Tobin Hatch."

"Yup. And if I'd been him, with Curtis taunting me like he did, I'd have done it right then."

He opened the door to his vehicle, then turned back, Columbo-style. "Oh, one more thing: How would you like to help? I mean, more than just fishing."

"You mean—with the investigation?"

"Sure, why not? Two days ago, I would have said the worst thing in the world would be to have an amateur involved with something like this. But what the hell, I'm practically an amateur myself. And now that I'm up to my armpits in this cesspool, I wouldn't mind having someone else in here with me."

His friend grinned, then looked over at the friary's old red pick-up. "I'll have to check it out with the Brothers; I'll let you know."

As he drove away, Brother Bartholomew felt strangely elated. He had a hunch that Anselm and Dominic would approve it, and that he would find it challenging.

And then the suspicious side of his nature kicked in, and he wondered if the reason he felt this way had anything to do with the fact that one of those holes in the sand back there belonged to Laurel.

31 | our own brother cadfael

BROTHER BARTHOLOMEW PARKED the red pick-up behind the friary and went inside. Seeing Brother Dominic, he asked if he knew where Brother Anselm was. "Probably down at the goat barn. Esmeralda's close to her time."

At the barn he found Anselm kneeling beside their white goat, who was lying on her side, her belly distended with the imminence of birth. As Bartholomew opened the gate to the barnyard, the Senior Brother got up, took off the barn apron, and came outside.

"Sorry to bother you," Bartholomew said.

"It's never a bother," the older monk smiled, "and you don't do it as often as you think."

Without going into details, Bartholomew told him of his meeting with the Chief of Police that morning, and of the Chief's inviting him to become part of the investigating team.

"So," Anselm mused, "it would seem we will have our own Brother Cadfael." He looked carefully at Bartholomew. "How do you feel about it?"

"Well, I'd like to do it," the younger monk admitted. "It certainly would be a break from my normal routine which, as you may recall, I was beginning to find a bit—routine."

"I'll check with Dominic, but I see no problem with it; in fact, it might be exactly what you need right now. To take your mind off—other things."

When Bartholomew didn't respond, Anselm asked gently, "What is it you're not telling me?"

"Laurel Winslow may be involved in the case."

"Is she a suspect?"

"I'm not at liberty to say. In fact, I shouldn't have even mentioned her."

"I'm glad you did. If I were you, I would avoid contact with her, as you help the Chief, or in any other context." He tapped the tips of his fingers together. "You may not be aware of it, Bartholomew, but there is a battle for your soul going on right now." He smiled. "There's no point giving the enemy any weapons he does not already possess."

The old monk thought for a moment, then added, "Could you take Brother Ambrose with you on your investigations?"

"Oh, Anselm, come on! He's—"

"You don't have to tell me," the Senior Brother smiled. "We've all had our turn with him. Now it's your turn."

"But I *have* been shepherding him! I thought—"

"Yes, you have, and Dominic and I are pleased with how you've put your heart into this assignment. I'll tell you something else: You are making a difference in his life. He's settling down. And he gives you most of the credit for it—after God, of course."

Bartholomew sighed. It was useless to try to persuade Anselm to change his mind.

"Cheer up," his friend smiled, "I think you'll be surprised at how well you do. You have the common sense and the balance for it. And as for Ambrose, ask God to change your heart. I think you'll also be surprised at what he has to offer."

He held up his hand. "Just one caution, other than the one I just gave you: Be careful that you don't let your adventuring interfere with your spiritual life. I don't want to see an empty place at supper or at the offices. You won't be able to make them all, but you should be at every one you can."

"I will."

"And don't neglect your roses, either, now that you've made such a good start with them."

"I won't."

"I'll pray for you."

"Thanks, Anselm," he grinned. "You're sure there's not anything else?"

"Well, as long as you've mentioned it, don't let this cause you to neglect your calligraphy."

"Oh, dear Jesus!" Anselm had hit a hot button. "Will you please tell me why Mother Michaela wants me to learn calligraphy?"

Anselm smiled. "She didn't say."

"But we've got a computer program that can generate perfect characters far more quickly than I'll ever be able to!"

Anselm turned to Esmeralda, who had just groaned. "Sometimes we have to do things which don't seem to make sense," he said, trying to help her be more comfortable. "You know that; it goes with our call." The younger monk scowled—but nodded.

"And sometimes," Anselm went on, "when we do them without knowing anything beyond the fact that we've been asked to do something that makes no ordinary sense, we receive an even greater blessing."

Bartholomew smiled. "Don't start sounding like a Zen master."

"Maybe we have to do some things, simply because it's God's will—is that better?"

"Marginally. For your information, I *did* pray about the calligraphy, and I *do* believe it's God's will. I just wanted to know why."

Anselm smiled and shrugged. "Who knows? Maybe someday there'll be no electricity to run the computers." He stroked Esmeralda's head and flanks. Then he looked up at his young friend. "Did you ever wonder why God values obedience more than sacrifice?" No response. "Because obedience is someone else's idea of what you should sacrifice."

"There you go again," Bartholomew smiled, "and I don't have time to go there with you. I'd like to go over to Teal Pond, to check out the crime scene."

"Fine. Don't forget Ambrose."

"Don't worry," he said, opening the gate to leave.

"Bartholomew," his old friend called after him, "maybe you're learning calligraphy simply because we can't have a friary cat named Pangor Ban without having a scribe, too."

"That's not fair!" Bartholomew laughed. "*I* named him that!"

"You see? You're the master of your own destiny, after all!"

32 | requiescat in pace

NEGOTIATING THE POTHOLES on the dirt track that led to the Royce cottage, Chief Burke questioned the wisdom of following his intuition. When Andrew—Brother Bartholomew, he corrected himself—had suggested it on the beach yesterday, it had seemed like a good idea.

But Royce had no phone; there was no way to make sure he was home. Well, he'd at least have a look around. There was a time when you could size people up by the books on their shelves; nowadays, with nobody reading much anymore, you could still get a feel for them by the way they kept their homes.

The path ended at a one-room cottage whose shingles were black with age. In the never-mowed clearing in front stood a vintage VW diesel, a rusting relic from the gasoline shortage in the early '70s. That model boasted 50 miles to the gallon, but if one were in your neighborhood, you were likely to hear or smell it before you saw it.

The Chief knocked on the front door. While he waited for an answer, he noted that the paint on the cottage's trim had peeled off years ago. He knocked again. Still no response. He went around the cottage, past the carefully fenced, carefully weeded herb garden with each row meticulously labeled, and down the sloping ground toward the pond.

He stopped. There, at the edge of the woods, was Royce, kneeling on the ground. He seemed to be placing an inscribed, rectangular stone on top of a mound of earth. Next to it were three other mounds, each covered with a new stone. Moving silently, he came up behind the kneeling man, until he was close enough to make out what was carved on the stone:

OLD MOSE
REQUIESCAT IN PACE

The Chief noted that the second line was spelled out. Some people would have saved money by having merely "R.I.P." inscribed. He realized that he needn't have been so quiet; Royce was weeping.

He cleared his throat, and Royce turned. "Chief Burke?" He scrambled to his feet. "What are you doing here?"

"I was about to ask you the same question." He gestured toward the graves.

Royce glanced down at his handiwork. "The stones I ordered, just arrived. I've been putting them on the graves of four friends who were killed two weeks ago." The Chief's eyes widened. "A family of turtles. The pond was their home, long before I came."

"When was that?"

"About twelve years ago."

"You live alone?"

"Not if you count the turtles—of course, you can't count them anymore," and his eyes started to fill again.

"How did they die?"

"They were murdered! With a rifle. Two of them lived long enough to crawl out of the water and die here together." He pointed to the grassy section between the deck and the pond.

The Chief nodded. "We've been getting complaints about a couple of boys over in Brewster with .22 rifles. Out in the woods, taking pot-shots."

Royce shook his head. "It wasn't them. When I was getting my friends ready for burial, a bullet came out of Young Mose. It was a lot bigger than a .22 caliber. It was about this size." He held up the tip of his little finger.

"Did you save it?"

Royce nodded toward the cottage. "It's inside somewhere."

"You know who did it?"

"I have an idea."

"Want to tell me?"

"Not until I'm sure."

The Chief walked over to the little graveyard. Without taking his eyes from it, he said quietly, "Last week I had to put down the best hunting dog I've ever had. Diana. She'd been with me fourteen years. Towards the end, she was too old to hunt, so the only time I went was when the boys were home for Christmas. Diana came, too; she couldn't bear being left home, any more than we could bear leaving her. But the trip was really for her benefit. She'd tire quickly, and we'd practically have to carry her back to the car."

He looked up at Royce. "The worst part was when I realized that, while she never complained, the cancer was causing her all kinds of pain. I had to do it; it would have been cruel not to. But that last day, in the car on the way to the vet," he could barely continue, "she just looked at me. It was as if she knew—where we were going—and why." He forced himself to finish. "I had the feeling that she was—forgiving me."

He put a hand over his eyes and turned away. It was a long time before he could turn back. "So you don't have to tell me what it means to lose an animal you love."

Royce stared at him, his own eyes brimming—this time, not for his own grief. "Come inside," he said, "and have some tea."

He led the Chief up the steps to the deck, past a long object with a tarp over it, and in the back door.

"I was going to make some green tea," he said, pointing to an old wood stove with a battered kettle on it.

"Um, have you got anything else?" The Chief looked in vain for a refrigerator.

"How about Earl Grey?"

"Huh?"

"It's an English tea."

"Fine."

Royce fixed two mugs, then from a shelf above the metal sink retrieved an old canning jar filled with a thick brown substance.

"Would you like honey in it? I collected it myself."

"Uh, sure."

When they had their steaming mugs, Royce had the Chief sit in the only stuffed chair, while he perched on the end of the unmade bunk. With a rapid glance the Chief took in the unwashed utensils in the sink, the books and papers stacked everywhere. He noted the absence of modern technology—no range or microwave, no fridge or freezer, no TV or VCR or radio or stereo. Not even a clock. He couldn't see a bathroom, but since there was a sink, there was running water, so presumably—

His eye was caught by a sharp incongruity: In the corner opposite the stove were a computer, monitor, and printer—the latest, hottest equipment money could buy. The Chief knew it was, because his sons had recently dragged him over to Cape Cod Computer in Orleans, to get him to upgrade the family computer.

Following the Chief's gaze, Royce smiled. "I have no use for modern conveniences, as they're all made and powered by energy gained from burning fossil fuels. But I'm a writer, and for that I must have the latest and best tools available." He smiled. "You wouldn't try to do your job in a ten-year-old patrol car, would you, Chief?"

The latter laughed. "I would, if the FinCom had its way!"

"The FinCom?"

"The town's Finance Committee," the Chief explained. "New England towns are reckoned to have the purest form of democracy, and for that, I suppose, we should be grateful. But I've got to say, sometimes the FinCom moves in mysterious ways."

Getting up to offer his guest some more tea, which the Chief declined, Royce said, "Well, this has been one of the most pleasant visits I've had. But I don't suspect that you came all this way to talk about the arcane ways and means of the Finance Committee."

"Right," said the Chief, taking out his Pearlcorder. "Mr. Royce, I've got to—"

"Roland."

"Huh?"

"I think we know each other well enough for you to call me by my first name; in fact, I'd like that."

"All right, Roland, I've got to ask you a few questions: First of all, did you know that your neighbor," he gestured in the general direction of the Curtis place, "was murdered?"

"*What?* Which neighbor?"

"Mr. Curtis."

Royce exhaled with relief. "Thank God, it wasn't Allison!"

"Allison?"

"Mrs. Curtis. I got to know her at their reception. She's a wonderful person."

"And Mr. Curtis?"

"You were there. The man's unstable, a real sociopath! In fact, if you hadn't been there, he might have killed someone!"

The Chief nodded. "Now someone's killed him."

"When?"

"Last Thursday afternoon. By the way, where were you then?"

"Right here. Where I usually am. I don't go out much. Last time was a week ago, to pick up some groceries." He gestured at a large cardboard carton on the floor by the stove, filled with flour, dried milk, and assorted cans waiting to be put away.

"Last Thursday, about the time the storm hit, can you remember?"

"Sure," Royce smiled, "working on an article for Barry Jones. Mrs. Curtis introduced me to him."

"What's it on?"

"The anticipated environmental impact on the Mid-Cape region in the first decade of the new millennium."

"Sounds impressive."

"Would you like to see it?" asked Royce, going to the straight-backed chair in front of the computer.

"I'm afraid I don't have time," the Chief said, glancing at his watch. "I've got to get back."

"It'll only take a minute," Royce assured him, as he booted up the computer. The Chief came over and stood behind him.

"Here it is," said Royce, getting up from the chair and offering it to the Chief, to give him a better view.

The Chief sat down and started to read about what the growing pollution in the bay, abetted by Boston's outfall pipe, was likely to do to the quahog and razor clam populations in the bay's southeast inner corner.

He looked up. "Were you affected when the Teal Pond transformer went down?"

"Was that what happened? I had started the final version that afternoon and lost over an hour's work. And they didn't get the power back on until after midnight."

"What did you do, go to bed?"

"Are you kidding? I got out my laptop, started again, and kept on working."

"And when the power came back on?"

"I transferred the new file to the desktop."

"Did you have any trouble keeping track of them? Whenever I try something like that, I usually wind up working on the wrong version."

Royce smiled. "No problem, Chief. Just check the times." He showed the Chief his document file, in which the previous version of the millennium article had been saved at 3:37 on the 13th. The newer, laptop version had been transferred at 12:34 on the 14th. Which didn't prove anything, except that he had been physically present at those two times.

"I've really got to go," the Chief said, getting up.

Royce sat down at the computer and called for it to print the millennium article. "I insist you take a hard copy of the work in progress. Here, hot from the printer," and he pressed the new pages into the Chief's hand.

"One more thing," the latter said, heading for the door. "Did you ever have any personal dealings with Mr. Curtis?"

Royce nodded. "He wanted to buy this property, to complete his ownership of the pond. But we never came to an agreement."

"Well, thanks for your time," said the Chief at the door.

"No, thank *you*," said Royce. "You're a very understanding person."

He's really lonely, thought the Chief, as he said good-bye. Especially now that the turtles are gone. He almost said something to that effect. But he did not want to open that door again—for either of them.

33 | wine and roses

AT KAREN MACALLISTER'S HOUSE, the Chief rang the bell. No answer. This was getting to be habit-forming, he thought, ringing again. From somewhere inside, he could hear what sounded like a television set. The thought crossed his mind to go out to the Bravada and call her on the cellular phone. He'd say he wanted to come see her, and she'd say when, and he'd say I'm in your drive-way—

"Oh, the hell with it," he muttered, trying the door, which was not locked. Entering the house, he called out loudly, "Mrs. MacAllister? Are you here? It's Chief Burke."

"In here," she called back.

He found her in what he assumed was the family room. The draperies were drawn, and the only light was from the television screen. In the darkness he could make out her form on the sofa in a sweatshirt and sweatpants. There was a half-full bottle of red wine on the coffee table. He recognized the movie she was watching. *Sabrina*— the original, not the remake. Bill Holden had just picked up Audrey Hepburn at the train station in his Nash-Healey.

"Want to see a great movie?" asked Karen, not getting up or turning on a light.

"I never watch when I'm on duty," he smiled. "But it *is* a great movie."

"Want a glass of a great wine? Cabernet—Mondavi '76. I'm working my way through Cal's collection."

"I only drink red wine when I'm watching movies. But it *is* a great wine."

She sighed. "Do I have to get up and be hospitable, Chief? I really don't feel up to it."

"Not on my account. But how about putting it on pause for a moment."

She did, just as the William Holden character was about to sit down on the two champagne glasses that he had forgotten were in his hip pockets. Smiling at the scene, the Chief sat down carefully in the chair next to the sofa and took out the ubiquitous little recorder. He came right to the point: "Where were you last Thursday afternoon, when the storm hit?"

She turned to him, and his eyes having adjusted to the dim light, he noted that her eyes were red and puffy. Probably from the wine, he thought. Or crying. Or both.

"Why?" she asked acidly. "Was that when Mac the Knife got a taste of his own?"

The Chief was taken aback. "How'd you know that?"

"The whole town knows it! I heard it at Norma's this morning. And I heard it again on that local talk radio station in the car."

"Sweet Mary!" the Chief murmured under his breath. Then he asked, "What are they saying, exactly?"

"That Curtis was killed with the knife he had used in Viet Nam. That the police—you, actually," she pointed at the Chief, "they mentioned you by name—have no leads and no idea how long it will be before they do have one."

Under his breath, the Chief muttered an epithet that he'd promised the Blessed Mother he would never use again. Then he asked, "So, where were you?"

"Last Thursday? I was here. Watching an old movie. Drinking an old cabernet."

The Chief noted that there were two other videos on the coffee table, *Casablanca* and *Roman Holiday*, both from Eastport Video. "Did you call or talk to anyone?"

"I don't know; Tobin Hatch may have called. No one else, though. Funny how the calls fall off about three days after the memorial service."

"You really miss Cal, don't you."

"Chief, we were married 27 years! How would you feel, if you lost Peg?"

Staring at her, he realized how much he had just hurt her. He nodded. "I would miss her. And I might just drink wine and watch old movies." He thought for a moment. "No, to tell the truth, I'd probably go hunting. With no dog and no sons. And—I just might think about climbing over a fence with the gun's safety off, to make what happened look like an accident."

She looked at him and slowly nodded. "You do get it."

"One more question, and then I'll leave, so you can let him," he nodded toward the TV set, "sit down on those things."

She smiled.

"How were things between Curtis and your husband?"

She stopped smiling. "You're probably going to hear it anyway: When the backers pulled the plug on Teal Pond—my God, was that only eleven days ago? It seems like last year!—it turned out that Curtis had taken care of himself in the event of a worst-case scenario. Which he'd hid from his partners. So he came out smelling like a rose—and we came out smelling like something you fertilize roses with!"

She refilled her glass. "Well, if you came over here looking for motive, Chief, you just found it! All wrapped up with a bow on it! *In vino veritas*, as they say." With difficulty she got to her feet and delivered his exit line: "And frankly, my dear, I don't give a damn!"

"I'll find my way out," he said, putting the recorder away. "By the way, have you seen *Bridges of Madison County?*" She shook her head. "Well, it's not an oldie, but it *is* a goody. And so honest, it'll tear your heart."

"Great," she smiled, "Sounds like just what the doctor ordered." And with that, she unclicked the pause button and let the Holden character finally sit down.

ॐ

When Chief Burke got back to the station, he called Sgt. Bascomb and Officers Whipple and Allen into his office. Otis Whipple, 32, was tall and beanpole thin, the first officer he had hired after being made Chief. Two other towns on the Cape had tried to lure him away, but he preferred to work under the Chief, who was urging him to take his sergeant's exam before the Fourth of July. The Chief knew he could trust Otis, and right now that particular quality was in high demand.

Trish Allen, with a brunette ponytail and a spray of freckles across her nose, was barely a year out of the academy. Smart and sensitive, "and consistently demonstrating a high level of competence," as the phrase in her last fitness report put it, she came from one of the abbey families. In the Chief's eyes, her best feature was her capacity for accepting responsibility with maturity. Those who did that, invariably got more than their share; so at 24, with only nine months in the department, Trish had more responsibility than some who had been there several years.

The Chief addressed her first: "Officer Allen, how would you like to be involved in the Curtis investigation?"

"I would, sir."

"Well, you and Otis are the two I'm assigning to the case. You are to report to Sergeant Bascomb and myself."

"Yes, sir. When do I start?"

"Right now." Unlocking the bottom drawer of his desk, he withdrew the Ziploc bag with the gold watch in it and handed it to Otis, who inspected it and passed it to Trish. "That is the sum total of our evidence so far. It was on the deceased when we found him. It's not much, but it has given us a pretty good idea of the time of the murder."

Next he took out a manila folder and opened it. "Here's the file containing everything I've been able to put together—a chronology of events, and the start of a dossier on each suspect, with the emphasis on motive and opportunity." He pointed to a legal pad at the back, the top page of which was filled with handwriting. "This is the start of a hypothesis for what actually happened. It will be updated regularly, as we gather more evidence. And we're going to keep all of this the old-fashioned way, by hand. I don't want anyone accessing it off of one of the computers."

Handing the folder to Otis, he said, "After you've familiarized yourself with its contents, return it here," he indicated the open bottom drawer, "and lock it up. We'll keep the key—" he looked around the office, then picked up the paper clip holder on his desk, "here." He dumped the paper clips into his hand, put the key in the bottom of the dispenser, and replaced the clips. "Whatever you do, don't leave the file out. No one knows about it, and let's keep it that way."

Seeing their faces, he added, "I know it sounds paranoid, but until the investigation is completed, a little extra caution is a healthy thing."

He turned to Otis. "The autopsy report won't be ready until Thursday. As soon as it is, I want you to go to Hyannis and talk to the pathologist." Reading the question on his face, he added, "Be sensitive to anything, however insignificant, that might have a bearing on the case. And add your report to the file."

He stood up. "Meantime, get up to speed on where we are with the fingerprints and the foot impression. I've put Officer Carey in charge of the crime scene, and he's to report to you or Sergeant Bascomb. Keep it cordoned off. In fact, the whole Curtis place should be off limits."

"I'll get on it," said Otis, turning to leave.

"Oh, and one more thing: One of the abbey's monks is an old friend of mine, Andrew—or rather, Brother Bartholomew. I've asked him to give us a hand. He's to have access to the crime scene and to any leads we might develop. Think of him as part of the team."

After Otis departed, he turned to Trish. "Officer Allen, I want you to go over to Eastport Video and have a look at the rental record of Karen MacAllister for the last," he looked at his desk calendar, "eight days. That's when she lost her husband. I'm particularly interested in the ones she checked out and returned just before and after the 13th."

Extracting a pad, she started taking notes, writing in real short-hand, as the Chief continued. "Next, I want you to get in touch with the phone company and get a printout of her phone calls for the same period."

She tucked the pad away. "Is it fair to ask who I'm looking for?"

The Chief smiled. "By the time you go over the call list, you should have a pretty good idea."

34 | thinking forensically

IT WAS A COLD, GRAY AFTERNOON, as the old pick-up made its way along Bridge Road. Brother Ambrose looked over at Brother Bartholomew, who was driving. "You don't want me with you, do you." Since it was a statement, not a question, Bartholomew decided it did not require an immediate answer.

"Well if it's of any interest to you," Ambrose continued, "I don't want to be here, either."

Great, thought Bartholomew, resisting the urge to do a 180-degree turn, go straight back to Anselm, and dump Ambrose in his lap.

"I'm fed up with having to follow around after you like some dumb pack animal," Ambrose declared, his voice rising. "Do this, do that, carry this, don't use that hoe, don't water over there—"

Gripping the steering wheel, Bartholomew's knuckles whitened. He slowed the truck, looking for a place to turn around.

"I'm fed up with roses and hedges and mowing and planting and digging and weeding and—"

All at once Bartholomew started to smile. He was wrong to have taken it personally. Ambrose had a full head of steam up, and it was best to just hear the whistle blow.

"What's so funny?" the young monk demanded. Bartholomew was grinning broadly now.

"I said: *What's so danged funny?*" Ambrose shouted.

"What's so funny," said Bartholomew, laughing, "is that a dozen years ago, I sat in that same seat and shouted those same words at Brother Anselm." He laughed again. "We didn't have roses then, and this is a different truck, but otherwise the script's identical."

"Well, I don't think it's funny!"

"I didn't think so, either, at the time," admitted Bartholomew. "But you know what? I still don't care a whole lot for weeding, but I really don't mind the rest. No, the truth is, I enjoy it. And as for the roses, they're the most fun of all. They're like us, Ambrose—willful, with a mind of their own. And they don't appreciate being trained, not one bit."

Bartholomew sighed and smiled. "But the more you prune them, the better they do. Look at how well our espalier experiment along the front wall is doing. I even hear the *Revelator* may do a story on it."

Ambrose was unconvinced. "But is this all I'm going to do for the rest of my life? Rake and mow and—"

Bartholomew did not answer, as he turned off Bridge Road into the Teal Pond development. The guard at the gate waved them through. "Yes," he said, resuming his train of thought, "I'd say we're a lot like roses, you and I. We don't like it when God takes the pruning hook to us, but He knows what He's doing. He's making us into a new species. And if we cooperate with Him, when He's done, we're going to be a work to His glory. And after all, isn't that what it's all about?"

Ambrose smiled. "How do you always manage to come up with the right words to settle me down?"

Bartholomew laughed again. "I once asked Anselm the same thing."

He slowed as they approached the two stone columns marking the entrance to the Curtis estate.

"What are we doing here?" Ambrose asked. "I was so angry, I forgot to ask where we were going."

"We're going to investigate the murder."

"What?"

Bartholomew didn't have time to explain. There was a police car parked just inside the columns, and the officer standing next to it, now came over. Bartholomew got out. "Officer—" he checked the name on the latter's badge, "Carey, I'm Brother Bartholomew from Faith Abbey. Chief Burke suggested I come out and have a look."

"Wait here, please." The officer went over to his patrol car and called the station. "Let me speak to Sergeant Bascomb," Bartholomew heard him say. And after a moment, "Lieutenant? Uh, sir, I need to talk to Sergeant Bascomb . . . At the Curtis place, sir . . . Well, there's a Brother Bartholomew here from the abbey, who says the Chief has authorized him. . . . Sir, I really need to speak to Sergeant Bascomb." He lowered his voice, and in a moment returned. "You're cleared." He glanced over at the pick-up. "Who's that with you?"

"Brother Ambrose. He's sort of my assistant."

The officer made a note on his clipboard. "Well, anything I can do, let me know."

"Could you fill me in on the situation here?"

"It's pretty quiet now. But it wasn't this morning. We had a bunch of reporters here, and keeping them out was like trying to herd cats. But I think we've got things pretty well under control now."

Bartholomew thanked him, and the officer described the location of the crime scene. They had outlined the position of the legs with red string.

Bartholomew parked in the circle at the end of the driveway, and he and Ambrose ducked under the yellow police barrier tape. As they started down toward the pond, Ambrose could hardly contain himself. "We're actually going to the murder site?"

Bartholomew gave him a sidelong glance. "Of course, if you'd rather be back hoeing peas or raking—"

"No, no! Forget what I said in the truck. How did you—"

Bartholomew held up his hand. "Don't ask. It's confidential."

"Can you at least tell me what we're doing?"

The older monk stopped, as if this was the first moment he'd thought it through. "I guess we're going to try to think forensically."

"I don't even know what that means."

"I'm not sure I do, either," said Bartholomew, starting forward again. As they walked, he filled Ambrose in on the facts of the case, concluding, "Anything we can do to help them figure out who did it—and why—would be, shall we say, most appreciated."

"You mean, like Holmes and Watson?"

Bartholomew nodded. "Though we're about twenty levels below them." He stopped again and faced the young brother. "Now listen, Ambrose: If you breathe a word of this to *anyone*, you'll never be trusted with a confidence again. Is that clear?"

The young monk nodded with great solemnity.

When they reached the outline of the legs, Bartholomew bent over them, peering intently at the ground just to the left. "Look at this," he said, indicating two slight, oval impressions in the muddy grass, about eight inches apart, parallel to the ends of the outline.

"What are they?"

"I don't know—maybe toe prints."

"Toe prints?"

Bartholomew pointed to where the outline of the each leg ended. "You see, a similar dent inside each one, but slightly bigger?" Ambrose nodded. "Heel prints."

Ambrose was mystified. "What does it mean?"

Bartholomew straightened up and winced, putting a hand on his lower back, as if that would ease the pain. "I think that originally the body was face down in the water, and that the murderer subsequently turned it over."

"Why?"

"That, my dear Watson, is a key question." He paused. "When we have the answer, it should unlock an interesting door to the murderer's psyche."

"What we're doing is thinking forensically, right?" Bartholomew nodded, as Ambrose studied the red outline. "Well . . . the most obvious reason to turn him over would be to make sure he's dead."

"Go on."

"But the toe prints—if that's what they are—are not blurred.

Which they probably would have been, if the victim was in the process of drowning."

"So?"

"So—it must have been for some other reason. And it wasn't robbery; if he wanted to go through the victim's pockets—"

"Or she," Bartholomew interjected. "We don't know that it's a man who did it."

"—it would have been easier to get into them with the body face down. Also, they would have taken the watch." Ambrose looked at Bartholomew. "It had to be for some other reason."

The older monk was intrigued; his apprentice was showing an unsuspected agility at this.

"It must have been to retrieve the murder weapon," Ambrose concluded.

"Eureka! I think you've got it! Now—why?"

Ambrose frowned. "Not because of fingerprints. From what you told me, this was premeditated; whoever did it would be wearing gloves. Could it be because he—or she—wanted to keep the knife as some kind of trophy, the way Curtis did?"

Bartholomew's expression grew serious. "I hadn't thought of that." He frowned. "I just hope they're not planning to use it again."

Bartholomew took one last look at the crime scene. He was about to leave, when the overcast parted and the afternoon sun briefly warmed them. It glinted off something just under the water's surface at the edge of the pond—something metallic. Oblivious to the mud, the older monk bent down and scrutinized it. It was metal, all right—and without bothering to roll up his sleeve, he reached down, got hold of it, and pulled it out. It was the buckle of a dark green nylon watchband, attached to a black plastic sports watch. The pin that held the buckle to the strap was broken.

Ambrose came over to see it. "Do you think it belonged to the murderer?"

"I don't know," Bartholomew mused. "It belonged to some-one—who didn't know where they'd lost it."

Before the overcast closed back over the sun, he noticed some-thing else glinting in it—in the distance, across the pond.

እ

"You want a cup of coffee?" asked Bartholomew, as the red pick-up entered town.

"You mean, at Norma's?"

"Sure. You've earned it." Ambrose glanced at him, eyebrows raised. "You did a good job back there."

The young monk grinned. "I enjoyed it—I mean, if thinking forensically is something you can enjoy."

"I wouldn't know about that," Bartholomew shrugged. "I just know it was good having you along."

"Unlike the beginning of the trip."

"You could say that."

Inside Norma's, they took a table by the window. "Now remember," said the older monk in a low voice as his mother approached, "not a word to anyone about anything."

"Yours I know," Isabel Doane said to her son, by way of a greeting. "What about your friend?"

"I'll have what he's having."

"Really?" asked Isabel. "Black, no sugar?"

"Sure," he replied, with decidedly less enthusiasm.

When she returned and placed the steaming mugs in front of them, she said quietly, "I hear you boys were out at the Curtis place, helping Dan Burke with the investigation."

Bartholomew stared at her. "Whatever gave you that idea?" he said, keeping his voice low.

"Emmet was in here, talking about how you two were over at Teal Pond. They've got the place sealed off now, but apparently you'd been passed through. By the Chief himself."

There was a look of alarm on Ambrose's face, but he remained silent. Bartholomew looked around slowly, ascertaining that no one was within earshot. Then he said to her quietly, "I *am* working with Dan on this, but no one's supposed to know. So, Mother, I would appreciate it if you kept that to yourself."

She scowled at him. "Andrew, you always knew how to rile me—and you've just done it again!" She glared at him, but she, too, kept her voice down. "Are you accusing me of being a gossip?"

Bartholomew's jaw muscle tightened—then he forced himself to relax. As he did, he realized that he might be able to turn a potential liability into an asset. "Not at all," he said, smiling. "But a lot of people in town come through here on a regular basis. Just by keeping your ears open, you probably know more about what's going on than practically anybody in Eastport."

She smiled. "Now that's true. But I don't gossip about it!" She nodded at the red-headed waitress behind the counter. "Now Suzie over there—she's incorrigible! I keep having to shoo her away from the listening post."

"The listening post?" asked Bartholomew.

His mother nodded. "The acoustics in this place are weird. You see table number four over there in the corner? The one between the window and the Coke machine?" Bartholomew nodded. "Well, people pick that table when they want to have a really private conversation, because it seems so—private."

"I would," piped up Ambrose. "In fact, that's where I thought we should have sat when we came in." Bartholomew threw an annoyed look at him, and the young monk fell silent.

"Well, for privacy," said Isabel, "where you're sitting is fine. But number four over there isn't. I don't know whether it's the rafters or the heat ducts, but if you're standing back there in the kitchen area, at the end of the skillet and next to the left door of the refrigerator, you can every word at that table. I call it the listening post. But ever since Suzie discovered it, I've told her she can't stand there when there are customers at that table."

"Mother," Bartholomew said, adopting a conspiratorial tone, "as long as you know what I'm doing, I could use your help. I want you to keep me posted on what the town is thinking, so I can pass it along to Dan. I particularly want to know if you see or hear anything that might be remotely pertinent to the investigation." He paused. "But *nobody* can know you're involved. Don't even tell anyone at the station." He smiled. "Of course, if it's an emergency, obviously you can tell Dan. *But no one else.*"

She nodded gravely, and he continued, even more quietly. "It's going to have to be a one-way street. I won't be able to tell you anything about the case. It'll be a strictly don't-ask, don't-tell situation. Will you do it?"

"Of course!" she whispered without hesitation.

As they left, she was beaming; it was the first time in 18 years that her son had asked her for anything.

35 | double feature

THE CHIEF RANG THE TOMLINSONS' DOORBELL and was pleased to hear someone coming, for a change. Sarah Tomlinson invited him in and called out the window to her husband, who was out with his beloved roses. The slight man entered and greeted the Chief warmly, and Sarah said, "Would you like some tea? It'll just take a minute."

Recalling the tea Royce had served him, the Chief shuddered. "No, thanks; I'm not thirsty." Through the window he admired the rose garden. "It really is magnificent," he said. "You've done a lot of work out there."

"It's nothing," demurred Maurice.

"It is *not* nothing, darling!" objected his wife. "The Chief's right: It *is* magnificent! And *you* are going to win the prize for the Eastport Rose!"

Maurice winced. "Sarah, the Chief is one of the judges; that might be construed as undue influence."

The Chief smiled. "Don't worry; I'll be objective."

Maurice reached in his pocket for a pack of cigarettes, took one, and offered the pack to the Chief, who waved them off. "It took me two years to get off them," he explained, "and my friends who've tried to quit tell me that that the next one will taste as good as the last one did 15 years ago."

Maurice nodded. "Your friends are right. I was off them for a few years myself."

"I wish you were off them now!" exclaimed Sarah, as her husband lit up.

"You can't refuse a dying man his last wish," Maurice commented laconically, as he took a deep drag and exhaled.

His wife explained his encounter with the defoliant in Viet Nam, the fact that his lungs were deteriorating, and that the doctors were unable to arrest the process, let alone reverse it. As for the smoking, while it obviously exacerbated the situation, it did not appear to be a contributing factor. The trouble was, they didn't know what *was* causing the illness.

But Maurice knew. And he did not hesitate to tell the Chief: It was a witches' brew that he himself had concocted. There was talk of a class-action suit by those exposed to the defoliant, but he figured he'd be dead before it ever happened.

Anxious to change the subject, Sarah said, with forced brightness, "But that's not why you came, is it, Chief? Nor, I suspect, did you come for a preview of our roses."

The Chief nodded. "You've undoubtedly heard about Mac Curtis." They nodded. "Well, I need to know where you were last Thursday afternoon." He took out his recorder, set it on the coffee table, and looked up expectantly.

"We went to the movies," Sarah said quickly. A little too quickly? "Where?"

"At the Harwich Cinema. We saw the new Clint Eastwood."

"Till There Was You?"

"Yes, have you seen it?"

"As a matter of fact, my wife and I caught it the weekend it opened. Lucky thing; since then, I've been—a little busy."

They laughed, and Maurice started to cough. The cough deepened into a wracking spasm that shook him so deeply, the Chief wondered for a moment if he needed to call for help. But gradually the spell subsided, leaving Maurice exhausted and trembling.

"That happens almost daily now," Sarah lamented. "He won't stop smoking, and—"

"What's the point of stopping?" managed Maurice in a small voice, so as not to bring on a fresh paroxysm. "Other than my dear wife, it's about the only pleasure I have left in life."

The Chief returned to his line of questioning. "So, you were at the movies. Do you remember when you got there?"

"No," replied Sarah. "Not exactly. We like to go to the late after-noon show at Harwich and then get a bite afterward. They usually start around three-thirty or four o'clock. If they start earlier than that, we go down to the one down at Patriot Square in Dennis. We like to get out around six."

"So at 5:13, you were watching Clint Eastwood trying to figure out what to do with Meryll Streep."

"Yes," recalled Sarah with a smile, "though I thought that was a little far-fetched."

"What did you think?" said the Chief turning to Maurice.

"It didn't bother me."

"It didn't bother me, either," the Chief admitted. "I knew she wasn't going to get on that plane. But your wife's right; the part with the dog was a bit much. Or do you think those x-ray machines would show a diamond ring in a dog's stomach?"

Maurice hesitated and looked at his wife. "Yeah," he finally said, "I had a hard time with that, too."

The Chief's eyes narrowed. "With which part? When the guard didn't stop the dog from going into the machine?"

"Uh, I guess so."

"But the dog caught him by surprise, suddenly taking off after that cat—"

"What cat?" asked Sarah.

Maurice fell silent.

Watching him, the Chief said, "Mr. Tomlinson, I think you'd better describe the ending of that movie to me. In detail."

Maurice looked out the window and then quietly said, "I can't."

"Why?"

"Because I didn't see it."

"Were you there at all?"

The sick man took a long drag on his cigarette before replying. "I started seeing the movie with Sarah, but I'm not much of one for romantic comedy. So I ducked out and went into the Mel Gibson one next door. It had started about the same time."

The Chief got up and walked over to the window. "Why didn't you tell me this in the first place? A friend of yours has vouched for your character. Now you've gone and cast suspicion on yourselves."

"It's my fault!" exclaimed Sarah. "I knew that sooner or later you'd be coming by, and I thought we'd better get our story together."

"Why?"

"Because of what happened at the reception."

"Well, you've really muddied the water," he said to Sarah. "D'you think husbands and wives always see the same movie? I *almost* did what your husband did! The only reason I didn't was because Eastwood got La Gravanese to adapt the book to the screen, and he's the best in Hollywood."

He returned to his chair. "So now you're going to have to tell me the whole plot of the Mel Gibson one—what's it called?"

"Hell Hath No Fury."

"Yeah, that's the one."

"Okay," he sighed, making sure there was plenty of tape in the little recorder, "start from the beginning and don't leave anything out."

Maurice, his hands shaking, stubbed out his cigarette and immediately lit another. He described the early action in great detail, and then the story grew vague. Why, the Chief wanted to know.

"I went out for a smoke."

"You left *then?* Just when the bad guys had commandeered the Statue of Liberty?"

Maurice scowled. "You've obviously forgotten—when you've got to smoke, you've got to smoke."

"So you left the theater and had a cigarette."

"Two, actually."

The Chief looked at Maurice's hand holding the cigarette. It was still shaking. Following his intuition, he asked, "Were you upset about something?"

"No," he answered quickly. Too quickly. "I mean, no more than usual."

"Did it have anything to do with what happened at the reception?"

"No!"

The Chief looked at Sarah, who also seemed distraught. He addressed his next question to her. "Okay, what *did* happen at the reception, Mrs. Tomlinson? Obviously it was not the first time you and Mr. Curtis had met."

It was a long time before Sarah spoke. Then she told him that she had dated Curtis when she was a nurse in Viet Nam, and that Maurice had been one of her patients. She and Maurice had fallen in love, but when she had tried to break off with Curtis, he would not accept it. She finally had to request a transfer. When she got back to the States, it took her a long time to locate Maurice, but she married him and brought him to Eastport. She'd read that Curtis was active in real estate on the Cape and hoped they would never meet. But they had, a couple of months ago at Sovereign's.

"About the time of the bee incident?" asked the Chief.

"Yes," she said slowly, her eyes widening. "You think they were—connected?"

The Chief shrugged. "As far as I'm concerned, everything's connected. Tell me about the reception."

She'd been worried about going, but since Maurice was one of the rose growers, she couldn't very well *not* go. But she was right to worry: Curtis had made a huge pass at her—which had precipitated all the rest. That's why, when they heard about the murder, she'd felt they'd better get their story straight.

There had to be more to it than that, thought the Chief, because from what he'd observed, Curtis had made passes at half the women present. But he sensed it would be wiser to pursue it later.

He turned to Maurice. "Let's go back to the movie: What exactly was happening, when you went back in? And tell me everything, in detail, until it fades to black."

Maurice did his best to comply, concluding that when his movie let out, Sarah was waiting in the lobby.

"Well," said the Chief, "thank you both for your time. And speaking of time, we'll save a lot of it next time, if you'll just tell me the truth."

ऩ●

Back at the station, the Chief called Trish into his office. "How's it going?"

"Well," she smiled, "now I know why it's called legwork. I'm beat! But you were right: The phone records showed a lot of calls from one person."

"Tobin Hatch."

Trish nodded. "He's been calling her every day since her husband's accident, usually late in the afternoon. And the calls have been getting longer: fifteen, twenty minutes; yesterday it was for half an hour." She tilted her head. "I get the feeling this is turning into more than just commiserating with his best friend's widow."

The Chief pulled out his tape recorder. "Well, I'm going to give you a break from legwork. Some sit-down work: I want you to go to the movies."

"What?"

"I want you to see *Hell Hath No Fury* at the Harwich Cinema."

"Thanks, Chief, but I've already seen it."

"Then you're going to see it again. This afternoon. But before you do, I want you to listen to this tape." He handed her the little machine. "That's Maurice Tomlinson's alibi." Explaining the situation to her, he took an old stopwatch from the top drawer of his desk. "Listen to the tape, make a log, and then watch the movie. I want to know, as close as you can tell me, when he left the theater, and when he came back inside. To the minute, if possible."

"Okay, Chief," she said, leaving somewhat mystified.

36 | the tell-tale clue

QUAINT WOULD BE THE WORD most visitors to Eastport would use to describe the little jewelry shop on the corner of Front and Bayview. Knowing this was an asset, D. Alan Jones, the owner and proprietor, went to considerable lengths to enhance the unique charms of Dickens Brothers Jewelers. He served fresh-brewed coffee and had several comfortable chairs and newspapers available for husbands who were weary of being dragged from store to store by their wives. And he would chat with them, even if they had just come in for a breath of air-conditioning, or to sit down for a spell.

It was a small store but an up-scale one: Dickens Brothers was the only place you could buy a Rolex on all of Cape Cod. For the wives, Alan Jones had a traditional assortment of gems in modern, stylish settings, balanced by a case of unusual, family-heirloom, estate-sale pieces. And for the sentimental, he had a whole corner of the store devoted to nine-inch tall felt figures of Christmas carolers, based on the characters in Dickens' *A Christmas Carol*. The tie-in with the store's name was the ostensible reason, but in truth Alan Jones was a bit dotty on them. He would tell his customers

that every so often he was almost certain he'd caught the little figures singing, when they thought no one was in the store. Each
Christmas Eve, on several of the Cape's radio stations, he would
sponsor a recording of himself reading *A Christmas Carol,* which
he had edited down to exactly 56 minutes and 30 seconds.

As he was also a member of Faith Abbey, it was to him that
Brother Bartholomew, with Brother Ambrose in tow, now repaired.

"Alan," he said, after he'd helped himself to a cup of coffee
and made sure no one else was within hearing, "what can you tell
me about this?" He handed the proprietor the watch they had
recovered.

"What would you like to know?"

"Well—how old is it? Were was it bought? How did it break?"

Alan took the watch and held it up to the light. "Since it's not
something we carry, I've no idea how old it is, though the styling of
these watches does tend to change every year. It's a fairly standard
sport watch, Japanese, retailing in the thirty-five to forty-five dollar
range."

"Any idea where it was purchased?"

Alan pursed his lips. "Well, at that pricing point, it's a little
higher than you'd find in Bradlee's or K-Mart." He thought for a
moment. "Try the Duck Blind or EastSports."

"Thanks," said Brother Bartholomew, smiling. "How about the
band?"

Alan held it up to the sunlight streaming in the front window
and squinted at it, much as Ebenezer might have examined a gold
coin. "The pin's still attached at one end, but it's bent." He paused.
"I'd say it took a pretty severe blow."

Brother Bartholomew thanked him again, and they left. As
they passed by the carolers, he whispered to Ambrose: "Do you
hear singing?"

At the Duck Blind they had no luck, but at EastSports they
struck pay dirt. "Yeah," said the young clerk with blond hair close
cropped at the sides but long on top, who looked like he'd rather
be surfing. "We carried that model last Christmas. In fact," he
brightened, "we just sold the last one to someone who'd gotten one
earlier and lost it."

"Who?" demanded Brother Bartholomew, then concentrated on trying to appear only casually interested.

"I don't know, man; I was on break."

"Was it a man or a woman?"

"I don't know that, either."

"Well, who does know?" He was not doing a very good job of keeping the impatience out of his tone.

"Natalie."

"Can I speak to her?"

"Not now, you can't." Surfer dude seemed to be enjoying this.

"When can I?"

"When she gets back from vacation."

"And when would that be?"

"Beginning of June."

He had to be careful now; he'd already asked too many questions. "Any chance of reaching her by phone?"

"Doubtful, man. She's on a windjammer cruise in the Caribbean."

"Thanks," said Bartholomew smiling, "you've been a real help."

"Hey, man, that's what we're here for!"

ॐ

"The last time I was aboard," said the Chief on a stool in the Commodore's galley, "it was under less than pleasant circumstances. I'm afraid that's true again, too."

"How is he?"

"Who?" responded the Chief, a little startled. He couldn't be referring to the deceased!

"Old Bull, of course."

"Oh, you mean, your cannon."

"Who else?"

"Well, it's—he's fine. Down in the station's storeroom." He smiled. "And you know, we haven't received a single complaint."

"He wishes he were home."

"I'm sure he does," the Chief nodded. "But I'm not sure your neighbors do."

The Commodore folded his hands on the counter. "You said you were here under unpleasant circumstances. Since you've already got Bull, I imagine it has to do with the death of MacArthur Curtis."

The Chief reminded himself that this old man was sharper—and sounder—than he appeared. "Yes," he said. "I need to know where you and your daughter were a week ago today—specifically, late in the afternoon."

"About the time the storm began."

"Yes."

"Is that when he got it?"

The Chief looked at him. "You didn't care for him much, did you?"

"Did *you?*"

"I didn't know him."

"Me, neither," said the Commodore, picking up a small brass telescope on a stand where the galley counter met the bulkhead. He extended it to its full length and scanned the Atlantic horizon. "But you're right: What I saw, I didn't care for."

"How about your daughter? She works for Curtis Investments, doesn't she?"

"Not anymore."

"I need to talk to her; will she be home soon?"

"Not any time soon. She's up in Maine, at Bar Harbor with her mother." He passed the telescope to the Chief, who looked through it and couldn't make out anything, not even the tops of waves.

"When did she leave?"

"Thursday morning."

"What time, exactly?" The Chief passed the spyglass back to its owner.

"Reveille for me is two bells. She was already gone."

The Chief shook his head. "For us landlubbers, what time would that be?"

"Oh-five-hundred."

The Chief asked for his wife's phone number and said he would probably be calling her. "Meantime," the Chief smiled, "how about the ancient mariner? Where were *you* a week ago at," he looked at his watch, "just about this time?"

"I was here."

"Doing what?"

"Watching *Victory at Sea*. I think by then I'd gotten to 'The Battle for the Mindanao Straits'; I'm not sure." He reflected a moment. "And then, of course, the lights went out."

"What did you do then?"

"There's a back-up generator down in the engine room. I fired her up."

"And went back to the battle?"

"No, I didn't feel like watching any more."

"So—"

"So, I settled down with a good book. I'm rereading the Hornblower series."

The Chief nodded. He noted that even the gray wall phone appeared to be Navy Issue. "By any chance, did you make or receive any calls?"

"No. Wait a minute; that's not true. I called Bar Harbor, to see if Pat got there all right."

"You were worried about her?"

"Yes," replied the Commodore and then looked as if he'd regretted saying it.

The Chief walked over to the big bay window and gazed out at the darkening ocean. "This is quite a view! If I had a view like this, I'd never get any work done." He turned his back on it and asked the Commodore, "Why did your daughter leave?"

"She wanted to see her mother."

"But it was sudden, wasn't it? I mean, driving off while it was still dark; wasn't that a bit—extreme?" Noting the Commodore's hesitation, the Chief pursued this line. From his hip pocket he extracted a Day-Timer and started thumbing through it. "My paper brain," he explained with an apologetic smile. "My trouble is, I should use it more often. My wife says: 'What's the point of having one of those things, if you don't write in it?'"

He found the note he was looking for. "Your daughter was Curtis's personal assistant, wasn't she?" The old man nodded, and on a hunch the Chief said, "After the MacAllister memorial service, Curtis went back to his office—by any chance did she go back there, too?"

The Commodore made no further acknowledgement. He stared at the Chief as if he were a flight of enemy dive bombers, and his own planes were a hundred miles away.

"What happened, skipper?" asked the Chief softly. "What made her up and go?"

The old salt just shook his head, and the Chief realized he was going to get nothing further but his name, rank, and serial number.

"Well, I've learned enough about Curtis to know what an unsavory piece of work he was," he said getting up to leave. "So whatever it was, it wouldn't surprise me."

"He had the morals of a Barbary Coast pirate!" the Commodore spat out.

"Care to elaborate?"

The old man shook his head. "The smoking lamp is out," he declared. "All hands return to duty stations."

The Chief sighed and made a mental note to have Trish check the time of his call to Maine—and any other calls that night. Also, exactly when the power went out at East Bluffs.

He stood up. "Request permission to leave the ship, sir."

"Permission granted."

"I'll probably have to come back."

"You'll be welcome. Give my regards to Bull."

"I'll do that," replied the Chief over his shoulder, as he went out into the gathering dusk.

37 | a mycean vase

THE DASHBOARD CLOCK SAID 6:30. The Chief shook his head; it felt later than that. Since Curtis's body was discovered four days ago, he had been averaging about four hours of sleep a night. Except you couldn't really call it sleep; according to Peg, he spent most of that time rolling and groaning. Then he'd wake up, and once the gerbil in his mind got on its exercise wheel. . . .

It was taking its toll; his reactions were in super slo-mo, and his mind felt like oil sludge in the bottom of a crankcase on a 12-degree morning. Plus, he was starting to cough. If he didn't get some real sleep soon. . . .

One day at a time, he told himself; no, make that an hour at a time. And right now, he had a hunch he ought to go over to the Teal Pond Country Club.

When he got there, the dining room was closed—which was odd for a Thursday evening. The sun hadn't been out, but it was still warm enough for golf. Then he remembered that Teal Pond was in the throes of bankruptcy. He was about to get back in the Bravada when he noticed that there were lights coming from the Tap Room. He went in.

It was the sort of room he really liked—overstuffed chairs in dark red leather, paneled walls, card tables with wheeled captain's chairs around them, a red carpet, trophy cases with inscribed silver cups in them, an antique wooden propeller mounted on the wall above the bar, and behind it, bank upon mirrored bank of single-malt whiskies. In the old days, in tap rooms like this, in metropolitan men's clubs around the country, bachelors would spend much of their lives in such surroundings.

This evening a foursome was having a drink at a card table prior to having some supper, and by the window another couple was doing the same. Behind the bar stood Tommy in his red jacket, a fixture of the place. The Chief took a seat at the end of the bar farthest from the other guests.

The tall, gray-haired bartender with the faint Boston Irish accent came over. "What can I get you, Chief?"

He looked at the various draft beer handles.

Following his gaze, Tommy asked, "How about a pint of Harp?"

"I'm not a member."

"Let's just say it's on the house."

The Chief sighed. "That would be great."

Tommy pulled him a beer, taking care to fill it to the rim. He set it in front of the Chief.

After he'd taken a long draught, he said, "Tommy, tell me about Mr. Curtis."

The bartender rubbed away an imaginary spot on the spotless cherry wood bar. "My mother told me never to speak ill of the dead."

"But you'd probably have a lot to say, if she hadn't."

"Probably."

"Okay, we'll let it go at that. What about Tobin Hatch? He's not dead."

Tommy smiled. "Mr. Hatch is a stand-up gentleman, that he is."

"Does he come in here often?"

"He didn't use to."

"But he has been, since the bankruptcy proceedings started?" prompted the Chief.

"It was more since the death of Mr. MacAllister," the bartender replied. "Now there was another stand-up gentleman! The two of them almost made up for their senior partner."

"They were good friends, weren't they—Mr. Hatch and Mr. MacAllister?"

"The best! They would come in here sometimes, after sailing. So happy, they made everyone around them happy."

"Mr. Hatch must have taken it awfully hard, when his partner drowned."

The bartender nodded. "We all did."

"Did he ever talk to you about it?"

"He did," Tommy said, not volunteering any more.

"Did he blame Mr. Curtis for what happened?"

"Didn't everyone?" Then he said something the Chief wasn't expecting. "I think somebody must have told the backers about what happened at the reception."

"Why?"

"Because just before that, we'd been told the club was going to expand, then two days later, it all hit the fan." He looked at the door to the kitchen. "The cook and I are the only ones left."

Tommy took his empty glass and was about to refill it, when the Chief waved his hand. "That's all, Tommy, thanks."

The bartender put the glass in the sink.

"Last question," said the Chief, getting up to leave. "Was Mr. Hatch in here last Thursday?"

Tommy rubbed the bar. "Mm-hmm."

"What was he drinking?"

"Bushmills Malt, 16-year-old."

"How many did he have?"

"A few," said Tommy carefully.

"Was he still here when the power went out?"

The bartender shook his head. "No, sir. I sent him home at the first flicker. You know what our power on the Cape is like, Chief. We knew how big the storm was, and I figured it was only a matter of time before the power would be gone completely. I told Mr. Hatch he'd be better off at home than here."

The Chief zipped up his windbreaker. "Before he left, did he say anything about Mr. Curtis?"

"Nothing he hadn't said before."

"Tommy, your loyalty is commendable. But I haven't been trying to get you to say anything against Mr. Hatch; I'm just trying to figure out what happened."

The bartender nodded. "You gotta do your job, Chief. And I'm just trying to do mine."

The Chief tried Tobin Hatch's doorbell. It didn't ring. He tried the brass door-knocker, shaped like an anchor. No response. But there were lights on inside, and one of the garage doors was up. In that bay, he noted, was the burgundy Jaguar sedan that was Mr. Hatch's everyday car, between Mrs. Hatch's Mercedes wagon and Mr. Hatch's old Morgan. The Chief knocked louder with the brass anchor. Inside the house, he heard a dog bark. Nothing else. He slammed the brass anchor so hard that it shook the door.

That did elicit movement inside. Someone was coming. Then there was a shattering of crockery, and the door opened. It was Tobin, as many sheets to the wind as it was possible for a vessel to be before keeling over.

"Evening, Chief," he smiled lopsidedly, slurring his words. "What brings this out on a night like you?" He opened the door wide, and the Chief stepped inside, avoiding the shards of what appeared to be an ancient vase that had smashed on the foyer's black-and-white marble floor.

Tobin looked down at the wreckage and mournfully shook his head. "Andrina's going to be terribly upset about that. That was a Mycean vase, genuine article. It just arrived yesterday—all the way from Greece. According to the card, it was a gift to her from someone named Ian." He looked down, crestfallen. "Humpty's all Dumptied now, I'm afraid. No king's men, no king's horses. Just ol' me 'n ol' Tiff." He nodded at the golden retriever watching from the far end of the foyer. The Chief fought back a smile; the dog's expression was as forlorn as her master's.

"I stopped by to ask you a few questions, Mr. Hatch, but I think I'll come back tomorrow."

"No, listen, Chief, I'm fine. Fire away." He turned and led his guest into the study. Looking around, the Chief realized it was another room that he liked. On the coffee table that had once been a wooden deck hatch, there was a nearly empty fifth of Bushmills, and a brandy snifter with a little of the golden liquid still in the bottom. The Chief smiled to himself; that's the way he would drink it, too, if he had any. Straight—no ice, no soda, nothing but the fragrance and the mellow—

"Have a drink?" asked his host.

"No, thanks; I'll only be a minute. I need to know where you were a week ago, when the power went out."

Tobin started to sit down, then lost his balance and, fortunately, collapsed into his chair. "Well, I would have been at the club, 'cept Tommy shoveled me out of there. He used the storm as an excuse to cut me off and send me on my way."

"So you were here."

Tobin scrunched up his eyes and wagged his forefinger. "Not—exactly."

"Where were you?"

The erstwhile sailor frowned mightily. "Officer, I cannot answer that question!"

"Why?"

"Because—I don't know where I was."

"What do you mean?"

"I mean—it's an awfully good thing you didn't run across me out there," he gestured in the general direction of the great outdoors, "or I'd still be in the hoosegow! I was so pickled that I got lost! And then the storm came, and all the street lights went out, and trees came down. . . . I spent two hours trying to stay off the rocks and shoals and find my into home port!"

The Chief shook his head. "You have no idea where you were."

"Not—a smidgen!"

"Well," said the Chief, watching him, "could you have gone to Curtis's house, taken that knife he'd threatened you with, and used it on him, the way he was going to use it on you?"

Tobin's expression registered that he was dimly aware that things had gotten a whole lot more serious than they'd been a moment before.

"You think *I* did it, Chief? Is that it?"

"I don't know; did you?"

"Nope. But I'm sure glad someone did. They ought to give a medal to whoever did in old 'one for all and all for one.'"

"You really despised him, didn't you?"

He poured the last of the Irish whiskey into the snifter. "Chief," he said, shaking his head, "you don't know the half of it."

"Do you hold him responsible for the death of your best friend?"

Tobin eyed him narrowly. "Cal's death was an accident," he said slowly. "But I will say this: If Curtis hadn't done what he did, he'd probably not have gone out sailing that day."

"Did he treat Cal worse than you?"

"No. But my lovely wife who owns this home has vast hordes of filthy lucre. Cal and Karen didn't have anything. When Teal Pond went belly up, Cal went to him for a loan, and Curtis turned him down. And broke a couple of his ribs doing it."

"Did you know that a week ago?"

"You mean, could that have been part of my motive?"

The Chief shrugged. "Sure."

"Yup. I knew."

The Chief stood up to go. "One more thing: I stopped by the club, before I came here, and talked to Tommy about last Thursday afternoon. He said that before you left, you had some things to say about Curtis."

Tobin looked into the bottom of the snifter. "Did he tell you that I said he was not fit to walk the face of the earth?"

The Chief shook his head. "No, as a matter of fact, he refused to go into specifics."

"Like I just did."

"Like you just did."

"So, if you quote that back to the poor guy, he'll have to admit I said that."

"Something like that."

"Pretty smooth, Chief," he said with sad disgust. "I hope you can sleep tonight."

38 | on the beach

East Bluffs, about three fingers north of Cape Cod's outer elbow, had the little-known distinction of being the first land the Pilgrims sighted as they arrived aboard the *Mayflower* in November of 1620. Upon viewing the looming sand cliffs, that good ship turned south to beat its way around Monomoy Point (the elbow). Bound for the northern tip of the Virginia Colony where it met the Hudson River, she encountered fierce headwinds that made the passage impossible. When after three days they had not moderated, the Pilgrims decided that perhaps God had something else in mind for them.

This noon, a light haze enveloped that vast, desolate beach, as it stretched away to the north. The bluffs, with their steeply slanted sides and crown of unruly vegetation spilling over the top, seemed almost primordial. To the north, a line of gentle, gray-blue breakers curled ashore. The whole scene was reminiscent of a French Impressionist seascape. There was even a solitary stroke of red—the band that girdled the lighthouse barely visible in the distance. Treading over the soft sand, Brother Bartholomew half expected to encounter a bearded gentleman in a broad-brimmed hat and a white linen duster, trying to keep canvas on easel in a lifting gust of wind.

But the only figure on the beach that day was Chief Burke. Absorbed in improving his casting technique, he was startled when his friend came up behind him and said, "Try using a little more wrist, as if you were trying to skip a flat stone."

With disgust the Chief reeled in and thrust the heel of the rod in the sand. Then he turned and smiled. "Thanks for coming on such short notice."

"What's up?"

"What's down would be more like it."

"Okay, what's down?"

"I am. I did something so skuzzy last night. . . ." His voice trailed off, and he stared at the incoming waves.

Bartholomew said nothing. It was best to let a person unburden himself in his own time, without prompting.

Slowly, painfully, the Chief related the events of the previous evening, concluding with how he had trapped an inebriated Tobin Hatch into incriminating himself. He looked imploringly at his friend, apparently hoping that somehow he might offer absolution, or at least a measure of relief.

Bartholomew offered neither. "What's done is done," he said. "You can't rewind the tape now. But—you *can* act as if it had never happened."

"What do you mean?"

"Well, you can simply choose to 'disregard the previous testimony,' as it were."

"You mean—forget I heard it?"

"Something like that."

The Chief scowled. "Easy for you to say; you don't have to solve this case."

Bartholomew watched a brown-flecked sandpiper peering intently down his bill for signs of lunch, as it scurried along. Totally focused on the sand directly in front of its nose, it nonetheless managed to keep just out of reach of each incoming wave. "Do you believe he did it?"

"Right now, he's at the top of my short list—though 'short' is something of a euphemism. He's got the most motive. *And* the least alibi. Though from the sound of it, it's a miracle he got home without killing himself, let alone anyone else."

Bartholomew chuckled. "You didn't mention his size. Last time you said that of all the suspects, he was the one big enough to handle Curtis—"

"Only that's no longer a factor," said the Chief, sourly. "Otis Whipple—he and Trish Allen are the two officers I've assigned to the case—talked to the pathologist. Apparently the murder weapon was so sharp that *anyone* could have done Curtis in." He watched as a gull glided along the crest of a breaker. "Which sort of puts us back to square one."

"Meaning?"

"Now that I've talked to them all, I'm running into a lot of shaky alibis—and a whole lot more motive than I expected." Abruptly, the gull plunged into the wave and emerged with a fish that had swum too near the surface.

"You didn't answer my question," his friend persisted. "In your gut, do you think Hatch did it?"

The Chief whirled on him. "I don't think *any* of them did it! Yet one of them *had* to! So at this point I'm not trusting my gut anymore, or anything else. Just the facts, ma'am!"

Brother Bartholomew threw up his hands, as if his friend had just pulled a gun on him.

"Sorry," murmured the Chief, "but frankly the whole thing's one helluva backlash!"

The monk picked up a rod and examined its reel. "Well, you know the first rule about undoing a backlash: You've got to take your time. The moment you lose patience, you—"

"Right now, I'm about to lose patience with *you!*" the Chief exploded. "I don't *have* time!"

"Whoa, Dan!" His friend took a step backward. "I'm one of the good guys, remember?"

The Chief exhaled and smiled. "Okay, okay, go on."

His friend rotated the barrel of the reel slowly, back and forth, as if he were examining a prime example of every angler's nightmare. "Well, you know the drill: You test the tension here—and here—and here—and sooner or later, you find one bit that has a little give to it. You poke it and give it a little pull and see if that loosens anything." He turned the reel. "Then you try the other side." He turned the reel in the opposite direction, listening to the clicks, as if he were listening to the tumblers of a safe.

"Pretty soon, you've got it sorted into a couple of major possibilities. Keeping your patience, you work one against the other until—the backlash unravels. So easily, you wonder what all the fuss was about."

The Chief just glowered at him, and Bartholomew put the rod back in the sand. "Let's start with what you know."

"Well, for one thing, I caught your friends, the Tomlinsons, in a flat-out lie." He related how they had tried to alibi each other, and that Trish was checking out Maurice Tomlinson's revised story.

He then told him that the widow MacAllister—and Tobin Hatch—seemed to hold Curtis responsible for her husband's accident. "Apparently he had turned down MacAllister's request for an emergency loan—and had broken two of his ribs in the process."

The Chief yawned and picked up the tackle box. "Let's walk; I'm so tired that if I stand still, I'm going to fall asleep."

They strolled down close to the water, taking advantage of the firmer footing at the end of the sliding surf. "What about Royce?" Bartholomew asked.

"He's an odd duck. But there doesn't seem to be any bad blood between him and Curtis, other than that he wouldn't sell Curtis his cottage." He told his friend about the computer log, which only proved Royce was at the computer at those two specific moments in the afternoon and evening.

"Did you get a look at what he was working on?"

From the inside pocket of his windbreaker the Chief produced the opening page of the interminable environmental exegesis that Royce was preparing for the *Revelator*. His friend glanced at the first paragraph: "It is doubtful that of all the people who have strolled the flats of Eastport at low tide, even one has ever stopped to consider what life out there might be like from the point of view of the clam. How does one protect oneself against 'Red Tide?'

What must it feel like to be harvested? Thrown into a wire bucket and then ripped open by a blade specifically designed for that purpose?"

Brother Bartholomew handed the document back to the Chief without comment. "What about Mrs. Curtis?"

"I called up her friend in Kennebunkport: She did not get there last Thursday until almost midnight." He squinted at his friend: "How long does it take *you* to drive up to Kennebunkport?"

The monk laughed. "I haven't done it in 20 years! But I'd guess about four hours—maybe five, if I stopped to get something to eat."

"But not nine."

"No, not nine. Although, there *was* a 'hundred-year weather event' under way."

The Chief nodded. "I thought of that. I called our State Police. And New Hampshire's. And Maine's. All the main arteries were open."

"What about motive?"

The Chief moved adroitly to avoid a wave that was sliding a bit further than the others had. "They weren't getting along. My sense is, things between them got a lot more sour after the reception."

They came to the smooth, gray trunk of a tree with three gnarled roots remaining—an ancient sea voyager that had been adrift for ages, before washing ashore here. The lines of the remaining roots were astonishingly graceful.

"What about the Commodore and his daughter?"

The Chief related his interview with the father. "I checked: The daughter got to her mother's a little after lunch on Thursday. She's not a suspect."

"But her father is?"

The Chief nodded. "I have a feeling Curtis did something to her the night before he was killed. But instead of reporting it or telling anyone, she hightailed it out of town. Her father wouldn't say anything, but—" he looked at Brother Bartholomew, "if she were my daughter. . . ."

"So much for motive. Opportunity?"

"Who knows? The man was home alone, watching old 'Victory at Sea' tapes. Impossible to check."

"Well, that's it then," said his friend, turning to retrace their steps. "Come on; I've got something in the truck I want to show you."

But the Chief did not move. With a smile he said, "Aren't you forgetting something?"

"What?"

"The eighth hole in the sand."

Bartholomew frowned. "You don't mean Laurel? I told you: She's not the murdering type."

"But you haven't seen her in what, eighteen years?"

"Doesn't matter; I *know* her!"

The Chief looked away to watch a tern skimming over the sand. "People change," he observed quietly.

"Not Laurel."

"*You* changed. Look at you: You're a monk now."

Bartholomew thought for a moment. "Some things don't change."

The Chief smiled. "She said the same thing."

"You talked to her?"

"Of course. She said she was at the library Thursday afternoon, but no one else was."

"So she has no alibi—is that what you're saying?"

"Will you relax? From what she told me, she barely knew the deceased."

"He's hardly her type."

The Chief gazed at a sloop a couple of miles out. "She asked about you," he said, not taking his eyes off the distant boat.

Bartholomew fought the urge to ask what she'd said.

"I told her I didn't know much about you, that I really hadn't seen you since school." He paused. "Then I told her that we *had* met recently—I didn't say about what. I did tell her that despite your present, um, circumstances, we were still friends." He picked up the tackle box. "That's when she said that some things don't change."

"But sometimes they do," his friend insisted.

The Chief shrugged and started up the beach toward the parking lot. "You said there was something in the truck you wanted to show me?"

39 | a pastoral call

AT THE OLD PICK-UP, which he'd parked some distance from the Chief's vehicle, Brother Bartholomew unlocked the glove compartment. Withdrawing a sandwich bag containing the black plastic sport watch with the dark green nylon band and broken clasp, he presented it to his friend.

"What's this?"

"Maybe your first real clue." Bartholomew related how he and Brother Ambrose had found it and checked it out.

"I've got to hand it to you!" said the Chief, marveling. "I figured your biggest help would be as my sounding board, someone I could be honest with, so I wouldn't have to dump it all on poor Peg." He smiled. "I didn't think you were really going to *help* me!"

"It's fun," admitted his friend. "I'm beginning to get the hang of thinking forensically."

"Huh?"

"You know, seeing what isn't there, or what *is* there but shouldn't be. Hearing the word not spoken. It's a little like chess: When you first start playing, you merely react to what the other guy's just done. Or maybe you try to figure out what he's going to do next. But as you build up chess muscles, you try to stay mentally three moves ahead. It gets addictive once you start working traps, pitfalls, and swindles. Ultimately, you try to get inside the other guy's head—only to find that he's been inside yours."

The Chief shuddered. "Sounds too arcane for me."

"Oh, come on, Dan!" Bartholomew chided him, "you do it all the time! That aw-shucks routine is strictly for those who don't know you."

The Chief slowly smiled. "Most of the time I haven't had to deal with anything deeper than 'I couldn't have been doing more than twenty, when I hit her' or 'I have no idea how that got in there.'" He looked at the sport watch. "We're on a whole other level here."

Bartholomew opened the door to the red pick-up. "Now what?"

"After I check in at the station, I think I'll pay the Widow Curtis a pastoral call."

Otis Whipple flagged the Chief down as he came in the front door. "You're not going to believe this! Mrs. Curtis—"

The Chief held up his hand and waved him into his office. "Do you understand the meaning of 'confidential investigation'?" he growled, as soon as the door was shut.

"Sorry." Otis's remorse lasted a millisecond. "But wait till you hear this! Mrs. Curtis's car was seen in front of Chandler, Gilbert and Cooper's last Monday. At noon!"

The Chief stared at him. "You mean, when she came back from Maine, she went to her lawyer's first, and *then* went home?" Otis nodded, and the Chief slammed his hand on the desk. "*Everybody's* lying!" He looked up. "Who saw the car?"

"It was an anonymous tip."

"Otis! Was it from a man or a woman?"

"It was a fax." He handed his superior a sheet of paper with one sentence on it and no sender info across the top.

The Chief studied it. "If this is true. . . ."

"There's something else," admitted Otis with great reluctance.

"What is it?"

"There's a reporter down from Boston, asking all kinds of questions."

"Like what?"

"Mostly about why the investigation is taking so long, and how come there aren't any leads."

"So long?" the Chief exploded. "The body was only discovered four days ago!" He made an effort to lower his voice. "Anybody talking to him?"

"It's a her. Jill Easton from that Boston slick, *Bayview Magazine.* She's staying at the Eastporter. Everyone in the department has been no-commenting, except Leo, who hasn't told her anything."

"Good! People are finally following orders." He was about to leave, when he noticed the younger officer's expression. "Oh, God, Otis, what is it that you're not telling me?"

"Well, the way she was putting the questions, she'd already made up her mind that we're booting it."

The Chief put his hand over his eyes and left the station, muttering.

ॐ

Getting out of the Bravada in front of the Curtis house, the Chief paused to watch a Great Blue Heron take flight, its huge wings beating a slow, powerful rhythm as it skimmed across the pond in the late afternoon sun.

Allison Curtis's convertible, top down, was parked in front of the house. Which meant that she had probably just come in. And would be going out again shortly. Hmm, forensic thinking, the Chief thought wryly, as he rang the doorbell.

The door opened. Allie, in a white tennis dress, had a towel around her neck and was blotting a still-damp brow. "Chief Burke," she smiled. "I wasn't expecting you."

Welcoming him in, she asked, "Can I get you something? I'm going to have iced tea. But then I've got to grab a shower and change; I'm due back at the club for dinner at six-thirty."

The Chief declined but accompanied her to the kitchen, where she filled a glass with ice and tea from a pitcher in the refrigerator.

"I need to ask you a few more questions."

"Fine," she said, blotting again, "but I'm still warm. Let's go out on the deck."

"Friendly game?" he asked, following her.

"Not exactly—women's doubles against Ocean Edge. Three-hour match." She collapsed into an Adirondack chair.

As he sat on a bench near her, he noticed the sunlight reflecting off something across the pond and squinted at it.

Allie laughed. "He's probably watching us."

"Who?"

"Roly Royce. He's got a big old telescope over there. He and Mac used to scope each other out, during the turtle wars."

"Turtle wars?"

She explained about the imported teal ducklings being eaten by the pond's turtles. When her husband had brought in exterminators, Royce had threatened to sic his environmental activist friends on him. Since her husband did not want any bad publicity, and hoped to buy the Royce cottage, he had backed down. But he kept a pair of high-powered binoculars at the end of the bookshelf next to the living room window.

"I wish I'd known the little creep was doing that," she concluded. "The first six months we lived here, I never bothered pulling my shades down."

"Did your husband also have a high-powered rifle?"

She hesitated. "Why do you ask?"

"Just wondered—may I see the binoculars?"

"Sure," she said, putting down her tea and leading him inside.

She showed him the binoculars behind the set of first-edition F. Scott Fitzgerald novels. Raising them to his eyes, he adjusted them out the window—just in time to catch some movement on the deck of Royce's cottage. Had he just ducked inside?

Returning them to the shelf, he followed her back outside and took out his little recorder. "First of all, your friend Joan said you didn't get there last Thursday until almost midnight. Where were you?"

"There was a storm, remember?" she said with an edge to her tone. "You know, with trees coming down?"

"That's true," he replied, unperturbed. "But the roads were open, and you knew the way. What took you so long?"

"When the rain started sheeting down," she replied sharply, "I stopped in the worst of it and had a drink. I don't particularly enjoy driving with lightning all around!"

"Where did you stop?"

"How should I know?" she cried. "One of those places along Route One, north of Boston."

"How long were you there?"

She stood up. "All right, what are you getting at, Chief? Because I told you: I've got a dinner thing, and I've got to get ready."

"What I'm getting at," he said, resolutely maintaining his smile, "is that it's only 178 miles to Kennebunkport. Even if you took an hour for that drink, and couldn't do more than thirty because of the storm, that still leaves three hours unaccounted for."

She glared at him, brown eyes flashing. But she was in trouble, and she knew it. So instead of rushing the net for a put-away, she hit a safe lob to the backhand corner. "I also stopped to get something to eat."

"At another of those places along Route One?"

"Yes—no, it was further up," she said, sitting back down. "Around Kittery."

"Anybody see you?"

"No one in particular."

"What did you have?"

"A big old yummy, greasy, bacon cheeseburger," she smiled. "I was sick to death of ordering chicken-Caesar salads."

"How long were you there?"

She sighed. "Even if I say an hour, which it wasn't, that's still not enough, is it?" She looked pleadingly at him, but he said nothing. Then she shouted, "Well, suppose I told you that I drove along the Maine coast in the driving rain, thinking, getting lost, stopping, thinking, smoking, wishing I was dead, wishing Mac was dead— would you believe *that?*"

She looked surprised and relieved, when the Chief nodded and said, "I might." Then he added, "If you told me what you were so upset about."

"I already did tell you! Mac and I weren't getting along. Can I go now?" she asked wearily, getting up again. "I really *am* going to be late."

He stood up also. "Tennis, dinner at the club—not exactly what one might expect from a widow less than a week in mourning."

She didn't answer, going into the kitchen to leave the empty glass in the sink. He followed, tape recorder in hand, its tiny red light still on. Then she turned on him. "You know perfectly well what kind of a man he was! My friends know; the whole town knows. I seem to have been the last to find out. But I know now—and since we *all* know, why the hell pretend?" She headed for the front stairs. "Now I *have* to go!"

She was half way upstairs, when the Chief called to her, "There's just one more thing: What was your car doing parked in front of CGC Monday noon? Two hours before you reported finding your husband's body?"

She stopped. She thought she'd put the point away, but somehow he'd retrieved it and come back with a cross-court volley she wasn't expecting. "*My* car?"

"Unless someone else in this town has a white Saab convertible."

"Who told you it was there?"

"No!" he said, countering her weak return with a sharp volley. "The right question is: Why didn't *you* tell *me* that?"

"I'm not going to answer any more questions without my lawyer."

"In your present circumstances, Mrs. Curtis, I would say that was a wise decision."

Game, Chief Burke. He leads the first set. . . .

40 | attorney–client privilege

THE BRAVADA SCATTERED GRAVEL IN ITS WAKE as the Chief tore out of the Curtis driveway. He knew who Allison would be calling, and in less than three minutes he was there, at the offices of Chandler, Gilbert & Cooper. The reception lobby was decorated with quiet, tasteful elegance in muted, beach plum pastels. Watercolors of dunes and sea gulls graced the walls. The overall effect seemed to say, we may be Cape Cod, but we can hold our own against anything Boston has to offer.

The Chief asked to see Mr. Cooper. The receptionist asked if he had an appointment. The Chief informed her he was on police business. The receptionist said Mr. Cooper was in conference. The Chief asked how long he would be. Through his tone, he let her know that he was about at the end of his patience. She said she would inquire. Through her tone she let him know that she was not intimidated.

She went into Mr. Cooper's office and returned in a moment to announce that Mr. Cooper was through, and he might go in.

"Hi, Chief," smiled Alex Cooper, rising from his desk. "What can I do for you?"

"I think you can guess. That was probably her on the phone, telling you that I'd just left."

The overfed, overcoifed, overconfident junior partner of CGC indicated that his visitor should take one of the sumptuous chairs facing a circular coffee table. He took the other, making no comment on the Chief's opening remark.

So he elucidated. "I want to know what Allison Curtis was doing here last Monday at noon."

"Chief, you know I can't tell you that. Mrs. Curtis is my client."

"Well, your client originally told me that on the day in question, she came directly from Maine to her home, where she discovered her husband had been murdered. She neglected to mention that she had been here to see you, first. Did she inform you that Mr. Curtis was dead? Because if she did, you both could be in very serious–"

Cooper waved his well-manicured hand. "I didn't know, Chief. Mrs. Curtis didn't know, either; she'd not been home yet."

"You handle the Curtises' personal affairs, don't you?"

"Yes. Their corporate affairs–Curtis Investments and the Teal Pond Corporation–are handled by Bernard and Landstrom up in Boston."

"Mr. Cooper, how long have you lived in Eastport?"

"Three years."

"In that time, you and I haven't had any dealings, have we?"

"Not that I can recall."

The Chief nodded. "Most of my contact with this firm has been with Russell Chandler. And after he retired, with Parker Gilbert. But he's in Bermuda at the moment." Cooper nodded. "So it's you and me, Mr. Cooper."

He leaned forward. "Now I'm going to tell you what I think: I think that Allison Curtis came here Monday because she was afraid her husband was going to divorce her and cut her off with nothing." Cooper remained silent. He folded his arms across his chest, as the Chief continued. "I think she chewed on that all weekend up in Maine, and the harder she chewed, the worrieder she got–and the more determined to take preemptive action." Still no comment. Cooper leaned back ever so slightly and recrossed his legs. "What I want to know is: Was she right to be so worried? Was Curtis planning to dump her?"

Cooper nervously cleared his throat. "Sorry, Chief, as I said—"

"I know damned well what you said!" the Chief exclaimed. "And now *you'd* better know something: Eastport is a *very* small town, and you would be making a *very* big mistake to get on my wrong side!" He paused. "Now I'm going to ask you some questions about the deceased, and you'd better not pull that attorney–client crap again, or I'll subpoena your entire office, get a court order to impound your time-sheets and phone and billing records, and make you the sorriest creature that ever walked down Front Street!"

Cooper blanched. The Chief gave him time to contemplate how he would explain the resulting chaos to Parker Gilbert upon the latter's return from Bermuda.

At length, Cooper smiled and said, "You know, Chief, I see no reason why we can't work amicably here."

41 | karen & tobin

HAVING PULLED THE DRAPERIES CLOSED against the afternoon sun, Karen was watching a video when the phone rang.

It was Tobin. "What are you doing?"

"Watching a movie. What are you doing?"

"Calling you. What are you drinking?"

She smiled. "How could you tell?"

"Takes one to know one."

Pausing the VCR, she leaned over and examined the bottle. "The final bottle of Cal's cabernet collection, a Margaux '93. Thought I'd save the best for last."

"Isn't it a little early?"

"Hey, it's after two. The sun passed the yardarm ages ago."

"You know what I mean."

She held the receiver away from her and frowned at it. "I can't seem to remember," she said to it, "who appointed you my guardian?"

"C'mon, Karen, I just care about what happens to you, that's all."

"Look," she exclaimed, getting unsteadily to her feet to confront her accuser, as if he were in the room. "Tobin, you're a nice guy—a really decent guy. But I don't have any room for that in my life right now."

There was silence on the phone. Then he said cheerfully, "What are you watching?"

She relaxed and sat back down. "*Love in the Afternoon*. It's right at the part where Gary Cooper and the Romanian gypsy musicians are sending the teacart with all the booze on it, back and forth to each other." She giggled. "Each time they have a sip, I have a sip."

"Didn't that cart go back and forth a whole bunch of times?"

She scowled. "Well, if you think that's bad, you should have been here last night. The movie was *Kiss Them for Me*—you know, the one where Cary Grant's a Navy pilot? The war's on, and he's in San Francisco on a forty-eight-hour layover. He's trying to connect with Suzie Parker. They're bar-hopping, and each time they go into a new one, he says," she attempted a Cary Grant impersonation, "Bar-tendah, a stingah for my lady friend and a stingah for myself."

Tobin chuckled. "As I recall, they went into a lot of bars."

"Yup, and each time *they* had one, *I* had one." She put a hand to her forehead. "Ooh," she moaned, "stingahs give the meanest hang-ovahs of all!"

Tobin laughed. "You've got that right! Listen, the reason I called is, let's go sailing."

"When?"

"Now."

"Oh, Tobin, bad idea. In fact, that's the worst idea you've ever had!"

"Why?"

"Because I feel like hell! The stingers are only just now wearing off, and the cabernet hasn't kicked in yet."

"Not fit company for man or beast, eh?"

"Don't say 'eh'; you're not Canadian." But the expression rang a vague bell.

"The way you feel is the way *I* felt when *you* called, the last time we went sailing, remember?"

She smiled. "I *do* remember; you sounded ghastly! You could hardly put words together."

"But I came, right? Because you wanted me to. And you know," he chuckled, "we had a good time."

"It *was* a good day," she admitted. "The last good day."

He cut in quickly: "I'll pick you up in 20 minutes." And before she could say no, he hung up. Nor did he answer, when she rang him back immediately.

Burying her head in her hands, she tried to will the rest of the afternoon to go away. When it wouldn't, she went upstairs and began to work on her face, keeping in mind that the doorbell would be ringing in 17 minutes.

The face looking back at her from the mirror, however, was a disaster. A shower might help—a *quick* shower, she reminded herself. She soaped and scrubbed and was out in five minutes. That left ten.

There wasn't much she could do about the puffy eyes and the circles under them, but a long time ago she'd learned a secret from a model friend, and now she put it to good use. With the dry towel, she rubbed as hard as she could around her eyes, then her cheeks and her forehead and the bridge of her nose. She was taking off layers of dead skin cells, and when she had finished, her face was definitely fresher looking. But she would still need her big Jackie O sunglasses. Seven minutes.

She went to the fun section of her closet and selected a navy blue boater and a pale blue Hermes scarf. And a white windbreaker, in case it got cold. She inspected the white ducks—slightly smudged but still presentable. As she struggled into them and fought to close the zipper, she realized this would be the last time she would be wearing them. Lolling around, drinking wine, and eating nachos was fun, but it took its toll.

She was just pulling on the navy-blue Topsiders when the doorbell rang. She opened it—and laughed. She couldn't help it; he looked exactly as stiff as Humphrey Bogart did, when he called for Audrey Hepburn to take her sailing in the first *Sabrina*. Why was Tobin so self-conscious, instead of like last time? And then she realized: It was because this was important to him.

Well, it was not important to her. Not with Cal gone barely two weeks. . . . She looked at him and giggled.

"What's so funny?"

Oh, dear, she'd hurt his feelings. "I was just remembering how much you didn't want to go, the last time," she improvised. It wasn't very convincing, but he accepted it.

"Do you know," she said, as he opened the door of the Morgan for her, "this is the first time I've been in this car?" She gracefully swung her legs aboard. "I've admired it for years, of course, as you motored about our little town on Saturdays like Jay Gatsby."

That did it; he was hers.

His boat, *Dream Away*, was twice the size of the *True Love*, but not as trick. Good, she thought, getting aboard; she didn't want anything to be the way it was with Cal.

"What's in the Thermos?" she asked, pointing at the big red jug at his feet, "South Shores?" Tobin made the most delicious cooler of dark rum, frozen lemonade mix, and fresh mint, all whirred in a blender with lots of crushed ice.

"Iced tea."

"Long Island?"

"Lipton's."

"Oh. Dry flight."

He gave her something to do. "You know how to put up a jib?"

Had he forgotten that she knew as much about sailing as he did? "Give it to me!"

He tossed her the bag, and she made her way forward. Clipping the line to the eye at the top of the sail, she briskly pulled it up and had it ready by the time they had cleared what was left of the sand bar protecting the harbor. While he raised the main, she tautened the jib and cleated its line.

When both sails were set, she looked up at them and thought about how good it was to be back on the water. She liked how eagerly the bow sought the open sea and how quickly the shore receded behind them; already its details were barely visible. She liked the sound of the wind in the rigging and the way the surface chop shattered the sun's reflection, as if someone had thrown away handfuls of diamonds. Claiming this halcyon moment as reality, she watched the trees and houses on the shore blur together, till they were no more than remnants of a vague, troubling dream.

She glanced back at Tobin. It was not very sociable of her to stay up here on the foredeck, instead of joining him in the cockpit, but she did not feel like being sociable. Not until the stiffening wind had blown away the lingering cobwebs of sadness and loneliness. She didn't really think it could, but after half an hour, it had—a little.

Tobin never called her to come aft, never tried to engage her in conversation or make jokes to cheer her up. He left her alone—which was the kindest thing he could have done.

When she was ready, she went aft and sat across from him, with the wheel between them.

"This was my father's boat," he said, apropos of nothing. "My grandfather bought her in 1959. Instead of a new house. He figured my dad—and I—would feel about her the way he did. And he was right. Mother didn't mind, as long as he invited her. But she got jealous if he went out alone."

So did I, Karen thought, and suddenly all the darkness came flooding back.

"Sorry," he said, seeing her expression.

"It's all right," she sighed. "I've got to get used to his really being gone. I keep thinking he's just away on business. I suppose if they'd found the body. . . ."

Tobin tacked to port, which required her to shift the jib. When she returned, he said, "My experience with losing someone I cared about is pretty limited. It took me a long time to get over my father's death. For years I'd get really down around the end of June and not know why. And then I'd remember: That was when he died."

She knew he was trying to help, but it wasn't helping. "Can we talk about something else?"

He looked downcast—oh, God, she'd hurt him again! Why did he have to be so damned sensitive?

"Okay," he said with forced cheerfulness, "how about this: We're both on Chief Burke's A list—and his A list is getting shorter."

"What do you mean?" It worked; she was genuinely interested.

"People who might have killed Curtis." Checking the mainsail for luffing, he tightened it slightly and fell off a bit. "He talked to Tommy last week."

"Tommy, the bartender?" she asked. Tobin nodded. "How did you find out?"

"The Chief told me. And got me to admit I'd told Tommy that Curtis was not fit to walk the face of the earth."

She grimaced. "You said the same thing to us. And we whole-heartedly agreed."

"Welcome to the list."

He alerted her that he was coming about, and they smoothly shifted seats. The sun came out from behind a cloud and warmed the boat. It really *was* a gorgeous day, she thought.

"You see?" said Tobin, reading her mind, "Just what the doctor ordered."

She decided to pull the cloud back across the sun. "I have to be out of our house by the end of the month.

"How much longer until the insurance clears?"

"I don't know; they've been to see me twice. Very polite, very considerate," she said with disgust. "Very anxious to find some evidence that Cal took his life."

He looked at her meaningfully, and she knew he wanted to ask her if Cal had. It was a pivotal moment, she realized. Because if he did ask, nothing further would ever develop between them. She would lie to him—because she could not burden a friend with having to lie for her. But that's all he would ever be, a friend.

He opened his mouth, then turned to check the windward horizon. "There's a front coming. In half an hour we'll have to head in. What are you going to do?"

"Find an apartment, I guess. Until the insurance thing gets settled. Actually, I'll probably keep the apartment, or maybe a condo if I can find one with enough bedrooms for the boys when they come home from school."

A real cloud passed over the sun, big enough so that it would be a while before it was warm again. They donned their windbreakers.

"You want some tea?" he asked. "And I think there's some stale cookies down in the galley somewhere."

"What I'd like is a good, stiff martini."

"That brings up something I've been meaning to talk to you about."

"Oh, God!" she yelled at the wind. "Don't turn this into the boat trip from hell!" And she didn't care how badly that hurt his feelings.

But he chose to laugh. Asking her to take the wheel, he disappeared down the hatch and in a few moments reappeared with two tall, green plastic glasses, full of iced tea. He had even put sprigs of fresh mint in them. She took a sip. "This is actually good," she said, surprised. "What's in it?"

"It's my mother's recipe—a little orange juice, a little ginger, a little brown sugar, and some fresh lemon."

She took another sip. "There's something else in here—what's the secret ingredient?"

"Strawberry jam."

"Ah, the old strawberry jam ploy."

He smiled. "My mother knew the way to my father's heart. They never went sailing without it."

"I like your family," she decided. "Did Andrina like them?"

He didn't answer at first. "She never really got to know them."

"Too bad. Did they die before you were married?"

"No, about five years after. Andrina was always too busy."

He looked up at the cloud, which had been joined by others. "Front's almost here," he observed. "We'd better head in."

That was the last thing he said, until they reached the harbor. Which she liked. It was nice to be with someone who wasn't made nervous by silence.

By the time they got to his car, the weather was cold enough that he put the top up. As they were leaving the parking lot, she shuddered.

"Don't think about it," he said—as if she could stop. Then he asked, "You want to get some supper?"

She shook her head. "I don't think that's a good idea."

"Okay." They drove on in silence. Then he said, "When you get home, are you going to watch another video?"

"Probably."

"And have wine with it?"

"Probably."

"I thought you said you'd come to the end of the cabernet."

"That's right," she frowned. "I'll have to get some."

They were at her house. "Drink the rest of this, instead," he said, reaching behind the seat and producing the red Thermos.

She glared at him. And then she smiled. "Okay, hot shot, then you've had your last Bushmills. Or Dos Equis. Or any other kind of Equis."

He stared at her, speechless.

Ah-hah! she thought. Sir Galahad wasn't expecting that! The gauge thrown down in the middle of his own banquet hall! I guess chivalry has it limits, after all.

"Deal. Until we both agree to go back on the good stuff."

She was shocked. She had not expected that. All right, but he would never outlast her. She stuck out her hand, and they shook on it.

He held her hand for a moment, before releasing it—but not longer than she wanted him to.

"Farewell, good knight," she said, smoothly swinging her legs out of the car. "Happy tea-leaves to you!" And she waved and went up the walk to the front door. Alone.

Yes, we have no bananas, she hummed as she let herself in, we have no bananas today.

42 | a refill

BROTHER BARTHOLOMEW CHECKED HIS WATCH. They were bringing a load of mulch for the new vegetable garden, but they had just enough time for a cup of coffee. The problem with coffee was, once you became a heavy hitter, you always needed another hit. He knew he ought to give it up. That he needed to give it up. That God would grant him the grace to give it up, when he wanted to. And he did want to—but not today. I'll stop tomorrow, he told himself. Just like he'd told himself yesterday. And the day before.

As usual, Brother Ambrose was in the passenger seat, and as usual, he was nattering on. "So how come we don't have anything else to do with the investigation? Aren't you still helping Chief Burke? Incidentally, I want you to know that I understand that you couldn't take me with you, the last time you met with him. He's got to be able to speak freely to you, and my being there might have kept that from happening. But I really enjoyed going to the crime scene with you, and frankly, I thought we made a pretty good team. I was dying to tell the guys about it, but you'd have been proud of me: I didn't say a word to any of them. Not a word. Because I—"

"Don't say another word *now!*" Bartholomew cut him off. "Not until we have coffee in front of us. Okay?" He smiled, so the young monk would not be overly hurt.

It worked. Peace, perfect peace, reigned in the cab of the old pick-up.

They turned down Front Street and were two blocks from Norma's, when Ambrose nudged him with his elbow. "What are you doing?" demanded Bartholomew, then realized that his young charge was only being obedient to the discipline he'd imposed on him. Ambrose was pointing out someone coming out of Dickens Brothers. It was Tobin Hatch.

On an impulse, Bartholomew swung into the little parking lot, even as the burgundy Jaguar was leaving it. "You wanted to be back on the case?" he said to Ambrose. "Well, now you are. But remember: You're the *silent* partner."

A little bell above the door, very Dickensian, tinkled as they opened the door and entered. Alan Jones was with a customer, so they went over to the display of carolers. There were Scrooge and Marley, and Tiny Tim and even Tim's little terrier. "Is that, 'God Rest Ye Merry, Gentlemen'?" Bartholomew whispered, listening with a cocked ear and a serious mien. Ambrose looked at him, looked at the felt figures, listened, and realized his mentor was teasing him.

Alan was free now, and they went over to him. "What was Tobin Hatch doing?" he asked Alan, trying to sound as casual as possible.

"Picking up his watch."

"What kind of watch?"

"A Rolex Submariner. A sailor's watch."

"What was wrong with it?"

"Nothing. He was just getting it serviced."

"Do you do that here?"

"We used to," Alan nodded towards his watchmaker's bench. "Until our watchmaker got so old that it was more than he was comfortable with. Now we send them to Rolex headquarters in New York."

"How long does it take?"

"About three weeks." Alan looked at him, his eyes narrowing. "This has something to do with that sport watch you brought in last week, doesn't it? Which means it must have something to do with—"

Bartholomew looked him in the eye and ever so slightly, shook his head.

"Well, he wasn't using that sport watch in the interim, if that's what you're thinking," Alan volunteered. "The Hatches are good customers. I gave him a nice Seiko as a loaner." He reached for the workbench. "This one. He turned it back in, when he picked up his Rolex."

"Thanks," said Bartholomew with a smile, and he left quickly, with Ambrose in tow.

"Now I *really* need a coffee!" he exhaled, when they were back in the pick-up.

⁂♦

Norma's was buzzing when they got there, filled with customers taking a Monday morning break. The safe table by the window was taken, but as they stood looking for a table, two older women sitting there got up, and they were able to get it.

Suzie came over to wait on them, but Isabel Doane signaled her that she would take care of them as soon as she was free. In a few moments she approached with two steaming mugs of black coffee. "You boys haven't been in for a while." She lowered her voice, "Are you still on the case?"

"Mother!" said her son a voice even lower. "Don't even talk about it."

"Well," she murmured, smiling as if they were merely passing the time, "I thought you wanted me to keep you informed."

"I do."

"How can I do that if you don't come in?"

Bartholomew didn't answer. Then he smiled, "Sounds like you're sitting on something right now."

She nodded—very slowly, very meaningfully.

"Well?" prompted her son, a little impatient. Coffee nerves, he thought. He took a sip from the mug, but it was too hot for him to take as big a swallow as he wanted.

"Well," she confided, "for openers, Emmet Adams was in here Thursday with Vic Malcolm. They made a point of sitting at number four, the 'private' table," she nodded to the table in the corner, "so I made a point of standing at the listening post."

Someone waved to her, and she waved back. "That's Ed Melcher. His daughter Anne and Tim just had their first baby. You'd think *he* had it, he's so proud."

"Mother," said Bartholomew edgily, "*what* did you hear last Thursday?"

"I'm getting to that," she chided him. "Emmet told Vic how angry he was at being kept out of the loop, and muzzled where the press was concerned. And how Dan should have gotten an investigator from the State Police involved long before now, and probably the FBI, too."

"What did Vic say?"

"He was real sympathetic, sort of encouraging Emmet to feel sorry for himself, then assuring him that things would all be different soon enough."

Bartholomew frowned. "What did he meant by that?"

Isabel started to reply, when Ed Melcher came over with pictures of his day-old granddaughter for everyone to admire. To Bartholomew, all newborn babies looked like Winston Churchill, and he could not work up much enthusiasm for them. But his mother was delighted, and her delight was genuine. And that, her son realized, was why she had so many friends.

Finally, they were alone again. "I think," said Isabel, "that Vic wants to see Emmet become chief so that he can finally have some say in this town. Nobody listens to him now, but with the Chief of Police tight with him and his nephew running for selectman in the fall—the combination might be something to reckon with." She shuddered. "I might just move to Orleans."

She next told him that Tobin Hatch was seen taking Karen MacAllister sailing Saturday. And that he'd been calling her every night. "They're becoming an item," she concluded.

"How in blazes did you find that out?" exploded Bartholomew, barely remembering to keep his voice down. As it was, several people turned to see what was happening.

"You watch your language, young man!" Isabel scolded him. More heads turned. She lowered her voice and put on a smile. "You keep a civil tongue in your head; I'm your mother!" She shook her head. "And you, a religious! You ought to be ashamed of yourself!" Norma's Café grew very silent.

Great, Bartholomew thought. This is supposed to be a clandestine operation, and now I've managed to make myself the center of everyone's attention. I might as well be wearing cap and bells! Blast! She really knows how to get to me! No—it's not her fault. She's only trying to do what I asked her to.

"I'm sorry," he said, meaning it. "You're right."

She was mollified, and the rest of the Nosey Parkers turned back to their coffee and conversation.

"But how *did* you learn about the phone calls? Because if there's a leak—"

"Suzie's cousin works at the phone company, and she told Suzie that the new girl in the police department—"

"Trish Allen."

"—had made an official request for her records."

The Chief wasn't paranoid, after all, Bartholomew thought. Trying to investigate a murder in this town *was* like working in a fishbowl. He looked up at Isabel. "Okay, so they're an item, to use your quaint expression—what of it?"

"Well, aren't they both suspects?"

"Maybe."

"Now, Andrew," she said, her voice starting to rise again, "don't get all Inspector Dalgliesh with me; I'm your mother!"

"I know," he muttered through clenched teeth, "you keep reminding me." He took a deep breath, exhaled, and smiled. "Remember what I said when we started: This would have to be a one-way street." He chuckled ironically. "But it seems like everybody and their dog, to use the Chief's expression, is up on the latest developments. Sometimes before we are." He looked over at Ambrose, who was concentrating on the contents of his mug.

"Well, they're not going to hear them from Dan. And they're not going to hear them from us." He paused. "And I don't want them hearing anything from you, either."

The line of her jaw hardened, and Bartholomew braced himself for another piece of her mind. But then, to his intense relief, she thought better of it. She told him that basically the town was divided into two camps: Most of the women were convinced that Mrs. Curtis had done it. And they didn't blame her; apparently the guy was a total creep. She started to tell him some of the creepy things Curtis had done, but he interrupted her and asked her to go on.

Most of the men, on the other hand, were of the opinion that Tobin Hatch had done it. They didn't blame him, either, but for different reasons. Guy reasons—Curtis had lied to his partners and betrayed them.

Bartholomew thanked her and tried to pay her, and as always, she wouldn't hear of it. "And don't be in such a hurry," she added. "I haven't told you everything."

Her son started to chuckle. "You mean, there's more?"

"Now don't you get smart with me—"

He held up his hand and smiled. "Mother, I'm sorry, believe me! It's just that you've turned out to be the most incredible secret agent!" He bit his lip to keep from laughing. "You've already given me more than I ever imagined!" He wiped the smile off his face. "I can't thank you enough, and you've been a real help to Dan."

"Well," she beamed, "he's a good boy. You both are. Except sometimes you get me so riled up!"

"Don't," he cautioned her. "Just tell me what else you have."

She bent close to him. "Barry Jones thinks the two of them did it together."

"The two of whom?"

"Karen MacAllister and Tobin Hatch. I overheard him talking with another reporter."

"What was the gist of it?"

"Well, they'd been doing a lot of digging into the financials of the Teal Pond collapse. Apparently the two partners went bankrupt, but Curtis came out in clover. They'd also heard that Karen

MacAllister is one bitter lady! Anyway, Barry thinks the two of them planned it, even if only one of them carried it out."

Bartholomew finished his coffee without comment. The watch they'd found couldn't have been Tobin Hatch's. But it might have been Karen MacAllister's.

He stood up and whispered: "Mother, you are one amazing Mata Hari!" And grinning, he gave her a kiss on the cheek.

The crowd in Norma's almost applauded.

43 | let's be friends

THE ROYCE COTTAGE COULD HAVE BEEN SO DIFFERENT, Allie thought, as it came into view. Freshly painted and scrubbed, with the yard groomed, and the overhanging limbs trimmed back, and flowers planted around the front step, it could have been charming. Instead, the music track in her mind was playing something in E minor. The setting was dark and ominous, and the tall, unkempt grass in the clearing in front had a sinister glint. Maybe it was just a trick of the late afternoon lighting, but the place looked like the opening scene of a rural Gothic.

She shivered as she got out of the Saab and retrieved the coffeecake from the passenger seat. Against the gloomy grays, greens, and drab browns, her car's gleaming whiteness seemed hideously out of place—which was exactly how she felt as she approached the front door.

There was no doorbell to ring, so she knocked—timidly at first, then a little louder. When no one came, she thought: He's not here. I tried; I can just go.

She turned and was about to leave, when the door opened. Royce seemed genuinely shocked to see her standing there.

Probably because she was suddenly a whole lot more up-close-and-personal than the way he usually saw her—framed in a little circle and magnified 150 times.

"Mrs. Curtis? What are you—"

She thrust the coffee cake toward him, and the words came rushing out: "I've felt badly ever since the reception, and I thought I'd try to make it up to you, so I made this coffee cake. Here."

But he didn't take it from her, didn't thank her for it, didn't invite her inside. He let her stand there on the step, coffeecake extended. He said, "I don't eat things made with animal fat."

She tried to remember the ingredients that had gone into the cake. Was he referring to the butter she'd greased the pan with?

"The reason I didn't hear you knocking right away, was because I was planting daffodils on the graves of my family."

Startled, she took a step backward. Coming here was definitely a bad idea! It was time to just take the cake and go home.

Alarmed, he reached for her. More alarmed at his gesture, she took another step back—and slipped off the front stoop, which was what he'd been trying to prevent. Arms flailing, she fell backward into the tall grass. The coffeecake landed nearby, upside down.

He came quickly to her and crouched down beside her. "Mrs. Curtis—Allison—are you all right?"

"Yes, I think so," she gasped. She looked at the bottom of the broken cake. "But I'm afraid my peace offering is ruined."

"Never mind," he said, reaching out to her, "let me help you up."

She did, and was surprised at how strong he was.

"Would you like some tea?"

"I don't think so," she said, straightening her blouse and brushing off her skirt. "You said something about graves—are there people buried here?"

"I'll show you," he said, leading her around the house. At the four small mounds, each covered with a stone, were fresh plantings and a trowel. A border of sunken bricks set off the little graveyard, and as she made out what was carved on the stones, she gradually realized that these were—turtles. She had known they had meant a lot to him—she had never dreamed how much.

"Your husband did this," he said bitterly.

"I'm so sorry, Roland," she said softly, placing a hand on his arm. He looked at her, his head cocked. "You really are, aren't you," he said slowly, a little in wonder. "You're not just saying that."

She shook her head. "I am not unacquainted with grief myself just now," she said quietly. "We have both suffered a loss."

He looked across the pond at her house. "I often think of that evening—not the bad part," he hastily added, "The good part. When you and I were alone in the study. You were so—understanding."

She smiled. "I remember it, too. In a way, that's why I came over: I wanted us to be friends. We're the only neighbors we've got, you and I."

He nodded. "I'm sorry I was rude when you came." Then he brightened. "Listen, can I show you something I've been working on? You remember when you introduced me to Barry Jones? Well, a major article is going to be the result of that, and in a way, you were responsible for it."

"I'm afraid I really have to get going," she said, but he was already halfway up the steps.

"Please come; it'll only take a minute."

Unable to think of a decent excuse, she followed him.

The first thing she noticed when she entered the cottage was its smell. As the weather was warmer and more humid than when she and Mac had come to call two weeks before, the smell was much stronger now, almost enough to make her eyes water. The place needed a complete cleaning—and so did its occupant. And all his sheets and attire. She wondered if his mother had ever been over here. It was certain no other woman had.

Absorbed at his computer, Royce could not see the furrows on her brow or the wrinkles on her nose. "Here!" he said proudly, as a page of densely-packed print appeared on his monitor. "It's almost done."

She noted that it was the first of 28 pages. "Isn't it—a little long for a newspaper article, even a feature?"

He frowned. "You think so?" He looked crestfallen. "How long do they usually run? I forgot to ask Barry."

"I don't know," she said. "I'd guess a longer piece might run 2,000–2,500 words max."

He paged down to where he had just finished polishing, then highlighted the above and checked the word count: 13,128. He was stunned.

"Maybe Barry will run it as a series," she offered.

"You think he might?" he asked, daring to hope.

"Well—it's possible."

Turning to her, he suddenly took her hand in both of his. "Allison, would you—speak to him?"

Good grief, she thought, wanting to take the hand back, but not wanting to hurt him, how did I get into this? "Of course, I will, Roland. The next time I see him." She did not offer to call Barry Jones, though he was plainly dying for her to. Nor did she mention that it might be weeks before she ran into the editor.

She glanced at the watch on the wrist of the trapped hand. "I really do have to go," she said, taking the hand back.

"Well," he replied, getting up from the computer, "I'm awfully glad you came. Now we have a good shared memory to put on top of the—other one."

"I've already forgotten it," she smiled.

"I wish I could," he said with a haunted expression. "When he took that knife out and showed us how to eviscerate people, telling us to always cut from lower left to upper right. . . ." He shuddered. "I'll never be able to forget that."

Allie nodded, and saying a firm but friendly good-bye, she walked out into the gathering dusk. As she backed out, he waved from the front door, and she waved back.

But she was frowning as she drove away.

44 | a foggy day on the wild side

When Brother Bartholomew left the friary that Wednesday afternoon, the sky was clear. The sun glinted off the white charter boats, bobbing in their slips in the harbor. But the wind was from the east, and as he drove the short distance across the Cape to the Atlantic side, the afternoon began to change. Fog was rolling in, thick and damp, and the temperature was a good ten or fifteen degrees colder. By the time he reached the seashore, the ocean was barely visible in the mist. It was hard to believe it was the same afternoon—and that barely three miles separated the two shores.

The Chief's message had sounded urgent, and he had hurried. The Chief was already there, not casting this time, just sitting on the sand with the rod stuck next to him, its line stretching out over the breakers. He was paying no attention to it, just gazing at the horizon.

"Dan?" Bartholomew called to him, concerned.

His friend turned—and momentarily brightened at the sight of him. Then the gloom returned.

Bartholomew sat down beside him and waited.

"*Bayview* just hit the stands," the Chief finally muttered. "They roasted us. In twenty years of police work, I've had my share of bad publicity. But nothing like this. They make us sound like Andy Griffith and Don Knotts!"

His friend said nothing.

"And all our critics got their oars in, especially Vic Malcolm. Emmet Adams comes off looking like the only person in the EPD who doesn't belong hanging from the back of a Mack Sennett police wagon."

When he finally subsided, his friend had a thought for him. "You can't change what they've written. And you'll never be able to get them to retract it. You won't even be able to persuade them to present your side of the story."

He put a hand on the Chief's shoulder. "If you let it get to you, eventually it will paralyze you, and neutralize any effectiveness you might have. You're just going to have to learn to live above it, Dan."

"Or turn in my badge."

"Whoa! No one's stamped UNSOLVED on the cover of that file in your desk. Man, we've not even *begun* to fight! We're going to solve this thing, and the moment we do, everyone's going to forget some off-Cape magazine's half-cocked take on it. Meantime, no one in this town's going to pay any attention to that sort of thing." He chuckled. "That's one of the *good* parts about living in a small town: People really *know* you." He paused. "And they also know Emmet Adams and Vic Malcolm."

The Chief turned to him. "Thanks."

His friend shrugged. "So, how goes the investigation?"

"To tell you the truth, it was the *Bayview* thing that made me really want to talk to you. I haven't turned up a whole lot else." He coughed—a deep, wet, rattling cough.

"You sound terrible!" said his friend. "You'd better get some rest, or you're going to get really sick." He told the Chief what he had learned at Norma's, or rather what his mother had learned, and also about Tobin Hatch's loaner watch from Dickens Brothers.

"That pretty well rules out Mr. Hatch," the Chief observed. Then he smiled. "I'm glad. I kinda like the guy." He told

Bartholomew about Allie. "Turns out, Curtis was hot to divorce his wife—so hot that he made an appointment to meet with Cooper Friday morning. When he didn't show up, and no one answered at his home or office, Cooper didn't think much of it; there was a helluva storm going on."

Bartholomew zipped up his windbreaker. "I remember," he said.

"Well, on Monday Mrs. Curtis went to see him—*before* she went home and found her husband's body. He wouldn't tell me what they talked about, but he didn't have to: It's pretty obvious she was trying to find out if her husband had been successful in freezing her out."

"You think she already knew he was dead?"

"That's the 64,000 ruble question, isn't it?" He started coughing again, worse than before.

"Dan, you've got to get out of this fog. It can't be helping—"

"I know, I know," the Chief gasped. "Change the subject!"

"How did you hear about Mrs. Curtis being at her lawyer's?"

"An anonymous tip, if you can believe it."

"From a man or a woman?"

"That's what I asked," the Chief acknowledged ruefully. "It came in as a blank fax."

"I wonder who sent it," Bartholomew mused.

"I wondered, too—but frankly, I forgot about it; too much else going on."

His friend looked up at the sky, searching in vain for a break in the clouds. "Why was it anonymous?" he asked. "If it was someone just trying to be helpful, they'd have called." A sandpiper skittered away from the reach of a sliding breaker. "I think it was someone who knew why the timing of her visit to her lawyers would be significant."

"Whoa, slow down for them curves, pardner! You just lost me back there."

Bartholomew was lost in thought. "I think it was sent by the killer," he finally said. "To deflect suspicion from themselves."

"Well, the timing was significant, all right," the Chief concurred. "But they couldn't have known how significant: Curtis was one day shy of divorcing his wife and cutting her out of millions. Right now, she's got more motive than anybody."

He started to cough again, and this time he allowed his friend to guide him to the parking lot.

They had not taken two steps before a figure emerged from the mist and came towards them.

45 | the wraith

STARTLED, Dan Burke and Brother Bartholomew stared at the form materializing out of the fog. And then they relaxed; it was Trish Allen. "Chief, I've been looking all over for you! Then I remembered when you went fishing with him," she nodded toward Brother Bartholomew, "so I called the friary. They said *he'd* gone fishing!"

"That's fine, Officer Allen," said the Chief. "What's so urgent?"

"I went to the Harwich Cinema, like you said to, and saw *Hell Hath No Fury*. Keeping track of everything in the dark was going to be too much trouble, so I audiotaped the soundtrack and played it back when I got home and could make a detailed time log of everything that happened. Then I played your interview tape and compared it to the log." She looked at the Chief. "The movie lasted an hour and 52 minutes. From where he left to where he went back in, I'd say he was gone a little over an hour."

"A long time to be out for a couple of smokes," the Chief said.

"That's what I thought," said Trish. "And by the way, that movie was as gripping as *Ransom*. I don't see how anybody could leave, even if they did crave a cigarette. Also, I timed how long it took to drive down to the theater from Curtis's house, going no more than thirty, as the storm would have broken by then." She consulted her notes. "It took eighteen minutes. I timed it the other way, too, going the limit, but not over it, figuring he would not want to risk a ticket on that leg. It took fourteen minutes, for a total of thirty-two. That leaves half an hour unaccounted for."

Brother Bartholomew was impressed. But not the Chief: "I gave you that assignment five days ago! How come you haven't made a report before now?"

Her enthusiasm was undampened. "Because it didn't occur to me until Monday to talk to the staff person in charge of the lobby the afternoon of the murder, to see if they'd seen anything. And she wasn't on duty until today."

"Well? Did she see anything?"

"Yes! That's why I'm out here! Hardly any moviegoers were in the Cineplex on the afternoon of the thirteenth, because everyone had heard the weather report. But she remembered a man fitting Tomlinson's description coming out of the Mel Gibson movie soon after it had begun. She wouldn't have remembered him, except that he had a terrible coughing fit. At first, she thought that was why he'd come out: to keep from disturbing the audience. His seizure, or whatever it was, got so bad she was ready to call 911. But when she asked him if he was all right, he waved her off. And it did calm down. He went outside. She thought he was going for a breath of fresh air—and could not believe it, when he lit up a cigarette!"

"Then what?" demanded the Chief.

"Then, after a couple of minutes, he left. She remembered when he came back, a long time later, because his jacket was pretty dry. That surprised her, because she'd seen him walk off in the storm. He should have been soaked."

"Not if he got in his car and drove to Eastport," the Chief stated. He turned to Bartholomew. "You *still* think it's not Tomlinson?"

His friend shook his head. "I know everything now points that way. But—I don't think he did it. And I can't tell you why; it's just a feeling."

"Well, that's the second time Tomlinson's lied to me, and the second time his wife has covered for him. There's not going to be a third." He turned to Trish and patted on the shoulder. "You've done really good work, Officer Allen. Sorry about chewing on you back there."

"That's okay, Chief," she smiled. "It looks like we've got our man."

"We'll see," said the Chief. "I'm going over there now. You go back to the station and bring Leo and Otis up to speed." He turned to Bartholomew. "You coming?"

His friend shook his head. "I think I'm going to stay out here for a while."

❧

Brother Bartholomew sat on the sand, about fifty yards up from the surf, arms clasped around his knees, watching the breakers. In sunlight, this late in the afternoon, they would have been an iridescent emerald, shot through with silver and gold. But in this billowing fog, they were only a dull gray. He shivered, but did not leave. And his mind was far from the recent developments.

It was on an afternoon exactly like this one eighteen years ago, that an Irish ghost had materialized out of the fog. And his world had never been the same.

What if—he had taken the other path? Their first child would be a senior now, about to graduate from Nauset High. He would not have pressured him—it would have been a boy—about going on to college; he would have already taught him the important things. But his mother would probably have insisted, and how could he object? His own mother had done the same.

There would also be a girl, about fifteen now, going through her latest *crise de cœur* over this boy or that.

He shook his head vigorously, as if to scatter the thoughts, and got to his feet. He'd best get back. To the friary. To real life.

Just to his left, there was a movement in the fog. He stared, not believing what his eyes were telling him. This tall, shrouded figure coming towards him. . . . His eyes widened, and he felt frost on his backbone. He knew what the focused power of the soul was capable of, but—could it do *this*? Could it materialize—*a wish*?

Seeing his expression, Laurel smiled. "Don't worry; I'm real. And I still like to walk in the fog. When I saw the old red pick-up, I thought of you." She smiled. "And then I wondered if it might actually *be* you."

She came closer, so close he could see the emerald of her eyes. "It was."

Everything in him wanted to take her in his arms. In her eyes, he could see how much she wanted him to. And she could see that if she so much as moved, or said another word, he would.

But she remained perfectly still. Whatever happened, it must come from him.

He was trembling from the effort to keep his arms at his sides. In that suspended moment, he could see the path dividing before him. With calm, icy clarity, he knew that whatever he did next would irrevocably alter his life—and hers—forever. And he knew that he could never claim or convince himself that he had been overwhelmed by the emotion of the moment.

As they stood there, less than a foot apart, tears filled his eyes—and then hers—till he could not bear to see them and closed his own. And still he did not move.

Then he felt the back of her fingers gently brush the tears from his cheek.

When he opened his eyes, she was gone.

46 | the right to remain silent

THE FIRST DROPS BEGAN TO FALL as the Chief went up the steps to the Tomlinsons' front door. At his knock, Maurice Tomlinson opened it and led him into the kitchen. "Perfect afternoon for cocoa, Chief; you want some?"

"No, thanks, I'm afraid this isn't a social call." He pulled out the tape recorder and switched it on, putting it on the kitchen counter. Next to it, he spread Trish Allen's log and the typed transcript of Tomlinson's description, with time estimates in the margins. "I had one of our officers corroborate your account of the movie with what actually happened on the screen." He checked the notes on the log. "It seems that you missed quite a bit more of the movie than you indicated, the last time we talked."

Tomlinson patted his shirt pockets to locate his cigarettes. "I told you," he said quickly, "I went outside for a smoke—two, in fact."

"Yes, you did. But an hour is an awfully long time to smoke a couple of cigarettes."

Finding his pack, Tomlinson fumbled one to his lips. He lit it and inhaled deeply. The tremor in his hands diminished only slightly. "Ever since Viet Nam," he said, "I've had trouble remembering details."

"On the contrary," retorted the Chief, "your memory was quite accurate—as long as you were in the theater." He tapped the transcript in front of him. "That's how we can be certain to within a few minutes how long you were gone."

"Darling," called Sarah Tomlinson as she came up the basement stairs, "who's here?"

"It's Chief Burke," her husband replied, "with a few more questions."

She emerged, wiping her hands on her apron. "I won't shake hands," she said, smiling, "I've just come from the darkroom."

"What are you developing?" asked the Chief.

"A close-up of a rose for the feature story the *Revelator* is doing. Fortunately, they want it in black-and-white, so I can do it myself. It's one of yours, of course," she smiled at her husband, "but we won't tell the judges that." She winked conspiratorially at him, but her husband was stone-faced.

"Oh, by the way," she added, "could I borrow that watch I gave you last Christmas? The one with the stop-watch function? The darkroom timer is acting up, and I don't trust it."

"Sarah, the Chief—"

"I looked in the middle drawer of your bureau, but it isn't there."

"Where did you get the watch?" the Chief asked her.

"At EastSports."

"What color was it?"

"Black," she looked at him, puzzled, "with a dark green band, why?"

"Mrs. Tomlinson, I'm glad you came up, because—"

"Call me Sarah," she said smiling.

"I'm glad you're here, because I need to talk to both of you." He looked up from the logs and transcripts spread out on the counter. "I don't think you told me the whole story about your relationship with Mac Curtis."

He went back over what she *had* told him, about breaking off with Curtis in Viet Nam, then running into him at the bookstore a month ago. He stopped there. "You see, Mrs.—Sarah, I don't think that 'chance meeting' was a coincidence. And I don't think you think so anymore, either."

Sarah pursed her lips but did not say anything, and the Chief suspected she was wondering how much else he had put together. He would not keep her in suspense. "That was the first time you saw him?"

"Yes!" she said emphatically.

"But you don't think it was the first time he saw you."

She thought for a moment. "He did mention that he thought he saw me coming out of Baxter's Pharmacy, but he couldn't be sure it was me."

"Do you remember what you were picking up there?"

"Um, the bee-sting antidote for Maurice."

The Chief nodded. "I think he found that out somehow, and that it was he who took the epinephrine from where you normally kept it, and who released the bees that nearly killed your husband."

They stared at him, shocked—not at what he was telling them, he suspected, but at how much he'd deduced.

"What's more," he went on, "I think you figured that out, too. And, if Curtis would go to that extent to get your husband out of the picture, there was no telling what he was capable of."

The Chief walked over to the rain-blurred window and gazed out at the roses. "In fact, you probably suspected that he had found out about your husband's interest in roses and cooked up the entire Eastport Rose contest so he would have an excuse to get close to you."

He turned around. She did not look shocked anymore; she looked—scared. Very scared. And her husband's hands were shaking so badly he clasped them together and kept them in his lap. "The reception was Curtis's perfect excuse. And when he got you out on the deck, just the two of you, I imagine he made his full intentions clear to you. Which was why you told him, loud enough for the whole reception to hear, that you were going home." The Chief shrugged. "Then came the episode with the knife, and we *all* went home."

Tomlinson was seized with a coughing spell, and this time the Chief did not worry about losing him. He let the paroxysm run its course, which eventually it did, leaving Tomlinson exhausted and trembling.

"Here's the part where you're going to have to help me," said the Chief. "Because I don't know whether one or both of you was in on the planning."

"The planning of what?" Tomlinson gasped. "I told you I went out for a smoke, that's all. So maybe I was out there quite a while, so what?"

The Chief strode back to the counter and slammed his fist down on it. "You've just lied to me for the third time! And in this ballpark, three strikes means you're out!"

"What are you talking about?" said Tomlinson, mustering a semblance of indignation.

"We have a witness who saw you come out of the movie and go outside. You lit up a cigarette, stood there for a couple of minutes, and then walked off towards the parking lot. When you came back an hour later, your jacket was almost dry—which surprised the witness, because the storm had started. You had gone somewhere in your car."

Sarah started to cry.

Totally focused on her husband now, the Chief asked, "Do you want to tell me where you went?" When Tomlinson wouldn't answer, he said, "Then let *me* tell *you:* Curtis had tried once to take your life. He was determined to take Sarah away from you, one way or another. Plus, he could offer her much more than you could—most of all, his health. He would be there for her, in her old age, whereas you—"

"Stop it, stop it, stop it!" screamed Sarah. *"This is cruel!"*

"No, it isn't," said the Chief in a low voice, but with intensity that matched hers. "It's the simple truth." And for confirmation he turned to Tomlinson who sat mute, his eyes fixed on his shoes.

"So," he resumed, "you got in the car, drove to Curtis's house, probably parked out on the road and walked in, to avoid being seen or heard. You saw that Mrs. Curtis's car was gone, and watched Curtis making preparations for the storm."

Tomlinson would not look up, but he was absorbing every word. "When you saw him go outside," the Chief continued, "and go down to the pond to feed the ducks, you saw your opportunity. You went into his house, broke into the display case, got the knife, snuck out, and finished him off—just the way he'd showed us!"

With an imaginary knife, the Chief made a vicious thrust, in and then up. Both of them flinched.

"You were using the watch she gave you for Christmas, because the whole thing needed split-second timing. You knew exactly how long the movie would take, exactly how much time you had to drive up here, do the job, and get back. Only he knocked your watch off when you attacked him, and you didn't have time to look for it in the dark. You had to get back to the theater, before your wife came out of her movie, which ended five minutes before yours did."

"That's a remarkable hypothesis, Chief," said Sarah bravely. "Too bad it isn't true."

He looked at her. "We found the watch. EastSports was the only store that carried it, and it was the only green-strapped model they stocked last Christmas. Be sure to let me know, if you ever find your husband's."

Now he fixed Tomlinson with his gaze, but the latter appeared to be incapable of speech. The silence grew protracted.

At length, the Chief asked, "Well?"

When Tomlinson found his voice, it was barely audible. "I'm going to tell him," he said to his wife. "I can't bear this any longer." He turned to the Chief. "Everything happened pretty much the way you said. When Sarah told me what had gone on between them, and of his nickname and reputation, I figured that the bees had probably been arranged by him. Obviously he was capable of anything, and when he went into that knife routine at the reception, I really felt it was me he was carving up in his mind. I knew he wouldn't stop till he got what he wanted." His voice broke. "I couldn't bear to lose Sarah."

"Oh, darling!" exclaimed Sarah, kneeling next to his chair. She put her head on his knees and wept.

Now that he had started, Tomlinson was determined to finish. "As you know, I–"

The Chief held up his hand. "Before you go any further, I have to tell you that you have the right to remain silent. You have the right to an attorney. If you cannot afford one, an attorney will be provided for you. You–"

"Does this mean–he's under arrest?"

The Chief nodded. "That's exactly what it means."

"Then I don't think he should say any more," Sarah declared, "until we talk to a lawyer."

But her husband shook his head. "No, Sarah, now that I've started, I want to tell it *all*. It'll be a relief, after all the lies!"

"I think it's a mistake," she said through her tears.

Tomlinson got up out of the chair and went over to the window. Staring out at the rain, he said to her, "I trust the Chief. I want him to know what really happened."

That would be nice for a change, thought the Chief, but he said nothing.

"When I drove up here," Tomlinson resumed, his voice growing firmer, "the storm hadn't started. And I did just what you said: turned my lights off, so I wouldn't be seen. I was about to get out and walk up the driveway, when–I realized I couldn't go through with it."

He shook his head sadly. "I sat there in the dark, trying to will myself, force myself, to do what I'd imagined: kill the man who was trying to kill me. In fact, I'd run that loop in my mind so often, it played in my sleep. I'd go into the house and get the knife and–do it. He was bigger than me, but with a knife that sharp, plus the element of surprise. . . ."

He shrugged and laughed wryly. "I even had the glass cutter from Sarah's craft drawer with me."

"Glass cutter?"

"I'll show you." He went over and opened the bottom kitchen drawer at the end of the counter, fishing out a slender, long-handled metal tool with a tiny, sharp wheel at the end of it. "I was going to use this on a window to get in, and on the case to get the knife out, without making any noise."

The Chief whistled in appreciation. "You really thought of everything."

"Darling, don't say any more!" cried Sarah. "Can't you see? He's trying to establish premeditation."

"Well, it *was* premeditated," said Tomlinson. "I'm admitting that. Only, I couldn't make myself do it."

"You just sat there in your car?" said the Chief, incredulous. "For half an hour?"

Tomlinson nodded. "When the storm started, it snapped me out of it. I realized I'd better get back to the theater."

The Chief's eyes narrowed. "But if you didn't kill him, you wouldn't need an alibi."

"I didn't want Sarah to worry. She had no idea what I was planning, and I never would have told her. Except when we heard that someone else had done what I wanted to do, at about the same time, I realized I *was* going to need an alibi."

He looked over at his wife with great tenderness. "That's when I told her what I'd been contemplating."

"I didn't believe him at first," Sarah added. "But when I saw that he was telling me the truth, I told him that if the police came, we'd better agree that he had been with me in the Clint Eastwood movie."

"And the watch?" asked the Chief.

Tomlinson sighed. "I took it off, because—it reminded me of why I'd put it on."

"But you can't remember where you put it. And your wife can't find it, either."

"That's right."

"Well, it's all plausible," the Chief admitted. "And I might even believe you—if you hadn't lied to me so convincingly before. Twice before. I'm afraid that now you're going to have to be as convincing to twelve of your peers."

He switched off the tape recorder and stood up. "Time to go."

Leaving Sarah sobbing behind him, he went out the door ahead of the Chief into the gathering twilight.

47 | once more onto the beach

THERE WERE SEVERAL CARS in the East Bluffs parking lot when Brother Bartholomew got there, but none were at the lower end. As he got out of the old pick-up, he thought of locking it, then smiled; there wasn't anything in it that anyone would care about.

He checked his watch: one o'clock. For once, the Chief was not here ahead of him. Not too surprising, since this time the meeting had been his idea, not the Chief's. The beach was almost vacant. To his left about a quarter mile away, a father was teaching his ten- or eleven-year-old daughter how to fly a kite, showing her how to pay out line when the kite started to dive, and how to quickly reel in to get it to climb again.

As he watched, his mind went back to the previous afternoon. He had been sitting just about here, watching the surf as it came out of the fog, sounding like a hollow, booming echo. Then the impossible had happened—and he had wondered if he had imagined it into happening.

"You're not even pretending to fish!" scolded the Chief, startling him out of his reverie.

"Sorry," he said, smiling.

"Well, it's your nickel. What's on your mind, that we couldn't have handled over the phone?"

Bartholomew looked at the surf and slowly said, "I think you've got the wrong man, Dan."

The Chief glared at him, then closed his eyes and drew a deep breath. When he exhaled, he was smiling. "I just reminded myself that you were, as you put it the other day, one of the good guys." The deep breath started him coughing, a deep, rumbling cough which ended with him spitting out a mass of ugly, yellow-gray phlegm.

His friend, searching his red-rimmed eyes, said, "Man, you have got to get some sleep! Whatever you've got, it's getting worse fast, and there's only one place it can go—pneumonia."

"You sound like Peg," said the Chief with disgust. "I can't stop now. Not with the whole country watching."

"It's not worth your health, Dan. Nothing is."

The Chief changed the subject by relating the details of what went on the previous afternoon at the Tomlinsons'. "If it weren't for that missing watch from EastSports," he concluded, "I might—just might—have been willing to believe him. But he has no idea where it is. Neither of them do."

Eyeing the kite-flying father and daughter, he suggested they walk in the opposite direction. "So Maurice Tomlinson is now down in our guest quarters, until Judge Randall decides how much bail to set—which I doubt they'll be able make. I gather she has some money, but not a whole lot—certainly not as much as it's likely to be."

"They'll mortgage the house," mused his friend, half to himself. He turned to the Chief. "Everything in me, all my intuition, tells me he's innocent."

"And all the facts tell *me* he's guilty!" the Chief retorted. "Or I should say, *they're* guilty. She's in it as deeply as he is. She's already an accessory after the fact; it shouldn't be too hard to prove she had foreknowledge."

His friend just shook his head. "I think he was telling you the truth. And I don't think she had any idea what he was planning. She just loves him so much, she'd do anything to cover for him."

The Chief stopped walking. "Well that's it, then; we're at logger-heads."

"I can't help it, Dan," said his friend sadly. "Over the years I've come to trust my intuition." He paused. "Just like you trust yours."

But the Chief would not be placated. "Right now, I'm getting so many conflicting signals from my own gut instincts, I don't trust the lot of them! And I trust yours even less!"

He turned back towards the parking lot. "So we're going by the book. And the book says we've got a good case. So does the DA down in Barnstable, incidentally, and we're going ahead with it."

"All right," Bartholomew sighed, "but you won't be going ahead with *anything*, if you don't start taking care of that cold."

Neither of them spoke, until they were back at their vehicles. Then Bartholomew said, "If he had the glass-cutter with him, why didn't he use it?"

"I told you," the Chief replied, "Curtis was home, so the house wasn't locked."

"But the display case was. Why would he smash it and risk alerting Curtis, if he had the glass-cutter in his pocket?"

"You know," said the Chief with consummate irony, "I don't know. And frankly, I don't care!" With that, he got in the Bravada and drove away.

Watching him leave, Bartholomew told himself that his friend was under a lot of stress, about as much as a human could handle without exploding. And obviously he had not slept in several days. And his cold or flu or whatever it was, probably had a fever with it by now. But the words still hurt.

He turned to the old pick-up and opened its door. On the passenger seat was a cassette tape that had not been there before. It was an old one, of Judy Collins singing "Both Sides Now" and some other songs. He looked around, but the parking lot was empty.

He got in, but instead of driving away, he inserted the tape in the truck's player and played it—just the title song, over and over, as he stared out at the Atlantic.

On a distant dune far above and behind him, a figure shrouded in wool stood watching him.

48 | hard choices

IT WASN'T WORKING, thought Brother Bartholomew, as he turned the page of the old leather-bound book. A long time ago, some kind minister's widow had made the friary a gift of her husband's nineteenth-century Bible commentaries. Whenever Bartholomew knew that his mind was far from ready for sleep, he would read one of the bound volumes in a corner of their library during Grand Silence. Invariably, he would soon be nodding off and more than ready for bed. Until tonight. This evening, it was not the rising and falling cadence of Compline's chant that lingered in his mind. It was the lyrics of that song—their song. "Moons and Junes and Ferris wheels, the dizzy-dancing way you feel. . . ."

He forced the haunting melody out of his mind and focused on the page before him: "And Gideon, fully aware that he had been called by Yahweh to this singular task, looked up to—ice-cream castles in the air, and feather canyons everywhere. . . ."

He shook his head and marshaled the full power of his will to the task before him: "But Gideon contended with Yahweh through the night, until—tears and fears and feeling proud to say 'I love you' right out loud. . . ."

Slamming the book shut, he went to find Brother Anselm. In the kitchen he came upon his old friend stirring a mug of tea. Keeping his voice low out of deference to the Grand Silence, Bartholomew said, "I've got to talk to you. And it can't wait until morning."

Anselm looked at him and nodded, leading him to two chairs at the end of a long table in the empty refectory. Bartholomew told him what had happened the afternoon before, when Laurel had appeared to him out of the fog, and then that afternoon, when she had left the tape—which he had listened to. For more than an hour. And now he was hearing their song in his mind, no matter what he did—and he feared he would go on hearing it all night long.

"It would seem," said Anselm when he'd finished, "that the time has come to make the hard choice I told you about."

"But why?" said the younger monk angrily. "I mean, I *did* choose! I went through all this years ago!"

"But it has not been sealed—or you would not be so tormented now."

Bartholomew did not answer. There was nothing to say. Then, by way of confession, he added, "I've been imagining what life would have been like with her, had I—gone the other way. In my mind I've seen our children growing up, seen myself teaching my son how to fish, my daughter how to drive. And I've seen my wife and me sharing middle age—and old age—together. And I'm remembering all the times we shared silence, never needing to say anything."

Anselm nodded. "You're seeing a romantic illusion of what might have been. It is powerful. And compelling. And so *real*. But it's an *illusion*, a fabrication of your imagination. And I have no doubt where the inspiration for it is coming from."

He looked at his younger friend. "Nor do you. You know the nature of fantasy—and who its author is—as well as I do."

Bartholomew said nothing. He did not care for what Anselm was saying, not one iota. But neither could he argue the truth of it. Besides, he told himself, wasn't this why he'd sought him out?

Anselm seemed to know what he was feeling. With gentle compassion he said, "Since you've been dealing in alternate realities, let me suggest another." He took a sip of tea. "Suppose you *had* turned your back on God's call, and responded to the desire of your heart. Suppose you had married and started a family."

He spoke slowly now, letting each phrase register. "Every time you looked at the ocean, or a sunset, or a still lake, or a field of wildflowers, you would wonder: What would it have been like, had you yielded to His call?"

Anselm's eyes fell to the mug, and without taking them from it he said, "There *would* come times of stress. They come to everyone. They even come to us," he smiled, gesturing to the refectory. "And yet the world, with its unreal, romantic notion of our life, envies the tranquility it senses here. The peace *is* real. But we know at what price it's earned."

Bartholomew smiled as his old friend continued. "I have never known a relationship in real life, in which both parties 'lived happily ever after.' Man is an imperfect creature; there won't be perfect harmony until we get to heaven."

The younger monk nodded. There was no arguing with—any of it.

"Suppose," Anselm went on, "in your alternate reality, you grew frustrated as fulfillment eluded you? Suppose you and your wife—though neither of you ever dreamed it could happen—grew apart. Suppose, for any number of reasons, you separated—"

Bartholomew recoiled, his face revealing the extent of his unbelief.

"Is it really so unthinkable? In a marriage that God may not have joined together?"

Bartholomew remained silent.

"What would happen to the children then? Your desire for the world's romantic ideal of happiness might ultimately do incalculable harm, not just to one life, but four."

Anselm was unperturbed by his younger friend's sullen stare. "Bartholomew, you are ruined for the world. You know too much of the ways of God to ever deny their reality. If you choose to leave your call now, you will never find real peace, the kind that surpasses human understanding. And you will spend the rest of your life trying to convince yourself that you have." He looked the younger Brother in the eye. "You *know* that."

Bartholomew shook his head. "No, I do *not* know that. If I did, I wouldn't be sitting here. All I know is, I don't have peace now, and it doesn't feel like I'll ever have it again. If I stay. If I go, I may not have it, either. But at least I'll have tried!"

"Well, then," Anselm concluded, standing up, "you'd better find out if you're going or staying. Because right now, you're in hell." He put his hand on Bartholomew's shoulder. "I can't help you any more, my brother. It is now between you and God."

ॐ

The chapel was dark when Brother Bartholomew entered it. The only source of light came from a votive candle beneath the small icon of Jesus in the front right-hand corner. He went there and knelt before it. He had come here at other critical times, yet none so critical as the present moment.

I am not going to play games here, he prayed, looking into the eyes of Jesus, illuminated by the steady candle flame. I know You called me. Once before, I asked You to rescind my call. I am asking that again now.

At other times when he had knelt here alone in the darkness, deep within he had been able to hear the still, small voice of God's Spirit. But not tonight.

Father, the desire of my heart is overpowering. I love her. I want to be with her. I know she wants to be with me.

The candle flame flickered. Through the eyes of the icon, he could feel God looking into his eyes, into the depths of his heart. And still he heard nothing.

You may not have put this desire in my heart, he prayed, but You allowed it to be there. And You know how strong it is. I cannot remember ever wanting anything so much. What is it that I want? The love of one person—is that so bad? Are You jealous that Your love is not enough for me?

Silence.

Forgive me for that. I have known Your love in the past. I have not forgotten the times, the many times, I have been dazzled by Your love, sun-struck by it, with all my circuits blown out. And I can remember the times, the many times, when You were so close that I would gladly have spent eternity there—not moving, not thinking, just being there with You.

Silence.

But—it has been a long time since I felt that close to You. And now, someone who was once close to me, wants to be close to me again. Is that so bad?

He groaned aloud. I am twisting on these horns. And You know it. And You won't speak to me.

Silence.

I know why. It's because this choice must be made by faith alone. If You were to speak to me now, then one day I might blame You for influencing the choice I must make entirely by my own free will. But has anyone ever told You that it's like expecting someone to walk backwards to the end of a high diving board, without looking down or even knowing if there's water in the pool, or if You're there. And then, stepping backwards into Your arms?

Silence.

I thought You were supposed to be love! This isn't love! This is hell! Saint Teresa was right: If this is how You treat Your friends, it's no wonder You have so few of them!

Silence.

He fell silent himself and stayed that way for a long time. Then, without taking his eyes from the gaze of the icon, he prayed, I—surrender. Absolutely. Unconditionally. By faith alone. You *are* love. You love me beyond all comprehension. And You have called me to be Your servant. In this place. In this way.

Silence.

I accept my call. Again. It is the hardest choice I have ever made. Even harder than the first time I chose You. And You chose me. But I have made it.

Silence.

But as Brother Bartholomew arose, he smiled. He would sleep tonight.

49 | a private conversation

IN THE MORNING, everything seemed to sparkle. Brother Bartholomew felt as Dorothy must have, when she opened the door and found the world was Technicolor. Outside the window of the friary's library, the dew glistened in the first rays of sun. Shafts of light came down through the locust trees like fingers pointing— to a gathering of daffodils, an arrangement of rocks, a green hedge.

Bartholomew settled into an easy chair by the window, to enjoy the quiet of the early morning. He put his hand out into the stream of sunlight and felt its warmth. He watched a mote of dust suspended in the light. He listened to the silence. He smiled at the inexpressible peace he felt.

He would have been content to just remain there—

Ambrose came up behind him. "There's a phone call for you; it's your mother."

Bartholomew got up and took the call in the front hall. "Mother?"

"I wouldn't have called," said Isabel defensively, "if it wasn't so important."

"That's all right," he said cheerfully, "What's the matter?"

"I can't talk about it on the phone. You're going to have to come over here."

"I'll come over right after Lauds and Mass."

"Can't you come now? It's really important!"

"So are Lauds and Mass." He refrained from adding that they were the most important Lauds and Mass he'd been to in a long time.

"Well—all right. But hurry."

The sun was streaming in through the tall south windows, as the community processed in, two by two, passing through one slanting beam after another and another. . . .

The offices were exactly the same as they had been the day before, the week before, the month before. The year before. And yet, to Bartholomew there was freshness to every aspect of this morning, as if each had been burnished for his appreciation. In the ceiling above the altar, the backlit, stained-glass dove seemed alive, and the candle flames on either side of the altar cross seemed to dance. . . . He was grinning now, a lopsided, foolish grin. And couldn't stop. And didn't want to.

And the chant! He rode its swells, as if he were a small boat on a vast ocean. He delighted in blending his voice with the voice of his Brother on his left and his Brother on his right—matching his voice to theirs, fitting it in, tucking it under. Till they were one voice, like a line of geese over the bay, heading north in perfect formation. Their sound was the sound of a single heart, seeking the heart of God.

He felt tears on his cheeks. And he felt the closeness of God. Again. The tears came faster. He was home. And, O God, he had been away too long.

❧

"Bartholomew," Ambrose called from the phone, as the older monk entered the friary. "it's your mother again."

He took the phone. "Mother, I said I'd be there as soon as—"

"You've got to know how important this is!"

"Look, Mother," he said, keeping a firm grip on his temper, not wanting anything to disturb the radiance he felt within. "I will be there. In ten minutes." Gently he replaced the receiver on its cradle.

"Ambrose?" he called to his young charge, "Get a move on! We've got business to do!"

"Police business?" the latter replied, suddenly excited, then chagrined at what he had just announced to the friary.

"Just be in the truck in two minutes."

As Bartholomew drove out, slowly, sedately, he realized that the joy he had known a few moments before was dissipating. But it was all right; he knew where he could find it again.

In seven minutes they were walking through the door of Norma's. The place was packed, but Isabel had saved them a table, and now she brought them two mugs of black coffee.

"Did you know the Chief's got Manchurian flu?" his mother exclaimed in whisper mode, as soon as they had tasted—and expressed their appreciation of—her coffee.

"No, I didn't," her son replied, "but I'm not surprised. I've been begging him to get some rest."

"Doc Finlay has confined him to bed. He says it's serious. He's got him on antibiotics now, but unless the Chief gets complete rest, it could get really dangerous."

Bartholomew looked up at her. "Well, that's important, but that can't be—"

"Of course not!" his mother snapped. "I wouldn't have bothered you with that." She lowered her voice. "Apparently Emmet Adams sees this as his golden opportunity. With the Chief off the bridge and confined to quarters, as it were, he's taken command of the ship. It's not exactly a Caine Mutiny, but it's pretty close."

"Okay, that *is* serious," agreed Bartholomew. "But how do you know all this?"

"That's why I called," his mother retorted. "Emmet and Vic Malcolm were in here early this morning, having another 'private conversation' over at number four in the corner. From what I could gather, Emmet is getting less than full cooperation from the officers assigned to the case—and he's furious. Before the Chief arrested Maurice Tomlinson, Emmet had wanted to bring in the

State Police to help. Now he's determined to do that, as soon as he has a pretext. And maybe even the FBI."

"Why?"

"I think our boy has set his sights higher than just taking over Dan's job. I think he wants to run for the State Senate." She glanced around to make sure no one was eavesdropping, then continued. "Anyway, he's getting ready to take over the case. And now that he's the man in charge, he's already giving interviews."

"Poor Dan," murmured Bartholomew, shaking his head. "As sick as he is, I'm going to have to tell him what's going on."

Isabel frowned. "Are you sure you should?"

"If I were in his place, I'd want someone to tell me. And if he were in my place, I think he would."

Bartholomew started to get up, but Isabel put a hand on his shoulder and gently, but firmly, pushed him back down. "I'm not finished," she said quietly. "There's one more thing you need to know: Vic left, but Emmet didn't. I thought that was strange, but I soon saw why. Barry Jones came in and went over to his table. It must have been prearranged."

She paused to signal Suzie that table number seven needed their check. "Emmet told Barry that he wanted to regard the *Revelator* as his main support base in the media. He said he would tip Barry off to breaking developments and make sure he scooped the other papers. In exchange, he would appreciate favorable coverage—and a strong endorsement, when the time came for him to widen his horizons."

As Bartholomew listened, he grew increasingly uncomfortable at absorbing all this overheard conversation—and guilty at having put his mother up to it. Was the end suddenly justifying the means? It depended how the information was used, he decided. We are called to be wise as serpents, but harmless as doves. Nowhere does it say we were to be dumb as doves.

"But Barry surprised him."

"What did he do?" asked Ambrose. The other two were startled; it was the first time he had spoken. Isabel looked at her son, who nodded, and she went on.

"He told Emmet that he would be grateful for the exclusives, and if they led to a favorable report on Emmet, he would certainly write one. But he was going to continue calling things the way he saw them. If Emmet did a good job, he would say so; if he messed up, he would also say so."

"Good," said Bartholomew, again starting to get up.

"I'm still not finished," Isabel warned him, and he sat back down. "Then Barry told Emmet there was one thing he would not do: run down the Chief. He had too much respect for him, even if he had arrested the wrong suspect. In fact, the last thing he told Emmet was that if he ever saw him sabotaging his boss, that would most definitely color his approach." She smiled. "I don't think Emmet was expecting that."

Bartholomew looked up at her, and she smiled. "Now I'm finished."

He got up. "Mother, you've outdone yourself! Now I've got to go visit a sick friend."

BARTHOLOMEW PULLED INTO THE FRIARY'S GRAVEL DRIVEWAY and turned to Ambrose. "You know the only reason I'm not taking you with me, is that the Chief is used to talking to me alone. So don't go getting your feelings hurt. I'll be back as soon as I can."

"You don't have to tell me that! I understand!"

"Then why are you angry?"

"I just wish you'd stop treating me like a kid!"

Bartholomew was surprised. "I'm sorry, Ambrose," he said, and realized it was the first time he'd ever said that to his young charge.

The latter was instantly mollified. "It's okay," he smiled. "You'd better get going."

As Bartholomew turned the truck around, he caught a glimpse of Ambrose in the rear-view mirror—and smiled. To his surprise, he was actually beginning to like the kid—er, the young Brother.

At the Burkes' home, Peg answered the door. "Andrew? Come in—what brings you here?"

"It's Brother Bartholomew," he smiled.

"Sorry," she said, "I should have remembered."

"Is Dan up?"

"No, he's sleeping—finally. Really sleeping, for the first time since this whole mess began. He was wiped out. Totally. I'd never seen him in such a state." She squinted at her old friend in the morning sun. "In fact, I'm actually glad this flu thing hit him. Because if it hadn't, I don't know what it would have taken; I've never seen him so run down."

"Well, when he's up, would you call the friary and leave that message for me? It's important I see him."

"Can't it wait a few days? I really want him to get some rest."

"I wish it could, Peg. But it can't."

Back in the truck, he was about to turn the ignition key, when he hesitated: Where to? There was plenty of yard work waiting for him back at the abbey, but. . . . The thought came to him of the reflection he'd seen from the direction of the Royce cottage. With a bemused smile, he put the truck in gear and wondered what his excuse would be when he got there.

With difficulty he found the two-wheeled track to the cottage, and cutting the engine just before he arrived, he coasted silently into the clearing. There was Royce's black VW; he was home. Getting out, he closed the door of the truck soundlessly and walked up to the front door. He knocked softly. When he heard no one inside, he went around the side of the cottage, past the herb garden, till he could see the pond—and the cottage's deck. As he had anticipated, Royce was up there, sitting on a stool, peering across the pond through an antique brass telescope.

"Hello, up there!" Brother Bartholomew called cheerily. "I knocked, but there was no answer, so I came around to see if anybody was home."

Royce, obviously consternated at having been caught at the telescope, was less than hospitable. "Well, I'm home. What is it?"

"Chief Burke told me about the article you were planning for the *Revelator*. He said it was going to call for a complete ban on clamming in the bay, and I came out to appeal to you not to do that. I would have called, but you don't seem to have a phone."

Royce's attitude changed. He seemed pleased that someone would take his article so seriously that they would drive all the way out here to appeal to him. He smiled down on Brother Bartholomew and invited him to come up higher and enter his abode.

When Bartholomew was standing in his living/dining/bed-room, its owner asked, "Now, why do you want me to change it?"

"At the friary we enjoy making clam chowder. In fact, it's kind of our specialty. *In fact,* people have said that ours is as good as Gordie's, or the Land Ho's, or even Captain Linnell's. And we think that one of the reasons is that our clams are only a couple of hours old when they go into the pot." He snapped his fingers. "We have some in the fridge; I should have brought you some."

"No thanks," Royce replied hastily, "I don't eat animals. In fact, I think of them as friends—even clams."

"But you don't object to others eating them, do you?"

"I guess not. But I hope they'll become enlightened enough to stop. My article should help them."

"Is it finished?"

"The working draft is. I'm in the process of condensing it." He nodded in the direction of the computer.

Bartholomew took a closer look at it. But instead of para-graphs, there was a chessboard. And a chat room window. "Do you play e-mail chess?"

"I do," replied Royce, surprised that this monk would even know of such a thing.

Bartholomew noted the name of Royce's club—Chess Unlimited, and that one had to become a member of bpm.com. He also noted Royce's user name: FalconerRR. "How do you find out if anyone wants a game?"

"Since I'm a member of the club, I just ask. Here, let me show you." Royce sat down at the keyboard with his left hand on the mouse, moved the cursor to the icon for the game room. Though the mouse was ergonomically designed to be used with the right hand, Royce was using it with his left and had reconfigured it so that the right button was the primary one, for his index finger.

"What's your rating?" asked his visitor.

"I never bothered to find out," said Royce, even more impressed. "So you're a player, too."

"Not for twenty years."

"But you were, once," Royce persisted.

"In Nam. I used to play with the chaplain while my buddies were in the bars."

"We must have a game sometime."

Bartholomew shook his head. "I'm too rusty. But tell me, will you consider modifying your article?"

"I'll certainly think about it."

"Good! I'll tell the Brothers; they'll be relieved. Thanks for your time."

Royce started for the front door to show him out, but Bartholomew headed for the door to the deck, as if simply departing the way he had arrived. "Say!" he said, admiring the telescope, "is that a Stanley London? She's a beauty!"

"Yes," said Royce, astonished. "How do you know about—"

"Mind if I try her?" Royce frowned, but before he could object Bartholomew sat down on the stool and squinted through the eyepiece. It was trained on the Curtis living room, and the detail was breathtaking: He could see Mrs. Curtis clearly. She was on the phone—was this what he had been watching?

"Wow!" he exclaimed. "The definition is amazing!" He looked up. "Did you see us the other day when we were investigating the murder site?"

Startled, Royce for an instant considered lying, then said, "Uh, yes. Was that what you and the other Brother were doing?" His visitor nodded. "You're involved with the investigation then?"

"Not officially. Just amateurs—but you know, even amateurs can get lucky."

"How do you mean?"

"Well," he shrugged, "we found something."

"Really?"

Again his visitor nodded. "Yup, we were surprised, too. Did you, ah, happen to see us find it?"

"No, what was it?"

"A watch."

"Oh," Royce smiled condescendingly. "I don't use a watch. I refuse to bow my neck to that tyrannical yoke."

"Well said!" chuckled Bartholomew, as he stood up to leave. "I envy you!" He glanced at his own watch. "My taskmaster tells me I've got about fifteen minutes to get back in time for Vespers. Thanks very much," he said, extending his hand to say good-bye.

"My pleasure," said Royce, shaking the hand. "And I must persuade you to join me on the jousting field sometime." He nodded toward the chessboard on the monitor.

At that instant, still holding Royce's hand, Bartholomew appeared to catch his foot on one of the legs of the telescope's tripod. In an effort to regain his balance, he pulled Royce's hand towards him. The latter's arm extended from the cuff of his long-sleeved shirt, momentarily revealing a tanned forearm—with a slightly less tanned, half-inch wide band just above the wrist. Bartholomew appeared not to notice it as he profusely apologized—and Royce appeared not to notice that Bartholomew had noticed it.

51 | a call for help

By chance, Trish Allen had pulled switchboard duty when the call came in. "Please," said the caller, her voice taut, "I need to speak to the Chief. Right away!"

"Who's calling, please?"

"Allison Curtis. It's urgent that I—"

"May I have your address, please?"

"We—I live on Teal Pond. Look, this is an emergency! I've got to—"

"Mrs. Curtis, this is Officer Allen. The Chief's out sick. But I've been assisting him on the case. Can you tell me—"

"No!" she shouted, almost hysterical. "I can't tell anyone but the Chief!"

Trish tried for the most soothing, understanding tone she could muster. "The Chief's got the flu, ma'am. I'm afraid he's going to be out of action for a few days—and believe me, I want him back as badly as you do!"

By chance, just then Lieutenant Adams walked by the switchboard and stopped. "Who are you talking to?" he asked.

Trish pretended not to have heard him.

"Officer Allen, I said: Who are you talking to?"

"One moment, ma'am," Trish said, putting Allison on hold. "It's Mrs. Curtis, sir, calling for the Chief."

"Does she have a problem?"

"She won't talk to anyone but the Chief."

"We'll see," he said, picking up the switchboard's extra receiver. "Mrs. Curtis, this is Lieutenant Adams speaking. While the Chief is sick, I'm in charge here. Is there anything I can do to help you?"

Allison hesitated, then blurted out, "I do need help! Right now! As fast as you can send it!"

"Can you tell me what's the matter?" Adams responded with calm, professional concern.

"Someone broke in last night and left a note. I was up in Maine and just got home and found it."

"I'll be right there," Adams assured her, hanging up. To Trish he said, "You are not to tell anyone in the EPD about this, do you understand? No one."

Trish nodded and watched him hurry out to his patrol car. There wasn't anyone to tell, anyway, she thought. Otis was off-Cape on a department errand, and Leo was escorting the prisoner Tomlinson down to the Barnstable jail. Then she thought of Brother Bartholomew.

She reached him just as he was robing for Vespers. She told him what had just happened. "I know from the beach that the Chief trusts you. I wish you'd go out there. I think he'd be grateful if you did. And from the sound of it, so would Mrs. Curtis. Only be careful what you say: I could get in a heap of trouble!"

Hanging up the phone, Bartholomew was in a quandary. It would mean missing the noon service, and he would not have time to round up Ambrose. But it *was* an emergency. And Dan, if he knew, would want him to go. That settled it. He returned his robe to its peg and ran for the truck. He did not do well at keeping his speed sedate as he exited the friary drive.

There was one stretch of the road into Teal Pond that he particularly enjoyed. A construction crew was still doing some heavy landscaping on the way in, and the winding road was not yet paved. When he was a boy, his father had taught him how to hang out the rear end as he rounded a dirt corner, just like the Saturday night stock car racers up in New Hampshire. There were three such corners on this road, and his pick-up was old enough to have rear-wheel drive. He drifted through every one.

Nine minutes after he left the friary, he parked behind the patrol car and walked up to the door, still wondering what he would say. When Allie answered the bell, he said, "Mrs. Curtis? I'm Brother Bartholomew. I was sorry to hear of your loss, and if this is not a good time—"

"You don't have to introduce yourself," she smiled. "You were my guest, remember?" She took his arm. "Come in. Lieutenant Adams from the police department just got here, and frankly," she whispered to him, "I'm glad to have a friend here. He's the most self-important—" She left the remainder unsaid and gave his arm a squeeze, as she led him into the living room. Adams stood in front of the broken display case on the mantel, looking extremely displeased at the intrusion of a stranger.

"I'm afraid I'll have to ask you to leave," he announced to Bartholomew. "We're conducting police business here, and—"

"Wait a minute," Allie interrupted. "This is *my* house, lieutenant. And this is *my* friend. Brother Bartholomew," she turned to him, "you're welcome here. And after the lieutenant leaves, we'll have a cup of coffee."

"Whatever you say," said Bartholomew with a shrug, relieved that he would not have to trot out some improvised pretext in front of Lieutenant Adams.

"Mrs. Curtis," said Adams in his most authoritative tone, "this is a criminal investigation and—"

"Do you want to see the note or not?"

Barely able to contain his anger, Adams said, "May I remind you that you called requesting assistance?"

"And I'm grateful for your rapid response, lieutenant. But that does not give you the right to be rude to anyone in my house, especially a friend. Now wait here," she said, disappearing into the study. In a moment she reappeared, holding a sheet of white paper, which she handed to Adams. "I found it taped to the bottom of the display case, when I came in."

Six lines of copy were printed on the paper, which Adams turned so that Bartholomew could not see them.

Which further annoyed Allison. "What it says," she said to Bartholomew, "is essentially this: 'He who lived by the sword has died by the sword. He has died, just as he killed: with a single disemboweling thrust, from lower left to upper right. And by the very sword with which he took eight other lives.'"

She hesitated, then recalled the rest: "That sword, specifically designed for ripping its victim open, now has a ninth notch on its handle. When it has received its tenth, it will be returned to its resting place."

Adams glared at her, then said, "On the phone, you said that whoever left this had broken in. Where?"

"Through the laundry room door, off the kitchen. It looked like he used a crow bar or something."

Without waiting for her to show him the way, Adams went to investigate. When he was gone, Allie looked at Bartholomew and just shook her head. Then she frowned. "There's something in that note that I—"

The phone rang, and she answered it. "Yes? He's here. I'll put him on."

Adams called, "Is that for me?"

"No," replied Allie, "actually it's for Brother Bartholomew," and she handed him the receiver.

It was Trish Allen. "Brother Bart, don't say anything; just listen. Peg Burke just called. The Chief is awake, and he wants to see you right away. But don't let on where you're going, or why."

"Okay, Sister Elizabeth," he said loud enough for Adams to hear him. "I'm on my way. Yes, I'll stop at the vet's and pick up what we need. But call him first, will you? It'll save time."

He hung up the phone and explained to Allie, "Barnyard emergency. One of our goats is about to deliver. I seem to have inherited the job of being the abbey's midwife." And with that he departed.

As he drove out the long drive, Bartholomew frowned. The lie had come so easily to his lips and had sounded so convincing. Not having lied in years, he would have thought it would have been harder, more awkward. It was for a good cause, he told himself. But he wondered if the stricture against the end ever justifying the means was beginning to get a bit frayed at the edges.

52 | bed of pain

BROTHER BARTHOLOMEW STARED DOWN at the bedridden form of his friend. "You look terrible!" he exclaimed with a grin.

"Thanks," said the Chief dourly.

"Hey, what are friends for?"

"Your bedside manner is beyond belief!"

"All my friends tell me that."

"Try again," said the Chief with mounting disgust.

"Okay—do you feel as bad as you look?"

"That's an improvement?"

"Well, I'm afraid you're going to feel even worse when you hear what I have to tell you."

"Impossible—but go ahead."

Bartholomew proceeded to outline all that had transpired since they'd been on the beach—"Good grief, could that have been only yesterday? It seems like a week ago!" He then related what happened that morning, first at the Royce cottage, then with Mrs. Curtis and Lieutenant Adams, finishing with the note, as best he could remember it.

"You were right," the Chief said, when he'd finished. "I do feel worse. Before, I just wanted to die. Now, I'm afraid I won't."

"Well," said his friend, determinedly upbeat, "let's start with the note."

"Oh, God," the Chief moaned, "I picked the wrong day to get Manchurian flu."

"You want me to come back later?"

"No, no, go ahead," the Chief waved him on impatiently. "But I can barely follow you. You're going to have to do the thinking for both of us."

Bartholomew nodded. "Okay. We know one thing: Tomlinson couldn't very well have written the note and planted it out there, while he was a guest in your facilities. Which means—"

"That your intuition was right, all along."

"The way I see it," Bartholomew went on, "we're dealing with one sick cookie—somebody who's treating the whole thing as if it's some kind of game. He's taunting us—telling us that he's going to use the knife again, and there's nothing we can do to stop him."

"Or her," the Chief murmured.

"What?"

"You're assuming it's a man."

"At this point, I think that's a safe assumption."

The Chief hoisted himself up on his pillows. "Unless it's someone who wants us to think there's a psycho out there."

"Like—who?"

"Like Sarah Tomlinson." He reached for the glass of ginger ale and took a painful swallow. "I'm convinced she'd do anything to get her husband off."

"Well, supposing it isn't Sarah." The Chief groaned. "I mean, just supposing. Does that leave us—"

"The other woman," murmured the Chief, collapsing back on his pillows.

"What?"

"You forgot the other woman."

"You don't mean Laurel."

The Chief shook his head, exasperated that Bartholomew wasn't getting it.

"Mrs. Curtis?"

The Chief nodded.

"How do you figure?"

The Chief rolled over on his side and closed his eyes. But he kept speaking, though barely above a whisper. "If she did it, then she knows Tomlinson didn't, and that pretty soon we'd figure that out. She could have planted that note herself."

Bartholomew chuckled appreciatively. "You know, for a sick man, lying there on your bed of pain, the old engine is still ticking over."

"Did you all handle the document?"

"Oh. Yeah," Bartholomew said with regret. "Lieutenant Adams's prints will be all over it. Also Mrs. Curtis's."

Peg came in. "Trish is on the phone, Dan. She's really sorry, but she thinks you'd better take it."

"Okay." He fumbled around on the floor for the phone.

"Hello, Trish," he managed and then listened. His face grew progressively redder. "I can't believe it! That—" He listened some more. "All right, I'm coming down there!"

"Dan!" cried Peg, "You can't! You really will get pneumonia!" She turned to Bartholomew. "Can't you do something?"

The Chief hung up. "Emmet's called another press conference. For three o'clock. When Leo objected, he pulled rank on him. He said that without me there, he's in charge!" He turned to his wife. "Don't you see, I've got to go down there and put a stop to this. If he announces what I think he's going to, he'll blow our case out of the water!"

Peg didn't answer; she was crying. The Chief swung his legs out of bed and tried to stand up—and had to reach out to Bartholomew to steady himself. Then he pulled himself together. "You're going to have to help me," he said to his wife and his friend. "I've got to get dressed in that blasted uniform and go down there."

"Can't you just call him?" pleaded Bartholomew.

The Chief shook his head, as he groped his way to the closet. "No, he's out of control. I've got to go and suspend his ass!"

Slowly, with great difficulty, Peg and Bartholomew managed to dress him and help him down the stairs. "Whoa," he exclaimed, gripping the railing with both hands. "I'm woozy!"

Finally, they had him in his coat and bundled into the Bravada, which Bartholomew would drive for him. "Peg, call Trish and tell her to tell Leo and Otis I'm coming. But to keep it to themselves."

When they got to the station, there were three mobile units parked outside, including two down from Boston, with cables running everywhere. It was ten minutes to 3:00.

Otis Whipple came out. "When I saw your vehicle, I couldn't believe it! Here, Chief, let me help you." He put an arm around the Chief, and then Trish came out and took his other side, while Brother Bartholomew waited in the car. The two officers had to half-carry him up the steps.

Inside, in the conference room, Emmet Adams stood behind a battery of microphones. He was beaming at the sea of expectant faces, awaiting his fifteen minutes of fame. Then his face fell. At the entrance to the room, behind the lights and the television cameras, he spotted a familiar silhouette.

The Chief, accompanied by Otis, who tried his best not to look like he was supporting him, made his way to the lectern. "Wait in my office, please, Lieutenant," he said courteously to Adams. "I'll be with you in a moment."

He took a deep breath and turned to the waiting journalists. "I'm afraid this was not authorized, and you've been brought here under false pretenses. Whatever you may have been told"—he ran out of breath and had to pause a moment until it returned—"there are no new developments in the Curtis case to announce at this time. We have a suspect in custody, but you already know that." He turned to leave, when an attractive blonde in a Chanel suit called out, "Chief? Jill Easton, *Bayview* magazine."

"I know who you are, Ms. Easton," the Chief acknowledged, forcing himself to smile. "It's only been a week since your story on us."

"Is it true that you have another suspect? That you're about to release Maurice Tomlinson?"

"No, that is not true." He suddenly had to grip the lectern, to keep from falling. "Now that's it."

The red lights on the cameras winked out, the halogen spotlights went down, the reporters started to leave. The Chief waved to Leo to meet him in his office. Even with Otis helping him, he had to stop twice to let his head clear.

When they were in, and the door was shut, he glowered at Adams. The latter was trying to keep up a good front, but his whole body was trembling. The Chief pulled out his little recorder, turned it on, and rested it on his desk. "Lieutenant Adams, you have disobeyed a direct order and acted in full opposition to my express wishes and commands. I am therefore relieving you of all duties as of this moment. You are hereby suspended, until such time as a review board can consider your case. You are to turn in your badge and weapon to Sergeant Bascomb before you leave, which you will do immediately. Is that understood?"

Adams nodded sullenly.

"I'm sorry, lieutenant," said the Chief, "but you'll have to speak up. The tape recorder doesn't pick up nods."

"It's understood," growled Adams. "But you haven't heard the last of me!" And with that, he turned and left.

As soon as the door closed behind him, the Chief collapsed into his chair. "Sergeant Bascomb, as of this moment you are acting lieutenant. That means you're in charge here. And Otis, you just made sergeant. Now get me out of here, because I'm about to pass out."

Otis and Trish helped him out to the Bravada, where Brother Bartholomew was waiting to take him home.

As they pulled into his driveway the Chief chuckled.

"What is it, Dan?" asked his friend, surprised.

"I may die tonight," he smiled weakly, "but for the first time since this whole thing started, I feel pretty good."

53 | the tenth notch

SATURDAY MORNING DAWNED cold, wet, and forbidding. The long
Memorial Day weekend was beginning—with just the sort of weather
that the Chamber of Commerce would like vacationers to believe
never came to the Cape. But the rain streaking the windshields of
the steady stream of cars arriving at the Sagamore Bridge rotary
from Connecticut and points west, and Boston and points north,
did not dishearten them. Some were even grateful; without the rain,
they might be stuck in a two- or even three-mile back-up, waiting to
get over the bridge. Besides, it would probably clear and be nice
by this afternoon. That was how it was on the Cape: If you didn't
like the weather, just wait a while.

Brother Bartholomew was finishing his French toast when he
was called to the phone. It was Allison Curtis, and she was not
merely verging on hysteria; she was hip deep in it. "I know the
Chief is sick," she cried, the words rushing in a torrent, "but I
called him at home anyway. Only his wife wouldn't wake him up,
so I called you, because I know you're his friend, and you know
about the note, and I can't stand Lieutenant Adams, and—"

"Mrs. Curtis," Bartholomew cut in, as gently as he could, "what's the matter?"

"I've seen the knife! Mac's knife! I saw it this morning! And that's what's been bothering me for the past three days: 'Lower left to upper right'—but Mac never said that! And—*oh, no!*"

She must have dropped the receiver, because what he heard next sounded farther away. He heard her screaming and pleading, and then a shriek—and silence. Then the phone was hung up.

He called the EPD, got Trish on the phone, told her what had just happened, and that he was going out there. He ran for the truck, jumped in, and did not bother departing sedately.

❧

When he came to the unpaved portion of the road that led to the pond, it being Saturday, the bulldozers and front-end loaders, the scrapers and dump trucks, were standing idle. They looked like giant yellow Tonka Toys, abandoned by a boy whose mother had called him in out of the rain.

One bulldozer, however, was moving, ascending one of the two huge piles of earth that flanked the road. It reached the top and teetered there, just as the old red pick-up came drifting around the third corner. The diesel roared, black smoke belched from its stack, the Caterpillar tracks ground, and the bulldozer plunged downward, its heavy blade catching the little truck full amidships and crushing it against the hill of earth opposite.

When Bartholomew came to, the first thing he was aware of was that it had stopped raining. The next thing was that there was blood coming down his forehead, and he couldn't move his arm to wipe it from his eyes. Either arm. Or his legs. And then he smelled the gas.

He must have passed out again, because the next thing he was aware of was a sound—distant at first, but growing louder—*wheep, wheep, wheep.* It was a police alarm, he realized, and he smiled. Years ago they'd phased out the wail of the old sirens, in favor of modern, attention-getting sounds. He was just glad they hadn't gone to the two-tone European *ooh-aah, ooh-aah* that sounded so eerie and desolate in foreign movies. He still could not move. And the smell of gasoline was pungent.

When he came to again, Trish was looking in the shattered windshield at him. "Are you all right?" she said, immensely relieved to see his eyes open.

He nodded. "Don't smoke," he said, attempting to smile.

"What?"

"If you light up, we'll go to Kingdom Come a little sooner than we're meant to."

Her brow furrowed. "I don't understand."

He wrinkled his nose. "Gas."

Her eyes widened. "Otis," she called urgently over her right shoulder, "be careful! Leaking gas!"

"Roger," came the reply, as Otis shut off the bulldozer's engine. "I guess we're going to have to do this the old-fashioned way."

He came around to where Bartholomew could see him. "I was going to just back that rig off you," he said, "but Trish's right; we can't risk a spark."

He disappeared and came back in a moment with a spade. "Call for back-up and the rescue truck," he told his partner, "while I start digging." He went around to the hill side of the crushed vehicle and slowly, carefully, began to extricate it from the earth that had half-buried it.

By the time the others arrived, he had made enough of an entry to try the passenger door. It would not budge. It took forty minutes for the paramedics and back-up officers, working steadily and carefully with shovels and the rescue truck's Jaws of Life, to free him. By that time the shock, nature's novocaine, had worn off, and he hurt—everywhere. But the EMTs did not want to administer pain-killer until they could determine the exact nature of his injuries.

Remarkably—he said miraculously—other than the scalp wound and two broken ribs and numerous bruises, he was intact. So was his sense of humor, once the Demerol began to take hold. "There's a moral here: If you're anticipating a collision with a bull-dozer, it's wise to buckle up."

They wanted to take him home, but he wouldn't hear of it. He insisted on accompanying them to the mansion, where they were met by Trish and Otis. Inside, there was blood all over the kitchen, and a long smear of it on the tile floor, leading to the back door. In the living room, on a sofa by the window, Bartholomew saw a pair of binoculars lying on its side.

"She's out here," called Otis, holding open the kitchen door, "down by the pond."

As they walked down the grassy slope, it started to rain again—really more of a heavy mist. Bartholomew shivered; despite the pain-killer, he could feel the cold.

At the pond, lying on her back almost exactly where her husband had been found, was Allison Curtis. Her abdomen had been torn open by a great cut that ran from lower left to upper right. Her brown eyes, once so full of life, were open and staring up at the leaden sky. The mist collected on her cheeks, until it ran down them like tears.

BROTHER BARTHOLOMEW AWOKE feeling like he had been run over by a bulldozer. Then he realized that he had. Everything that moved, ached. But at least it moved, he told himself; it could have been so much worse. It was only the grace of God that it was not a double homicide yesterday.

It was Sunday morning, which meant Lauds was not until 8:30. What luxury! How appreciated by most of the Brothers, including the three forms burrowed in sleep who shared this room with him! Alas, it was wasted on early risers like himself, who invariably awoke an hour before dawn. Every dawn. If he ever needed extra sleep, he had to get it at the other end, by going to bed immediately after Compline. Or even earlier, as he did last night.

So concerned had he been about Dan's not getting enough sleep, he had forgotten that he himself had been running on about four hours a night. But yesterday afternoon, ribs taped up and aching, he had retired before supper, which meant he had slept about—he squinted at the alarm clock by his bunk—ten hours straight. With the result that, regardless of how battered his body felt, his mind was fresh. Too fresh to remain in bed.

As he started to get up, however, the darkened room began to spin. Easing a foot from under the covers and putting it on the floor (he had a bottom bunk—seniority had its privileges), he was able to stop the room from spinning. But that did nothing to ease the pounding in his head, and he realized that he must have a concussion. Moving very slowly, he took his shaving kit and towel to the corridor bathroom. At least he had it to himself.

In twenty minutes, about twice as long as it normally took, he was back in the room, dressing in the pre-dawn half-light. He pulled on his old sweats intending to go out on the flats. Of all the places on the Cape, none was more conducive to restoring everything to its proper perspective than a long walk on the flats. His father had preferred the wild beach at East Bluffs, yet even as a boy he'd found that for himself, peace of mind lingered about a mile out on the flats.

He had been meaning to get out there for several days, but with the accelerator jammed to the floor as it had been, there'd been no time. Well, now there was—a good two hours at least. Blessed solitude. And serenity.

He needed them just now. No sooner had he gotten his inner life sorted out, than a second victim had been murdered. And very nearly a third—himself. It was only the grace of God that he had survived yesterday afternoon.

All he needed now was some coffee to take out there with him. He would stop by the kitchen to see if by chance any other member of the dawn patrol might have brewed a pot; if not, he thought as he quietly descended the friary stairs, there was always instant.

Someone *had* brewed a pot of coffee; in fact, that someone was just pouring a mug, as he entered the kitchen. The half-smile of bemused anticipation vanished from his face. Ambrose. He liked him somewhat better now, but he still preferred to take him in small doses. Small, measured doses. Spaced as far apart as possible. Which meant *not* before breakfast. And *never* on Sunday.

"Morning!" Ambrose greeted him warmly. "You want some coffee?"

"Does a duck swim?"

"How're you feeling?" Ambrose asked, handing him a piping mug.

"About as poorly as can be expected," Bartholomew replied. He looked out the window; it was getting lighter by the minute. It wouldn't be long before the sun came up. "I'm going out on the flats," he heard himself say, "you want to come?" He could not believe he just said that! Was he some kind of masochist? So much for solitude and tranquility! That blow to his head yesterday must have loosened something.

"Great!" Ambrose exclaimed. "I'll get my coat."

For once, the young Brother kept silent, as they crossed the harbor parking lot and went out past the stone jetty onto the flats. Nor did he speak as they passed the first sapling marking the channel—and the second—and the third.

On the other side of the channel loomed a giant boulder, deposited eons ago by a receding glacier, as if to mark the harbor's entrance. On the sand bar nearest it, a flock of gulls had gathered. They were milling about, nattering, grubbing, preening, doing little gull things—as if they were passing time, waiting for something.

Suddenly they grew completely silent and motionless. A moment later, warm, red-golden light washed over the bar and the gulls. They looked east to its source, the white orb that had just appeared above the trees on the eastern horizon. In its light they were illumined, an almost incandescent white. Then, as one, they spread their wings and took flight, soaring away to the west.

The two Brothers watched them until they were small. Finally, Bartholomew spoke. "Lauds," he said in a voice barely above a whisper.

Ambrose nodded.

"I've never seen that before," Bartholomew added, still speaking in hushed reverence and wonder, as if he were in church.

"I have," said the younger monk, finally breaking silence. He, too, spoke softly, with the same awe. "I like to come out here before dawn. It's like being in a cathedral before the service. There's a feeling of anticipation—as if all creation was awaiting the coming of the Creator."

Bartholomew stared at him.

"When I come out here," Ambrose went on, "I try not to even think. There's such a sense of solitude and serenity, I don't want to disturb it, even interiorly."

Bartholomew felt his throat tightening.

"I wouldn't have spoken now," Ambrose smiled, "if you hadn't."

All right, God, Bartholomew thought, I hear You. Help me. I don't like who I am.

He started heading west toward the receding waters, and the young Brother fell in beside him. For more than a mile they walked without speaking—two lone figures crossing a vast and broadening expanse of sand that was in the process of shading from pink to gold to beige.

When they finally reached water's edge, Bartholomew looked at his watch. "If we go back now, we won't have to hurry." They turned, and Bartholomew was surprised to see how far they'd come. Even the new stone church looked small—no mean feat. But the sun was well up now, and the flats, though breathtaking, were normal. Magic time was over.

"Ready to think forensically?" he asked Ambrose, as they started back.

"Lead on, Holmes."

"Okay, here's where we are," and he recapped the investigation, including as many specific details as he could remember. As he filled Ambrose in on all that had happened since they'd been together at Norma's, he could not believe it had been only two days ago.

"The murderer is a man," Ambrose announced, when he had finished.

"Why?"

"Because bulldozers, with brake-handles for each tread, are a guy thing. I'm sure there are female dozer-jockies, but I'll bet there aren't any on the Cape. And to ambush you by waylaying you with one—that would never occur to a woman."

"Okay," agreed Bartholomew, "so–?"

"Well, since Tomlinson's in jail, and the Rolex ruled Hatch out, it's either the Commodore or Royce." He thought a moment. "Probably Royce, because he would have known about the road to

Teal Pond being under construction, and the heavy equipment being there. Remember, he had only a few minutes to improvise."

The moment Ambrose said it, Bartholomew knew it was true. Meeting Ambrose in the kitchen this morning was proving fortuitous in more ways than one. "That explains what's been bugging me about the note," Bartholomew said. "That phrase, 'ripping knife'—Royce used that in his anti-clamming manifesto."

"Plus," added Ambrose, "he lied to you about not having a watch!"

Bartholomew nodded. "And he was the only one who knew I was involved in the case; he'd seen us at the murder site."

All at once he stopped and turned to Ambrose. "I just remembered something Mrs. Curtis said, just before she was killed: she'd *seen* the knife."

"You mean, around her house?"

"No," said Bartholomew slowly, "I don't think so. There were binoculars in the living room. . . . I think she saw Royce at his cottage. With the knife. He was probably watching her and playing with it at the same time."

Ambrose shuddered. "That must have been why she called you."

Bartholomew nodded. "But first she called the station—and that's what gave him enough time to get there and kill her. With that telescope of his, he must have seen her with the binoculars and realized she'd seen the knife. He had to kill her, after that." He resumed walking and picked up the pace.

"What do we do now?" asked Ambrose. "Call the Chief?"

Bartholomew shook his head. "Church first, then Chief. The Eucharist always takes precedence over forensics."

Ambrose frowned and searched the shoreline. "It may be my imagination working overtime. But I've had the eeriest feeling we're being watched."

55 | a matter of time

PEG ANSWERED THE DOOR. "Brother Bartholomew, come in; he's been expecting you. Who's this?"

"This is Brother Ambrose. He's been, ah, assisting me on the case."

"Come in," she said, shaking hands. "And thank you for calling first," she said to Bartholomew. "I'm *determined* that he's not going to have a relapse like Friday. He's going to stay in bed long enough to get over this thing!"

Bartholomew smiled; she was like a lioness protecting her cubs.

"He finally got a good night's sleep last night, and he's doing better. But he's up now, and bored," laughed Peg, as she led them upstairs. "I think you'll be good for him." They entered the bedroom at the top of the stairs. "I'll leave you all to your crime solving," she said, withdrawing.

The Chief was propped up and scowling, obviously not pleased that Bartholomew had brought someone with him.

"This is Brother Ambrose," said Bartholomew. "He's been a big help, and don't worry; he's the only one at the friary who knows about what's going on."

The Chief said nothing and just looked at Bartholomew, clearly unconvinced that Ambrose needed to be there.

"I think he may have solved the case this morning."

The Chief's eyebrows went up. "Let's hear it."

"You know, Dan," said Bartholomew with a mischievous smile, "you look a *lot* better! Do you *feel* a lot better?"

"I feel fine! Will you get on with it?"

"Peg's right," Bartholomew mused, "bed rest is still the best remedy. After chicken soup, of course."

"Will you tell me what you came here to tell me!"

"Is everything all right up there?" called Peg.

"It's okay," Bartholomew reassured her, "I was just finding out how well he is." He turned to his friend, serious now. "It's Royce."

The Chief nodded. "I've been thinking that, too—ever since Sarah Tomlinson called the station yesterday morning, about the same time Curtis's wife must have called you. She'd found the watch; it was in the side pocket of the driver's door of their car. He must have taken it off, put it there, and then forgotten." He shook his head. "I've done the same thing myself."

"So you released him?"

"Of course! That missing watch was the only thing that could have put him at the scene of the crime."

Bartholomew turned to Ambrose. "Tell the Chief how you figured out it was Royce."

Ambrose told him, with Bartholomew filling in. When they finished, the Chief nodded. "It's him."

The phone was back on the nightstand, its place no longer usurped by pills and potions, Kleenex and stale ginger ale. The Chief called the station. "Put Sergeant Bascomb, make that Lieutenant Bascomb, on." Pause. "Leo? Take Otis and go out to the Royce cottage and arrest Roland Royce for the murder of MacArthur Curtis and his wife. Be sure to read him his rights and— *what?*"

The Chief's eyes widened in disbelief. "When?" A look of pain came across his face. "I don't believe this!" The pain worsened. "That was the only piece of concrete evidence we had!" And worsened more. "When are they coming back?" His face was red and getting redder. Finally, he sighed and threw off the bedcovers. "I'm coming down there." He slammed the receiver down.

"What is it?"

"You're not going to believe this! I just heard it, and *I* don't believe it!"

"*What?*"

"The watch and the case file are missing!" He headed for his closet. "We keep them locked in the bottom drawer of my desk. When Trish went to update the file after she and Otis got back from investigating the second murder yesterday afternoon, the drawer was unlocked, and they were gone."

"How could they be?" asked his friend. "It couldn't be a break-in; there's always somebody on duty."

"I said you'd have a hard time believing it," the Chief commented, putting on a weekend shirt. "Leo thinks Adams must have found the key and gotten it out of there day before yesterday, to get ready for the press conference. Leo figured it must have still been in Adams's desk, when I suspended him." He pulled on a pair of khakis. "When I gave him three minutes to clear his desk and get out of the building, he must have taken it with him."

"Well, can't you just get it back?"

"No," groaned the Chief. "He and his wife have gone on a vacation—a driving vacation. Down south. His mother, who lives with them, doesn't know where. They'd mentioned Williamsburg and Charleston, she thinks. All she knows for sure is that they didn't expect to be back until the middle of next month."

"Could the file still be in his house?" asked his friend.

The Chief shook his head. "Leo went over there last night and explained to her that it was police property, and we had need of it. She let him search through her son's desk and papers. It wasn't there. Leo tried to call me then, but I'd gone to bed. I was still asleep when he called back this morning."

"You think Adams took it with him?"

The Chief shrugged, as he tied his bootlaces. "It's the only place it could be. That—" he caught himself. "He got even, all right. But when I get done settling his hash, he's going to wish he'd never clapped eyes on the Eastport Police Department. He won't even be able to get a job as dogcatcher!"

"Dan!" Peg was at the bedroom door, in an Irish fury at what she was seeing. "Where do you think you're going?"

He explained the situation to her. His will was set. But so was hers, as she stood legs apart and arms akimbo, blocking the doorway to the upstairs hall.

Just before the irresistible force met the immovable object, Bartholomew intervened. "I'll make certain he doesn't overdo, Peg, and I'll have him back here within an hour, I promise."

She allowed herself to be placated—somewhat. "But you listen up, mister," she said, wagging her finger under her husband's nose, "there'll be no red beer and Red Sox this afternoon. You're going to take a nap! A *long* nap."

Confronted with the conditions of his freedom, he nodded grudgingly and hurried downstairs, Bartholomew and Ambrose following him.

"And Dan?" she called after them. "You let Brother Bartholomew drive! Do you hear me?"

"All right, all right!" he yelled, storming out the front door, and muttering "Women!"–but only after he was sure she couldn't hear him.

Leo met them at the station's front door. "I'm sorry about this, Chief."

"It's not your fault, Leo, but we've got some damage control to do here. Where's the rest of the team?"

"Waiting in your office. I called them as soon as you said you were coming in."

The Chief entered, and everyone got up. "Sorry to ruin your Sunday, people, but we've got problems." They were looking past him at the two Brothers standing in the doorway; the Chief waved them in and shut the door. "You all know that Brother Bartholomew has been helping with the investigation, in an unofficial capacity. Well, this is Brother Ambrose, and he's been helping Brother Bartholomew."

Otis said nothing, but the Chief could see from his expression that he resented the newcomer's presence. "Will it help, Otis, if I tell you that he solved the case? It helped me."

He asked the two civilians to tell the others what they'd told him. The Chief summed up the situation: "We know it's Royce. But with the watch and the note and the case file missing, we can't very well arrest him."

There were murmurs of agreement, and the Chief went on. "We're dealing with a shrewd customer here, who is also a psychopath. He may have already figured out why we haven't arrested him."

"So what's our plan?" asked Trish.

"If we had one," replied her superior not unkindly, "don't you think I would have told you by now?" He paused. "But I'll tell you this: We're not leaving this room until we do have one."

56 | sounds like a plan

LOOKING OVER AT THE CHIEF slumped in his chair, Brother Bartholomew grew concerned. The energy was literally draining out of him. He was good for about ten more minutes, then the monk would have to get his friend out of here. The trouble was, it looked like it was going to take a lot more than ten minutes to come up with a viable plan.

Otis spoke first, "My sense is that whatever we do, we'd better do it fast. Because he's ready to bolt. He's got to suspect we're onto him, and that it's only a matter of time before we can build a strong enough case to put him away." He shook his head. "If I were him, I'd just disappear. Go out to Montana and buy a shack."

"And start working on a new manifesto," muttered Leo.

Trish agreed. "I think we've got to bite the bullet, pull out all the stops to find Adams, and get our file back. He's bound to call his mother at some point. If she'll help us, no problem; if not, we get a court order for a tap."

Otis frowned. "What I can't figure is why he took it with him. I mean, sure, it would cause us grief, but it would ruin any future he might have in law enforcement."

"He's done that already," growled the Chief. "Believe me!"

Leo looked uncomfortable with what he was about to say. "I'm afraid there may be another reason: All the time I was over at his house, his mother kept talking. She thinks he's running the case and is some kind of hero. She's immensely proud of him, because he's working on a book about it. He even has a publisher."

The Chief smote his brow. "Well, now we know what he meant, when he said we'd not heard the last of him."

Leo smiled. "There's not a chance of his getting it ready quick enough to cash in on the publicity—which will die down fast once we have Royce in custody."

Otis sighed. "There's a reason they call them 'instant books.' A ghost-writer interviews the 'author' for a few hours, half a dozen people get the transcript done overnight, the ghost produces a working draft in a week. The publisher fast-tracks it with presses running around the clock, and voilà! Finished books in a month."

"I know who's going to ghost it!" Trish exclaimed. "Jill Easton. I saw them huddled at Norma's a couple of times, and she had her tape recorder out. I assumed he was giving her an 'exclusive.'"

"That settles it," the Chief declared. "I'm going to write Adams a letter—and Leo, I want you to take it to his mother and tell her to send it to him, the moment she hears from him—telling him that unless he immediately returns the police property in his possession, I'm going to prosecute him to the full limit of the law." He chuckled. "Not even Vic Malcolm is going to be able to save his bacon now! Okay, the pop publishing seminar is over. Time to get back on track."

Ambrose had a suggestion. "We wouldn't have to wait, if we could reach that EastSports clerk who sold him the watch and its replacement. The windjammer company must know how to get hold of one of their ships. If she could identify him from a faxed photograph—"

"Which we should be able to get easily enough," added Otis. "Isn't he the son of the Roland Royce over in Chatham?"

The Chief shook his head. "I'm not sure we want to tip our hand to that extent," he said, thinking out loud. "The moment we spook him, he's gone."

Bartholomew had waited until now to speak. "There may be another way. This man is a games player. He plays chess on the Net. And he probably figures he's a whole lot smarter than the rest of us."

He continued slowly, figuring it out as he went. "I agree with Officer Whipple: He's just about out of here. But before he leaves, he's got to make good on his boast."

"What boast?" asked Trish.

"In his note to us, he said that when the knife had received its tenth notch, it would be returned to its resting place." He smiled. "The chain-mail glove has just hit the flagstones."

The Chief frowned. "You just lost us."

"The gauge: he's thrown us a challenge. He's told us he's going to return the knife to the display case, even if we're waiting for him." He paused. "But it's crunch time for him, too. Because now he's got to deliver. If he doesn't, it's just empty words—confirming he's the failure and lightweight he's always feared he was."

The Chief looked at him with admiration. "You're doing it, aren't you?"

"What?"

"Getting inside his head."

"I hope so," Bartholomew admitted. "He wants to get out of here, and he will, as soon as he returns that knife."

No one spoke, as all weighed what he had just said.

At length the Chief summed up: "Well, it makes sense. All right, we'll expect him to do it tonight. Leo, what's the status at the crime scene?"

"We've had a car out there with two officers ever since the second body was discovered," the acting lieutenant reported. "We've got the whole area cordoned off. As you might expect, the media have been wonderfully cooperative and a pleasure to work with," he said wryly. "But we're handling it."

"Who's on this afternoon and tonight?" the Chief asked.

Leo checked his roster clipboard. "Buchman and Perkins are due on at four o'clock. I figured that by the next watch at eight o'clock, it would be quiet enough to get by with single coverage, namely Officer Carey. Besides, we just don't have the manpower."

The Chief nodded. "That's fine, Leo, and they're all solid; we'll stick with your arrangement." He leaned forward. "Now here's what we're going to do."

With quick precision he outlined a double stake-out. Leo and Trish would go out with Buchman and Perkins at four o'clock. They would get on the floor in the back seat, so that Royce, who was bound to be watching, would not see them. The officers coming off duty would also bring Mrs. Curtis's car back to the station, presumably for close inspection. That would open a space in the garage for the patrol car, and with the garage door down, the hidden passengers could get into the house without being seen.

At this point, Bartholomew interrupted. "Chief, we've been instrumental in this thing from the beginning. Let us go out in Officer Carey's car at eight o'clock."

"No way! I don't want civilians anywhere in the vicinity. Don't misunderstand me; you've been a real help. In fact, we couldn't have done it without you. But let's face it, when it comes to armed confrontation, you're amateurs. Now is the time for professionals. The ones with guns, who know how to use them. This guy has already killed twice. He wouldn't hesitate to slit you from your guggle to your zatch."

But Bartholomew, having anticipated this response, had a counter-move ready. "You said I was able to get inside his mind; I mean, that's what we're proceeding on here. You may need me to do that again—tonight, right when it's happening. And remember, his primary objective is not to kill any more people; it's to get that knife back in its case." He paused. "Think about it."

The Chief did. "All right, on one condition: You do *exactly* what Leo and Trish tell you. You don't argue; you don't have a better idea. They are in command, and you obey them without question or hesitation."

"That shouldn't be a problem," smiled Bartholomew.

"Well, if you can do that—you can come."

As for the other site, after dark he and Otis would make their way on foot through the woods to the Royce cottage. Then, at around 10:00, the duty officer at the station would call Carey—not on the house phone, but on the car radio. Until then, the station would maintain strict radio silence with Carey at the Curtis house. But he *wanted* Royce to intercept this call, because it would be to inform Carey that they were curtailing the police presence there, and for him to come on in. He would comply, leaving the four of them in the house.

Bartholomew nodded. "Good. Royce may suspect one, but not four. And he won't anticipate that we've also staked out his cottage." He looked around and frowned. "After my close encounter of the nasty kind with the bulldozer yesterday, I'm afraid we've got to assume he knows how many people are working this case, and who they are—"

"Everybody does!" grumbled the Chief. "Thanks to Adams's big mouth, all they have to do is read it in the papers."

"I think Royce is doing more than that," observed Bartholomew. "He knows too much about the movements of your vehicles. I think he's got a scanner."

"Isn't that pretty high-tech for someone who loathes technology?" Leo asked.

"He's selective in his loathing," qualified Bartholomew. "From what I saw, he's got about the hottest computer on the Cape."

The Chief got to his feet, then wavered and had to lean against the desk for support. He was close to passing out, but there was no question that for the next few moments, he was still in full command of the situation. "Otis, soon as we're done, go over to Eastport Electronics—they should be open on Sunday afternoon—and ask Dick Miller if there's any way we can change the frequency in our radios, so that after tonight he won't be able to pick them up. Dick ought to know; he probably sold Royce the scanner!" The officers laughed.

"Don't worry," the Chief said in an aside to Bartholomew, "He's sold us a lot of equipment over the years, and he'll want to keep our business; he'll be discreet." Back to Otis: "While you're there, pick up a couple of those new Motorola hand-held short-range radios—and make damned sure he can't eavesdrop on them!" He chuckled. "I'll have to justify the purchase to FinCom, but if we catch him, that shouldn't be a problem."

He swayed, and Bartholomew, frowning, said, "Dan, I've got to get you home, or Peg will fillet both of us."

The Chief raised his hand. "In a minute. Are there any questions?"

"What about backup?" asked Leo.

"We'll have be each other's backup. The fewer people who know about this, the better. But there should be one person back here in the know, in case there's a snafu. Leo, who's the night duty officer?"

"Morton, with Biggs on the switchboard and Buchman and Perkins in the cars."

The Chief grimaced. "Morton is Adams's hand-picked protégé—with all his unfortunate propensities."

"I know, but he's got the seniority."

The Chief thought for a moment. "Well, it should be all right; all he has to do is make that one call. Brief him strictly on a need-to-know basis."

"Snafu," Ambrose asked Bartholomew privately, as the meeting was breaking up, "where does that word come from?"

"Military expression," the older monk explained. "Situation normal: all fouled up."

The Chief turned to Bartholomew. "Nap time."

"You sure you're supposed to go tonight?" asked his friend when they were in the car.

"Are you kidding? I wouldn't miss this for anything!"

57 | snafu

THE SUN HAD NOT YET SET, but Teal Pond was already shrouded in shadows when Officer Carey pulled his patrol car into the Curtis garage and closed the door. Brothers Bartholomew and Ambrose, as much on the floor as it was possible to get in the back seat of the cruiser, now unfolded themselves. Getting down on hands and knees, so as not to be visible from any window, they entered the house. In the kitchen they joined Leo and Trish, who were sitting on the floor.

"Comfy?" asked Leo in a low voice. "It's going to be a long night."

"It helps if you crawl into the library and get one of the sofa cushions," suggested Trish. Ambrose did, returning in a moment with one for himself and one for Bartholomew.

Leo told them that Royce had indeed purchased a scanner three weeks ago–the day before he did the first murder. "But here's something: Two days ago, just before the second murder, he purchased four remote-controlled, time-delay switches. No telling what he has in mind." A possibility came to Bartholomew, but it was too disturbing to contemplate, and he brushed it away.

From where they sat, their line of sight outside was of the last rays of daylight. About half an hour after dark, the Motorola on Leo's belt crackled. "We're in place," came the Chief's voice in a whisper. "We're in the woods, about half a click west of the cottage. No sign of the suspect. But we can see both the cottage and your house. Which looks deserted, so be careful not to show any light."

Promptly at ten, Officer Carey, standing out on the deck, heard someone calling him on the radio in his patrol car in the garage. He went through the house to the garage, and took the call: He was told that the decision had been made to curtail the police presence for the night, and for him to come on back to the station.

After he left, those inside the house set up watches: Leo and Ambrose would take the first hour, then Trish and Bartholomew. In the darkness they crawled from one room to another, scanning outside in all directions. There was nothing to see, and time began to drag, as if the quicksilver wings on its heels had molted.

At 11:30, they were startled by the ringing of the phone. No one picked it up; it might be Royce, checking to see if the house was really as empty as it appeared.

Shortly before midnight, Trish, at the living room window, spotted what they had been waiting for: a form in the underbrush at the edge of the lawn, making its way towards the house. Alerting the others, she unholstered her sidearm and got her flashlight ready. Leo, upstairs in the bedroom, whispered that he, too, had the intruder in sight. Bartholomew, in the dining room, said a prayer.

Leo activated the Motorola and whispered, "Chief, we've got movement. Someone's approaching through the cover at the edge of the lawn. Contact in about three minutes."

"Roger," came the soft reply. "Keep your mike open."

And then the impossible happened. Headlights streamed into the house from the driveway, and a crunching of gravel announced the arrival of a car. Ambrose, on that side of the house, whispered that it was a patrol car.

The front door opened, the lights went on, and it was Officer Morton. "Hello?" he called with the door open. "Anybody home?"

Trish crawled in from the living room and startled him. "What the—"

With a furious gesture, she shushed him and signaled him to shut the door and go into the library, which was not visible from the pond side of the house. Leo slid downstairs on his stomach and into the library, signaling Trish to join him.

"What's going on there?" whispered the Chief. "I don't like what I think I'm hearing."

"It's Morton," Leo replied. "He just arrived."

"What in hell is he doing there? Put him on."

Leo handed the Motorola to Morton.

"Chief?" said the latter, matching the hushed tones of the others. "I tried to call on the phone, but no one answered. And since you wanted to maintain radio silence, I figured I'd better come out and tell you myself."

"Tell me what, you—"

"Lieutenant Gillespie from the State Police just arrived at the station. He's come to assist in the investigation."

"*What are you talking about?* I never asked for any assistance."

"No, but Lieutenant Adams did, just before he went on leave. I guess he didn't tell you."

The Chief was apoplectic, his voice rising to the point where Leo had to grab the Motorola and turn the gain down. "You blew a stakeout for *that?*" the Chief shouted. "The only difference between you and Inspector Clouseau is that Clouseau gets the perp in the end!"

Silence. When he spoke again his voice was lower, though no less intense. "You go back to the station and tell Lieutenant Gillespie that the request for assistance was unauthorized, and that I will explain the foul-up in the morning. Then you arrange the nicest accommodations for him you can find. You call Gordie's and ask them to give him anything he wants, and in the morning you call Norma's and do the same. And the cost of all that is coming out of your and Adams's paychecks. Now put Lieutenant Bascomb back on. I'm calling off this operation, as of now."

Bartholomew signaled that he would like to speak to the Chief, and Leo nodded. "Chief? Brother Bartholomew here. Listen: This could actually play to our advantage. If Royce suspected a stakeout, Officer Morton's arrival will have confirmed it. And the fact that it is obviously a blown op will confirm his impression of us as his bumbling inferiors." He thought for a moment. "Have someone leave with him– Lieutenant Bascomb probably, since the stakeout officer would most likely be a man. Then the rest of us just sit tight and wait."

There was silence, while the Chief thought it over. "It might work," he finally said. "Do it."

Leo pushed Morton out the door in front of him, turning off the lights and slamming the door behind them. Then he yelled at Morton, loud enough for those inside (and anyone else) to hear: "Get in the car, you idiot! No, the passenger side! From now on, you're not driving anywhere! You're going to be doing traffic detail at the mall!" Two car doors *thunked* shut, gravel crunched, headlights left–and darkness and silence returned.

With hand signals, Trish directed Ambrose to the dining room with its view of the driveway, and Bartholomew upstairs to the master bedroom, from which the entire back yard could be seen. Since she was the only one armed, she would stay on the first floor, where her weapon was most likely to be needed. She crouched in the corner of the living room, where she could see both the deck and the side yard.

Quietly they took their positions and waited.

58 | bishop's gambit declined

OUTSIDE THE CURTIS HOUSE, there was a full moon. The pond and lawn were brightly lit, but the bordering trees and shrubs were a series of silhouettes, some more dense than others. As Brother Bartholomew stared out at them, trying to force them to reveal some movement, some telling detail, his mind went back to a similar night, more than a quarter of a century before. He had been in a machine gun emplacement then, in a small perimeter atop a low ridge, with a platoon of badly scared, stumblingly tired young men who had been under fire for 36 hours straight.

They, too, had been searching for movement in the darkness. They knew the North Vietnamese were out there; they could hear them. Too many of them. But they couldn't see them. That was the night that he had said his first prayer. And God had answered; he had survived—one of the few who did. The enemy's final assault had begun with a flare.

Even as he recalled that moment, there was a sudden burst of flame in the underbrush at the edge of the yard. A fire had started. He whispered downstairs, but Trish had already seen it. "It's probably a diversion, meant to draw anyone inside to expose themselves," she whispered, "but we can't let all of Teal Pond go up in flames."

"Let me get a shovel from the garage, and see if I can deal with it," Ambrose volunteered.

Trish considered it. "All right. If his primary objective is, as Brother Bart says, to return the knife, you should be okay."

Ambrose left, but three minutes later a second a fire started in the woods a hundred yards from the first, and two were more than he could cope with. Two men, however, might still be able to contain them, and now she sent Bartholomew to help him.

"Will you be all right?" he whispered.

"I'm the one with the gun, remember? Now hurry up, before we have to get the fire department out here."

He went out the deck door and started running across the lawn. And then in the distance across the pond, near Royce's cottage, another fire flared up. And three minutes later, another. Bartholomew had the sickening realization that they—he—had been outmaneuvered. That's what the time-delay switches were for! The first fire was to bring out anyone waiting inside the house; the second was to flush out a possible backup.

Well, it had worked—perfectly. Royce had waited until he saw a second person leave the house to help the first. But he would not have counted on there being a third person—which meant he was probably entering the house at this moment. Bartholomew turned and saw a figure going in through the laundry room door, the lock of which had been broken at the time of the note.

In a quandary, he wondered if he should help Ambrose or go back inside to help Trish. Fire was fire, but a life was—he ran back and entered, as Trish, standing in the living room, switched on her flashlight. She held it just above her drawn .38 Smith & Wesson revolver.

"Stop!" she commanded to the ski-masked intruder, standing by the display case. "Police! Drop the knife! Do it *now!*"

At that instant, Ambrose cried, "I need help out here!" Momentarily distracted, Trish took her eyes off the intruder, who now sprang for the door to the deck. She ran to the door after him and fired two rounds, and the form sprinting across the lawn began to limp. But he soon disappeared into the total darkness of the trees.

Ambrose, meanwhile, was shuttling back and forth between blazes, and Bartholomew ran to help him, while Trish used the Motorola to call the Chief. "We've lost control of the situation over here. There's a couple of fires that are getting away from us. So did Royce. He was in the house, and I had the drop on him, but the fires—I may have winged him, though. Chief, can you guys get over here? These fires are more than we can handle."

"We can't! We've got a couple of fires of our own!" replied the Chief, from his position a mile away. "Call the fire department, Trish, and tell them to hurry. In fact, tell them to get the Orleans and Eastham trucks out here, too, or this whole place is going to go up!"

ॐ

In the early morning, after the fire equipment had departed, the Curtis house and the Royce Cottage were both intact. But much of the beautiful woodlands surrounding the pond was in ruins—naked stumps standing amidst gray ash. Gazing at the scene, the Chief shook his head. "For someone who fancied himself such a friend of nature, especially the nature around this pond, he sure had some way of showing it."

"I guess you sometimes have to kill the thing you love, to preserve it," Bartholomew observed wryly.

The Chief laughed without humor. "We'd better go. Peg's going to kill me. And to tell you the truth, I've had it. Fighting fires while you have the Manchurian flu is not the healthiest combination. Come on, Ambrose," he called to the younger monk, "I'll give you guys a lift to the station."

As they drove away in the Chief's vehicle, Bartholomew surveyed the wreckage. "This is my fault," he said quietly. "All of it."

"How do you figure?" asked the Chief.

"It was my plan."

The Chief turned and looked at him. "No, you're wrong. I'm the one wearing the captain's bars, and I'm the one who signed off on it. It's my responsibility. Besides, it was a good plan; it could have worked."

But his friend would not be consoled. "He simply outplayed me. I even figured he might have arranged a diversion—but not four. And I had an inner warning when I first heard about those time-delay switches—but I didn't do anything about it." He waved at the fire-scarred glade behind them. "I did that."

"Stop beating yourself up, will you? We nearly got him. We *will* get him the next time."

"If there is a next time."

"I said, knock it off!" the Chief commanded. "Get some sleep. So will I. Then we'll see where we're at."

They drove in silence back to the station, where he let his passengers out at their old, beat-up red pick-up. Seeing it, the Chief grinned. "Hey, wasn't that thing crushed to death over at Teal Pond Saturday?"

Bartholomew smiled. "This is another one. The abbey has an unending supply." All three of them laughed.

"My office," said the Chief, shifting into gear. "This afternoon, three o'clock," he called out as he drove away.

か

Bartholomew slept from before seven till after two. Then he went to find Brother Anselm. The Senior Brother was in the kitchen, supervising preparations for the friary's Memorial Day picnic supper. From the look of things, there were going to be enough hamburgers for a small army—which meant there might just be enough for the 30 Brothers. In the kitchen's brick hearth, a black cauldron was simmering with the makings of a delicious batch of chowder, awaiting only the fresh clams.

"Oh, Bartholomew! Good!" said Anselm, seeing him. "I was going to ask you to captain the over-40s volleyball team." He frowned. "Though with two broken ribs, I guess you'll have to be their coach, instead."

Bartholomew nodded. "Don't worry; I'll keep them from running up the score on the under-40s this year."

Ambrose, who was shucking corn with another of the younger Brothers, said, "The Geezers will be lucky if they even get close!"

Bartholomew grinned at Anselm. "Every year, they make a big noise, and every year–" he shrugged. "A balloon makes a big noise, too, when you suddenly let go of it." He made a gesture with his hand, indicating a balloon darting this way and that.

"This year will be different!" exclaimed Ambrose. "Just because you guys play dirty–"

"What can I say?" chuckled Bartholomew to Anselm. "We had a little more beach time in our misspent youth." He turned to Ambrose. "When you get older and have to conserve your energy, you, too, will learn to use your mind."

Then his smile faded, and he asked the older monk if he might have a private word with him. They went into the library, and Bartholomew started to tell Anselm about what happened the night before, and how the failed plan was all his fault, but the older monk wouldn't stop smiling. Finally Bartholomew asked him what was so amusing.

"I'm delighted with how well you're doing with Ambrose! You've taken that assignment seriously, and he's responding. For the first time since his novitiate, he seems to be settling down. And finding peace. I've talked with Dominic, and he agrees with me: Whatever you're doing, keep doing it."

"But that's not what I wanted to talk to you about. I want to talk about last night–"

"How do you feel about him?" said Anselm, undeterred.

"Ambrose? Well–I'm seeing sides to him, that I hadn't seen before. He's bright and intuitive. And sensitive. But at bottom he's got a good heart, and that's the most important thing."

Anselm nodded. "He thinks the world of you. Are you willing to keep him with you for a while longer?" It was a question this time, not a request, and the younger monk knew that if he said no, the assignment would be ended.

He thought a moment. "I think I'm supposed to keep on. At least for now."

Anselm nodded. "Good. I was hoping you'd say that." He stood up. "Now, I've got to get back to the kitchen." He paused, as if remembering. "Oh, and about last night? From what you've told me, you were asked to help. You did your best. Your plan nearly worked."

And then he surprised his younger friend: "I think it's your pride, Bartholomew, that's got you hung up. You thought you were going to win; you were sure of it, in fact. And instead, you got beaten. At your own game."

He started back to the kitchen, where he was needed. "Next time—and there will be a next time—trust God a little more, and your vaunted acumen a little less."

IT WAS TWENTY-FIVE MINUTES TO THREE when Brother Bartholomew swung the pick-up into the parking lot at Norma's. They had difficulty finding a parking place, and inside, all the tables were taken. The place was humming, but when people saw who had come in, it quieted.

In a few moments there was a table, and Isabel came over. "The usual?" she asked, and was about to get it when Ambrose said, "Actually, I'd like mine with milk and sugar."

"But you always have black," said Bartholomew, startled.

"No—*you* always have black," Ambrose corrected him. "And I wind up having what you have. Only now, I want what *I* want."

"Coming right up," smiled Isabel.

Bartholomew shook his head. "You never cease to amaze me," he said with a smile.

"I amaze myself sometimes," Ambrose admitted. He looked around. "I think these people are whispering about us," he said quietly.

"I'm *sure* they are," said Bartholomew. "Three Mid-Cape fire departments know that we were part of the stakeout. But hey, let them whisper; what difference does it make?"

Isabel came back with their coffee. "One black," she said, putting it in front of her son. "And one with milk and sugar," she announced, setting it before Ambrose.

Then she bent over for a *tête-à-tête*. "Everybody knows you're involved now. That you were trying to catch Royce, but he got away."

"How do they know?" Bartholomew asked in a low voice.

"Morton. He was in here, shooting his mouth off." She looked around and smiled. "Of course, *today* everybody knew it was Royce all along. Never a doubt. Living off in the little cottage, writing those weird environmental manifestos—Cape Cod's own Ted Kaczynski."

"Conventional wisdom's never wrong," mused her son, "until it's wrong."

"So now people are wondering: How come the police didn't get on to him long before now? And where *is* the fat little creep anyway?"

"That, Mother, as Dan would say, is the 64,000 ruble question."

❧

At three o'clock on Memorial Day afternoon, when many Cape men were home watching the Indianapolis 500 or the Red Sox–Yankees game or the insides of their eyelids, five of them and a woman were in Chief Burke's office at the EPD. Though they had gotten some sleep and a shower, they still looked tired and dispirited. The unrelenting strain of the past two weeks was getting to each of them, and the near miss the night before, followed by hours of fire-fighting, had taken their toll.

The Chief looked at them, one by one, as they concentrated on the pattern the sun made on the carpet, dimmed as it was by the fog of despair that seemed to permeate the room. Then, his voice dripping disgust, he said, "Well, what are we going to do, throw in the towel?"

No one said anything.

"He beat us last night," the Chief went on. "He was smart, and he got lucky. And he made us look bad." There were nods and murmurs of assent.

In frustration the Chief turned to Bartholomew. "You remember what you used to say to the soccer team at Nauset, when we were behind at the half?" His friend shook his head. "You used to remind us that we still had another half to play, and that the score of that half was zero-to-zero. And that we were not beaten, unless we believed we were." He looked around; their eyes were up now. "Well, truth is truth, and it doesn't matter how old it is. If you believe we're beaten, we might as well go home and try to enjoy what's left of the weekend with our families. And tell them: The winner is Roland Royce, the Fourth."

They were with him now. "But if you're not willing to concede victory to that pathetic little piece of excrement, then let's decide right now that we're going to win! And if you believe *that*, then we will!"

Nice speech, Knute, thought Bartholomew. But he was grinning like the others.

"Okay," said the Chief, "let's see what we've got. And I don't want to hear *anyone* say 'nothing'—even if it's true!" They all laughed. The fog had lifted.

Otis led off. "He's vanished without a trace. We've got an APB out for his Volkswagen, but he's probably ditched it by now and gotten another car. He took both his computers with him, and there's nothing left in the cottage that's of any use to us."

"I went to see his parents this afternoon," offered Trish. "They have no idea where he is, or might be going."

"How'd they take it?" the Chief asked.

"His mother, who's a bit of a flake, is in complete denial. His father, on the other hand, did not seem the least surprised. I felt that to him, it was the final, predictable chapter of a book he'd stopped reading a long time ago. He did us one favor, though; he called the head of the brokerage firm which handles his son's trust account, and got him to have someone go into the office and access it on their computer. His son had cleaned out all the cash in it Friday—just before he murdered Mrs. Curtis."

"How much was in there?"

"A little over five thousand."

"So," the Chief sighed, "he's got enough to go pretty much wherever he pleases."

"Does this mean—he walks?" asked Ambrose.

"Not exactly," responded the Chief. "We've got a good recent picture of him—two, actually: one that his parents gave Otis, and the one that the *Revelator*'s photographer took of the judges at the reception. We also have an excellent set of fingerprints from the brass telescope. We'll get him eventually."

"I'm not so sure," said Bartholomew. "He's gone to ground, and this guy really knows how to disappear. We won't see hide or hair of him—unless he wants us to." The fog seeped back in under the door and began to gather around their ankles.

Then Trish wondered, "I wish there were some way we could entice him out. . . ."

"Wait a minute!" exclaimed Bartholomew. "Maybe there is! Royce has an ego that just won't quit. He's also a chess-aholic, and he's just drawn the most important match he's ever played."

"I'd say it's more like a win," commented the Chief sarcastically.

"If you're counting the pieces he's taken, it is," answered Bartholomew. "Two murders, no arrest. But suppose—*we* don't regard it that way. Suppose *we* see it as a draw. We've got a positive ID, fingerprints, hard evidence, a character profile—we're bound to get him, sooner or later. If he thinks that *we* believe we've played him to a draw—which, for a player of his caliber is almost the same as losing—it'll drive him crazy!"

"It would," the Chief agreed.

"The main thing is," said Otis, catching Bartholomew's perspective, "to lay it on thick, portraying him as a rank amateur, a serial-killer wanna-be."

"How are we going to let him know this?" asked Leo.

The Chief groaned. "I don't think I like what's coming next."

Trish smiled, also catching it. "The Chief calls a press conference—the first *official* one. For the next-to-last chapter in the Duck Pond Murders."

All eyes turned to the man behind the desk.

"All right," he said with resignation, "set it up."

60 | contact

AT THE PRESS CONFERENCE, the Chief, who had gotten another good night's sleep, was in top form—cordial and confident, and parrying each reporter's thrust with grace and wry, self-deprecating wit. The media ate it up.

"So what we have here," he said in conclusion, "is a Ted Kaczynski wanna-be, who is not as bright as the Unabomber, and whose environmental polemics are, if possible, even more tedious. But the biggest difference between Royce and the Unabomber is this: We know exactly what he looks like," and he held up an enlargement of Royce's smiling face. "I give you Roland Royce, the Fourth. He's 35 years old, five feet, seven inches tall, and seriously overweight; his nickname at Harvard was Roly-Poly. But don't let his cherubic appearance deceive you: He's a cold-blooded killer. He's armed and extremely—repeat, extremely—dangerous."

Eight hours later, his presentation was the lead story on the Boston evening newscasts, and in the morning, Royce's picture was smiling on the front page of the regional dailies.

And nothing happened.

A week went by without a clue. There were lots of false sightings, but not a single substantial lead. The media, never known for the length of its attention span, soon turned elsewhere. Nor was there any attempt at contact by Royce, whom the press conference was supposed to flush out into the open.

Two weeks went by, and on police bulletin boards around the country, the photo and rap sheet on Royce began to get covered over by other, more urgent requests. Still no contact.

After three weeks even Eastport began to lose interest. According to Isabel Doane, the top of the town's mental bulletin board was now occupied by parades and other bicentennial festivities. Continuing interest in the Duck Pond Murders was desultory, at best.

The Chief called another meeting in his office. "Well," he said to the team, but especially to Bartholomew, who had been so certain that Royce would get in touch: "Now what?"

No one had an answer. Bartholomew felt that he had again let them down. Like the stakeout, which had also been his idea, the press conference had yielded nothing. At this point, he would have tendered his badge, if he had one.

"White to move and mate in three," said the Chief sarcastically, mimicking a typical lead of the *Globe*'s Sunday chess puzzle. It was not meant for Bartholomew specifically, but since no one else in the room was a chess player, that was the way he took it.

And then his eyes widened. And his mouth opened, though at first no sound came out. "That's it!" he shouted. "That's how we're going to reach him! Instead of waiting for him to come to us, we'll go to him!"

"What are you talking about?" asked the Chief.

"He plays cyberchess! And I know his handle: FalconerRR." He looked around at them. "Are any of your computers on the Net?" "Mine is," said Trish.

"Do you want to do this?" Bartholomew asked the Chief.

"Go for it."

Leaving the office, they went over to Trish's desk, and stood behind her while she logged onto the Net. "You remember what the name of his chess club was?"

"It was part of bpm.com—ChessUnlimited, I think."

Trish looked at the Chief. "We'll have to join bpm.com."

"Go ahead," he said, and she filled out the on-screen membership, and gave the department's credit card number for payment. They were in.

"What screen name shall we use?" she asked.

"DeeperBlue," Bartholomew immediately answered. "It's a reference to the IBM team and machine that finally beat Gary Kasparov, the world's greatest player. Royce will never be able to resist such a challenge, especially when he sees it's coming from Eastport."

Her fingers flew in a blizzard of keystrokes. "I'm in, and there's a message board. What should I say?"

Bartholomew frowned. "Type: 'Since you drew the last game, would you like another?' And leave it for FalconerRR." She did.

"What happens now?" Leo asked.

"Well, we check it periodically, to see if he's responded. He'll suggest a time, and when we agree to it, we start."

The Chief said, "Then we nail his ass! We find out from bpm.com exactly where Royce is playing from, and—"

"I don't think so," said Trish, shaking her head. "The Web service providers are awfully leery about revealing specifics about their clients."

"Even if it's a police emergency?"

"Doubtful. Last year there was a big stink about someone in the Navy who advertised himself as a homosexual on the Net. The Navy went to his service provider to find out who it was, and they gave him up. But then the ACLU raised a huge stink. I don't think they'll do it again for anyone now."

The Chief, suddenly weary of cybertalk, said, "Who wants coffee? I'm buying."

He started for the door, and they were about to follow, when Trish called, "Wait! Don't leave! It's Falconer! He's coming through—right now!"

They rushed back to her computer. A reply to their message had just appeared: "My dear sainted brother, I'm disappointed it took you so long to remember this way of contacting me. I expected to hear from you long before now! But I'm *really* disappointed with the Chief! Did he honestly believe he could provoke me into revealing my whereabouts? Bush league, Chief, very bush. But it is you, Brother Bartholomew, with whom I'm most disappointed. I had expected a better match from you. It was clever of you to stake out both sites. But I anticipated that gambit, too, and effectively countered it. Hardly what I would call a draw!"

Leo rubbed his eyes. "How could he write so much so fast?"

"He probably drafted it as soon as he left," explained Bartholomew, "and he's been waiting to post it ever since."

Trish pointed at the monitor. "He's in the chat room now. Do we want to dialogue with him?"

"Absolutely," said the Chief.

Trish looked up at Bartholomew. "You're the player; you take over."

Bartholomew looked at the Chief, who nodded. He sat down at the keyboard, and with a burst of strokes typed:

DEEPERBLUE: BIG TALK FOR SOMEONE WHO BARELY GAINED A DRAW.

FALCONER: WHAT DO YOU MEAN? I WON!

DEEPERBLUE: NOT BY YOUR RULES.

FALCONER: ???

DEEPERBLUE: YOU FAILED TO REPLACE THE KNIFE. ERGO, A DRAW.

FALCONER: BUT I OUTPLAYED YOU!

DEEPERBLUE: NOT BY YOUR PARAMETERS.

FALCONER: WANT ANOTHER GAME?

DEEPERBLUE: ANY TIME.

FALCONER: WE'LL PLAY ON THE THIRD OF JULY.

DEEPERBLUE: WHAT ARE THE STAKES?

FALCONER: MY OWN BICENTENNIAL SURPRISE FOR EASTPORT.

DEEPERBLUE: WHICH YOU WILL GIVE, DESPITE ALL EFFORTS TO STOP YOU?

FALCONER: EXACTLY!

DEEPERBLUE: AND IF YOU WIN?

FALCONER: THE CHIEF RESIGNS, AS HE PROMISED.

DEEPERBLUE: EXPLAIN.

FALCONER: IF THE CASE IS NOT CLOSED BY THE FOURTH.

"I never promised that," said the Chief.

"Sorry, Chief," said Leo, "but I heard you say that once in confidence to Lieutenant Adams. Which is the same thing as telling everyone."

Royce exited the chat room, but before he left, he typed one last line:

FALCONER: I PROMISE EASTPORT A CELEBRATION IT WILL NEVER FORGET!

61 | endgame

THE CHIEF HAD CALLED the investigation team to a final strategy session at 10:00 A.M., June 30. So at 9:30, Brothers Bartholomew and Ambrose stopped off at Norma's. Though it was as crowded as usual, there was a different clientele this morning—summer people and vacationers, getting a couple of days head start on the long Fourth of July weekend.

This time, it was seven minutes before they could get a table. Then Isabel came over with two mugs of her best—one black, one with milk and sugar.

"Have you got your rose ready?" she asked her son.

"I don't know," he said. "I've been too busy to pay a whole lot of attention to it—and I'm afraid the neglect kind of shows."

"How about yours?" asked Ambrose brightly.

She frowned. "I don't know. Mine looks kind of peaked. Too much rain and only two sunny days last week. It's past its prime, I'm afraid."

"That's too bad," said Ambrose, genuinely concerned. "Maybe you'll be able to—"

"Oh, can't you see she's gaming us?" Bartholomew cut in, with a wry smile. "Just like I was gaming her?"

Isabel laughed. "To tell you the truth, I think Maurice has got it in the bag."

"How's his health?" Bartholomew asked.

"His holiday behind bars didn't help it much. But other than that, he's about the same." She looked down at her son. "I know you can't tell me anything about the investigation, but—have you got anything at all?"

"You're right; I can't tell you about it." He paused and then said almost wistfully, "I just wish there were more I couldn't tell you about."

"Charlie Barker was in here yesterday. He told Eben Snow that he thought he saw Royce last Sunday, up at Plymouth. He had family visiting from the West, so he took them up to Plimoth Plantation. He thought one of the people in the cafeteria looked like Royce."

"People are seeing him everywhere. Well, come on, Ambrose; time to boogie. Good luck on Sunday, Mother."

"You, too, Andrew."

৵

In his office, the Chief gave them a situation report. "We've got three days left till the third, and we still have no idea what he has in mind. I'm calling in the State Police and the Feds. We need all the help we can get. I'm also thinking of calling off the fireworks. They bring 5,000 people down to the harbor, and with the Bicentennial, it'll be more like 7,000. It's just too dangerous."

"If you do," said Bartholomew, "we'll never catch him. He'll go to ground permanently."

"But we're dealing with a madman here. Don't forget that as a diversion, he was willing to burn down all of his beloved Teal Pond. He's capable of anything."

"At least wait until the morning of the third. If we don't have something by then—"

"All right," said the Chief, "but that's it. Unless we have an awfully good reason not to, I'm canceling them."

In the ensuing 48 hours, FBI agents and State Police undercover officers came quietly into town. Every possible precaution was taken.

And nothing was turned up.

On Friday morning the 2nd, Bartholomew woke up with the certainty that Royce was near. On a hunch, he went down to the harbor parking lot. It was a rainy, overcast day, yet a surprising number of people were out and about, most of them in their cars with the windows rolled up, making them practically invisible from outside. Yet the feeling persisted, until finally Bartholomew got in the old pick-up and drove over to the station. The Chief was in his office, and waved him in.

"This is going to sound really wacko, Dan, but I feel like Royce is around here somewhere."

"More of your intuition? Aren't we kind of O/D'd on that? I don't want to hurt your feelings, but let's face it: It hasn't been that all-fired impressive recently."

Bartholomew smiled. "I know; I'm not too happy about it myself. But I can't shake this feeling."

He looked out the window at the rain. The low clouds were shot through with sheet lightning. "I've got the eeriest feeling that he's stalking me. And you know, I had this same feeling that morning with the bulldozer."

He got an idea. "Would you mind if I used Trish's machine and tried to raise him?"

"Be my guest."

Trish was at her desk, and when he explained what he wanted to do, she relinquished the keyboard. In a few moments, he had ChessUnlimited up on the screen. He left a message for FalconerRR: "I know you're in town. I know you're ready to play. But you're not going to win. You're going down. In flames."

Immediately there was a reply message, as if Royce had been waiting for him to sign on. "Brave talk, sainted one. You're right about the flames, but it won't be me going down in them.

Meantime, be sure to keep the other campers' courage up, as you lead them deeper into the cave."

The lights flickered, and Trish, looking up at them, said, "Oh, no! Not now! Of all the times to have a power failure!"

But Bartholomew was too busy at the keyboard to pay attention. He had gone into the chat room.

DEEPERBLUE: YOU'RE THE ONE IN THE CAVE. DEEP IN.

FALCONER: I'D BE SCARED, TOO, BRAVE BARTHOLOMEW.

DEEPERBLUE: SO DEEP, YOU THINK THE SHADOWS OUTSIDE ARE REAL.

The lights dimmed, the image on the monitor wavered, and just before the power went out completely, Bartholomew noted that Royce's signal was still strong. "He's close by," he said to Trish, "but he's not on local power; his signal didn't waver. He must be in a car, using a cellular modem." He nodded toward the window. "See if you can see him out there."

Trish ran to the front door and out into the storm as the emergency generator kicked in. The lights returned, and in a few moments, the computer, shut off but spike-protected, was ready to be powered back up. Bartholomew hastily regained ChessUnlimited and went into the chat room. Royce was still there.

FALCONER: ENOUGH TALK. I KNOW YOU'RE TRYING TO FIND ME.

DEEPERBLUE: WE WILL FIND YOU!

FALCONER: NOT TODAY. I LOOK FORWARD TO OUR GAME.

Royce exited, and Trish came back in. "I saw him! In a Volkswagen! Not his old one, but another one! He took off before I could get the license."

Bartholomew turned to the Chief. "I know what his surprise is going to be."

62 | a rose is still a rose

THERE IS AN OLD SAYING ON CAPE COD: Summer does not begin until the Fourth of July. Surrounded by an ocean that is slow to warm up in the spring and slow to cool down in the fall, the crooked peninsula has a long, cold, wet winter, followed by a brief but intense summer, and a lingering, beautifully soft fall. Thirty years ago, year-round Cape Codders looked forward to Labor Day, when the summer people finally closed up their cottages and left. The Cape seemed to rise two inches out of the sea, and you could hear the birds again. September was their secret. It was still warm, and you could even swim. You could also find a parking place or shop without being crowded off the sidewalk. You could get a coffee at Norma's without having to wait, or a table at Gordie's right when you wanted one.

But the things the locals loved most about the Cape were the very things which drew so many tourists. Word got out about September, and by the 1980s there were as many off-Cape license plates in Eastport after Labor Day as before. The locals promised each other not to tell anyone about October which, though no longer warm enough for swimming, was still balmy, still bathed in golden sun and caressed by tranquil breezes (except when the occasional hurricane rumbled past).

Alas, word got out about October anyway, until there were almost as many foreigners then as there had been a month before. Summer-hibernating locals, deprived of their last month of cozy weather to enjoy by themselves, *swore* never to reveal to any off-Caper that a final whiff of Indian Summer sometimes graced the first week of November. . . .

There were many off-Cape visitors in June, though the weather was still chancy, but Fourth of July weekend traditionally kicked off the summer season. On that weekend, the parking lot at Eastport's harbor was suddenly crammed with cars and people, and would remain that way pretty much all summer. This Fourth was no different. The charter boats still entered and exited the harbor in single file, making a great, stately procession—Eastport's own not-so-tall ships, passing in review. Anyone who saw them sailing in at sunset with pennants flying and the last rays of sun bathing their hulls in golden light would never forget the sight.

Bartholomew, carefully potting his entry in the Eastport Rose contest that Saturday morning, had little time for the scenic beauty that others had driven hundreds of miles to enjoy. The judging would take place in front of the town hall at noon, but his thoughts were not there, either. He was dwelling on the fact that his intuition seemed to have let him down. Again.

When Royce had said that it would be *him* going down in flames, not the other way around, Bartholomew had had an epiphany moment. He *knew*—in his heart, not his head—that Royce was planning the same sort of surprise that he had used to divert them at the stakeout. Flash fires. At night. At the harbor, where the greatest number of people would appreciate his handiwork.

It made sense, Bartholomew reasoned. There were vast stretches of dune grass on both sides of the harbor. He would plant the fire bombs there, and the ensuing conflagration, on all sides of the harbor and its crowded parking lot, would panic the thousands that had gathered to watch the fireworks, and might actually imperil lives. It was so real to him that he could see it in his mind's eye, as he described it to the Chief. And he succeeded in convincing the Chief—to the point where he was more than ever ready to shut down the fireworks.

But Bartholomew had persuaded him not to. If his hunch were right, they would know what to look for and where, and this would be their one chance to catch Royce. Reluctantly, the Chief had gone with his friend's leading. But Trish had spent a full day on the phone, checking every retail outlet on the Cape that handled the sort of remote control switches that Royce had used before, and turned up nothing. And twice they had swept the dunes, to no avail. At three o'clock, the pyrotechnicians would arrive to start setting up that evening's display. By one o'clock the Chief would have to decide whether it was go or no-go, so that he could stop them before they started for the Cape.

At 11:45, Brothers Bartholomew and Ambrose took their rose to the town hall. The seven other finalists were already there with their roses, as were the five judges, with Barry Jones taking Royce's place. A small band of onlookers had collected, mostly family and friends of the contestants.

Bartholomew greeted his mother warmly, and Maurice Tomlinson, who was leaning on a cane, accompanied by Sarah. He did not greet Laurel Winslow.

So she greeted him. "I was afraid you were going to miss it," she said softly. She was wearing a pastel green summer frock, with her hair drawn back in a pony-tail.

"Wouldn't miss it for the world," he said lightly. He could feel her eyes seeking his, but he studiously avoided them. It was exceedingly unwise for a recovering alcoholic to go into a tavern, no matter how firm his resolve or how long it had been since his last drink.

"That's a beautiful rose you have there," she observed privately, watching him put it in place alongside the others. "I think it's the most beautiful I've ever seen."

Then he made the mistake of looking up. Two magical emerald pools, dancing with light, welcomed the swimmer—

"Brother Bartholomew, any further thoughts on that matter we were discussing earlier?" The Seventh Cavalry, in the person of his friend Dan Burke, arrived at the last possible moment. Smiling at Laurel, the Chief took Bartholomew by the arm and led him away.

"Listen," he said under his breath, "I've got to decide *right now* whether to pull the plug on—"

But Bartholomew wasn't listening. He was looking at his mother chatting with Maurice Tomlinson, and remembering something she had said in passing at Norma's, the last time he had seen her. He whirled on the Chief, whispering, "Can you get hold of Trish?" The Chief nodded. "Have her check the electronics outlets in Plymouth." He glanced at his watch. "Fast!"

The Chief took out his cellular phone and called the station, while Selectman Barb Saunders gathered the other judges and announced that the judging would now begin. Accompanied by the Commodore, Laurel, and Barry Jones, she corralled the Chief, and together they started down the row of roses, stopping at each and whispering among themselves.

When they finished, they came back up the row, and then requested that three entries be set aside—Isabel Doane's, Maurice Tomlinson's, and Brother Bartholomew's. These were now inspected—from above, below, and all around—for richness and originality of coloring, sturdiness of stem and leaf, and all-around health and beauty.

At length they reached their decision. On a little stepped platform for the winners, resembling the one for Olympic medalists, they placed Maurice Tomlinson's on the middle, highest step, Isabel Doane's on the second highest, to the left, and Brother Bartholomew's on the third. Then they announced the prizes (which, fortunately, been put in escrow before the collapse of Teal Pond). A check for two thousand dollars went to the winner. His rose would be installed in the new concrete Bicentennial planter which had just been poured, and his name would go on its brass plaque. A year's subscription to the *Revelator* went to Isabel, and a year's free coffee at Norma's went to her son.

Warmly applauded by everyone, Maurice was in tears as he accepted the check. Isabel laughed and said how grateful she was that she had come in second, not third, and her son quipped that today was probably the wrong day to give up coffee.

As the gathering started to break up, Laurel came over to Bartholomew and, putting a hand on his arm, said in an aside, "I still think yours is the most beautiful." He was trying to think of a clever but noninvolving response, when the Chief, cell phone to his ear, called him over to the Bravada.

"Okay," the Chief said to his friend, "I take it back about your intuition. Last Monday, Plymouth Electronics sold 17 remote-controlled, time-delay switches to a Mr. R. Falconer."

"Jesus help us, Dan! *Seventeen?*"

63 | the scent of a woman

THE SATURDAY EVENING SKY WAS CLEAR, the air stirred by a warm southwest breeze. At 8:19 the sun had slipped below the horizon, and now the sky was layered from deep lavender directly above to progressively brighter red-orange, with the brightest point being just behind the rusting prow of what was once the target ship. In the harbor parking lot, thousands of people were closely packed, awaiting the fireworks. It had been a perfect beach day, and the mood of the crowd was peaceful and patient.

The mood of Brother Bartholomew was anything but. He had met some of the FBI agents and State Troopers, all in plain clothes. They were an earnest group, and they augmented the entire EPD which was in uniform, and who were joined by all the officers that Eastham and Orleans could spare. The plainclothesmen were circulating among the onlookers, while the uniformed police were casually checking all vehicles and foot traffic en route to the harbor. Ostensibly they were there simply to discourage vehicular traffic from approaching and to keep the foot traffic from getting dangerously bottlenecked. In reality, each had a photo of Royce, which they had memorized. Even in that vast throng of people, it would be almost impossible for him to move in or out undiscovered.

As Bartholomew observed all this with Ambrose, from their vantage point where the abbey's front lawn met the asphalt of the parking lot, he could see something that should have reassured him. In the gathering twilight, fire trucks from all three towns were moving unobtrusively into position on either side of the harbor. If any visitors even noticed them, they would merely assume it was a wise precaution, in case falling fireworks debris should happen to start a grass fire in the dunes.

Behind him, upstairs in the glassed-in conference room of the abbey's Pastorium, the Chief, the FBI's agent-in-charge, and the senior officer of the State Police contingent had discreetly set up a command center, in touch by walkie-talkie and cellular phone with all key posts and personnel. The conference room was dark, affording them an excellent view of the parking lot, most of the dunes on both sides of the harbor, and the boats that had come to watch the fireworks from the bay. All in all, thought Bartholomew, they could not be better positioned or in a higher state of readiness.

And yet he was almost frantic with worry. Despite all their precautions, he knew Royce was here, somewhere. He could feel his presence. The game was going forward.

As the twilight deepened, on the lawn behind him, under a large open tent, the abbey's orchestra, without their lead French horn (Bartholomew) and second tuba (Ambrose), were playing the final selection of their pops concert for some three hundred dinner guests. After that, they would swing into their traditional encore, "The Stars and Stripes Forever," and the fireworks would commence.

Finally he could not bear standing still any longer. "Let's walk," he said to Ambrose.

"Where?"

"I don't know. Along the beach. Come on."

At the end of the parking lot there was yellow barrier tape cordoning off the boat ramp and the beach, along with the dunes and the dirt road leading into them. And in front of the tape, at intervals, uniformed police were keeping curious individuals well away from ground zero. The fireworks crew had been working there all afternoon, planting and aiming the rockets in their launch pipes for the various displays, stapling their fuses to boards for carefully-timed sequential firing. Now they were munching on Italian sausages, Chinese egg rolls, and Belgian waffles from the row of gaily-decorated food kiosks, waiting for the signal to commence the launching sequence.

Bartholomew recognized Otis and went up to him. "Can you let us through?"

"Sorry, Brother Bart; not without passes. You cannot believe how tight the security is tonight!"

"Where do we get them?"

"It's too late now, I'm afraid." Then he smiled and said, "just a minute." He activated his Motorola. "Whipple, Beach number three. I have two requests for beach access: Brothers Bartholomew and Ambrose." He listened for a moment, the radio to his ear. "Roger that." He turned to Bartholomew. "The Chief says you can go through. But he wants to hear from you in ten minutes."

Bartholomew nodded, and Otis held up the tape for them. They ducked under and made their way along the shore, heading west, past waiting rockets and waiting workmen, past a snow fence erected by the workmen as a temporary barrier. Out on the bay, held at a safe distance by the harbor master's launch, were about a hundred floating silhouettes—craft of all sizes, from kayaks to sailboats to large power boats, down from Wellfleet or over from Dennisport.

They walked about half a mile, until they came to a wooden walkway that led over the dune to the back yard of a family that belonged to the abbey. Ambrose turned in to mount its steps and complete their loop, when Bartholomew called to him: "Let's go a little further."

Ambrose shook his head. "If we want to get back within the ten minutes the Chief gave us, we'd better start now."

"We don't have to go all the way to the Skaket inlet. Just a little further." Ambrose dutifully fell in behind him. In the distance they could hear the faint strains of the opening bars of "The Stars and Stripes Forever!"

Despite the waning moon, it was so dark they could barely see a small sailboat, pulled up on the beach ahead of them, just above the line of dead sea wrack that indicated where the incoming tide was likely to stop. The boat looked like a big surfboard with a raised centerboard and tiller, and a well just big enough for two adults. Its sail was left up and was flapping in the light breeze. Someone had obviously come ashore to watch the fireworks—which was odd, Bartholomew thought, because the best view would have been out on the water, with the other boats.

"You recognize this boat?" he asked Ambrose, who was one of the abbey's lifeguards and was more familiar with the comings and goings at the beach than he.

"It doesn't belong to anyone in the abbey," Ambrose said.

Behind them, the orchestra was into the final refrain, all stops out.

Noticing an article of clothing in the boat's well, Bartholomew reached down to have a closer look at it. It was a dark woolen shawl. In the darkness he couldn't see what color it was. But he didn't have to; its texture was familiar. And—as he raised it to his nostrils, his blood ran cold—so was its scent.

64 | show time

WITH BROTHER AMBROSE SCRAMBLING behind him, Brother Bartholomew raced back down the beach, up the steps, and over the walkway to the yard. In the darkness there were perhaps thirty children sitting on the lawn. A few, excited at the prospect of the imminent fireworks, were running around with glow-in-the-dark wands in their hands or fastened around their necks. Bartholomew found the two young women in charge. "Has anyone come up here from the beach?"

"Just a couple of rowdy teen-agers, and we asked them to leave."

"Nobody else?"

"Nope."

He looked up at the little lighthouse on the end of the house to which the lawn belonged. In the faint light of the waning moon he could see a silhouette standing on its catwalk. "Who's that?"

"Trish," said the young woman. "And she's in uniform!"

Bartholomew ran across the yard and called up to her. "Get the Chief! Tell him he's here. I've found his getaway boat, a Sunfish, two hundred yards down the beach towards Skaket inlet. He's got to be in the dunes over there somewhere," he waved in the direction of the distant parking lot, "and he's got someone with him."

"Stay where you are," said Trish, as she got on the Motorola. But at just that moment the night sky above them exploded with a dazzling, rattling, multiple-star burst. On the lawn the kids cried "Oh!" And up on the catwalk Trish pressed the Motorola to her ear, trying to hear what the Chief was saying.

Bartholomew could wait no longer. Leaving Ambrose behind, he ran back across the lawn and over the walkway, down onto the beach and back towards the parking lot. As he suspected, there was a break in the snow fence. It had not been there this afternoon, but it was there now. He ducked through it into the dunes, flattening himself against the nearest one, as the second salvo went off, to the delight and applause of the vast crowd in the parking lot.

The delight, however, was not universal. On the deck of one of the houses overlooking the bay, an eight-year-old boy, badly scared but trying not to show it, announced that he was going inside, to see how his dog was doing. The large, black dog, also badly scared, bolted through the open door, out into the night.

After that came a series of single bursts, spaced by fifteen seconds of silence and darkness. It was during these pauses that he moved forward. To retain night vision in his right eye, he kept it tightly shut during the bursts of light. It was an old trick that he'd not used since 'Nam, and now he shuddered: This night was beginning to remind him more and more of the horror he had not thought of in more than twenty years.

And then he saw Royce.

He was intent on the parking lot, lying against a little hummock of a dune about thirty yards ahead of Bartholomew. That hummock was the last cover between Royce and the rockets, which were periodically streaking heavenward, each emitting a hollow-sounding *whump* as it left its launch pipe.

Whump . . . ka-bam, boom! Another burst went off directly overhead. Bartholomew pressed himself further into the little dune between him and Royce. When it grew dark again, he peered ahead with his right, night-vision eye—and saw what he had desperately hoped he wouldn't see. There *was* someone with Royce. A woman. Laurel.

He stood up in a half-crouch and stared at them, trying to make out exactly what their situation was. So intent was he that he forgot to duck with the next burst. He lost his night vision, but at least the burst clearly illuminated exactly what the situation was. Laurel's hands were tied—no, duct-taped—and there was a band of duct tape around her neck with a short strip of it leading to, and wrapped around, Royce's right hand. There was also a strip across her mouth. Lined up on the rim of the dune, within easy reach of his left hand, was a row of small black boxes, each with a red button. Bartholomew stood up straighter, and as the light died away he could make out, on the other side of Royce's hummock, a dense cluster of vertical pipes—which had to be the grand finale.

Whump, whump, whump—three rockets left, and in four seconds three bright starflowers blossomed. Bartholomew ducked, but not fast enough. For just as he had sensed Royce's presence, now Royce seemed to sense his. In the eerie green light that bathed everything, Royce turned slowly and faced his adversary. *Bappity-bappity, bam-bam-bam, ka-boom*—a new series of rapid explosions made everything starkly clear and devoid of its own color.

Royce was smiling. "Sainted one!" he exclaimed. "I was hoping it would play out this way!"

Bartholomew took a step towards him, and Royce reached for his waist. Instantly the combat knife was there in his left hand. "I've been observing your brief career as a sleuth with much interest," he informed his opponent, "and in the course of following you following me, I've discerned that this person is—or should I say, was?—of great importance to you."

Bartholomew took another step, and Royce whipped the point of the blade to Laurel's throat. Her eyes were wide with terror. "Uh-uh," he cautioned, shaking his head. "You know how hideously sharp this thing is. You don't want to do anything that might make me slip!" As another burst lit the sky, Royce barely moved the point along her throat. A dark gash appeared behind it and started oozing blood.

"You see? I've arranged this so that you'll be able to watch me light my fire, and you won't be able to stop me. And then, in the panic and pandemonium, my new friend"—he glanced at Laurel and gave a little tug on the strip of tape connected to her neck—"and I will simply slip away into the night."

A bouquet of explosions overhead indicated that the final salvo would not be long in coming. As the light died away, from the parking lot rose joyous shouts and vociferous applause. The grand finale was next.

"Well," said Royce, glancing at the black sport watch on his right wrist, "it's Show Time."

Behind him in the darkness, Bartholomew heard a whisper. "On my three-count, drop to the ground, and I'll kill the—"

Bartholomew smiled. The Seventh Cav rides again!

But Royce heard him, too. "Is that you, Chief? This is even better than I dared hope for!"

"One," whispered the Chief.

"Come out where I can see you," cried Royce jubilantly, as if he were hosting a tea party.

"Two."

"You see those?" Royce exulted, pointing the tip of the knife at the row of trigger buttons. "Those are for fire bombs, all right. But not where you were looking for them! Not here in the dunes, or over there," he pointed the blade across the harbor. "They're in the new church and in the friary and the convent and the old chapel, and in the parking lot scheduling booth, and in three of the charter boats in the harbor, and even in that lighthouse—I've outplayed you again! And now, checkmate!"

Sticking the knife in the sand, he reached for the triggers.

"Three!"

Bartholomew dropped, and Royce, surmising what they were doing, tried to jerk Laurel in front of him. The Chief fired. Unable to go for a kill shot for fear of hitting Laurel, he nonetheless hit Royce in the chest, just below his left shoulder. The wound partially shocked him and spun him around. But he still had movement in his arm.

Above, the night sky erupted with staccato explosions and a rising crescendo of boomers and blossoming light bursts. The grand finale had begun, and they could see each other clearly, as if in stop-motion freeze frame.

Again the Chief fired, this time hitting Royce in the upper arm. But he could still move the arm, and now he grabbed up the knife and returned its point to Laurel's throat. The last salvo of the grand finale was launching out of their tubes.

"Chief, you're too good a shot for her own good!" Royce cried. "But there's more than one way to skin this cat!" With a sharp tug on the tape around Laurel's neck, he yanked her with him to the top of the hummock, so that he could stamp on the triggers with his feet. "This is even better!" he screamed. "A fire dance!" The multiple blasts of the grand finale began overhead.

Royce shifted the knife to the horizontal and placed its upper edge against Laurel's throat, making it clear that he no longer had any intention of keeping her as a hostage. He was about to slit her throat. Laurel realized it, too, as she worked her jaw enough to loosen the tape over her mouth. "Oh, God!" she cried in despair, certain they would be her last words on earth.

Suddenly, out of nowhere a large black dog, in a blind panic to escape the cataclysm detonating above, hurtled through their midst, bumping hard against Royce as it passed, so that the knife jerked in his hand. Instead of slicing across her throat, it slipped downward and cut her neck, at the same time severing the strip of duct tape holding her captive.

In that instant, Bartholomew lunged for the triggers, imposing his body between them and Royce. The latter, more than willing to butcher his opponent to get to them, swung the knife toward him with savage intensity. But losing his balance in the loose sand, he toppled off the top of the hummock. He twisted to break his fall—just as the last, biggest rocket came out of its pipe.

The projectile caught Royce squarely in the chest, and he looked down at it, eyes wide in horror, as it blew him apart—in a misty haze of red, white, and blue.

Truly he had given Eastport a Bicentennial surprise it would never forget.

| epilogue

THE NEXT DAY, SUNDAY, was the Fourth, which for the EPD meant all hands on deck. No rest for the weary on the heaviest traffic day of the year. They sorted out minor accidents, reunited lost children with their parents, and persuaded those who had done a bit too much celebrating under the broiling sun, to let their wives drive them home.

Monday was also a holiday, but on this day the Chief did something unprecedented: He told everyone not on duty not to report until 10:00 A.M., and the investigative team was not to report at all. They were to take the day off, as he intended to himself, as soon as he and Otis took care of one last piece of business.

The Commodore answered the door, with his wife and Pat standing behind him. When he looked down and saw his beloved cannon sitting on the front step, he began to cry.

"You make an early morning racket one more time," said the Chief gruffly, "and he goes right back in the slammer! And this time we throw away the key!"

"Aye, aye, Chief," the Commodore replied, saluting. "Come on, Old Bull," he said, addressing the cannon, as he wheeled it into the

house, "from now on, we will hear from you at noon, not Reveille."
The Chief just shook his head as he went back to the Bravada.

That morning Brother Ambrose requested a meeting with
Brothers Anselm and Dominic. He informed them that at the next
vows service, he would like to take his final vow. And at that service, he requested that Brother Bartholomew be his shepherding
Brother.

That afternoon, Sarah took Maurice to a movie. A date movie
of her choosing, which they saw together.

Later that afternoon, Tobin, wearing a blue blazer and a white
yachtsman's cap and humming "Yes, we have no bananas," called
for Karen and took her sailing aboard the *Dream Away*.

Still later, a tall, willowy figure with a green Italian silk scarf
covering the bandage on her neck, entered the abbey's nearly finished great stone church. It was empty, and perfectly still. She
walked about a third of the way up the nave, her footsteps echoing
on the concrete floor, and stopped.

"So this is where you live," she murmured, looking up at the
high windows and lofty rafters. "After last night, I figured I owed
you a house call."

She looked around at the rows of stone columns, and the distant apse. "Nice house. But don't get any ideas about me starting
a relationship, or anything," she added hastily. "I just stopped by to
say thanks." The silence was unbroken. Outside, a cloud parted,
and behind her, through the high circular window above the
entrance, a shaft of sunlight limned her in silhouette.

That night, his head still aching from caffeine deprivation,
Brother Bartholomew composed himself for sleep. Though his
flesh was still letting him know how furious it was at being denied
its favorite substance, his will was set, and his spirit was graced.
Tomorrow, when he stood against the first-cup-of-the-morning
temptation, it would rage even more. But eventually it would come
to accept the new way things were—and one day might even appreciate them.

He awoke two hours later, dimly aware of a soft, heavy weight
on his lower legs. It was Pangor Ban, the friary cat, who had waited till he was asleep before settling in for the night. Moving his legs

vigorously from side to side, Bartholomew did his best to discourage him. But the old cat rode the billows unperturbed, like a small craft on a midnight sea.

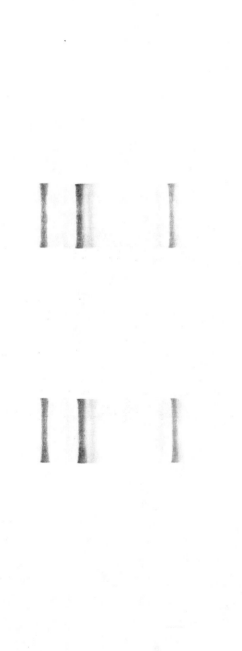

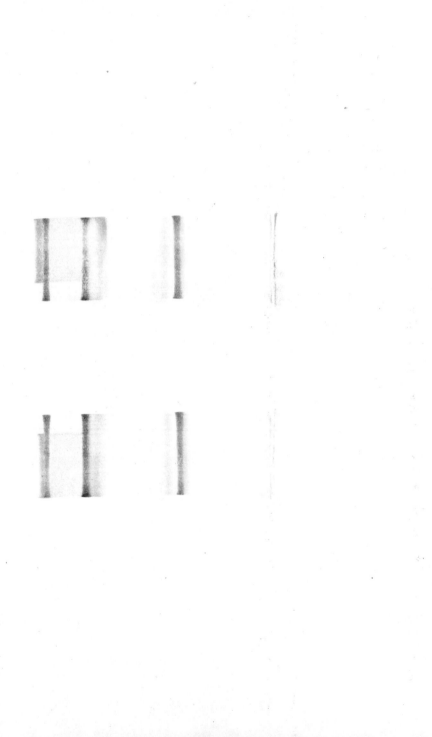